BREAK

THE GREYSON SERIES: BOOK ONE
BRENNA FERRELL

ISBN: 979-8-9919757-0-4 (Paperback)

ISBN: 979-8-9919757-2-8 (Hardback)

ISNB: 979-8-9919757-2-8 (Ebook)

Library of Congress Control Number: 2024924201

Cover Art: Covers by Combs

First Published: 2025, The Graphite Dove Co. in the United States of America

For therapists and mothers, who are often one and the same.
Thank you for listening.

For my family and friends. Thank you for your support and
giving me time to write.

"We are never so defenseless against suffering as when we love."
~Sigmund Freud

PROLOGUE

Thirty Years Before

Theresa Miller was seventeen years old, entirely alone—almost—and she hated herself. She hated herself because she had nothing, because she was nothing, and because she knew she could become nothing. But she hated herself most of all because she also hated her four-week-old daughter. No doubt for any teen girl, a pregnancy and subsequently becoming a young mother, would be an uphill climb—even for someone who wasn't lacking in resources. For Theresa, however, the lack of money, support, and maternal instincts, combined with her short, teenage existence made parenting feel like a hopeless task. Not something that if she tried harder, or cared more, she might be able to make work. It literally felt *impossible.*

When Theresa found out she was pregnant, her mother, Charlotte, better known as Lottie, said she couldn't provide the financial or physical support Theresa would need before and after the baby was born. Not wanting Theresa to become any more of a social outcast than she already was, very early in her pregnancy her mother sent Theresa a few states away, to Mississippi, to live with her aunt. Amelia, her late father's much older sister, and someone Theresa had never met, was willing to provide room and board for the pregnant teen. As much as she hated leaving her mother, Theresa knew this was the best option she had. Honestly, it was the *only* option her mother had given her, so there was no room for discussion on the matter. Amelia had spared enough money to provide for Theresa's care, along with a more comfortable life than Theresa was accustomed to, but that was the end of her generosity.

While she was clothed, fed and taken to see a doctor—and was grateful for those things—Amelia did not provide her niece with the love, nurturing or guidance the teen craved. It was almost like Amelia, a deeply religious woman, was doing this favor for Theresa as a resume builder for her interview with Saint Peter, but not wanting to go above and beyond.

Living alone for the entirety of her adult life, Amelia hadn't developed patience or compassion, and just days after the baby was born, decided it was time for Theresa and her newborn daughter to leave. Amelia gave Theresa only a three-day eviction notice, so the young mother had little time to prepare for her life back at home. Making matters more difficult was the fact that it had been weeks, maybe even months, since she had spoken to her mother, and Lottie still wasn't answering her phone. Due to all the anticipation, fear, pain, and recovery surrounding the birth, Theresa hadn't actually thought to worry about the lack of communication with her mom. But now considering she would not only be reuniting with her mother, but also moving back in, she found the inability to get ahold of Lottie more troubling by the minute.

The prospect of returning home to live with someone who had made it clear she could be of no help should have added to Theresa's woes. But Lottie was the only person who had ever cared about Theresa, and the feeling of being loved trumped all else. Theresa had almost convinced herself that surprising her mother by showing up unannounced with the new baby might be just what their family of three needed. However, given the way her life had gone so far, Theresa couldn't quite make herself believe it.

The last three days spent at Aunt Amelia's house yielded no results regarding reaching Lottie. Instead, longing for the raspy, comforting sound of her familiar voice on the other end of the phone line left Theresa feeling abandoned. On the bus ride back to Roseville, the small Florida town where she'd lived her entire life prior to her stay with Amelia, Theresa occupied her mind by coming up with excuses to justify away her worry. *The phone bill probably was overdue and the service disconnected*—although it rang when Theresa called. *Maybe she picked up a second job and was busy working. Maybe she's having one of her ill spells and is having trouble getting out of bed.* Regardless of the excuses or their validity, the fact remained that Theresa had no idea what was happening with her mother and couldn't prepare herself for how her life would change yet again.

Before arriving back at the only home she'd ever known, because Aunt Amelia's place was just a house, not *home,* Theresa had a fleeting thought: *Maybe I should contact the baby's father?* But there were countless reasons that was not a good option. As the end of her journey from Mississippi back to her hometown drew closer, Theresa's thoughts shifted from excuses to dread, and all the bad things that might have happened to Charlotte Miller filled her mind. Upon entering Roseville's city limits, Theresa noticed that nothing had changed in the past seven months since she'd departed. Theresa wasn't sure what exactly she was expecting, but she thought she would feel different returning as a mother and more of an adult than when she left. However, the same mutual disdain between the town and her was still there, and she felt no different at all.

The walk from the bus stop to her house seemed farther than she remembered, but she had never walked it before while carrying a baby in her arms. Relieved to see her old driveway come into view after a curve in the road, the pair headed toward the cozy cottage, as Theresa liked to think of the dilapidated bungalow. The front door was unlocked, but that was no surprise as the lock had been broken some years before.

"Mom?" Theresa called, her voice louder than necessary in a house where even a whisper could carry. "*Mother?*" When there was still no response, she shouted, "*LOTTIE?!*"—her tone desperate as a child lost in a crowd , searching amongst many "mothers" and "moms."

Still nothing. Theresa didn't feel too alarmed because her mother had no idea she was coming, so she wouldn't necessarily be home anxiously awaiting her daughter's arrival. After four days went by with no word from her mother, Theresa decided she should file a missing persons report. Not wanting to see anyone she knew, she chose to phone the police station as opposed to going in person. Her call was directed to the department that handled missing persons, domestic disturbances, auto thefts and traffic violations—it was a small-town police station, and resources had to be combined.

When she said the name of the person in question, the female voice on the other end said, "hold on."

Soon a different voice, a male, came onto the line and said, "Theresa? This is Bob Harrison, do you remember me?"

Theresa did remember him. He had come to their house once when she was younger, and he had been nice to her. He had brought her a stuffed animal puppy dog wearing a police hat, one of the few presents she had received in her life, so the memory was not easily forgotten. Officer Harrison had been the one to tell four-year-old Theresa that a man she never recalled meeting, who was apparently her father, was dead.

"Yes, I remember you. Do you know where my mother is?"

Theresa replied in a clipped tone, easily misconstrued as rudeness, but Officer Harrison knew better. It was the tone of someone trying to convince others, or maybe even themself, that they were not as worried about a missing loved one as they really were.

Then came the part of his job that he hated the most. Telling someone once was bad enough, but the fact that he would be the person to share the news with this young girl twice made it infinitely worse.

"Theresa, I am sorry to have to tell you this, but your mother, well… honey… she passed away about four months ago."

After a pause to process what the officer had said, Theresa responded in a trembling, childlike voice, "What? How?"

Officer Harrison knew a little about Theresa's situation that he had heard from the rumor mill. He also knew quite a lot about what had happened with her mother, but if this poor girl didn't know what went on, he was hoping to protect her from it. He knew how most of the town felt about the Millers, and he was not sure being dealt another blow could be tolerated by the girl.

"Well, she had gotten herself into some trouble with the law and was taken to jail where she proceeded to get sick and passed away. This happened out of town, from what I understand, and I don't know much more than that. I am very sorry sweetheart," said the kind policeman.

Theresa hung up the phone very slowly, as if it was so fragile it would shatter at the slightest click of the handset into the receiver. Processing the news while caring for her crying baby was not possible. Either task, on its own, would have been difficult, but the combination—insurmountable. She did not go to the child, but rather covered her ears, closed her eyes tightly, slid her back down the wall next to the phone until she was crouched on the floor. Raw emotion took over the reasoning part of her brain and she let out a wail that rivaled that of her tiny daughter. Theresa thought she had known loneliness before, but she quickly began to understand its true depth.

Waking up the next morning to what could only be described as screams, rather than cries, from her child, Theresa couldn't move. Frozen in place by something she couldn't identify, the young motherless mother lay on the ground, numb everywhere but her brain. Thoughts of the birth of her child entered her head and she remembered being so hopeful that the entrance of this young thing into the world would bring a joy to her life that she'd never known. That was the way she had heard people describe how they felt about becoming parents, so why wouldn't she have believed it would be the same for her? However, when a baby is born out of wedlock to a teenager with almost nothing, it's hard to find any moments of joy. Thinking about before the baby was born, and the tiny bit of hope she had then, made Theresa feel foolish. The idea of motherhood had never crossed her mind before the instant she found out she was going to be one. As it would be for most teens, she did not love the idea of being a young mother. Theresa had never even been around a baby before, and she had no idea what she should do. Her own mother, while she loved her daughter deeply, wasn't quite what one would call "maternal," but she could at least have been another set of hands.

Theresa, in her naïveté, believed that the two of them could do it together—raise her child and give her a loving home—but now that her mother was gone, she would have to do it all. The baby's father was not in the picture, and really had never been other than the few minutes it took to conceive the child. At first, Theresa thought she loved him, but she soon realized that he wasn't someone she wanted, or even knew very well. All of the hope Theresa had, even up to a few weeks ago, was now nonexistent, and she felt the lack thereof begin to drain the life out of her.

A few weeks had passed since her less-than-triumphant return to Roseville and the devastating news of the loss of her mother. All of the sadness, frustration, anger, and confusion—along with many other emotions Theresa couldn't put a name to—needed a place to go, and she began to direct it all at her daughter. The infant became the sole target of the blame for their situation, and it seemed as though the self loathing and disgust she had for her child had reached their peak. The only thing that gave her a bit of solace was that things *had* to get better because clearly she was already at rock bottom.

Theresa had little food, almost no money, and a shell of a home. She spent her days trying to find work, but even before the pregnancy, she was a black sheep in her town. Theresa knew she wasn't a "front of the house" caliber of employee, but she thought surely someone would hire her to work in a kitchen or stockroom. But no one wanted to hire the teen mother, and she felt more like a pariah than ever before. It didn't help matters that she had no suitable childcare, and her situation was the epitome of a "Catch-22:" if she worked, she couldn't parent, and if she parented, she couldn't work. In reality, that meant working was not possible unless she wanted to leave her baby alone. The lack of income made it impossible to pay for heat and electricity in the house in which she lived. The food she ate was purchased with found change she had saved or stolen from the local market's stockroom, her former place of employment—*before*. The lack of nutrients meant she produced little to no milk, and her growing lack of interest and resentment towards her child meant she did not steal formula. Failure to thrive would be a severely understated diagnosis for the baby, who at four weeks old, weighed only seven pounds.

The familiar feelings of hunger and exhaustion were constant companions, but six weeks after becoming a mother, she found a new feeling of complete hopelessness was starting to settle in. For the past few weeks, she could hardly get out of bed, but the lack of other stimuli made it clearer for her to feel something she hadn't in a very long time. Tormented by her daily fight to survive had made it extremely difficult to notice the spark that was beginning to ignite in her heart—she felt *love*. How had she been so blind to it before? Having felt alone for so long, she had become numb to the reality that beside her lay a tiny life full of unconditional love, and that wanted to be loved in return. Yes, she'd been at the lowest part of her existence, but that was going to change as she finally felt a reason to go on.

While things for Theresa did change, unfortunately they were not for the better. The motivation to improve did not help her get out of bed as she thought it would. It did not help her provide for her child. It did not help her become a better mother. Instead, she felt a sorrow so deep, it permeated every cell in her body, consuming her entire existence. The love she finally felt for her young daughter was supposed to be her salvation. Instead it magnified her despair, and made reaching her breaking point inescapable.

One day when her daughter was in her seventh week of life, Theresa had the most clear thought she'd ever had. Rising slowly from her bed, she made her way to the small, dingy bathroom with the intent to swallow every pill she could find in the medicine cabinet. The amber-colored glass bottles that bore her mother's name on the labels were one of the many remnants of her mother left in the house. Thinking of Lottie in that moment made what came next both easier and harder. Ingesting the contents of each bottle with handfuls of water from the sink made her gag and almost vomit, but Theresa managed to get them all to her stomach. She wiped her mouth as she looked at her reflection in the medicine cabinet mirror and didn't recognize the pale, emaciated shell of a person looking back at her. The Theresa she once knew was already long gone which made it just a bit easier to continue forward with what had to be done.

It took all the energy she could gather to make it back to the bedroom where her tiny, helpless child lay on the tattered comforter on the bed, and Theresa whispered her epiphany to the small girl.

"I will never be the mother you deserve. This world will never be good enough for you. Your life will be filled with nothing but pain because of me and I love you too much to let that happen. My gift to you is freedom from this world—a gift I wish my mother had given to me."

And with that, she carefully swaddled her small child in the same blanket her mother wrapped her in as a baby. Theresa then held her thin, ragged pillow over her daughter's face, closed her own eyes, and awaited their fate.

PART I ~ REAPER

CHAPTER 1

The woman who sat before me was a dark-haired beauty with striking light green eyes. It seemed obvious she believed she could use her looks as a bargaining chip, since society taught women to believe that beauty is power, often valued over most other attributes. In this case, I knew *her* beauty was only skin deep, and this woman held no power over me. The reason? I had *my* priorities in order. In an odd gesture, through her fear and her restraints, she flashed me a thousand-watt smile, undoubtedly to remind me just how fetching she was. *That wasn't going to work on me.* This woman disgusted me, yet ironically, was also exactly the type of person I was looking for.

"Why are you doing this to me? Do you want money? I can get you plenty of money if that's what you want!"

Not only was she beautiful, but she was also rich, and everyone knew money was power too. *Bargaining chip number two? Nope. This wasn't a situation she could buy her way out of.*

"Please!" she pleaded. "I'm a *mother!*"

She whisper-yelled as she gestured toward the sleeping infant who lay in a fancy bassinet. Even though he was within arms reach of his mother, she did not reach for him. No doubt she believed that if her looks and wealth hadn't worked, surely motherhood would. *Bargaining chip number three? Hell no. I care too much about my cause to let anything distract me. This child deserves better.*

"I know people who have influence in this city! I can get you whatever you want!" she pleaded.

I stayed silent. She likely mistook that for strength, but in reality, I didn't speak because fear had stolen my words. Carrying out the task hadn't been something I *wanted* to do, but rather something I felt *compelled* to do. Nonetheless, the young woman was not stupid, she could see her offers were not what I wanted.

Deciding to take a different tack, the woman said, "Please don't hurt my baby!"

I paused at the first unselfish thing out of her mouth, and it made me fleetingly question if I was doing the right thing. But what she said next confirmed I was doing what was best—*for everyone.*

"What do you *want?*" she said, growing more frantic each time she opened her mouth.

I continued to say nothing, but turned my gaze ever so slightly towards the bassinet, and frankly, I'm surprised she noticed.

"Do you want my *baby?* If it is him you want, take him! Just leave me alone!"

What likely felt like an eternity to her, in reality, was only about twenty minutes. That amount of time was all it took for her to give up the one thing that any decent mother—even any *mediocre* mother—would *never* have done... her child. I calmly walked closer to the young mother and she flinched. I didn't touch her; instead continued past her and reached for the slumbering infant. Cradling him carefully, I placed him in his expensive stroller, ensuring he stayed asleep. I clasped the handle, then pushed the carriage as I tiptoed my way toward the front door.

"*That's* what you want? *Him?"* asked the scared and confused mother.

I slowly turned to look at the young woman tied to a chair, and finally spoke, "For the most part, yes. I want your son."

A baffled look crossed her face, and in a rather calm, almost annoyed voice, she said, "*Why?"*

"Isn't it obvious?" I said, letting the words hang in the air to give her a chance to answer.

After a minute, when it became clear it was *not* obvious to her, I felt I owed her an explanation.

"I want him because *you don't*."

That would be the last thing I said to her because I had nothing left to say. I checked on the infant to make sure he was still sleeping soundly. Even if he was awake, I doubt he would remember any of it, but I didn't want to take any chances. I left him at the door then turned and walked past his mother.

Once in the nicely appointed primary bathroom, I turned the bronze faucet on high and proceeded to fill the large jetted tub. As the level of the water rose, so did my apprehension. In theory, my plan seemed foolproof, but in reality, I had discounted the emotions I might have associated with what I had to do. Even someone harmful and worthless was still *someone...* A thought I hadn't been prepared for at the onset of my planning. It had already gotten *real,* but if I followed through with this, there was no turning back.

I walked back into the bedroom and saw the fear in Juliana's eyes, but I didn't feel one ounce of sympathy for her. In fact, it was quite the opposite—I felt nothing but disgust. I did, however, feel sorry for the little boy asleep not far away. My mind was made up, so I approached Juliana and grabbed the back of the chair to which she was tied. As she began to scream, I located the duct tape I brought for just such an occurrence, ripped off a piece, and placed it over her mouth. Dragging her and and the chair, was awkward and heavy, but I managed to get her to the bathroom and wrestle the chair into the tub.

"You're welcome, Juliana," I said to her as she writhed and squirmed beneath the water.

I knew she hadn't understood my reasoning, but to me, it was crystal clear—I was doing what had to be done. I did her a favor—in more ways than one—and if she felt anything, it should have been freedom.

CHAPTER 2

The bright sun shone through a window on a brisk April morning, casting rays across the nameplate of Delores Shaw, M.D. Delores, more commonly referred to as "Lorie," would normally find joy a simple moment like that, but she didn't even notice. Instead, her blue eyes were trained on her phone, looking at the screen with irritation over the top of her tortoise shell glasses. It was 9:12 on Monday morning and her nine o'clock appointment had yet to show. *No call, email, or even a text to let me know she was running late,* the doctor thought to herself. *Typical.* While she rarely generalized, Lorie had no trouble finding patterns in her clients' behavior. Patients with lower socioeconomic statuses tended to be on time or early to appointments and rarely canceled except for dire circumstances. On the contrary, patients who were better off financially tended not to be as courteous. The "no call, no show" policy and corresponding fee did little to assuage the behavior.

Thinking about how valuable her time was and growing more displeased with each passing minute, Dr. Shaw took a deep breath, letting it out slowly, and reminded herself why she did the work she did. *My time is valuable, but not as valuable as the help I provide my patients.* The simple mantra always brought her back to why she became a psychiatrist in the first place: helping others. It was hard, exhausting, frustrating, draining, and often all-consuming work, but Lorie was good at it, which balanced out the hard parts and made it all worth it. Still, she was human and tamping down her frustration was not always possible, especially when no one was watching.

It was nothing out of the ordinary for a patient to be tardy, and Jules was often late. In fact, not long ago she missed an entire appointment without letting Lorie know. For more than a handful of those Dr. Shaw treated, getting out of bed could be a struggle in and of itself, let alone making it to appointments on time. But missing so much of a session without any notification rarely happened. It was now 9:22 and Dr. Shaw's frustration morphed into disdain. Two no-call, no-shows might be cause for her to terminate Juliana Stevens as a patient. Lorie decided that she needed to make her cancellation policy more strict.

Inactivity, both physically and mentally, was not something Lorie did well, and her patient had forced her to do nothing but sit for almost a half hour. Not about to let irritation get the best of her, Lorie did her best to make herself busy.

"You know what they say about idle hands..." she said aloud to herself.

Her words must have been a little louder than she intended since her assistant, Eddie Randall, called in and said, "What's that, Lorie?"

"Oh just thinking out loud," Lorie replied, unable to hide the vexation in her voice. "Any word from Juliana Stevens, by chance?"

"Sorry, I haven't heard from her today. Are you expecting her to call?" asked Eddie.

"No, she just hasn't shown up for her appointment yet," replied Lorie.

Eddie checked his copy of Lorie's schedule and said, "You're right, she was scheduled to be here at nine. Sorry, I should have caught that. Do you want me to give her a call?"

Lorie knew she was right, but resisted the urge to say as much in a too-sharp tone to her assistant, whom she greatly appreciated.

"No. She has already missed so much of the appointment, that even if she came in, we would have to reschedule. You can call her later today and set up another session," said Lorie.

At 9:33, Lorie determined it was unlikely Juliana would show, and she just couldn't continue to wait, so she decided to get to work. There was always research to be done. So. Much. Research. And organization, and upkeep with patient files, and registering for conferences, so Dr. Shaw certainly would not be lacking for choices of what she could do. As the computer mouse was moved and the photo slideshow screensaver of Freud, her golden retriever, switched to the Google landing page, Lorie was briefly distracted by the stories Google thought she would be interested in. She often tried to avoid this black hole, that even a highly educated woman could get sucked into, but for some reason, today she perused the offerings. The usual celebrities behaving badly, food recalls, and politicians putting their foot in their mouths were there, but so was a local headline that caught Lorie's eye: *Young Mother Found Dead* and the single click of a mouse opened the article.

Juliana Stevens, 24, of Wyndisburg, was found dead in her apartment at approximately 7:45 this morning. Cause of death is not yet being released, and it is undetermined whether or not foul play is involved. We do know that she had a thirteen-month-old son, Huxley, who was not found at the dwelling and that the child's father is not involved in his life. While we are hopeful he was spending time with a friend or relative at the time of his mother's death, we are not taking any chances and have issued an Amber Alert. We are asking that anyone with information about Ms. Stevens or her son to please call the Wyndisburg police department and ask for Detective Christopher Greyson.

Jules. The guilt Lorie felt in that moment hit her like a punch to the gut. She had assumed Juliana Stevens was being inconsiderate, when actually her young, troubled patient was not at all inconsiderate this time—she was dead.

With her phone intercom button pressed, in a dry, shaky voice Dr. Shaw said, "Eddie, please cancel my appointments for the rest of the day."

When Eddie asked why, Lorie got up from her desk and headed to the adjoining office to talk to him face to face. This was not an "intercom" conversation.

"Eddie, I'm afraid I have some deeply upsetting news," Lorie said as she moved toward his computer and pulled up the article.

"Oh my God. So, she wasn't…" he trailed off.

Lorie just shook her head, almost in disbelief.

The assistant, now visibly shaken, was told that after he canceled the day's appointments, he was able to take the rest of the day off, paid. Dr. Shaw wasn't sure if she needed to think or just find clarity of mind, but she knew she was too distracted to offer any consolation to Eddie. Given his reaction, he would likely be of little help to Lorie as well.

Within fifteen minutes, Lorie's schedule was clear and she was alone in her office with her thoughts. Too many unanswered questions swirled around inside her head for hours, like they were on a loop. She asked herself over and over: *Had I not done enough to help her? Did the strategies I gave her to cope not work? Did she not trust me enough to try? Did she kill herself? Was she murdered? Is this somehow my fault?* The chasm left between the questions she had and the answers she didn't left plenty of room for one off-putting question to creep into her brain: *Her baby is missing, but why am I not more troubled by that?*

CHAPTER 3

"**A**re you kidding me?" I said out loud while reading the comments below the short article about Juliana and her son.

There was an outpouring of sadness over the loss of such a "special person" with "so much living left to do." If they had only known. Most of the people commenting probably didn't know Juliana Stevens whatsoever, and strangers romanticizing her death was infuriating. They probably just wanted to insert themselves into the narrative, which was equally enraging. A commenter named Sara Skinner, claiming to be a best friend of Juliana, said, "It breaks my heart to think that her son, God willing he is alive, will never know his beautiful mother." She was not totally incorrect since the girl had been beautiful, but I knew that was not the sentiment she had been trying to convey. The worst comment by far? "I bet she gave her life to protect her son." Disgusting.

In a twisted way, I supposed she had saved her son. Her selfishness and lack of love for her child hadn't just begun yesterday. If she had shown an ounce more that she truly loved that boy, she may still be alive. Her son however, likely wouldn't be for long under her care, and I would be the fool… again. It wasn't easy, but I was glad I had the courage to follow through, and I felt better knowing Huxley was no longer in danger of his mother. The right choice wasn't always the easy choice. The thought put me in mind of a poster that hung on the wall of my fourth-grade classroom: "What's right isn't always popular, and what's popular isn't always right." I felt that sentiment rang true now more than ever before.

Satisfied the boy's fate was secured, I could move forward to the next steps. I was hoping—in vain, I now realize—that Juliana's life would be the only I would have to take. Disappointingly, that was not the case because people just weren't getting it. Briefly, I considered keeping Huxley for myself; he seemed like a sweet child, well tempered and he even looked a bit like me. Then reality set in… What was I going to do, keep them all? Keeping the boy was impossible, he didn't fit into the life I had created for myself. I needed to move forward with my original plan. Though I was not happy about what was to come, I knew from the beginning that making my point would likely require more than just Juliana Stevens' life.

CHAPTER 4

Detective Christopher Greyson arrived at the office of Dr. Shaw at almost exactly thirty hours after Juliana Stevens' body was discovered by her housekeeper. Each of Jules' appointments with her psychiatrist were listed in her phone calendar, which was easy to view once the police's tech department accessed her phone using her own birthday as the password. Even with her door shut, Lorie could hear the detective's deep voice in the next room as he spoke to Eddie. The lobby outside her office was typically silent, even with a patient present. The fact that she could hear the visitor so clearly made her realize she needed to soundproof her office to protect her patients' privacy. If she could hear the conversation in the lobby, surely that would work the other way around. A moment later, and what Lorie assumed was to maintain professionalism and confidentiality, Eddie used the phone's handset, not intercom speaker, to call Lorie to ask if she was available to speak with Detective Greyson.

"Of course," replied Lorie.

The detective was a tall, handsome man with dark brown hair, slightly graying at the temples. His tightly cropped beard was half salt and half pepper, and he had defined lines around his eyes that hinted at kindness when he smiled. Detective Greyson wore a well-tailored blue suit, crisp white shirt and a navy tie adorned with a pattern that looked like small brown and white blobs. Upon closer inspection, the dots were tiny embroidered puppies. Lorie's instincts told her she liked the detective already. Guessing he was somewhere between forty-five and fifty-five, Lorie hoped he leaned toward the older side, putting him closer to her age. While she found herself intrigued by him, she quickly pushed aside any thoughts of attraction, reminding herself of the importance of her professionalism in such a tragic situation.

"Dr. Shaw, Detective Greyson with Wyndisburg PD, but please call me Chris."

His deep voice was absent of any accent, which meant he was probably local, or at least Colorado born and raised. Lorie wondered if he noticed the faintest hint of Southern drawl in her voice that she had not been able to drop, even after years living in the Centennial State.

As he extended his hand for an introductory shake, the detective said, "Pleasure to meet you, but of course not under these circumstances. Thank you for seeing me on such short—well, I guess *no* notice."

His sheepish smile, coupled with his sincere gratitude, disarmed Lorie, making her warm to him despite the grim circumstances.

"Not a problem," Lorie said as she extended her hand to meet his. "My next appointment isn't for another forty-five minutes. How can I be of help?"

"I will make this as brief as I can. I'm sure you are very important to your patients and I would hate to be the cause of your schedule needing to be rearranged. I assume you know I am here regarding one of your patients, Juliana Stevens?"

The question was obviously rhetorical because the detective did not leave enough pause for Lorie to reply.

"I understand that you're a doctor, and that some level of doctor-patient confidentiality still applies here even though Ms. Stevens is deceased. I assume you can confirm that she was a patient of yours?"

"Yes, I was treating Juliana Stevens. She has—I mean had—been a patient of mine for close to a year now."

"Great, thank you. We are off to a good start. Can you tell me what you were seeing her—"

"Detective Greyson—" Lorie interrupted, but in turn was interrupted by the detective.

"Please call me Chris."

"Okay, Chris. Let me stop you there. I'm sure your time is as valuable as mine, and I do not want you wasting it asking me questions I am not able to answer. I do want to help, but I am afraid everything you are going to ask me from this point forward is going to fall under the aforementioned doctor-patient confidentiality. If you get a subpoena, please do not hesitate to contact Eddie to set up an appointment. I would be happy to discuss Ms. Stevens' file with you at that time."

"While I do appreciate that, Dr. Shaw—"

"Please, call me Lorie," the doctor interrupted again, something she rarely did in her line of work.

"While I appreciate your future *potential* willingness to help, *Lorie*, are you aware that her son, Huxley, is still missing?"

"I am aware he was missing yesterday when they found Jules—Miss Stevens—" Lorie corrected, feeling that by calling her "Jules" she sounded less professional. "I assumed that, since I have not heard otherwise, he still has not been found."

"Is there anything you can think of, that you are *allowed* to disclose to me, that might help track his whereabouts? The first forty-eight hours are of vital importance in these cases and we are approaching that number like a runaway train barreling down the side of Mount Elbert. I am sure you can understand my urgency here and want the best for that little boy too, right?"

"Of course I do, Chris. But I also value my license to practice psychiatry and help many people who are still *living*. I don't mean to sound insensitive, or imply that the child has already perished, but you have to understand that I am not being uncooperative either, my hands are just... tied," said Lorie as she held her hands out in front of her as if they were in invisible cuffs.

"Well, thank you for your time Dr. Shaw. I will be in touch soon. You have a nice day."

His words were filled with frustration as the detective walked toward the doorway of Lorie's office. When he was within the door frame, he turned back around to face the doctor.

"One last thing, and I am ninety-nine percent sure you can tell me this," he said with an exasperated tone. "Do you own this building or rent?"

"You are correct, Detective Chris, I *can* answer that. I rent and my landlord's name is Jack Russell. And no, it's not a joke, that is his real name. It is not even John," said Lorie with a smile hoping to lighten the mood in the slightest.

"Ya don't say. That is kind of funny. Thank you for the information. I will reach out if I have any additional questions."

A warm smile appeared within his well-groomed beard, and he gave a little wave as he disappeared out of the room. Lorie was relieved the meeting ended on a higher note than it began. As Chris exited Lorie's office, he paused, then again turned to look back at her with another smile.

"Lorie?"

A nervous excitement coursed through Lorie's body as she tried to anticipate what he might ask her.

"Certainly!" said the doctor exuding a little too much of that excitement. Quickly composing herself, she then said, "I mean what is it you need, Chris?"

"May I ask what you were up to last night?" inquired the detective.

A wave of tension gripped Lorie as the conversation took a more ominous turn. It appeared there was a level of duplicity to the detective's visit. For the first time, she thought, *Does he think I could be a suspect?* The notion sent a shiver down her spine.

The shiver did not go unnoticed by Chris, who asked, "Are you okay, Lorie?"

"I was home in bed, officer. And I was *alone,*" Lorie said, ignoring his second question about her well being.

The rational part of Lorie's brain took over after she responded to the detective's obviously routine question.

"I'm sorry for the tone, I am sure you ask that of everyone you talk to, right?" Lorie inquired.

"Right. Pretty standard. Thank you for your time, doctor," the detective said as his tone turned serious.

After Detective Greyson exited her office, Lorie was left with a feeling of anxiety that wasn't there prior to his visit.

CHAPTER 5

Lorie's eyes opened wide as she suddenly awoke. Sweat soaked her chest and neck, and hair clung to her forehead. The alarm clock read 3:37 a.m. It had been over a week since Jules died and this had been the nightly routine since Lorie learned of the loss of her client. Though not always at 3:37, the times were eerily close, making Lorie wonder if that might have been around the time that Jules was killed. Her brain conjured nightmarish images of what Jules' final moments must have been like, and left her deeply unsettled. *Had she been trying to communicate something from beyond the grave?* No, that was nonsense.

Lorie wasn't a child who believed in Ouija boards and spirits. She knew the fitful sleep was her brain's way of trying to process subconsciously, what it couldn't while awake. Lorie's beliefs were rooted in science, research, facts and practice and the dreams were less likely paranormal communication and more likely the product of concerning 3 a.m. thoughts too many nights in a row.

The day before, it was announced that Jules' cause of death was asphyxiation by drowning and it was classified as homicide. During a press conference broadcast on News 6, Detective Greyson informed reporters and the local community that Ms. Stevens' body showed "signs of a struggle," leading them to believe her death was neither self-inflicted nor accidental. No further details were disclosed, and Lorie knew the authorities would likely remain tight-lipped until Jules' killer was caught. Having seen enough police dramas on TV, and having consulted on a few cases herself, Lorie understood that the police needed to keep key details under wraps. Prematurely releasing information, that only the killer would know, could complicate the investigation and muddle the case.

Finding out that Jules did not take her own life brought Lorie a measure of consolation. It allowed for some of the latent blame she had been placing on herself to subside. The realization did not occur to her that she had been blaming herself until after the metaphorical weight was lifted. Lorie's treatment, at the very least, kept Jules from harming herself, and hopefully her child.

Knowledge was always power, and Lorie found it validating to know that her methods were still sound. But no thanks to Lorie's analytical brain, her brief feeling of comfort was edged out as more questions and unrest crept in. Patients of hers had passed away before, but it had always been from more expected causes like old age or illness. Juliana Stevens was her first, and hopefully last, patient to die from violence. It was no wonder her most recent patient's passing had been keeping her up at night. Certain that a subpoena would soon be granted, and Detective Chris would soon be back for her help, Lorie found it increasingly difficult to fall back asleep. Giving in to her restless mind, she decided to review Jules' file to help her prepare for the inevitable meeting with Detective Greyson.

Lorie, being somewhat old school, always kept hard copies of all her patients' records, both at the office and at home, along with electronic copies. In today's digital world, it was faster to share files via secure email when necessary and allowed; plus they were always easier to read as Dr. Shaw's handwriting was not the most legible. Furthermore, she had developed a shorthand early on in her career to help get her thoughts on paper more quickly during sessions. She did not like to type on a computer while with a client. Lorie had tried to simplify the process for a bit, but it not only seemed to make many patients feel self conscious, she thought it also seemed cold and disconnected.

All handwritten notes were transposed and typed at a later time, and for any client Lorie had seen for more than a year, she also created an overview summary. Though it created more work, and to a younger generation—like Eddie—it seemed unnecessary, she even wrote yearly summaries by hand. Reviewing each session, and writing the cumulative thoughts down, helped her better remember the past and create a direction for future treatment. Since time was not an issue when writing summaries, shorthand did not need to be used. Preferring to read paper at this time instead of looking at a screen, Lorie located her at-home copy of Juliana Stevens' file.

Initially, she thought the yearly summary would provide enough of an overview refresher, but as she began to leaf through all the notes in Jules' file, she opted for the individual visit summaries of her first eight sessions. It was during this time where Dr. Shaw learned the most about her patient, and the detailed, handwritten summaries made her feel more connected to the recently deceased.

Patient Name: Juliana "Jules" Sarah Stevens.

Session 1 Initial Observations: No job, art history degree from CO Univ. 1 2MO son, Huxley. SWF. Huxley's father, not involved, conceived as the result of sperm donation, according to parents—said she was desperate to be a mother, but had no relationship prospects. OC with what others think about her. LI in leaving apt. LI in child, parents told me during our IC. So far, Ms. Stevens has yet to speak to me, let alone look at me or even glance in my direction, however she is here, which indicates she is not vehemently opposed to treatment. Seems exhausted. Hygiene OK. Walks around the room and looks at herself in the mirror each time she passes. Fixes hair, messes with jewelry, applies lip gloss.

Initial Diagnosis: Inconclusive.

Treatment Plan: APP once per week.

Session 2 Notes: Arrived promptly to the APP. BL suggests she does not want to be here. It looks as though she has put less time into her appearance than first session—subtle change noted. wearing one gold diamond stud earring and one silver (white gold or platinum?) Wearing mascara, no eyeliner. A few hairs out of place on her head.

In the TBS of her therapy plan— I start with SL questions. Response
is the same, "I don't know," for the following questions: How do you
feel today? Do you want to be here? Do you think you need to be
here? Do you feel safe in this office? Is there anything you would
like to know about me? She does not make eye contact once during
the questions. I let her guide the rest of the session, as to give her the
illusion that she is in control. We sit in silence for the last 42M of
our 60M appointment. Progress made: she spoke to me.

    <u>Session 3 Notes:</u> Arrived 5 ML to the appointment. Still no eye
contact. Still does not trust me? Instead of beginning w/questions,
I offer up info about myself to jumpstart the process of making her
comfortable with me. I share info about my name. I always felt it
sounded like an old lady name. Now that I am getting to be an old
lady, I suppose it is not so bad. No response from J.S.S. I ask if she
likes dogs. I have a golden retriever named Freud. I ask if she wants
me to bring him in. No EC, but nods head in agreement. To the
untrained eye, this does not look like much, I know it's progress. I
continue to talk about myself a bit and other uninteresting topics: the
weather, favorite foods, etc. At end of session, still no talking, but has
made EC. EC = progress.

    <u>Diagnosis:</u> D or possibly DD, although she seems fairly con-
nected to reality.

    <u>Session 4 Notes:</u> Arrived 7ML. Sees Freud and sits next to him
on the couch. Gives him a faint smile and pets him for most of the
appointment. Towards the end of the hour, she speaks. "Thank you
for bringing your dog." We SIS for 12M then she asks: "How old is
he?" For the rest of the session, we talk only about the dog. Talking
= progress.

    <u>Session 5 Notes:</u> Arrives 3ML to the APP. Sits next to Freud.
We SIS for about 10M. J.S.S then says "I know why I am here. Do
you?" I explain to her that I know that she has been struggling to
connect with her child, a child she wanted badly, and to participate
in daily activities. "That's what they told you?" J.S.S scoffs. "Unbelievable. Of course, they coat everything in saccharin." Exaggerated
eye roll. I ask her why she thinks she is here if not for the reasons
her parents said. "I did not desperately want to be a mother. I didn't
want to be one at all. They told me I had to provide them with

a grandchild or they would stop paying for anything for me. Like completely cut off and cut out of the will." This changed the way I looked at her parents and how I interpret what they have told me, and anything going forward. *"But he is my son, a choice I did make, and, well, I guess they aren't wrong. I haven't found a connection with him. But, what landed me here is I left my baby home alone at my apartment for just under two days."* My expression remains clinical, nonjudgmental, stoic. I learned the hard way over the years that if you want to connect with someone so you can help them, the no. 1 thing is they cannot feel judged. Shock and awe is not something a therapist can wear on their sleeve. I ask: *"Why did you do that?"* J.S.S' response: *"Because I wasn't feeling it."* And with that, our 60M was up. Opening up = progress.

<u>Session 6 Notes:</u> Arrives 9ML to APP. SIS for 5M but makes EC almost whole time. Seems she's waiting for me to start after the unexplained bomb she dropped last session. Like a petulant child, she is waiting to be scolded. It is clear she doesn't care if it is negative, she just wants my attention. I give in. *"In our last session, you said you 'weren't feeling it.' What's 'it'?"* J.S.S' response: *"Motherhood."* For the first time, she is very talkative. She also asks that I call her "Jules" instead of "Juliana" because her parents hate the nickname. The words pour out like water from a faucet on full blast because for the first time she has a basin to catch them... me. Expresses she feels she cannot be a mother, says she's never been taught. Parents are in her life, but consumed by their wealth and status. Juliana's main responsibility as a child was to look, act, be perfect. Nannies provided for her primary care and weren't always loving. Parents were concerned with her lack of attendance at social gatherings and required she attend regular counseling to "fix" their daughter or they would stop paying for her expenses. Parents seem to want to use their grandson as a prop. They want J.S.S to attend social events they host only to bring the baby, and look attractive to maintain the look of a perfect family. They hired a lactation consultant to make sure Juliana was breastfeeding because their peers deemed formula "gauche." Parents named her son, her mother's maiden name, J.S.S. did not desire to. She did not hold her baby after he was born. J.S.S

mother held him first, that being the next day after he had been bathed and inoculated.

Additional Diagnosis: PPD.

Session 7 Notes: NCNS.

Session 8 Notes: Arrives on time. Does not acknowledge she missed her last appointment. Looks more disheveled than before, but also seems to be fidgeting with her appearance more than usual. Asks where the dog is and is disappointed I didn't bring him in. I told her it was because I wasn't sure if she would show up. Talks about how she is a busy person and therapy didn't fit into her schedule that day. Shares how much better her life was before motherhood and how wonderful she was before "that thing" came into her life. It is almost as if she is speaking about another person's life. The J.S.S. prior to motherhood seemed to have some narcissistic tendencies. Parents pay for a nanny for her son now after the incident where he was left alone and they want JSS to move back home with them. JSS is repulsed by the idea and considers her childhood home a "prison" of sorts, with better food, clothing, and accommodations. I ask if there is anything about her son that she loves or enjoys to which she responds, "Not one thing. He ruined my body, my freedom, my life."

Rereading through the intimate details of Jules' first few weeks with Lorie made her feel uncomfortable, mostly because she was being brutally honest with herself regarding how she felt about her deceased patient. After someone dies, people tend to canonize them, remembering only the good qualities, sometimes conjuring up some that never existed, and omitting all the negative aspects from their brain altogether. Lorie had always prided herself on her objectivity and professionalism; yet, as she reread her notes on Juliana Stevens, she couldn't help but feel a twinge of guilt. How could she, a therapist dedicated to empathy and understanding, harbor such unflattering thoughts about a patient who had trusted her? The realization felt like a betrayal—not only to Jules, who would never have the chance to defend herself, but also to her own ethics as a mental health professional. Lorie struggled to reconcile her disdain for the woman's feelings regarding motherhood with her duty to offer compassion and understanding. It felt wrong to think of Juliana as anything less than deserving of empathy, yet the truth lingered uncomfortable in Lorie's mind. While she understood the struggles of the young woman, she just didn't like her that much. Yes, she was a trained psychiatrist, but she was also human.

In her line of work, Lorie tried very hard not to be judgmental, but she was only human. She did, however, do a very good job at masking her dislike when the emotion would begin to bubble up inside her. The thought of someone feeling so loathsome about their own child made her stomach churn. So she found herself reaching, as she had before Jules' last few appointments, for the bottle of Pepto Bismol she kept in her desk drawer. The minty taste of the thick, pink liquid brought back such a strong memory of how she felt about that particular patient, that it almost had the opposite of its intended effect, causing her stomach to hurt more. Lorie's true feelings made her want to crawl out of her skin. Societal norms dictated that the dead should be remembered with reverence, not disdain. Yet Lorie couldn't suppress the uncomfortable truth—she had never liked Juliana.

CHAPTER 6

The following day, Dr. Shaw was pleased to see she had no patient appointments scheduled for the remainder of the day. It was rare when she had a full afternoon off, and she looked forward to spending it as she desired. A small notation caught her eye for 1:00 and she clicked to expand the comment. Eddie must have added the appointment as a "task," not an "event" within her calendar, and she actually did have one appointment... With Detective Greyson. It had been nine days since the discovery of her dead patient, so Lorie was a bit surprised—even a little disappointed—when she had heard nothing further from the detective in that amount of time. She was starting to think that a subpoena might not be granted for Jules' records, but alas, the detective would be arriving in less than 15 minutes for their one o'clock meeting. Perturbed, Lorie wondered why Eddie didn't feel a "heads up" about a meeting with authorities was necessary. A calendar notation hardly seemed sufficient, but that conversation would have to wait. The voice of Detective Greyson—*Chris,* she reminded herself—could already be heard in the lobby. Eight minutes early, not really a surprise, and Lorie felt the optics of reprimanding Eddie in front of the detective might paint Eddie, or even herself, in an unfavorable light.

With little notice for the meeting, and the detective's apparent "to be on time is to be early" philosophy, Lorie was glad she'd read through Jules' file the night before. A "shave-and-a-haircut" knock, minus the "two bits" was followed by Chris' entrance into her office. She thought his smile looked more "I told you so" than "I'm happy to see you," but either way, it was nice to look at.

"Good afternoon, Doc!" the chipper detective said. "Guess what I have?"

He waved a piece of paper, in a playful teasing gesture. Lorie imagined this is what a childhood exchange with an older brother might have felt like, if she'd had one.

"A yearly subscription to the 'Jelly of the Month Club?'" Lorie replied, cracking only a hint of a smile.

"Ha! So the good doctor has a sense of humor, too!"

Lorie wondered to what the "too" he spoke of was referring, as if there might be something more about her that he enjoyed, but left it alone. It was her nature to read into things others would say, but it was not something she often had the chance to do when it came to her personal life, and this visit clearly was not personal.

The detective waited long enough for her to guess again, and when she didn't, he said, "It's a sub-poe-na!"

His tone was lighter than it was during their first encounter, and it elevated the somber mood Lorie had been harboring for the past week and a half.

"I just need to take a look. I'm sure you understand, detective?"

"No problem-o, Doc. And, it's Chris, remember?"

"May I ask what's got you in such a good mood, Chris?"

"Well, any lead I have had in this case so far seems to be leading me *nowhere*, not that I've had many thus far. I am hopeful you'll be able to shed some light on a new path for me."

"While I hope I can help, I reviewed part of Ms. Stevens' file last night, and I just couldn't find anything I thought would be helpful to your case. It was from early on in her treatment, where I learned the most about her. After the first few months, it was more her 'playing the therapy game' to satisfy her parents, and it didn't produce anything significant," said Lorie.

"With all due respect, Lorie, you don't have the eyes of a twenty-seven year veteran of the police force. If you don't mind, I would like to have a copy of the decedent's file."

"You are correct, my area of expertise is not in detecting crimes, it is in detecting people's problems and helping them to be fixed. I have both hard-copy handwritten and electronic files. Which would you prefer?"

"I'll take a copy of both, please. You never know what small detail might be in one but not the other," said the detective.

"That is not a problem, I will have my assistant make a copy of the paper files and I will email you the digital version. There are many instances of shorthand in the handwritten reports that you should be able to translate after reading the electronic versions, but please feel free to reach out if you have any questions. I am happy to provide you with a key to my shorthand and my personal cell number if you like as well."

Lorie thought she would slide that in there, just in case he might also want her information for when he was *off* the clock.

"I appreciate your help and I will take that number."

Lorie then asked Eddie over the intercom if he would please make copies of the Stevens file, then proceeded to email the digital file to the detective. Pulling one of her business cards out of the top left drawer of the desk, Lorie wrote her cell number on the back then handed it to the detective. Chris thanked her for the card and the two let silence hang in the air between them. A few moments later, the beeping intercom pierced the growing awkward silence, and startled Lorie.

Eddie's voice came over the speaker and said, "I am sorry to interrupt you Dr. Shaw, but can you please come out here?"

"Excuse me, Chris. I will just be a minute, I'm sure."

Lorie moved out from behind her desk and as she walked toward her office door, she brushed against the sleeve of Chris' jacket. Lorie thought to herself, *Had that been on purpose?*

Once in the lobby, in a hushed voice she said to her assistant, "Is there a problem, Eddie?"

"I don't know what happened, Lorie, but Miss Stevens' file is not in the cabinet."

"Okay... Where is it?" replied a confused Dr. Shaw.

"No, I guess I meant to say that it's, well... missing." With a look that teetered between apologetic and concerned, Eddie said, "I don't know where it went. I only touch the files when you ask me to, and I have never taken them out of this office. And—"

Lorie interrupted her assistant before he could finish, asking in a quiet, yet irritated tone, "How could it be *missing*!?"

Eddie continued, "I've been trying to tell you... there's more. It's not just Ms. Stevens' file... The whole cabinet... it's empty."

Before Lorie could wrap her head around the fact that the office copies of her handwritten patient files were M.I.A., in walked Chris.

"Everything okay here, Lorie?"

Standing in the doorway and leaning against the jamb with his arms crossed, he gave her a quizzical look. It was a look that she mirrored back at him.

"Actually, Chris, we do have an issue. Eddie just informed me that my hard copy files are gone."

"Just Ms. Stevens' file?" asked Chris, his interest piqued.

"*All* of my paper files. I have a spare of each at home, so you will get the information, but it is deeply concerning to me. As you know, there is sensitive information within each file."

"When was the last time you were sure the documents were there?" asked Chris.

"I can't be sure each and every file was there, but I was in there just over two weeks ago. The day I last saw Jules, was the last day I added updates to the handwritten files. I added information to five files that day, and it appeared, at quick glance, that all the drawers were as full as they should be."

Opening his mini notepad and licking the tip of his pen, Detective Greyson said, "Let's start with the obvious: Do you have any idea who might have taken them? That question goes for you too, Mr. Randall."

Eddie responded first, addressing Dr. Shaw more than Detective Greyson, "I have no idea. Lorie, you know how seriously I take my job and how careful I am about making sure everything is in its place. I would never share with anyone about *anything* that goes on here."

Lorie replied, "I know you do, Eddie, and don't think for a second that I think you had anything to do with this. To answer your question, Chris, I cannot think of a single person. There is no one on my list of clients who I believe would benefit from having their own file, let alone them *all*."

"Okay, fair enough. But what about the theft being aimed at *you*? Is there anyone, a patient, a former patient, someone in your personal life, who might be angry with you?" asked the detective.

Lorie paused, acting like she needed a minute to think about his question, but the truth was she did not have much of a life. Personally, there were so few people she interacted with, that the answer was easy: no. Professionally, now that was a different story. Lorie had been a well-respected psychiatrist for many years and was good at her job. She knew how to connect with people in ways that were meaningful to each of them individually. Occasionally, she had to deliver unwelcome news to patients. While they might be upset at first, they usually came around by the end of the session or by their next appointment, often more grateful to Lorie in the end. So again, the answer to Chris' question was *no*. Lorie figured she gave enough of a pause to adequately "think" about what she had been asked.

"Honestly, there is no one that comes to mind. I will continue to search my brain to see if I can come up with any names, but I wouldn't get your hopes up," she said.

"Obviously, if you think of anyone, even if you just have a slight inkling, please let me know. While I'm here, could you answer a few more questions for me, especially in light of this recent development?"

While polite, the question didn't require an answer, as it was assumed the request wouldn't—or couldn't—be refused.

"Do you have security cameras anywhere on the premises?" inquired Chris.

"Unfortunately, for these purposes anyway, there are not. I had them at my old office, and I found that it made many of my clients uncomfortable, like they were being watched. Their mental wellbeing was the sole reason for my clients' attendance at my office, and it was counterproductive to interfere with that in any way," replied Lorie.

"That makes sense, and it is certainly well within your rights not to have them. I will check around to see if there are any neighboring businesses who might have some footage I can view. After walking around the building a bit before our appointment today, I noticed in the back there is another office belonging to a Dr. A. Jenks. Do you know her?"

"Yes, I know Alise Jenks, but she's not a doctor, she's a psychologist who I have collaborated with on a few occasions. From time to time, she will have a client who she feels could benefit from medication, and since she doesn't have the ability to prescribe, she refers them to me. We have also both been in attendance at a few of the same mental health conferences, but I only know her in a professional capacity."

"Do you know if doctor—I mean Ms.—Jenks has any cameras?" asked the detective.

"We briefly discussed it when she moved in, and we agreed that they wouldn't be in our clients' best interest. However, you might want to check with her to see if she has installed any since then."

"Okay thank you for the info. I will reach out to Ms. Jenks and have a conversation with her," said Chris as he wrote a few more things down on his notepad. "I think that that is all I need for right now. Lorie, would it be possible for you to clear your schedule for the remainder of the day? I would like to get some techs over here to dust for fingerprints and look for anything additional."

Even though she hadn't seen anyone else listed on her schedule for the day, she figured she should double check due to Eddie's error in recording Detective Greyson's visit appropriately.

"Eddie, is my schedule still clear this afternoon?" asked Lorie.

"All clear," replied Eddie.

"Thank you, both of you, I do appreciate your help. If you think of anything, even if it seems small, please call me on my direct line listed on my card," said Chris, handing a business card to Lorie and one to Eddie. "One last thing, please do your best not to touch *anything*. Leave doors open, light switches on, doors unlocked and open. Once the techs get here, you can leave if you like," Chris instructed.

While it seemed like the detective left the psychiatrist's office with next to nothing, Lorie noticed a spring in his step, like maybe he thought he was onto *something*. It was concerning to Lorie just what that might be, as she had no idea what was going on. The thought was even more disturbing considering it could be connected to Lorie's own world. While she couldn't think of a single person who would have had, not only a reason to steal her files, but also a reason to kill one of her patients, she thought about making a few arbitrary suggestions. *I mean, everyone is technically a suspect, right?* She thought to herself. *So what would be the harm in making a few suggestions?* Lorie could not believe that is where her train of thought was going. *Am I really willing to turn the life of someone I know upside down just to get a chance to talk to Detective Greyson again?* Quickly shaking off that terrible idea, she grabbed her laptop, purse, and briefcase and patiently awaited the arrival of the crime scene techs outside her office with Eddie.

That evening, Lorie was at home doing her usual routine: Takeout Thai food from her favorite restaurant which she graciously shared with Freud. His veterinarian said he could stand to lose a few pounds, but who was she to deny him one of his favorites, Chicken Pad Thai sans onion? The pair watched the nightly news while finishing their dinner. The sitcoms that followed played in the background while she mastered the art of checking her email with one hand and rubbing behind the ears of her buddy with the other. After clearing out some of the junk emails, her heart began to race when she saw at 7:42 p.m. she had received an email from *Det. C. Greyson.*

Dear Lorie,
So sorry to bother you after office hours, but I am reading through some of your handwritten notes and I think I will take you up on your offer of a key to help me better decipher them. I will be in touch soon if I need anything further from you. Have a wonderful rest of your evening.
Sincerely,
Chris

To Lorie's dismay, the email was only about work. She had hoped that it might be inquiring about something more personal, like coffee or lunch together, but apparently a working relationship was all he was interested in. *Why do I keep thinking like this?* She wondered. It was so unlike her to be interested in something other than work, and she found it a bit unsettling. While Lorie was particularly adept at reading the emotions of others, she sometimes misread her own. It is possible that she thought she was feeling a glimmer of something that just wasn't there with the detective, and that was all right. Life was orderly and manageable and Lorie liked it that way. No sense in letting a silly crush make things complicated and messy. She responded to Chris, in a very professional manner:

Good evening, Chris,
No bother at all. That is the beauty of email, you can send it when it is convenient for you, and the receiver can read and respond on their timeline. I am happy to help whenever I can, and I just so happened to be doing a bit of work from home tonight anyway. Below you will find a key to my shorthand. I tried to make it comprehensive, however if I may have missed something, please do not hesitate to reach out again, at any hour. I hope you are having a delightful evening as well.
Fondly,
Lorie

Dr. Shaw's Shorthand Key:

Any capital letters separated by periods are initials.

#WO = number of weeks old, SWF = single white female, OC = overly concerned, LI = little interest, IC = initial consultation, D = depression, DD = dissociative disorder, APP = appointment, BL = body language, TBS = trust building stage, TP = treatment plan, SLQ = surface level questions, EC = eye contact, SIS = sit in silence, # before M = minutes, W/Qs = with questions, PPD = postpartum depression, NCNS = no call no show.

Before hitting send, Lorie replaced *fondly* with *regards*, not wanting to suggest she sought something more. Her life was her work, and that was the way it would stay. However, her shorthand list may have not been quite as comprehensive as it should have been…

CHAPTER 7

Another few weeks passed with little news about Jules, no updates about her son's whereabouts, and not a peep from Chris. Lorie couldn't help feeling a twinge of disappointment—about all three really—but she thought she would have at least maintained regular contact with Chris. Not only for updates, but also for her own selfish reasons. Though unwilling to admit it, even to herself, she was struggling to stifle her bubbling excitement at the possibility of what could be with the detective. The doctor also desperately wanted to know what happened to Jules and if the loss of her records could somehow be connected. As much as she had tried to put the theft out of her mind, the feeling of violation was inescapable. Someone, who shouldn't have been, was in her space, messing with her things, and now they held onto some of the most personal and intimate details of her patients' lives. How would she explain to her clients what had happened? It was possible she might even lose some of them given the nature of the breach, a thought that made Lorie even feel a bit sad.

Lorie had spent most of the time in between patients and after work making copies of the records she had brought from home and organizing the office files. Still bothered by where they could have gone and why, she found it soothing regaining some order in her life. Lorie had gotten good at practicing what she preached when it came to the serenity prayer, so she was doing her best to accept what she could not change and change the things she could. Admittedly, she was lacking a bit of the "wisdom to know the difference," and often found herself lost in thought about her patients that were so recently there, but then gone forever. The life of Dr. Shaw was normally very orderly and predictable, in which she took comfort, but the past few weeks had thrown her off balance.

After finishing up an appointment with one of her patients, Lorie had an hour break in her schedule. She was going to use the time to finish the arduous task of refilling her file cabinet, but instead was startled when Jules' parents barged into her office.

Without so much as a "hello," Jules' mother, Caroline Stevens launched in with her demands.

"We need to see the patient records you have for our daughter! There has to be *something* in there to help locate our grandson!"

Although startled, Dr. Shaw responded to the irate woman in a calm, collected tone.

"I am truly sorry for the loss of your daughter, and of course about Huxley. I cannot imagine what you must be feeling. Regrettably, I am not able to provide you with a copy of her file, for two reasons: First, anything I have pertaining to Juliana is part of an ongoing police investigation. Second, since Juliana was an adult, without a court order, I am not able to give them to anyone."

"EVEN THOUGH *WE* WERE THE ONES FOOTING THE BILL?!" screamed Juliana's mother.

Doing her best to maintain her professionalism while feeling somewhat under attack, Lorie said, "I truly am sorry, but that does not matter. What your daughter shared with me in session is held in confidentiality by doctor-patient privilege."

Apparently Lorie's "professionalism" had her sounding a little to calm and collected for Caroline's liking.

"Do you have no heart? Do you not care what has happened to my grandson? Huxley is a *minor*! He is a *child*! Surely his whereabouts trump my dead daughter's right to privacy! Clearly it is of no consequence to her now."

Now Mrs. Stevens' tone had Lorie feeling off put. It was almost like Jules' mother couldn't have cared less that her daughter had passed. Chalking it up to the different, sometimes strange, ways people grieve, Lorie tried to let it go. Not really knowing what else to say, and already feeling like she was a broken record, Lorie simply responded with a *very* unprofessional shrug.

"Will you please excuse me for a moment?" Lorie said to the couple.

Mrs. Stevens' eyes widened in disbelief as the doctor exited the office, clearly expressing that they were not yet finished with the argument. Mr. Stevens did not even look in Lorie's direction acknowledging he had heard her speak.

As soon as Lorie was out of the office, Eddie whispered, "I am so, so sorry Lorie!"

Lorie waved him off then held her pointer finger to her lips, silently shushing her assistant. She hadn't stepped out to scold Eddie but rather to escape the suffocating tension in the room. Hoping the pair would follow her lead and leave her office, instead Lorie found herself eavesdropping on their conversation as they stayed a few minutes longer.

"This was our best shot at getting custody of our grandson and now look what has happened!" said Mrs. Stevens in hushed tones to her husband, who up to this point, had been weirdly silent.

In an even quieter tone than his wife, Mr. Stevens replied, "I know dear. We should have never let him out of our sight. We will find him and he will be ours."

Had she heard that correctly? Their callousness was startling. If Lorie wasn't mistaken, Jules' parents sounded like they might even be *glad* their daughter was out of the picture. Even though people expressed grief in a myriad of ways, that still seemed off. Could they have played a role in their daughter's death? That would definitely be something worth reporting to Chris.

When Lorie did not return to her office after a few more minutes, the Stevenses finally decided to leave, but not without Mrs. Stevens first making her feelings known as to how the meeting went. In lieu of a "goodbye," she slammed the frosted glass door behind her so hard that it rattled loudly. After the coast was clear, Lorie let out a deep breath she had been holding, likely in anticipation of her door shattering.

Again, Eddie apologized, "I am so sorry! I tried to stop them!"

"There probably was not much you *could* do to stop them, Eddie. They are grieving parents whom I am sure are being torn apart by wondering where their grandson is, and that would not make for a force that could be reckoned with."

"But did you hear what they were saying?" asked Eddie. "That was kind of strange, right?"

"I agree, it seems like they were almost waiting for this kind of situation to arise so they could get custody of their grandchild."

Normally, Lorie would not discuss even the smallest detail about a patient with Eddie, as fond as she was of him, but Jules' parents had opened the door for the conversation. Eddie was aware that Juliana's son was missing, that his name was Huxley, and that the angry people who just came in were her parents. He couldn't help what he overheard them say, and Lorie felt validated in her feelings about the odd interaction.

CHAPTER 8

I watched as twenty-eight-year-old Brandie Amstell smoked a cigarette with one hand while using the other to push her child in a well-used stroller. The pair was headed toward the entrance of the Tender Age Childcare Center, a place Brandie dropped off her daughter each day. The toddler, just over a year old, was not strapped into her stroller, and seemed unfazed by the flakes of ash that were falling onto her red hair. I had been watching their routine for almost a week, and not much had changed. It was as if Brandie's muscle memory had taken over, making her oblivious to the child in the stroller. I could have swapped the baby for a stuffed animal and there was little doubt in my mind the mother would notice. It was as if the "lights were on, but no one was home" when it came to Brandie Amstell, and she was barely managing to function through life.

That was day five of my same routine: watch and wait. The right moment was bound to present itself, but I couldn't afford to wait forever. Each day I came prepared and wondered if *today* might be *the* day, but "the day" had not yet arrived. I was beginning to think I might have to abandon the idea of Brandie altogether. As she entered the daycare facility, I could see through a large window that the drop-off seemed a little different from the others that week. Every other day I had observed Brandie check in at the front desk then give the requisite kiss goodbye to her daughter when the childcare provider took her. On *that* day, Brandie had just entered the lobby of the building and as the daycare worker approached, Brandie gave the stroller a big push, as if she couldn't get the child away from her fast enough. Without a word to the worker or her daughter, she turned and walked out. The shocked employee ran towards the runaway stroller and stopped it just before it ran into the pony wall separating the children's play area and reception. *Looks like today is the day after all* I thought to myself, as an unnerving mixture of relief and dread filled my body.

I approached Brandie as she walked past the alley behind the daycare center, ready to give her an offer she couldn't refuse.

"Excuse me?" I said politely, as not to startle her.

It was apparent she had no idea I was talking to her, let alone that I was even *there*, so I spoke again, in a louder voice, but not so much so as to draw attention to our exchange.

"Excuse me? Miss?"

This time, Brandie turned toward me and asked, while pointing to herself, "Me?"

"Hi! Yes, you. I was wondering, do you have a few minutes to spare, I—" but she cut me off before I could finish.

"I'm not interested in whatever you're sellin'." Her voice was slurring, likely a combination of sleep deprivation, despair, and of course, drugs. "Have a nice day," she said as she began to walk away from me.

"Oh, I think you might be!" I said in the same, elevated tone of voice as before. "Would you be interested in making $200?"

As predicted, that piqued her interest, so she stopped and turned her head ninety degrees, so I could just see her profile.

"What would I hafta do? I'm not sucking any—"

I cut her off, "No, no nothing like that. I know you are not that kind of woman," I added as a reassuring measure. "I have some, um, 'brown sugar' that I need to unload. Do you think you might be able to help me with that? I would make it worth your while, financially speaking."

As I said the words, I felt a bit disgusted with myself. I have never once even tried drugs, let alone *dealt* them. I took a deep breath, that I'm certain Brandie didn't notice, and reminded myself that there weren't actually any drugs involved. Brandie's short-sleeved t-shirt revealed needle marks in her arms, that I used as leverage. To make my offer more enticing, one that she likely couldn't refuse, I added to my original offer.

"In addition to cash, I can give you something *sweet* too."

By then, Brandie was facing me with a wary "I'm listening" look, but I could still sense her skepticism. I thought it might be because she was wondering why I would just assume that she would be interested in selling drugs. I was right about the skepticism, however I was wrong about the why.

"You don't look like someone who, well, ya know... sells the stuff," Brandie said to me. "Are you a cop?"

The suspicion was not about her, but about me.

"No, I'm not a cop. And don't you know you shouldn't judge a book by its cover? I have a mind for business, and selling illicit substances happens to be a profitable one."

My response seemed to satisfy her doubt, so I continued on. I told her that it would look better if she were seen as a mother out for a walk with her baby, rather than a single woman—what I was really thinking was a lone *junkie*—wandering the streets. She agreed, and promptly went back into the daycare facility to retrieve her child. I instructed her to meet me behind the center so I could give her the drugs out of the eyesight of any passersby. Within five minutes, Brandie and her daughter were in the alley behind Tender Age ready to receive the package I had for her to sell, or at least the one she *thought* I had.

Slowly, I reached into my bag as if pulling out the drugs, but instead, I brandished a six-inch steel knife. Brandie didn't see what came next since she, too, was looking around trying to avoid getting caught. I would guess another arrest, landing her in jail like her baby's daddy, was something she'd like to avoid. Turning towards me, her eyes caught the glint of the steel blade as it sailed through the air.

With wide-eyed confusion evident in her expression, Brandie said, "Wait, what—"

I interrupted with, "You should be thanking me,"—because I firmly believed I was doing her a courtesy—just before Brandie's world went black.

CHAPTER 9

Lorie's final appointment of the day—and the week—was with Jeff Stuart. As usual, the session was filled with Jeff's whining and complaining—technical term, "venting." Lorie, as always, responded minimally with affirming "mmm hmmms" and head nods, signaling not only that she was listening but also in agreement, which seemed to satisfy Jeff. Thankfully, Dr. Shaw had mastered the art of concealing her annoyance—a skill any good therapist must acquire quickly, and one she had perfected over the years. Jeff also had a habit of pushing the time limits of his appointments, squeezing in extra minutes almost every time. That day, however, Dr. Shaw wasn't in the mood. She found a natural stopping point four minutes before the session's official end. Jeff protested slightly, but Lorie reassured him that she would make up the lost minutes next time. By 6:07 p.m., she was out the door and heading home, pleased with the personal record she had set for leaving so quickly after her last patient. Usually, she stayed an hour longer, but that night she was eager for a much-needed hot bath, a glass of wine, and snuggling on the couch with Freud. She looked forward to giving her overworked mind a well-deserved break.

After an evening of some much needed R&R, she was tucked into bed with a snoring golden retriever next to her. In order to help drown out both her thoughts and the snores, Lorie turned on the television tuned to the eleven o'clock news. Just as she was drifting off, the high-pitched voice of Janie Jones, a news anchor, jolted her back to full attention.

"One last thing to share with our viewers before signing off for the night. News 6 has just learned that a local woman has been reported missing."

Followed by the other anchor, John Haskins, saying in his much lower voice, "If anyone has any information on the whereabouts of Brandie Amstell, a twenty-one-year-old woman and mother, please call our station or the police."

Even when halfway to dreamland combined with the dulcet tones of John Haskins, the name Brandie Amstell was enough to rouse Lorie from her sleepy state. *Brandie Amstell. Could it be the same one?* Lorie's patient was twenty-eight, not twenty-one, but Wyndisburg wasn't a metropolis, so there couldn't be that many Brandie Amstells. *And after what happened to Jules…* It seemed not only possible, but probable. The news offered no additional details, leaving Lorie desperate to know more. Grabbing her MacBook from the nightstand, she quickly searched for anything else on the story.

Brandie Amstell was a more common name than Lorie had thought, but what she was looking for was not hard to find. After Googling the girl's name, many things came up, first of which was the website of an adult film star. The second Brandie was an up-and-coming country singer. The third Brandie Amstell appeared to be the one she was looking for, so she clicked on the link which took her to the News 6 website. On the screen appeared a brief blurb, with the same information Lorie had heard on the news, except her age was listed as twenty-eight. As she scrolled down the page, there was a photograph that had not been shown on TV, confirming it was *her* Brandie. One other thing was listed on the website that surprisingly hadn't made it onto the short news segment: Brandie's fifteen-month-old daughter was also missing.

Lorie struggled to wrap her head around the fact that another patient might be dead and their child missing. Even though Brandie had only been reported missing and not dead, Lorie could not shake the feeling that it was probably true. It was a lot to process, and not knowing what else to do, Lorie continued to search for more information that she soon realized just wasn't there.

Going down one rabbit hole after another—many not at all related to Brandie's disappearance—was mind numbing, which was compounded by her lack of sleep. Lorie's phone began to ring, and the unexpected sound made the on-edge doctor jump. The caller ID said "unknown," which she usually would not answer, especially at 1:32 a.m., but the timing of the call made it so she couldn't resist.

"Hello?" Lorie said with a timid voice.

"Lorie? It's Chris. I hope I didn't wake you."

"No, it's fine, I was already up. What's going on?"

"Did you by any chance catch tonight's news?"

"Briefly, but I heard a familiar name so I looked into it. One of my patients, Brandie Amstell, is missing. Is that why you called?"

"It is, and I am sorry to say she is more than missing at this point. Or rather what I meant to say is she is not missing now."

Lorie was a bit confused by what he was saying, and to clarify, asked, "So it's good news you're calling me with then?"

"I'm afraid not. This is not even news yet since her next of kin has yet to be notified, so I must ask you to use the same discretion on which you pride yourself. Lorie, Ms. Amstell has been found… but the outcome isn't what we'd hoped. When I heard about another young, single mother's death, I had a hunch. I compared your records against her name and, unfortunately, I was right. I am afraid that the theft of your files may be far less innocent than we first thought. Are you able to meet me, either at your office, or at the station tomorrow morning, first thing?"

"Of course. Tomorrow is Saturday, so I don't have any appointments. I will meet you at the station. Does 8 a.m. work?"

"Perfect, see you then. Oh, and Lorie? If there is anything you have pertaining to your two deceased patients that you can bring with you tomorrow, I would very much appreciate it.

You know I will have the proper subpoena in due time, but I could use all the help I can get A.S.A.P."

CHAPTER 10

The only mention of Brandie Amstell in the news that evening—that she was *missing*—left me disappointed, impatient and frustrated that my work would have to continue. Adding insult to injury, there wasn't a single word about her child, who was also nowhere to be found. Making my point was taking more time and effort than I'd hoped. I really just wanted to be done with all of it because it was extremely difficult. It was not a passion, hobby, or game; on the contrary, it was something I wish I never had to do. It was a *calling* that required more time and effort than I originally thought and was both physically and emotionally exhausting. *Was it all necessary? Was it all worth it?* I had asked myself on a handful of occasions thus far, and each time my answer was the same: *Yes.*

Brandie Amstell was an obvious choice for my second mother to *save*. In many ways, Brandie was the stark opposite of Juliana—not rich, not popular, and not pretty. On paper, she was a wreck, but in actuality, she was a colossal disaster. Brandie had been the only child of two absent parents, and was raised by her paternal grandmother, Arlene. While it appeared Arlene did her best to provide for her grandchild, this meant long shifts at one of her three jobs that left Brandie on her own often. Even a loved child—who was properly fed, clothed, and sheltered—without proper supervision, was still a neglected child.

Middle school Brandie, lacking guidance, found herself drawn to an older crowd, presumably looking for adult role models. She frequently attended parties with her older "friends." Not long after, she was given the opportunity to try various drugs, and wanting to fit in, she did so without hesitation, following her older companions' lead. By the time high school began, she was hooked on the feeling that, ironically, made her feel *nothing*. It felt good to feel nothing—to escape the void caused by a lack of structure, role models and love. A few years later, she was running with an even tougher crowd, always chasing a high and lacking resources to get help, even if she'd wanted to. Brandie spiraled out of control. While it was surely a sad story, it wasn't uncommon and not my problem, until the part where she got pregnant and threatened to perpetuate the cycle.

Surprisingly, her pregnancy had prompted her to get clean—an unusual turn of events that left her friendless and battling withdrawal. When she removed the drugs, she removed everyone from her circle who still used. Brandie managed to stay away from mind-altering substances for the duration of her pregnancy, but her tumultuous and sometimes abusive relationship with the baby's father, Keith Wicklow, combined with the stress of an infant, and eventually single parenthood, were enough to drag her back down. Despite Arlene's best efforts, she couldn't be everything Brandie needed to pull through the turmoil and trauma that consumed her life.

It didn't take long before Brandie's own child, Corie, began suffering from neglect. Soiled diapers stayed on far too long. Feedings were irregular and infrequent. The little girl was often left alone. Arlene did what she could to help, but the more of a positive influence she tried to be for her grand-daughter-turned-daughter and great-granddaughter, the more Keith wanted to cut her out of their lives. Corie Wicklow was underweight, unhealthy, and unhappy, her chances at a better life dwindling with each passing day. I feared the little girl wouldn't survive much longer without intervention—so I had to take action.

CHAPTER II

On her way to the police station the next morning, Lorie swung by her office and looked for anything she could give Chris to help him out. He sounded a bit desperate and it did not suit his naturally jovial demeanor, which she much preferred. Not that she expected she would find much, but she was still disappointed. Other than the records she had already provided, the only thing she had that contained any reference to her patients was her appointment book. One was electronic that both she and Eddie had access to while the other was an old-school leather-bound calendar that had four days for each week on one page and three on the next. Writing her appointments by hand was double the work, but fas with her files, Lorie still found still it necessary to have a handwritten copy. Embracing new things, including technology, was not a problem for the psychiatrist, but she didn't feel that something new should necessarily replace something old every time.

Even though she arrived at the police station just before eight o'clock in the morning, Lorie almost felt tardy. She would have been willing to come in much earlier, as sleep was not a luxury she had last night. A few days ago, Lorie had stopped waking up at what had become her new normal—around three-thirty in the morning—and had been appreciative of the short respite of full night's sleep. Over three weeks worth of fitful nights had drained Lorie and she had not been 100% on her game. When the nights began to feel normal again, she was pleased, although it was short lived. Last night, thoughts of Brandie and Jules filled her mind and kept her from the restorative slumber she craved. Two patients dead, both with young children who were missing, and she was hoping Chris would be able to tell her that at least one, if not both, had been located.

The odd feeling she'd experienced before, when she'd learned Jules' son had been taken, returned. *If she was still alive, was Corie Wicklow better off without her mother?* Brandie, like Jules, was not a great mother, or even a good mother. Getting in some trouble with the law due to drug use and theft had landed Brandie on probation, and one of the requirements of that probation was that she see Dr. Shaw for counseling. In addition to providing her typical counseling services, Lorie, as well as a representative of children's services, was tasked with determining if Brandie was, in fact, even a fit mother. Decisions, such as those involving custody, had never been something Lorie took lightly, and they often took some time to reach a conclusion. Though she had not yet submitted her formal recommendation, she was leaning towards recommending Corie be removed from her mother's care. Even if that outcome was best for the child, the thought of separating her from her mother didn't sit well with Lorie. It certainly wasn't happiness that she was feeling that she no longer needed to make that weighty decision, but quite possibly relief.

Lorie introduced herself to the receptionist at the station's entrance and was promptly escorted to a room that she assumed was a conference room, as it seemed too spacious for interrogation purposes. The detective arrived just after Lorie and greeted her with an appreciative yet tired look and a firm handshake. He looked like he could use a shave and if she had to guess, he might still be wearing the same clothes he wore the day before.

"Hiya, Doc. Thanks again for meeting me. Can I get you a cup of coffee? We even have espresso here."

Needing a jolt of caffeine, and curious about the quality of police-station espresso, Lorie opted for it. With demitasse in hand just a few minutes later, she wanted to get down to business.

"I understand why I am here, but I am just not sure how I can help," said the psychiatrist.

Almost as if changing the subject, Chris responded, "So what were you up to the past few days? And might you have had the chance to look over Ms. Amstell's file last night? It's fine if you didn't; I know it was very late. But after seeing how diligent you were with Ms. Stevens' file, I thought maybe..."

The weary detective trailed his rapid-fire questions off with a yawn.

Lorie wondered if Chris was making a feeble attempt at small talk before diving into the nitty gritty, or if he was casually trying to inquire if she again did not have an alibi for yet another murder.

"Oh it's been a fairly typical few days," she said.

Lorie instantly regretted the casual nature of her comment considering that *two* of her patients were now deceased.

She quickly added, "Other than Brandie, of course. It's been work at work, work at home, a little television and dog walking. I did not look at Brandie's file with fresh eyes, but I thought we could go over it together now. Have you read it yet?"

"Honestly, Lorie, I've been swamped. My suspicion led me to look at the names of your patients, but that is it. Looking over the file together now would be fine. And while I have you here, there's something else I want to run by you. I spoke to my lieutenant, and given your knowledge of the victims, ability to keep information confidential, and your expertise, we would like to hire you as an official consultant on the case. Before you answer, please know that what is discussed regarding the cases of Ms. Stevens and Ms. Amstell, including your own thoughts on the matter, would be strictly confidential. Additionally, there would be no expectation for you to violate any of your other clients' right to privacy. I already told my lieutenant, that if you do agree to work with us, confidentiality would not be a problem for you," Detective Chris said with a wink in Lorie's direction.

"What kind of time commitment would it be? I cannot jeopardize the needs of my patients, but I would like to help."

"There is no set schedule. It would be on an as-needed basis, and I would get a hold of you with updates or to run things by you. If you have prior commitments, those would come first," Chris explained.

Lorie took a moment to think about it before she replied, "I would be happy to help. Well, *happy* might not be the most appropriate word in this case, but I am more than willing to do what I can. And if there is any monetary compensation involved, I won't accept it. These are my patients and I want to know what is going on."

"Great! The city of Wyndisburg thanks you for your service," he said with a mini bow and handed her a contract to sign.

"You're very welcome. Oh, and I stopped by my office, but all I could think of that had anything to do with my patients was this."

The doctor handed her leather appointment book to him with an apologetic look.

"No worries, I will take anything I can get," said the detective. "Not sure this will be of any help, but I want to exhaust all my options before ruling anything out. And now that we're officially working together, I can tell you I spoke with Alise Jenks, and she had nothing to share that would be beneficial to the investigation. When I asked her about cameras, she shared your sentiments about not having them and not wanting them. Ms. Jenks assured me that she did not know or treat Ms. Stevens or Ms. Amstell, and I have not been able to find a connection or another reason to question Ms. Jenks any further. Same as you, she doesn't have an alibi, but again, at this point, she is not on my radar."

Lorie nodded in agreement since she was not surprised by anything Chris said, as she had figured as much about her colleague and office neighbor.

"Let's get down to business then," Chris continued. "What I know so far is that Brandie Amstell was found deceased behind the Tender Age Childcare Center where her daughter Corie attends. The M.E. has not yet completed her autopsy, but preliminary findings suggest that Ms. Amstell died from stab wounds. Brandie was reportedly seen by a staff member at Tender Age when she dropped her daughter off at 7:30 Thursday morning, then again when she picked the child up shortly thereafter, at 7:43 a.m., which is highly unusual, but since she was the child's mother, there was nothing the care center needed to report at the time. The front door camera captured Brandie's arrival and departure, but no other footage showed anything concerning. On a regular basis, Arlene Amstell, the child's maternal great-grandmother, picks her up from daycare on Thursdays around six, but this time, Arlene was informed that Brandie had already picked her up much earlier in the day. While this news was of some concern to Arlene, because Brandie was supposed to have gone to work that day, but again there was nothing to report.

According to Arlene, Brandie isn't always the most reliable, and even when he was not locked up, you could count on Keith, Corie's father, even less. However, after Arlene's many attempts to reach her granddaughter that day were unsuccessful, she promptly filed a missing persons report at 7:13 a.m. Friday morning for both Brandie and Corie. We found Brandie yesterday, just before the 11 p.m. news aired. That's why it was reported that she was missing, not dead. Earlier in the day, a tip was called in stating that a person had noticed a dark liquid substance on the ground and walls by a dumpster. The person who took the tip didn't think much of it considering that the area around dumpsters wasn't known for cleanliness. However, when I was made aware of the tip, I followed up with the caller who left their information and it turns out the dumpster being referenced was behind the daycare center where Brandie was last seen. I headed over there right away along with a few uniformed officers and at 10:37 p.m. we located a body believed to be that of Ms. Amstell. We got a positive I.D. on Brandie's body from Arlene close to midnight. Since it is such a new case, that is all we know at this point. I'm still waiting on forensic evidence from the scene to be processed, but from what I heard, there wasn't much, just like in Jules' case. Now that I have filled you in, I bet you know more than I do about Ms. Amstell."

Lorie asked with trepidation in her voice, "What about Brandie's daughter? Was the child found? After what happened with Huxley…"

Lorie trailed off as there was no need to elaborate because it was obvious what she was thinking.

"I am not sure if it is a good thing or not, but at least the child hasn't been found deceased, but no, we haven't found her at all," Chris replied.

With his answer, he could see Lorie look more drained than she had a few moments earlier.

"I have worked with Brandie for the past few years, so I feel like I knew her well," Lorie said, then paused and looked off into the distance. "It's just hard to lose one patient, let alone two in such a short time period. It's hard to believe they are gone and the circumstances surrounding their deaths make the situation all the more troubling."

Chris gave Lorie a gentle squeeze on the shoulder and said, "I know this is difficult and I know how hard it is to lose people you care about. If at any time it gets too overwhelming, just tell me. You are here as a favor to the department, not as a requirement."

"Thanks, Chris. I think I will be fine, helping here is better than letting my mind race at home."

"Do you have any idea who might have wanted to cause harm to Brandie, but leaving Jules out of the equation? While the similarities in these cases seem to add up to the same killer, there are still enough differences at this point that we need to look at them as independent incidents as well," Chris said.

"Brandie did not have any real friends. She had people she hung out with, but I wouldn't say they cared for her as friends should. But from what I can tell, she also didn't have any enemies—well, other than herself. Brandie was her own greatest adversary, along with her addiction," replied Lorie.

"Based on what I know about her injuries, I'd guess it is unlikely she committed suicide. That means there is at least one person out there who wanted her dead. It is possible that it was a drug deal gone bad, a targeted kidnapping or even a random act of violence, but I have found in my experience that these kinds of murders are rarely random without some other motive, like robbery. From the sound of it, Brandie did not have much in the way of possessions that someone would like to steal," said the detective. With nothing new to add, Chris said, "I have the copy of Ms. Amstell's electronic file you previously shared with me right here."

Chris cast the display of his laptop onto a projector screen at the front of the conference room. The pair then began looking over the file to see if it held any clues or helpful information as to what happened to Brandie Amstell.

CHAPTER 12

The detective and his new partner finished reviewing and discussing Brandie's file just before 11 a.m. Lorie hoped they would pause their work soon for lunch together, but was disappointed with what Chris said next.

"I think we have made all the progress we can today. We've gone through this file backward and forward, and without new evidence, I fear we are at a standstill. And I apologize, but I do have another meeting to get to. Believe it or not, this is not the only case on my plate right now. You're more than welcome to stay here and review anything you want. The department, *and I*, greatly appreciate you working with us on this case." Chris placed a ten-dollar bill on the table and said, "There is a hot dog stand right outside the front door if you feel up to eating. Just avoid the monster dog," he added, patting his stomach. "Speaking from experience."

He then gave her a salute and headed out the door.

Lorie gave a little wave and sighed as she watched Chris walk away through the glass windows of the conference room. A minute later, she watched him walk backwards past the windows, like he was on rewind.

Chris stepped back into the room and said, "I almost forgot—I spoke with the owner of your building. Good news! He said he does have a few exterior cameras for me to review."

"He has cameras!?" Lorie said, unable to hide the surprise in her voice. "He promised Alise and me that there weren't any on the premises!"

"Mr. Russell said you might not be happy about it. He told me that at the time he promised you there weren't any cameras on the building, that was true. But he was able to get a discount on his property insurance if he had cameras installed. Needless to say, they're discreet, as neither you nor Ms. Jenks noticed them. I am guessing none of your patients knew they were there either. Don't be too upset, Lors—this footage could provide a break in the case. I will let you know if there is anything usable or helpful retrieved."

With two taps on the doorframe being his "goodbye," the detective left for a second time. Though the discovery of the hidden cameras left her feeling angry and violated, she couldn't help feeling a small flutter of excitement in her belly at hearing her new nickname.

CHAPTER 13

Thirty Years Before

Theresa awoke in a bright, cold, and unfamiliar room. Before her eyes fully adjusted, she could hear sounds: beeps, clicks, whirs. Everything looked so white. *Am I in Heaven?* she wondered. As she tried to sit up, she was met with restraint and realized she was stuck to the bed. Theresa felt the cold steel dig into her wrists before her eyes focused enough to see the handcuffs. Still not completely aware of her surroundings, she thought, *Are there handcuffs in Heaven?* As her senses sharpened and she began to take in her environment, her brain became less foggy too and her last memories began to materialize.

I was feeling like a weight had lifted. I was lying in my bed and I was talking to my baby. I felt a little dizzy and slightly sick to my stomach. Then I fell asleep? No. Her lips parted as she sucked in a gasp of air, the realization of her last memory flooding her mind: *I put a pillow over my daughter's face. I killed my baby.* She slumped in her bed as tears began to stream down her cheeks. *But I am not supposed to be here either. I am not supposed to be… anywhere.* Theresa knew where she wouldn't be going after her death, so by process of elimination, she determined that *this must be Hell.*

Through waterlogged weepy eyes, Theresa noticed a figure near the corner of the room. Without context, she thought it might have been a specter due to the figure being dressed in head-to-toe white. As the figure moved closer, Theresa could see it was a woman, a nurse whose name tag read "Nancy." Not looking at Theresa's face, the nurse checked the machines to which her patient was attached.

Noticing her patient was now conscious and crying, the nurse said in a monotone voice devoid of concern, "Oh. You woke up."

Without another word, Nurse Nancy turned and exited the room. Theresa knew she deserved that treatment, and it appeared her caregiver knew why she was there, but where exactly was *there*? It felt like a hospital, but also not. As she further acclimated to her sterile surroundings, she noticed a wooden plaque hanging by the door with a man's picture on it. Below the photograph, a small metal plate read:

Dr. Clifton Hall, Director
WyldeWood Mental Institution

She was in a mental hospital. Her comprehension of the situation descended upon her like the dark of night falling over a town—inevitable and complete. *I must be alive, and of course, they think I'm insane.* She wanted out of the bed and out of the igloo-like room, but she had absolutely no argument to precipitate her release. How could anyone in their right mind do what she did? Although Theresa had felt like she was of sound mind when she made the decision to end two lives, she also knew that wasn't what a sane person would do. At the time, Theresa believed with certainty that she had done what was best for her child, and for herself, but it now felt so wrong. Thinking about her child's last moments, and what should have been her own, felt like watching a movie about someone else. The fresh perspective made her question her mental state leading up to this point.

Nurse Nancy entered the room again, maybe an hour later, or maybe many hours later. Time was hard to discern since there was no clock, heavy shades on the windows, and nothing to do. The harsh fluorescent lighting amplified the situation, almost making it seem as if time stood still. This time, Nancy spoke to her patient.

"How are you doing?" the nurse asked, without a hint of bedside manner.

Stuttering a little and speaking rather softly, the patient replied, "I-I feel tired, and thirsty."

Nancy reached toward the small nightstand next to the hospital bed to retrieve a glass of water. The nurse held the cup close enough to her patient's lips so she could sip through the straw.

"Thank you," Theresa said.

"If you need anything *important*, there is a button you can press here."

Nancy indicated a red button, near Theresa's hand, that was attached to a long cord that ran down the side of the bed. Turning to leave, the nurse was stopped by a question from her patient.

"Wait. Can you tell me how long I have been here?"

Nancy replied, "About a week." She looked at her chart in the plastic holder by the door and said, "10 days, to be exact. And now that you are conscious, it is expected that you will begin treatment tomorrow. I will be back at eight in the morning to take you to your first session."

The nurse continued on her original path and left the room.

Calling out to Nancy, Theresa asked, "What is my treatment? What is a 'session?'"

Her queries were met with an empty doorway and no response from her nurse. At that moment, Theresa began to understand that most of her questions—and she herself—would likely not be considered *important* enough for her caregiver.

CHAPTER 14

There must not have been any new information in Brandie Amstell's case, because in the past two weeks, Lorie had not heard from Chris. The *hope* of hearing from him made the time feel even longer. Trying to get back to normal felt like she was doing a disservice to her two murdered patients, and their missing children, but there wasn't much else she could do. For a minute, she thought a vacation might be in order. She hadn't taken a proper vacation in a long time, and reading a book on white sands overlooking turquoise waters or in a cozy cabin by a lake somewhere with Freud sounded rather nice. But then Lorie thought of her other patients, who were in need of her listening ear and sage advice, and she decided it would be a disservice to the living if she took a vacation at this time. Plus, what if there was a break in the case and Chris needed her help—or even just *her?*

She could feel herself wanting to protect her remaining patients like they were her cubs and she the mama bear, but how exactly would she do that, she wondered. Warning them about the office theft and murdered patients would not only cause undue alarm, it would also violate her code of ethics. She would just have to help Chris solve the cases as fast as possible and hope that none of her other clients were in the killer's sights. That realization made Lorie feel utterly helpless, even more so because her life's work had been to *help* others. Then a thought crossed Lorie's mind that made her feel an enormous sense of unease… *What if they were never solved?* Unable to bear the thought of the murders going unsolved and her life remaining in a state of limbo, Lorie grew even more certain of her decision to focus on her work and living patients.

On a Monday morning, during an hour she did not have booked that happened to be over Eddie's lunch break, she had an unexpected visitor. The light rapping of fingertips on the door to her office startled her more than she would have liked to admit. As she got up to see who it was, the closed door was gently pushed open and Chris stuck his head in.

"Chris! Hi! What are you doing here?" Lorie said, surprised, all the more because he entered the room before she gave the okay.

"Sorry if I startled you, Doc! But long time, no see and I figured I would swing by as I was in the neighborhood and there are a few things I would like to discuss with you. I saw Eddie was not at his desk, so I figured a knock on the door would be all right. In hindsight, I guess it probably wasn't the right move considering you could have been in session."

"True, but I wasn't, so it's no bother. I was actually just thinking about you," replied Lorie.

She was starting to notice a pattern of spontaneity with the detective, and to her own surprise, she didn't hate it.

"You were?" said Chris, as a slight grin crossed his lips.

A little embarrassed, Lorie said, "I mean yes, I hadn't heard from you in a while and I was wondering if there was any movement with the case."

"Gotcha," replied Chris, with a wink as his grin grew into a full smile. "Anywho, I did stop by to discuss some new developments, but it is also nice to see ya."

Nice to see ya, she repeated silently in her head. Did he really mean it, or was it just a pleasantry, like "how are you?"

"Is there something new with one of our cases?" inquired Lorie.

"Not nice to see me too?" Chris asked in a playful tone.

Again, he flashed a smile in her direction, which made Lorie feel the unfamiliar nausea that is associated with the beginning stages of a crush.

Not waiting for a response from the doctor, he got to his point and said, "I just finished reviewing the footage from your building's exterior cameras this morning and I wanted to share with you what I found. Can I plug this drive into your laptop?"

Chris pulled a chair around to her side of the desk and handed her the small storage device. His eagerness both excited her and frightened her as to what she might see on her screen. Chris instructed Lorie to click open the drive, then another click on the file contained within labeled "front."

A black and white image popped on the screen that was shot from an angle above. It was the entrance to Lorie's office. The subtle rustle of the leaves of the young maple tree in the front yard of the building was the only indication that it was a video and not a photograph.

Chris said, "I won't bore you with the hours of footage I've watched of nothing but that tree," as he placed his hand over hers, which rested on the computer's mouse.

Without thinking, Lorie pulled her hand out from under his, almost as if she'd received a static shock from his touch.

"Sorry, doc, I didn't mean to make you feel uncomfortable."

"Oh no, it is totally fine… It just surprised me a bit, that's all."

In a playful move, unlike her to do, Lorie put her hand on top of his, and moved the mouse's cursor to the fast forward button. They smiled at each other as she removed her hand, and the detective proceeded to the point in the video he wanted her to see.

"I thought that three weeks before the first murder, when you said you knew you still had your files, would be a good place to start. As you can see, even at a fast speed, the comings and goings are you, Mr. Randall, and your patients. Nothing seems out of the ordinary to me. Does it to you?"

"I'd have to take a closer look at regular speed, but as of now, nothing seems to be standing out," said Lorie.

Chris moved the video forward a bit more, and then said, "What about *this*?" as he paused the clip.

Frozen on the screen was a person, dressed in dark clothes, entering the front of the building eight days after the dated timestamp at the start of the video. Lorie normally wouldn't have found that unusual, since many of her patients wore dark clothing, but the timestamp on the still shot read 2:13 a.m. and *that* was not normal.

"Do you recognize this person?" Chris asked Lorie.

The time of night, the only light being from the streetlamp nearby, and the proximity of the camera to the person made it impossible for Lorie to tell who it was. All she could definitively say was that it wasn't her. She also felt a sense of relief that from the angle of the camera, it was unlikely that any of her patients had noticed their comings and goings were being recorded.

"I'm sorry, Chris, but I have no idea who that is. I have burned the midnight oil here more than a few times, as I am sure you saw on the footage, but I have never *arrived* at such a late hour."

"I'm thinking this might be the person who took your files, and if it is, my money would be on this also being the murderer of Ms. Stevens and Ms. Amstell."

CHAPTER 15

It had only been three days since Lorie saw Chris, and yet again, it felt like it could have been at least twice as long. With little to no correspondence in between visits, she began to feel like she was reading too much into feelings that weren't mutual. *But then why did he keep giving little hints that he was interested?* she often wondered. On Thursday, when Lorie was on her way home from her office, she received another unidentified call.

Hoping it would again be Chris calling, Lorie pushed the "answer" button on her steering wheel, and tentatively said, "Hello?"

"Hey Doc, did I catch ya at a bad time?"

There was no need for identification, Chris' voice was unmistakable. Lorie had to try hard to keep the excitement out of her voice.

"Hi Chris. Not a bad time at all, I'm just on my way home from work."

"Okay good. Might you be able to meet up for a quick bite tonight? I have something I want to ask you about."

Caught off guard, she reflexively blurted out, "Like *a date*?"

"Oh, well, I mean sure. I just—"

Lorie cut him off, embarrassed about what she'd said, and tried to gracefully recover by saying, "Chris, I am just messing with you! I assume it is work related!"

Relieved that this sounded somewhat believable, Lorie secretly hoped he would say it really was a date.

"Oh, I suppose it is a kind of date, I just hadn't thought about it that way because I'm still on the clock," replied Chris.

Lorie thought about faking checking her schedule again, but felt silly. Plus, she was too concerned with what he wanted to discuss.

"Well, okay then. And yes, I can do dinner tonight. When and where?"

"Meet me in a half hour at Sutton's?" asked Chris.

"That works. See you soon," replied Lorie.

Sutton's was a casual dining spot in the heart of the city's charming downtown. Her work attire would be appropriate, so at the next stoplight, she checked her hair and makeup in the rearview mirror, and decided she was presentable. When the light turned green, she made a U-turn and headed in the direction of the restaurant, which was only about seven minutes from where she was. Lorie was anxious because she had no idea what he needed to discuss, but excited about the "kind-of" date.

Lorie hoped to beat Chris to the restaurant, to allow a little extra time to compose herself. She figured since she had not been far from the place, she'd definitely be the first there. To her surprise, as Lorie was telling the hostess she needed a table for two, a waving hand caught the corner of her eye. Excusing herself from the hostess, she made her way toward the table at which Chris was seated, wondering if he had already been there when he called to ask her to join him. The detective was smiling, but for some reason, Lorie felt like he was slightly less excited to see her than usual.

As Lorie approached the table, the detective stood to greet her in a gentlemanly manner. What followed was a mildly awkward exchange: Chris seemed about to kiss her on the cheek, but hesitated and opted for a half hug, half pat on the back, just as Lorie extended her hand for a handshake. Their unexpected moves caused them to bump heads. They both laughed in embarrassment, making the encounter feel like an awkward blind date. Continuing with his manners, Chris pulled out her chair and motioned for Lorie to sit just before the server approached and asked for the couple's drink order. Feigning indecision, Lorie told Chris to go ahead and order first. If he ordered a drink, then maybe this wasn't just a work thing. If he ordered coffee or something non-alcoholic, this most likely was strictly business.

"I'll have a Glenlivet single malt neat, please."

The server turned to look at Lorie in anticipation of her beverage order.

"I'll have a glass of your house chardonnay, thank you."

So you didn't give me a peck on the cheek, but you ordered some decent booze. Is this a "date date" or not? It seemed that her internal dialogue as of late was causing a rollercoaster ride of emotions over what may or may not be, and Lorie didn't much care for it. *I understand the human brain and human emotions better than most people. How can I not control either of my own better?* she wondered. But the answer was simple: *she was human.* Breaking from the thoughts that she hoped had not caused her to noticeably zone out, she saw Chris was staring at her.

"What's on your mind?" he asked.

"Oh, sorry…" Lorie said, feeling a bit self conscious. "I didn't mean to drift off. I was just thinking that maybe I should have stopped home first to let Freud out, but he'll be fine, I'm sure. May I ask the reason for our impromptu meet up?"

"You may," he said as he pulled out Lorie's appointment book and a paper which appeared to contain a handwritten list. "I want to be thorough, so I'm scrutinizing everything I have pertaining to the Stevens and Amstell cases. I was looking through your datebook here and comparing it to the list I have of your patients. Can you go through the list I made from the files you provided and let me know if I have missed anyone?"

He handed her the list of patients he'd written in his distinctly masculine, all caps penmanship.

JULIANA STEVENS
SHARON MCCAFFREY
BRANDIE AMSTELL
JEFFREY STUART
OWEN SCHRAEDER

GRANT ELLIS
AMY PACKARD
CHARLIE SANCHEZ
MARNIE SANDERS
MISCHA TAYLOR
ELOISE ROSENBAUM
GORDON SHUTZMAN
CAMDEN WILLIS
ELIZA MARTZEL
DEVONTE SANDERS
BRENDA ULLUM
KILEY FELLER-DANIELS
ELLIOT NUSSMAN
DANIELA ORTEGA
OSCAR NASMYTH

Lorie looked the list over twice, and determined it was accurate.

"It is not every patient I have seen in my career, but I would say it is a comprehensive list of those I have treated in the past five years."

Chris opened the leather-bound book and Lorie could see there were a half dozen or so neon-colored sticky note placeholders.

Opening to the first one and pointing, the detective asked her, "Can you tell me who this appointment was for?"

The notation on the fifth of August, would be the same on the 5th of the following five months, presumably matching the sticky notes.

Before Lorie could answer, Chris asked, "Who is A.J.?"

Shit. This is not good. Lorie's brain wasn't processing what she should say fast enough. She had not intentionally kept these appointments a secret; she did provide Chris with her appointment book. But she also had not intentionally been forthcoming with the information, because up to this point, doctor-patient confidentiality had trumped all else.

"Remember how precious my patients' confidentiality is to me?" said the doctor in the same tone a child might have who didn't want to tell her mother she'd broken her favorite vase. "A.J. stands for Allison Jenkins, whom I currently do not keep a file, electronic or otherwise."

"Why would you not keep a file for a patient? Are there more patients without files who are missing from your list? Why does the name *Allison Jenkins* sound familiar?"

As he looked as though he was about to ask another question, Lorie stopped him before he'd fired off so many she wouldn't be able to keep up.

"No, this is my only patient without a file, or rather the file is just in my brain, kind of... Since we are working on official business together, and I know you would just end up trying to get a subpoena for the file in my head anyway..." Lorie said with a snarkier tone than intended while trying to bring a little levity to the conversation, "I will save you the trouble and just tell you about her. Allison Jenkins was, and is—well sort of—my patient."

Chris interjected, saying, "What's with the 'kind ofs' and 'sort ofs'? You are being awfully cryptic here, Lorie."

"I'm getting to it, it's just that, as you will see, it is a delicate situation. Chris, Allison Jenkins is *Alise Jenks*."

Chris pondered what Lorie said a few moments before he replied, "Okay... I still don't get it."

"I have been treating Alise for the past six months. As a professional courtesy, in case such a situation might arise where someone would gain access—legally or otherwise—to my records, Alise did not want hers to be commandeered. Looks like she was right to feel paranoid about the possibility. She felt that if it got out that she was seeking therapy, it would undermine her expertise with her clients."

"You told me you only know Alise Jenks in a *professional capacity*. Lorie, why did you lie to me?"

"Chris, think about it... Did I really lie to you? I *do* only know Alise Jenks in a professional way. And, until now, I didn't see a reason to elaborate on that statement."

"Okay, okay. Semantics, don't you think? But I guess you're right, it doesn't appear you were deliberately trying to withhold information," replied Chris.

Lorie was beginning to see the argumentative side she knew must be hiding under his cheerful exterior. As a detective, there was no way he didn't have one, she just hadn't seen it before and she did not like that it was aimed at her.

Chris continued, "So that explains the lack of file, but what do you mean Alise Jenks *is* Allison Jenkins? And do you have a file for Allison?"

"Allison was a patient of mine a long time ago, and while I did have a file on her at one time, I don't anymore. I only keep patient files for five years after I stop treating them. After Allison successfully completed the treatment program required by the courts, she decided a name change was in her best interests… thus becoming Alise Jenks."

"Hmmm. This is not what I was expecting. It's tough feeling like I am late to the party with this information you have known all along, but I suppose I can see the logic in your actions. I'll admit, when I found these notations in your book that didn't correspond to any files, I was concerned you might be hiding something," said Chris.

"Well, do you feel better about that now?" asked Lorie.

"I think so," replied Chris, traces of skepticism still in his voice. "Might anything in the file you have in your head for Alise have anything that could lend help to our case? Because it looks a hell of a lot like Alise, I mean Allison—what should I call her?"

"You should call her Alise. She had her name legally changed over ten years ago," said Lorie.

"Well, it's clear she has hidden something in the past, and wants you to continue to do some hiding for her in the present, since she asked you not keep a file on her. Do you think it's possible there's more to all this? It's all a little too cloak-and-dagger for me. I mean, why the name change?"

CHAPTER 16

Just as Lorie opened her mouth to elaborate, the waiter returned and asked if the pair would like to place their food order.

"Sorry, I haven't looked at the menu, but I have a feeling I am going to need another drink first," said Chris.

He took the liberty of ordering one for both himself and his date, and asked Lorie to continue.

"Alise, or *Allison*, had been my patient twelve years ago, and then again more recently. I didn't think much of it when Alise asked if she could start seeing me again, as many mental health professionals need counseling of their own, and we had a history together. Before Allison became Alise, she had gotten into some legal trouble. Do you remember the abortion clinic bombings around the state of Arizona about thirteen or so years ago?"

A look of recognition came across Chris' face, and he said, "Oh shit. That's why the name sounds familiar! I do remember them. That group of twenty-something pro-lifers thought they were saving babies' lives by killing the doctors and patrons of the clinics, essentially becoming the ones who terminated the very babies they claimed to be saving. Such backward thinking. They were sent away for life, if memory serves."

"In a nutshell, yes, but you're wrong about the prison time. All but one member of the group went to prison. Allison Jenkins, who was the youngest of the group at eighteen, did not serve any time behind bars. The group all had the same story about Allison; she was more on the periphery and while she attended planning meetings, she never actually contributed to the plans. Allison was also reportedly never at any of the bombings. But Allison wasn't above reproach, or disciplinary action. The courts determined that while they could not give her any time behind bars, they could impose mandated counseling and community service."

"And you were the court-appointed counselor," Chris said, as a statement, not a question, since he could tell where she was going.

"I was," Lorie confirmed. "I suppose I was expecting Allison to be just as angry and irrational as I suspect they all were. It was hard for me to believe that she wasn't more involved than the others claimed. Groomed to be angry and gravitate towards violence, it could be expected that Allison would be a near-feral person, and one would think I would have seen that side of her right away. However, that person didn't appear to exist when she walked into my office. Allison Jenkins seemed to be a scared, insecure kid who fell in love with an older man who wielded power and control over her. I know that our year of sessions together made a world of difference in helping her heal and adjust to her new reality. As you can see, Alise Jenks is a productive member of society now. I think sometimes going through some tough stuff might make for a better counselor, you know?"

"I can understand that," Chris said as he nodded. "And I would imagine the name change would be to protect her true identity from her clients."

"Right," Lorie agreed.

"And you started seeing her again not long ago?"

"I did. She has been having some strong feelings, even flashbacks, that have surfaced in light of the new pro-life laws being enacted across America. Conflicted, and tormented by too many old memories, Alise thought that seeing me again would be a good idea."

"And…?" Chris said, hoping Lorie would add more to the story.

"*And what?*" said Lorie, although she knew what he meant. "That is all I have to say about Alise right now."

Lorie did not like the way the maybe-date was feeling more like an inquisition.

Chris, realizing his tone sounded like he was frustrated with Lorie, when really he was just more frustrated with the case, said, "I'm sorry, Lors, I didn't mean to sound so tense. I do appreciate all that you have shared with me, and all I ask is that in the future, you let me know about *anything* that could have even a minuscule impact on the case."

Lorie smiled and nodded politely, but was kind of taken aback by the whole meetup so far. Not really sure what to say at this point, she was relieved to see the waiter with their second round of beverages. Taking a long slow sip as a stall tactic, hoping Chris would be the next one to speak, Lorie felt that their time together was ending—for the evening, or maybe the whole partnership.

"Now, how about we end the 'business' portion of our evening and make this more pleasurable?" Chris said with a toothy grin. "Let the date commence!" he exclaimed as he motioned the server back to the table and ordered a bottle of decent prosecco.

As happy as Lorie was with the positive vibes emitting from Chris changing the mood, she couldn't ignore the little seed he had just planted in her brain: *could Alise be involved with this case?*

CHAPTER 17

I became so frustrated that *the point* I had been working so hard to make was not getting the respect it deserved. Part of it might have been my own fault, as I thought the breadcrumb trail I was leaving would have been easier to find. Apparently, I was wrong, and I vowed to remedy that. I was hoping there would be a longer run about Jules in the media, but the story of devastating wildfires in California dominated the news shortly after hers hit the headlines. The public seemed to view Jules' murder as an isolated incident, which was further reinforced by the news stations' diminishing media coverage. The only reason there was still any buzz about her at all was because her parents had enough money to buy airtime and printed pages and the missing grandson of white, wealthy people was still newsworthy.

Brandie's fifteen minutes of fame was more like two, if that. While I wasn't surprised, it sickened me further to know that people on the fringe of society: the poor, the addicted, the minorities and the downtrodden, primarily women, who need extra help and care, were so easily brushed under the rug. Corie Wicklow needed to be saved, but I thought at least *she*, a *baby*, would make a headline or two. Since news of Brandie's death hit the media, it had been, at best, a page-three story or a mere mention at the end of the news. I knew I needed to make a bigger impact with the next one, and soon. But I was confident that I could get the story back in the headlines, so that was just what I did.

CHAPTER 18

The police-interrogation-turned-lovely-evening had Lorie on a high she wasn't accustomed to that lasted through the weekend. Chris wasn't available to get together again for a few days, since he had to put in some overtime on both Saturday and Sunday, but she received a "Hope you're having a great day!" text, or the like, at least once daily. Getting a little closer to Chris had also made her want to focus on her role as "civilian consultant" more than ever. Most of the free time Lorie had over the next few days was spent reviewing the footage she'd seen of her building. Initially, Lorie was not that into taking a second look at the monotonous and lengthy videos after viewing them with Chris at her office. But, with her recent uptick in interest in the case being twofold—helping solve the murders of her patients and finding any excuse to see Chris—she became singularly focused on anything related to the case. The time she would ordinarily spend watching game shows, reading books, and doing clinical research was put on hold as she delved back into the security camera footage.

When Chris was at her office, they hadn't even opened the file labeled "back" for the back of the building, which contained footage of the entrance to Alise Jenk's office. That video was shaping up to be as uneventful as the footage from the front camera, and Lorie felt like her eyes might cross from the intense scrutiny she gave each frame, searching for something without knowing what that something was. She wondered if she was looking for evidence to help bring her patients justice or if she was hoping to find a reason to reach out to her favorite detective. Either way, her careful examination of the footage couldn't hurt, so she chose not to dwell on the thought.

Her slight obsession with the boring movie even continued into her sleep a few times. Her dreams would be bits and pieces of the reels, peppered in with things that happened during her day, sometimes even bits and pieces of her childhood. One dream contained a giant pink hamster walking into her high school science room at 2:13 a.m. and was greeted by the teacher, Freud, the golden retriever. Lorie wished she could hear the *real* Freud's explanation of what *that* meant.

On one particular night, she awoke much like she did when she was not sleeping well after Jules passed, sweaty and breathing heavily. It turned out that nights of dreaming of the "front" and "back" video recordings had paid off. Her subconscious had noticed a small detail that neither the awake Dr. Shaw nor Detective Greyson had. To confirm her suspicion, even though she'd seen it more times than she cared to recount, she had to rewatch the "front" video starting at the part where early morning intruder had been present, until she saw—or rather *didn't see*—what she was looking for. After that, she watched the "back" footage, fast-forwarding, pausing, and rewinding until she could see with her eyes what her dream had directed her to find.

Lorie tried her best to wait until a reasonable hour to call Chris. As *reasonable* as she could be was waiting to text him until 5:48 a.m. to inquire if he was yet awake.

5:48 a.m.

Hi Chris, sorry it's so early. Are you awake?

5:59 a.m.

Good morning, Sunshine! Yes, I'm up.

6:00 a.m.

You sure I didn't wake you?

6:02 a.m.

Positive. What can I do you for?

6:03 a.m.

I know you're working today, but are you able to meet me at some point? I think I might have found something on the footage from the office.

6:04 a.m.

Yep, not a problem. Let me shower quick and we can meet wherever. If you have coffee, I can come to your house.

6:04 a.m.

I could be ready to roll in 20.

6:06 a.m.

Sure that works fine. My address is 324 W. Willow Rd. See you soon. X

6:06 a.m.

Sorry, the "X" was a typo!

6:10 a.m.

No worries! See you soon. XO ;o)

CHAPTER 19

C hris arrived at Lorie's house just shy of seven o'clock that morning. Coffee was already waiting for him in an "I heart my golden retriever" mug. It was the least Lorie felt she could do considering the sun hadn't even peeked over the horizon when she sent him the day's first text.

"Good morning! Early bird catches the worm with you, I see?" said the detective, who looked more tired than his voice suggested.

"Normally, I am not much of a morning person if I don't have to be, but I haven't been sleeping all that well as of late," responded Lorie.

"I hear that. Nothing like a string of murders, let alone people you *know,* to keep you up," Chris said, stating the obvious.

Lorie handed Chris the cup of joe and he smiled at the mug's design.

"I figured it was better than the mug that says, 'Keep talking, I'm diagnosing you,'" Lorie said with a laugh that was matched by Chris. "Plus, I remembered that you like dogs."

"How do you know that?" inquired Chris.

Even though she was a little embarrassed to admit it, she still said, "I remember the first time we met, you had tiny little dogs on your necktie."

"Ahhh, I see. Attention to detail. As a detective, I'm sure you can understand my appreciation for that! Might it be the same attention to detail that brought me here today?"

"We shall see…" Then she asked, "Do you take cream or sugar?"

"Do you happen to have any of those candy bar-flavored creamers?" Chris inquired.

A laugh escaped Lorie's lips and then she caught herself when she realized he was serious.

"Oh sorry, I don't. I'll add some to my grocery list for next time, though! What is your favorite?"

Wanting to hit her forehead with her palm, Lorie thought to herself, *Seriously, Lorie? First, you accidentally sent him a "kiss" over texting. Now you've offered to go grocery shopping for him, and you haven't even been on one proper date!*

It was clear there was some inner dialogue going on with Lorie, and she could tell by the look on his face that Chris noticed her faux pas. She was grateful by what he said next, and appreciated his need to put her mind at ease.

"Well, that would be great! Snickers is my favorite," he added.

Chris took his coffee with both extra cream and extra sugar, no doubt to compensate for the lack of confectionary flavoring.

"Okay, whatcha got for me, Lors?"

While *he* appeared to be able to concentrate on the task at hand, it was obvious Lorie wasn't.

"What, huh?" said Lorie. "I mean, right, you're probably really wondering why I asked to meet you so early!"

Completely changing course, Chris said, "Lorie, might you be free Wednesday night?"

Caught off guard, she looked at Chris and said, "Wait, what? Why? I mean, I'm not sure, let me check."

She knew that her nightly routine involved a standing reservation at Chez Shaw, takeout food, and spending time with a very hairy redhead who was a messy eater but a good listener. For show, she pulled out her phone and checked her calendar.

"Looks like I happen to be available. Is there something related to the case we need to do?"

"You might want to keep your day job, doc, because it appears that you aren't quite as good at catching those little details as I thought," Chris said with a smile.

Lorie gave him a perplexed look, even though she thought she knew what he was getting at.

"It would seem you're not the best detective since you can't seem to figure out that you have just been asked on an official date," he said winking again.

Lorie felt her cheeks flush, and with a conspicuous grin said, "Oh. Well… This may come as a *shock* to you, but I don't get asked out on many dates. And our last one, well, a date wasn't your initial intent."

"I do find that hard to believe, and I am lucky your Wednesday evening wasn't already full. Pick you up at seven? And don't ask what we're doing, it's going to be a surprise."

Feeling more comfortable, Lorie said, "Okay then. It's a *date.*"

Wanting to see if his guess as to why she appeared unable to concentrate was correct, he asked, "Are you able to focus now that you no longer have to wonder if I'd like to see you outside of work?"

Blushing and smiling, Lorie replied, "Yes I am. Now Detective, you were implying just a moment ago that I am not as good a detective as you, correct?"

"Well, I mean I do have the word *detective* on my name plate, so…"

"Did *you* spot anything unusual on the videos then? Because *I did*," said Lorie proudly.

"Do tell! I have been waiting with bated breath since nearly 6 a.m. in anticipation for what you have to show me!"

Lorie pulled up both videos on a split screen on her Mac-Book. "Here we see the unidentified person going into my office at 2:13 a.m. It's hard to tell with the poor lighting, but does it look like they are breaking in to you?"

Chris carefully examined the video and said, "I mean, they could be a pro at picking locks, but at first glance, it does not appear they are actually 'breaking in.' But you do realize that the definition of 'breaking and entering' does not mean the person has to bust a window or kick down a door or something like that, right?"

"I guess I'd never really thought about it, but what I meant to say is it does not look like this person is struggling to obtain entry and I am positive that I lock my door each night. But let's circle back to this. I want to show you what else I found."

Lorie fast forwarded the film at speed six, all the way until Eddie arrived at 8:47 a.m.

"See?"

"That was a great video of leaves rustling, Lors, but that is all I saw," said Chris.

"Exactly! No one came out of the door in which they entered. Now look at this."

Lorie cued up the "back" footage beginning at 2:12 a.m. she set it to fast forward speed two and they watched as the first movement on the camera was at 8:54 a.m.

Lorie paused the video and said, "I don't recognize this woman, but it isn't Alise Jenks."

"So do you think she's a patient of Dr. Jenks?" inquired the detective.

"Based on the arrival time, I'd guess so. But if that's her patient, where's Alise? No one entered her office prior to this mystery person," said Lorie.

"Good point," said Chris as he began to progress the video forward again, at the slowest fast speed. "Let's see who else comes and goes on this day."

The camera trained on Alise Jenks' entrance had the expected traffic of a normal day. Patients would go in and out at just over one-hour intervals.

"Pause it!" Lorie exclaimed louder than she meant to.

Lorie leaned her face closer to the monitor to make sure, for a second time, that her eyes did not deceive her.

"*That* is Alise," said Lorie pointing to the screen.

The timestamp read 18:10, which meant that was Alise Jenks leaving her office at 6:10 p.m. Chris clapped his hands together and, without thinking, kissed Lorie on the cheek.

"Hot damn! I guess I stand corrected—you are a much better detective than I gave you credit for! Lorie, unlike anything up to this point, this is information that might *lead* somewhere. From the looks of it, it appears the intruder entered a stranger and left as Alise Jenks."

"There's more. If you have a half-hour or so to spare, I can show you," said the doctor-detective.

"This is an open and active investigation," said Chris. "I am scheduled to work today, and that is precisely what I am doing. Even if it was my day off, I wouldn't miss what you have to show me. Where are we going?"

CHAPTER 20

L orie offered to drive, so the pair got into her maroon
Volvo SUV and headed out. When they pulled into the
parking lot of her office building, Lorie could tell Chris was
buzzing with excitement about what would be better shown
than told. They got out of the vehicle and walked up the sidewalk to Lorie's entrance to the building. Just to double-check,
Chris carefully inspected the front door to make sure he hadn't
missed any small signs of forced entry, and he hadn't. Lorie was
right, the intruder was able to get into the office with ease.

"Lors, what is going on? Why are we here?" inquired
Chris.

Lorie didn't say anything; she just motioned with her
hand for him to continue following her. They passed the small
waiting area, reception with Eddie's desk, Lorie's office, a small
kitchenette, and a bathroom, ending up in a closet at the back
of Lorie's half of the building.

Looking around confused, Chris just said, "*Okay*?"

Lorie walked to the far back left of the closet where a
curtain hung shut. Chris didn't think much of it, assuming
there was a window behind the covering. Pulling the curtain
back, Lorie revealed that there was not a window behind it, but
rather a door.

Lorie pulled her keyring out of her pocket and flipped
through the keys until she found the right one. She inserted
the key into the doorknob, turned it, and a small clicking
sound indicated it was unlocked. While Lorie was searching for
another key, Chris noticed what appeared to be two deadbolts

above the knob, one facing in, and the other facing out. Lorie found the second key and put it into the deadbolt that faced in.

"This may not work," she said, but after turning the key and twisting the knob, the door opened.

Looking into the darkness, Chris was unsure of what he would see when a light was turned on, but once illuminated, he saw he was in a closet identical to Lorie's.

"Alise Jenks' office mirrors mine," Lorie said as she crossed the threshold into the twin closet and Chris followed. No further explanation was needed because Chris was able to easily see what Lorie was trying to show him.

"I can see how Ms. Jenks could enter through one door and exit another without needing to go out and around. But if this door exists, why would she have to do that? Couldn't she have entered through her own door, then through the closets, then to your office if she wanted to retrieve the files?" asked Chris.

"It's unlikely because we only use this door when she has an appointment with me. The doorknob key for both sides of the door is the same, and Alise and I each have one, but we each have our own individual deadbolt lock and key. If I lock my deadbolt, she cannot enter through this door. I am diligent about keeping this door locked except for the hour and ten minutes or so from the time just before she arrives until shortly after she leaves. On occasion, I have Eddie do it for me, if I run over an appointment time with a patient. It would have been difficult for her to gain access to my office outside of her scheduled appointment times."

"So does the key that opens this door's knob also open both of your exterior doors as well?" Chris asked.

"No, we have our own separate main office door locks and keys, however my closet deadbolt lock is also keyed to match my front office door. If Alise was able to somehow make a copy of my front door key, she would also be able to use this hidden door. Another possibility is that she borrowed a key and unlocked the door at another time."

Chris continued, "Is it possible Eddie might have left the door open?"

"I suppose it is possible, but unlikely. He is good about checking it too."

"So, if Alise wanted access to your documents, she would have to come through your front door, at a time when you weren't here," said Chris.

"Correct. And, since neither of us knew about the security cameras, she wouldn't have been concerned about being detected. Sometimes Eddie unlocks the deadbolt on my side a little prior to her appointments, so I will have to check with him to see if he remembers it ever being *already unlocked* when he got there."

Chris understood that this was all starting to make a lot of sense, but one thing still bothered him about the scenario.

"But why do you think she took your files, if you don't have a file on *her*?"

"I don't know for sure, but while I don't have a current file on her for professional courtesy, twelve years ago when she first became my patient, that was not the case. Maybe she thought I still had her 'Allison Jenkins' file and for some reason she is concerned about it getting out now?"

"Could be, or maybe…" Chris' eyebrows raised, and he looked at Lorie as if she should be reading his mind.

"Or maybe?" she said in a tone that indicated she wasn't sure where his thought process was going.

"Lorie, look at the evidence. Two murdered mothers—both of them were your patients—two missing babies—and your files were stolen by…"

Lorie sucked in her breath sharply as her conscious brain was now forced to accept a possibility that her subconscious had already suspected.

"You think *Alise Jenks* murdered my patients?"

"She had motive and access, and she has a past that could be argued tracks with what is going on here. I think it's time I pay Ms. Jenks another visit."

PART 2 ~ REVELATIONS

CHAPTER 21

Twelve Years Before

The group of seven was gathered in the small living room of The Leader's apartment, six of whom were sitting in a semicircle around the room listening intently. The Leader was in the center of the room and had been a commanding presence. A trifecta of compelling characteristics: charisma, charm, and the ability to completely captivate an audience, made them a perfect candidate for the role. Thus far, the group had been all talk and hype, but no action—just like many young wannabe-vigilantes-with-a-cause. But tonight's meeting was the beginning of *all* the action.

With a group of this nature, code names were deemed essential, therefore each member of the group had been given one. There was Philomena, chosen because she was the patron saint of babies and infants. Magdalen, named for Mary Magdalen, the patron saint of sinners. Jerome, an abbreviation of San Jerome Emiliani, the patron saint of abandoned children. Nicholas, eponym of the patron saint of protecting children. Eugenia, after Eugene de Mazenod, the patron saint of dysfunctional families. Eulalia, for the patron saint of strong-willed children. Based on their cause, and the way they felt about themselves, each member of the group had chosen a code name that corresponded with a patron saint—all except one... The Leader.

The Leader detailed every aspect of their plan, which would commence in two days, thus setting their bigger-picture goal into motion. In just over forty-eight hours, their literal boom was going to be figuratively heard around the country, and finally they would be taken seriously because people would have no other choice. Magdalen had graciously volunteered to plant the first bomb at the OCWC—Opuntia County Women's Clinic. Posing as a patient a few weeks earlier, Magdalen was able to scope out the building and determine a plan for placing their first bomb. Since it was her first visit, she said she would feel more comfortable if she had the "lay of the land" first. The building tour allowed for her to familiarize herself with the layout and exits. Before she left her first visit, Magdalen made a follow-up appointment for the first time slot of the day, on *the* day.

On the day all their plans would be set in motion, Magdalen would arrive at her appointment at the OCWC five minutes early, with her messenger bag across her body. Once in the exam room, she would ask to use the restroom and leave the bag behind. As to not draw suspicion, she would enter the restroom if anyone was around, but if the coast was clear, she would continue down the hallway to the door marked "emergency exit." Magdalen knew from her own recon that the door would not sound an alarm if opened. If all went as planned, Magdalen would exit through the door into the back parking lot and disappear into the wooded area behind the clinic, where she would remotely detonate the bomb in her satchel. The group would then reassemble at headquarters, AKA the living room of the apartment, the following night at 9 p.m.

The plan went off without a hitch, except for one detail; there was either an issue with the detonator, or Magdalen took her devotion to the cause to the next level, because the bomb exploded while Magdalen was still in the room with her bag. As planned, the whole group, minus one, assembled in the small room at the prescribed time the next night. There was a heaviness to the silence in the room, and grief was visible on the faces of every member except one: The Leader. They, too, were saddened by Magdalen's death; however, it was not the time for mourning. Electricity seemed to course through The Leader's veins and they were wired. The palpable sorrow could not be denied, so The Leader addressed the issue and tried to rally the troops.

"I know we are all mourning the death of our faithful Saint Magdalen, but know she did not die in vain," said The Leader. "Look at this…"

The Leader turned the volume up on the television as the local evening news was playing and the top story was the bombing. Reggie Dayton, an anchor with a voice smooth as silk, began explaining what had happened at the clinic that day. The details of the bombing sounded so good coming out of his mouth, almost like he was hired to narrate a movie made about their cause, which further excited The Leader.

"We have an update on the tragedy at the Opuntia County Women's Clinic yesterday morning. It has been confirmed that twelve people perished in the explosion. While we cannot yet release the identities of the victims, we can tell you that two doctors, three nurses, a receptionist and six patients were killed. All six patients were reported to have been pregnant at the time of their death."

With haste, The Leader muted the television and changed the channel to a station that was airing news of the bombing at a national level. Having trouble believing the new detail that had just come to light, The Leader needed a few moments to compose themself. Heading into the kitchen for a long pull from a bottle of cheap vodka, The Leader steadied themself against the counter and took a deep breath. After another minute, they rejoined the group, anticipating much discussion about the new revelation. Instead, The Leader was met with the same quiet, solemn faces they'd left minutes before. No changes. No new questions. Knowing they could only move forward, The Leader summoned all their strength and continued to lead.

"See! We made *national* news! Wouldn't Magdalen have been so happy about this?" Still feeling like the group was collectively questioning their actions, The Leader continued, "Magdalen knew the risks involved in what we were doing, what we *are* doing, we all do. But isn't it worth it? We all deemed it was during the planning, so we cannot change our minds now that we are getting noticed! While the outcome of our plan had the intended effect, we do need to be better about buttoning up our safety measures. Magdalen's loss will be felt greatly for a very long time, and we must honor her memory by continuing on. Who's with me?"

For a few minutes, no one moved, then Eugenia spoke first.

"You're right, we do know the risks. I am heartbroken at the loss of our friend, but what we are doing is dangerous in more ways than one, and we *all* knew that prior to yesterday. I do have a concern though… How are we saving unborn babies if we are murdering the vessels that house them? I guess I didn't realize that part of the plan included killing pregnant women."

In addition to the previously discussed qualities, The Leader was also smart and could think quickly on their feet.

Always knowing the right thing to say, The Leader added, "Eugenia, I hear you, but there are going to be a few aspects out of our control. We don't know exactly who will be at each clinic when we take them down. We cannot think small scale, we have to think big picture. Just like the death of Magdalen, the death of a few unborn babies, as unfortunate as it may be, are part of the collateral damage required to affect real changes. Those babies, sad as it was to lose them in this way, were going to be lost anyway even if we hadn't stepped in."

Feeling a renewed sense of purpose, Eugenia slowly stood and said, "I am with you."

After that, the dominoes fell, or rather stood, and The Leader and Eugenia were joined by Philomena, Eulalia, Jerome and Nicholas. The Leader was convincing, as usual, and was only a tad worried this might be more than a setback.

Before discussing their next steps, The Leader said, "I'll be right back," and left the room.

Returning with six mugs and the almost-full bottle of vodka from the kitchen, The Leader handed a mug to every group member and poured a shot of vodka in each.

Raising the cup, The Leader said, "To Magdalen!" and the sentiment was echoed by the others.

The Leader could tell forward movement was again possible and phase two could soon begin.

"Let's raise our glasses again for everyone who died in yesterday's explosion. Each of them deserves a toast too. Each death on our conscience will further our cause, and we owe the twelve who died yesterday a debt of gratitude."

CHAPTER 22

Twelve Years Before

Aftﾫer the toasts were done and everyone was back on board, The Leader said, "I think our next order of business should be to give ourselves a name. It is clear we are very serious about our mission and any group with such devotion should have a moniker. Does anyone have suggestions?"

Jerome spoke first, "How about 'Better for Babies'?"

"Great start! Thank you for sharing your ideas! That is a possibility, but let's get a few more options and then we will take a vote."

The Leader's response to Jerome was more supportive than they actually felt, since they thought the name was a rather juvenile offering.

"'Magdalen's Cause' might be a good way to honor our fallen friend," said Philomena.

"That's a good suggestion, too. I think we're getting the hang of this name game!" said The Leader. "But I think we can do better."

The Leader already had a name in mind, but all effective leaders make their followers believe they have more say than they really do. The Leader was encouraging the ridiculously lame names the group was tossing around just long enough to lend validity to their ideas, like everyone had a fair chance at making suggestions.

"Anyone else?"

Nicholas said, "How about 'They Don't Have a Choice,' you know, like the babies don't have a choice."

"Thanks for sharing your thoughts, Nick!"

Again, a silly suggestion, but The Leader didn't let on. Nicholas wasn't the sharpest knife in the drawer, but boy, was he sure good at taking orders and The Leader wanted to keep that one happy.

"I have an idea too," said The Leader in a timid tone. "Thoughts on 'The Righteous and Just'?"

The Leader's voice was slightly elevated at the end of the suggestion, to make it sound like a question instead of the statement it really was. The Leader knew that by sounding unsure of the idea, the group would be far more likely to agree with it. Just like every other time, it worked like a charm and that night the group became The Righteous and Just.

The next day the group had already seemingly put the trauma of the first bombing behind them and were focused on the plan for the rest of the "big booms." The Leader knew that immersing the team in the next plan would be the only way to keep Magdalen off their collective mind. While they knew it would be effective for the team as a whole, it wasn't so easy for The Leader, though they would never let anyone know. The Righteous and Just were on a mission to protect the sanctity of life, which according to them, begins at conception. The plans were well thought out and executed with precision because they learned from the mistakes of the OCWC. The Leader was able to convince the group to orchestrate and execute five more abortion clinic bombings, in the state of Arizona, over the next six months. As the death toll rose from the initial twelve to thirty-seven, so did the group's aspirations. The plan was to make their point all over the country, with at least one bombing in each state. Even localized in Arizona, the group was already big news all over the United States. This not only made them feel untouchable, but also gave them the sense that they were on the verge of making significant changes to protect the lives of many unborn children.

The night before the seventh bombing, the group had its usual pre-game ritual at headquarters. A virtual run through of the plan, followed by pizza and beers, as one would expect a group of twentyish-somethings would do. While relaxing and enjoying the party, the group heard a soft knock on the door. Not expecting any visitors, The Leader held a finger to their lips, indicating the group should be silent. The person outside the door knocked again, harder and louder this time. Figuring the unwanted guest had likely heard them talking and the TV on, The Leader felt they had no choice but to answer, which ended up being irrelevant. If The Leader had waited another minute to go to the door, it would have been knocked in by a battering ram.

The next few minutes were a blur of running, yelling, pepper spray, billy clubs, and men in navy blue uniforms rounding up the six remaining members of The Righteous and Just. As it were, the pizza delivery boy overheard a comment about another bombing and he felt it warranted a call to the police. Law enforcement around the state of Arizona had been on high alert since the first bombing, and were following any lead they received in hopes they could thwart any further bloodshed. Numerous leads had been followed, all of which turned out to be false alarms, except for this one. Jerome, Philomena, Nicholas, Eulalia, and Eugenia were all placed in the back of separate police cruisers, as was The Leader, Allison Jenkins.

CHAPTER 23

Twelve Years Before

O nce in police custody, the true identities of the remaining group members were revealed. Jerome was actually Marcus Duvall. Philomena's real name was Ellory Byrd. Nicholas' legal name was Johnny Gustavson. Eulalia was Susie Inkster and Eugenia's actual name was Candace DeLeon. Each of the five members of the anti-abortion group admitted to the bombings and was almost happy to discuss the mission of The Righteous and Just in order to continue to "spread awareness." Allison's story was the only one that was different, and she was not eager to discuss the group. Allison claimed that she had no part in the planning or execution of any of the bombings, and as a young and impressionable girl, she got caught up in something that she could not escape. Allison was only eighteen, making her the youngest member of the group by a few years. Marcus, the twenty-six-year-old person in charge, was also Allison's boyfriend. The significant age gap made it plausible that Allison might not be a guilty party, but a victim herself. Never wavering from her story, Allison said when she was just seventeen, Marcus began grooming her to think like the others. She fought him when it came to any part of the bombings, but he still required her presence at the meetings, and he threatened her with violence if she were to leave the group. Allison was small, timid, and very weepy.

Every other member of the group had a story that was nearly identical, and their responses all went something like:

Detective: "Who is The Leader of this group?"

R&J member: *"There is no leader, we are all involved in the planning and execution. All except for Allison. She was just, well, there."*

Detective: "Whose idea was it to bomb the clinics?"

R&J member: *"It was all of our idea, except for Allison."*

Detective: "Who placed the bombs?"

R&J member: *"Each one of us placed one bomb, except for Allison."*

Detective: "Why was Allison even there if she wasn't helping with *anything?*"

R&J member: *"Allison was Marcus' girlfriend and he wanted her around for moral support. She was so young and naïve, she would not have been much help anyway."*

The district attorney, Sam Callaghan, under pressure from the governor, media, and the public, decided to prosecute all six members of The Righteous and Just, including Allison. The stories were too consistent between each person in the group, and he was confident he would break one of them, or at least when the stories were told to a jury, surely the jury would see through it all. Six trials were held, six verdicts were handed down: Marcus—determined to be the mastermind behind the group—was sentenced to life in prison without the possibility of parole. Johnny was found guilty and sentenced to life in prison with the possibility of parole. Ellory was found guilty and sentenced to life in prison without the possibility of parole. Susie was found guilty and sentenced to life in prison without the possibility of parole. Candace was found guilty and sentenced to life in prison without the possibility of parole. Allison... was acquitted. She knew that, had Magdalen—A.K.A. Melinda "Lynnie" Westerly—survived, she, too, would have received a life sentence. It had been their plan all along—to ensure Allison's freedom—and Lynnie would definitely have stuck to it. For the first time since her death, Allison felt a bit of relief that Lynnie, her best friend, was no longer there and wouldn't have to waste away in prison like the rest of their group. Allison didn't care for the others like she did for

Lynnie; they hadn't been there since the beginning—not just the beginning of the group, but the beginning of Allison's life.

The D.A. had underestimated the group's allegiance, not only to each other, but especially to Allison. The girl was good. She was able to convince the members of her group, with less effort than one would think, to save her to make sure the cause could continue. And why shouldn't it have been her? Allison was the brains of the operation, by far. Her trial jury was also easily persuaded to believe the seemingly young and innocent girl was just that, young and innocent. That was absolutely no surprise to Allison; she was confident her plan would work. What was a revelation to her was that she couldn't convince *everyone*, as she had always had before. D.A. Callaghan was not buying her story, rightfully so, but Allison did her best to remind herself that what he believed didn't matter. She was tried and acquitted, end of story. Though Allison was acutely aware there could be a loophole that might still land her in prison for her past actions, and any future crimes wouldn't be protected by double jeopardy, she knew she had to lie low and avoid the spotlight. Making it believable that she was not a part of anything serious was a priority because she knew she would likely still be watched.

CHAPTER 24

Twelve Years Before

H er exoneration did not come without strings; Allison was required to complete enough counseling to the point where she was deemed able to function in society and had no threatening tendencies. Relocation was the second requirement imposed on her by the courts. She would have to move to a different state, wherever the courts found a suitable counselor, and reside there until the counseling was successfully finished. Three weeks after her acquittal, Allison was relocated to Wyndisburg, Colorado and would begin her intense therapy with renowned psychiatrist, Dr. Delores Shaw. Her recent convincing performance of a poor, impressionable young girl worked better than she could have hoped, so she was ready to keep up the act for her new psychiatrist. Allison was certain that, just like the jury, Dr. Shaw would be eating out of her hand in no time. If she played her role well enough, she might even finish treatment in record time.

The transition from Arizona to Colorado was fairly smooth. Even with an innocent verdict, Allison was still despised in her home state, so the move was a breath of fresh air. With zero remorse felt for her former—and quite literal—partners in crime, she headed North to her new home. Colorado was more beautiful than she had pictured, which was an added reward for all her hard work. With no criminal record, and not *everyone* in America knowing her name and/or face, the mastermind was able to rent an apartment and find employment with ease. Two weeks was the allotted time for "getting settled," and on the third Monday after her arrival, she attended her first session with Dr. Shaw. As she walked into the front door of the psychiatrist's office, Allison thought to herself, *let the games begin.*

Dr. Delores Shaw, or "Lorie" as she said her new patient could call her—if it made her feel more comfortable—looked pretty much like what Allison expected: mousy, boring, and kind of old. Not at all the typical type of company Allison would keep, except the psychiatrist had something about her that Allison instantly found likable. Allison couldn't put her finger on what this quality was—off-putting since she could usually read people well—and there was a little voice in the back of her head telling her it could potentially be problematic.

Their first meeting was more of a get-to-know-you sort of thing; what are your likes, dislikes, family background, etc. Other than seeming more timid and more messed up over the bombings than she actually felt, Allison found there wasn't much acting necessary. For the first several appointments, Allison played the intended role of innocent bystander, and it appeared that Dr. Shaw was believing the narrative.

Thus far, Allison assumed that she had been in the driver's seat, controlling the tone of the appointments and telling the doctor everything she wanted to hear in between tears and sobs. "I'm sorry I ever met Marcus." "I hate that I was even a peripheral part of something so terrible." "Even though it would have been so dangerous for me to do so, I should have gone to the police." "I promise I will do better from now on." "I can't wait to do something good with the second chance I have been given." "I just feel lucky to be alive." However, about six months into her three-times-a-week treatment plan, Dr. Shaw surprised her patient, and the potentially problematic situation reared its head. That day's appointment started just like the others with Allison making promises, apologies and saying what she believed were all the right things. That is, until Dr. Shaw took off her glasses and looked Allison directly in the eye.

In the polite and caring doctor tone she had used up to that point, Lorie said, "Allison, cut the B.S."

"What do you mean—"

She tried to speak, but Dr. Shaw cut her off. Allison didn't have to fake the shocked look that appeared on her face because it was real.

"Oh I *know* you know what I mean. Do you think your placement with me was just the judge throwing a dart at a map and finding the first available appointment in that town? I was chosen because I am one of the *best*."

Allison just stared at her, blinking. It wasn't often that she couldn't come up with a lie on the spot. Wondering silently, *How did I read this situation so wrong?* Allison sat without speaking for several minutes, thinking how she wanted to steer this conversation, and ultimately the remainder of her treatment. Doubling down on her lies and "poor me" persona was her first thought, because that was what she had always done. But there was something about Dr. Shaw that made her want to tell her *everything.* Maybe it was because no one had ever seen through her like that before. Sam Callaghan came close, but even still, that outcome went her way, not his.

Allison realized she had allowed for the pause in the conversation to stretch too long, and it must have been obvious to Dr. Shaw that Allison knew she was caught.

In a tone that attempted to convey authority as opposed to innocence, Allison said to Dr. Shaw, "Okay. So what do you want to know, *doctor*?"

Lorie responded, "Well then. Now we can actually make some progress. What do you think I have already surmised about you, Allison?"

The skillful psychiatrist phrased the question in a way that was probing and opened Allison up to providing answers to questions that Lorie didn't yet know she had. From that moment on, Dr. Shaw became the only person to know the whole truth. Allison's former partners didn't even realize the depth and breadth of her knowledge, and for the first time in her life, as far back as she could remember, Allison dropped the act.

CHAPTER 25

Lorie finished reading over Alise's, or rather *Allison's*, twelve-year-old file, moved it to her virtual trash bin, then hit the "empty" button. She hadn't meant to lie to Chris when she said she didn't keep files for past patients longer than five years. It wasn't until after their dinner that Lorie remembered that she had moved Allison's file from its original location. It was buried in a separate folder on her computer labeled "important," tucked inside another folder named "courts," which was hidden within yet another folder called "Christmas Lists." At the time, Lorie figured she should keep her files pertaining to court-ordered patients in a separate location that was more private than the others. She wasn't sure why she did this when technically all of her files were private, but at the time, it made sense. Surprisingly, there had been no additional court-appointed clients, and she had strictly treated private, law-abiding citizens as patients—as far as she knew—since treating Allison Jenkins. Lorie thought labeling a folder with something ordinary like "Christmas Lists" would keep potential wandering eyes out, should she hire an assistant with whom she developed trust issues. Looking back on it, she realized how silly it all seemed. *Why would she hire someone she thought she couldn't trust?*

Lorie grappled with the possibility that Alise Jenks might be responsible for yet another string of murders. She knew that if she didn't delete the original file, it would be incredibly damaging to Alise now. Awareness of what Alise had been capable of in the past did not cloud Lorie's judgment of the person Alise had become: smart, caring, professional. The facts, however, could not be denied and all signs were pointing toward her former patient-turned-friend of many years being responsible for these present-day killings. Had the recent trauma of women's rights in the news brought up more emotions than Alise had been letting on in their sessions together? Had Alise reached her breaking point? That seemed so unlikely, as Alise had always—since Lorie had called her on her lies—been completely forthcoming with her actions and feelings. At least, in her professional opinion, that was what Lorie believed. In addition, everything Alise had done since her arrival in Wyndisburg had been for the good of others.

Whether or not Alise was guilty was almost irrelevant at this point since Chris had her squarely in his sights. And how could Lorie refute his findings, say, "I know she tells me everything because she has in the past?" Alise had been tried and found not guilty for the crimes related to the clinic bombings, therefore, she could not be tried again. Lorie just couldn't see what good would come of sharing the entirety of Alise's story with anyone, including Chris. It was clear he already believed she might be culpable and had some compelling evidence to support it. If Lorie shared everything she knew about Allison, Alise would be finished and would *never* get a fair trial. Alise was now a good person—had been for over a decade—and was deserving of the fresh start she had earned years back. Lorie couldn't reconcile what she knew about the current Alise with what she would likely be accused of. There was just something nagging at the back of her mind, a lingering question, a "what if" she hadn't been able to let go. *Could Alise be guilty... again?* And with whom did Lorie's allegiance lie: Chris, Alise, or her dead patients?

It would appear Lorie had made her choice when she remembered about the hidden file and then deleted it; her devotion was to Alise. Although she didn't have to say what she saw on the security camera footage or mention the shared back office door to Chris. Perhaps that was a way to ease her conscience and straddle both sides of the fence. Either way,

Lorie knew then she was officially interfering with a police investigation by withholding the evidence she had. But if no one knew the file existed, she wondered if it even mattered. At that point, Lorie was torn between right, wrong, and self preservation. At the time, choosing not to disrupt what she had already put in motion seemed like her best option. Although it had felt necessary, it hadn't feel good to prioritize her own needs. Still, her conscience definitely was not clear. Going forward, Lorie vowed not to keep anything from Chris, but that would be something that might prove to be easier said than done.

Lorie wanted to give Alise a heads-up that Chris would be contacting her again and to explain why. However, given her feelings about the recent decision to withhold then delete information, reaching out to her colleague, patient, and friend before the detective would definitely cross the proverbial "line." *Was treating Alise as my patient, by its very nature, already crossing the "line?"* Lorie wondered. The investigation was becoming increasingly more complicated when it came to Lorie's relationships, which was something she never thought she'd have to worry about. The life of a psychiatrist could be a lonely one, as carrying the weight of others' worlds on one's shoulders leaves little room for anything else. But now, Lorie felt like she had many relationships precariously balanced in the palm of her hand, and she felt increasingly uncomfortable in her own skin.

Before she was asked to consult on the cases, her primary concern was that her doctor-patient relationship would suffer due to the loss of her patients and the loss of confidential information, but it had grown to so much more. Agreeing to work with Chris had given her a front-row seat to witness the investigation as it unfolded. Knowledge was power, but knowing too many details about the ways in which her patients died was difficult. On the plus side, she had the chance to work with Chris, someone she was eager to get to know better. Adding another shade of gray to the situation was the worry over Alise's innocence or guilt, and how her being under a microscope once again would threaten the life she created as

Alise Jenks. Withholding information from Chris, should he ever find out, could cause an abrupt halt in whatever was blossoming between them, and possibly cause delays in solving the cases. The doctor's normally quiet, boring life felt like it was exploding, and with every fire she extinguished, a new one ignited. Paralyzed with indecision, the psychiatrist decided she would do... nothing.

CHAPTER 26

To her surprise, doing nothing actually produced *something*. On Sunday evening— unprompted—Alise texted Lorie, asking to set up a counseling appointment without any further explanation. Normally, that would not have been out of the ordinary for the two to have a session, but with all that Lorie had been thinking about as of late, she could barely wait the three days until their meeting. Lorie was hoping that if Alise, as her patient, brought up the topic of missing files or Chris contacting her, it wouldn't technically count as interfering. Her duty to patient confidentiality would ensure their conversations remained private. Unless, of course, Alise confessed to killing Jules and Brandie, and if that were the case, Lorie would have a huge problem.

The next morning, Alise's upcoming appointment had Lorie feeling like her brain was buzzing. Wanting to keep her cool and let her patient lead the session as usual was going to be harder than she'd anticipated. Lorie was skilled at guiding her patients' thoughts and responses in the direction she desired so they could have breakthroughs in their treatment. In this instance, however, she was careful not to lead Alise into self-in-crimination or reveal that she knew more about the case than Alise realized. Questioning again whether keeping Alise as her patient was a conflict of interest in and of itself, Lorie thought she should either cancel with Alise indefinitely or excuse herself from helping Chris. She did neither. Lorie needed to know what Alise had to say, and she was not about to step away from the case—at least, not yet.

After exchanging a few brief texts upon learning Alise Jenks could be central to their case, Lorie hadn't seen or spoken with Chris, and she figured that, sadly, was probably for the best. There was too much at stake to risk saying or doing the wrong thing in his presence. Not hearing from Chris with regularity had been his typical M.O. anyway; Lorie had grown more used to it and took it less personally. If her relationship with the detective were to develop further, she would need to get accustomed to the demanding nature of police work, knowing she might not always be at the forefront of his thoughts as he was of hers. For now, Lorie chose to let Chris be in the driver's seat regarding their correspondence—whether work-related or personal—to help her more easily manage both aspects of her life.

On the day of Alise's appointment, Lorie was on "autopilot" during her first two sessions, which was not a problem for veteran patients Eloise Rosenbaum and Gordy Shutzman. Both Eloise and Gordy had been in treatment with Dr. Shaw for years. Eloise had been seeing her for depression since her husband, Marvin, passed away from cancer four years prior, while Gordy had been in therapy following a series of panic attacks that began five years earlier after being mugged while on vacation. Both had been model patients during each phase of their treatment and done everything as they should with great success. In truth, Lorie thought that either could stop seeing her at any point and be just fine, but therapy was good for anyone at any time, and she knew both were lonely. It was no coincidence that their appointments were scheduled back-to-back whenever possible. Lorie didn't feel it was appropriate to play "matchmaker" with any of her patients, however if they happened to meet in the waiting room and strike up a conversation that led to getting coffee, what would be the harm in that?

Alise was her third appointment and she arrived with the usual, preplanned tardiness of a high schooler with "senioritis." Both Lorie and Alise had agreed that in order to maintain further confidentiality, considering she was housed in the adjacent office, her appointments would begin ten minutes late and end ten minutes early. Forty minutes wasn't much time, but they could increase the frequency if needed since their close proximity made it so convenient. Upon her colleague's arrival into her office, Lorie knew Alise was worried and stressed, as it was written all over her face.

"Alise, hi, are you okay today?" asked Lorie, now in "Dr. Shaw mode."

She transitioned between doctor and friend when it came to Alise's appointments depending on the topic and what Alise needed from her.

"I am not," Alise responded, and without further probing she got right into the nitty gritty of the appointment. "Lorie, they think *I* murdered Juliana Stevens and Brandie Amstell!"

Lorie held up one finger, indicating for Alise to "hold on," as she walked to her desk and pressed the intercom button on her phone.

"Eddie, I don't need you here until my one o'clock appointment. Why don't you go ahead and treat yourself to a nice, long lunch."

Eddie knew that meant Dr. Shaw needed additional privacy for her patient, and after hearing the muffled exclamation through the office door, he understood why.

"Of course, Dr. Shaw, thank you. See you in a few hours."

Lorie, feigning surprise, said to Alise, "What do you mean? Why would they think that?"

She avoided the real question she wanted to ask: *Did you do it?*

"Lorie, I did something stupid—but with good reason!" Alise said, as Lorie braced herself for the verbal impact of a murderous confession—even though it wouldn't be the first time Alise admitted as much. "I am the one who stole your files, but I felt like I had no choice."

CHAPTER 27

Not sure if it was a gasp of shock or a sigh of relief, but a noise forced its way out of Lorie's mouth that she was able to cover by clearing her throat. Even though she knew that it was likely Alise who took the files, the surprise was real. Lorie hadn't expected Alise to so readily admit to anything, and was on the literal edge of her seat, wondering what Alise would say next.

Alise, noticing Lorie's attempt at covering her surprise—a technique she had used many times herself—said more calmly, "I *really* am sorry. In retrospect, I should have *known* I could come to you."

Lorie, detecting a hint of Allison in Alise's voice, proceeded cautiously.

"Why did you take them?"

Lorie had been careful not to sound angry; she also didn't want to make Alise feel worse, as surely the reason has been justified. But either way, the outcome of the theft wasn't good: either Alise was a killer, or she wasted valuable time by inadvertently being a red herring.

Alise didn't speak for what felt like a long few moments and Lorie knew why there was such a pregnant pause. Alise had put her past behind her as best she could, and every time it was necessary to broach the subject again, it took a bit for her to gather enough internal fortitude to find her words.

Alise finally spoke, but only said one word.

"Magdalen."

Lorie let the name hang in the air, hoping Alise would continue of her own accord, but when that didn't happen, Lorie said, "What about Magdalen?" Again, Alise was silent, so Lorie repeated her question one more time, and said, "Alise, *what about Magdalen?*"

After letting out a huge breath, Alise responded while looking at the floor, "Do you remember who Magdalen was?"

Lorie nodded as she said, "I do."

"She was the only one who gave *everything* for the cause," Alise said, even though Lorie already knew who she meant. "Melinda—Lynnie—she was my best friend and I'm the reason she's dead."

This information was not a revelation for Lorie, she had heard the whole story before. Not sure what it had to do with her missing files, but it didn't matter. Lorie had to stay the course Alise had begun.

"Alise, while you may have played a part in her death, *Lynnie* is the reason Lynnie is dead."

"But if she wouldn't have been the one to go into the clinic that day…" Alise trailed off.

"We have been over this, dear. You may have had the ideas, but every single person in that group…" Lorie was careful not to call it *your group*, "…was a willing participant. The blame for the death toll associated with the acts of that group can be spread equally amongst the seven members… even Lynnie."

Alise squirmed uncomfortably in her seat as if she was sitting on a cactus and not full-grain leather.

"I understand what you're saying Lorie, and I even believed you for a long time."

"So what changed?" Lorie asked.

Discreetly, Lorie looked at the clock on the wall behind Alise. It read 11:45, which normally meant there would be only five minutes left of their session. Thankful that Alise's appointment bumped up to the lunch hour, Lorie figured it would likely be a working lunch today. It would depend on where the conversation went, but she hoped she wouldn't have to cancel the day's remaining appointments.

"Sam," said Alise with the same intonation she used when she said Magdalen's singular name earlier, except this time, Lorie had no idea who Sam was.

It was also the first time since her most recent confession that Alise had looked Lorie in the eye, which showed the seriousness of the name drop. Unsure if she was supposed to recognize the name, Lorie chose her words carefully to remain vague.

"Tell me more about Sam," prompted Lorie.

"Samuel Westerly is Lynnie's older, half brother," Alise said as if she had mentioned him before, but she could see the recognition in Lorie's eyes just wasn't there. "I have never told you about Sam before, have I?"

Lorie shook her head indicating Alise was correct.

Alise continued, "Sam and Lynnie shared the same father, but Sam is considerably older than Lynnie would have been… seven years older."

"So what has happened between you and Sam that would lead you to want my files?" Lorie asked.

Another carefully chosen word—*want* instead of *steal*. It was important that no matter what they said, that her office be a safe space for her patients.

Another sigh escaped Alise's body as she slumped her head down and looked back at the floor. They had been through so much over the past twelve years, Lorie wondered why Alise was acting like she couldn't tell her anything anymore.

"Sam and I share a half sister. He blames me for her death. And he is looking for proof to make me pay for it now."

Lorie's eyes widened in response to what Alise had just shared with her and this time her surprise couldn't be contained.

"Alise, Lynnie was *your* sister too?"

Alise nodded. This was brand new information for Lorie that she was having trouble sorting out.

"How were you related? Obviously, Lynnie and Sam share a father, since they both have the same last name, right? So you and Lynnie have the same mother. Alise, with all the sensitive information you shared with me about your past, why leave that detail out?"

Alise began to shake her head back and forth with her eyes closed, looking like she was trying her best to hold back tears.

"Because it hurt too much. I let my own sister die for something that, looking back, was so ridiculous. We were willing to kill to punish murderers? It is just insanity. And if I hadn't put those ideas into her head, she might still be here. And so would her *baby*."

"Her *baby*?" said Lorie with obvious shock and confusion. Then it hit Lorie what Alise had meant, "Ahhh. Lynnie was pregnant when she died then."

Alise began to cry, real tears this time, no faking it like years before. Although, with what she just learned, Lorie thought maybe it wasn't all smoke and mirrors when it came to Allison's behavior when they first met.

"I didn't know Lynnie was pregnant when she volunteered to plant the bomb. If I had, I would have never let her do it. I am guessing she knew that, and that's why she didn't tell me. I found out when the news aired the story about the bombing and they said that *all six* patients who had been killed were pregnant. I wonder if she even knew when she went to the OCWC the first time that she was pregnant, or if they told her at that time after doing some basic tests as part of her 'recon' mission. I thought we told each other everything…"

Unsure of how to respond to what she just heard, Lorie focused more on the "Sam" aspect.

"Just to make sure I understand the lineage here, Lynnie's father had Sam with one woman, then Lynnie with your mother. After their relationship ended, your mother had you with a man with the last name Jenkins. Have I gotten things right?"

Alise lifted her head but looked out the window instead of at Lorie, before saying, "That's not quite it. It is more complicated than that. Lynnie's father, Henry Westerly, was also my step-father, and very much involved in raising me."

Alise paused to let that sink in. Lorie didn't catch it at first and wondered why there was a lull in the story. Then it registered.

"Wait, if Henry was your step-father, that means he was married to your mother at some point after you were born."

"Henry had Sam with his college girlfriend. They were never married, and they split up when Sam was two. When Sam was five years old, Henry married my mother, Diane, and together, two years later, they had Lynnie. About a year after Lynnie was born, my mother had an affair with a man named Elliot Jenkins, and you are looking at the product of their indiscretions," Alise said, arms extended out at her sides, palms up. "Apparently, my mother wanted Henry to believe I was his child, but when my biological father found out that my mom was pregnant, he insisted on a paternity test. He had no children of his own, but was very excited about being a dad, and was not about to let another man raise me while he sat on the sidelines and watched. I was too young to know better, but I had heard that things got ugly for a while as Henry and my mom went back and forth about staying together or breaking up. They decided to stick it out and stay married, but you know what they say, 'Once a cheater, always a cheater,' right? My mom went on to have more affairs, I don't know how many, but Henry turned a blind eye. He would rather keep his family together and stay in an unhappy marriage than leave Lynnie and me alone with our mother, who was growing more unstable by the day. Henry was a wonderful, selfless father because he not only loved me as one of his own, but he also had no issues with my biological father loving me too. I have had no contact with either of my dads since I moved to Colorado. I didn't want to make their lives any more difficult than I already had.

As Lynnie and I got older, we noticed mom would be gone a lot. We were told she was in the hospital, visiting friends, on work trips, etc. But Sam, who was older and wiser, and had followed mom a few times, was able to confirm and fill us in on her additional extramarital activities. He also told Lynnie and me why she didn't have any more children. According to Sam, my mother had at least four abortions to try to hide from Henry the subsequent affairs she'd had. And I suppose that is where my idea to save the babies came from. I should have had more siblings, and it posed the burdensome question of why she decided to keep me. The closest thing that I can relate it to is that maybe I have a form of survivor's guilt?" Alise said, as a question, likely hoping Lorie would confirm her self diagnosis.

It was a lot for Lorie to take in, but she managed to process it fast enough to keep up.

"It's possible you have a version of survivor's guilt, however did you ever think that the way you were going about trying to stop abortions was subconsciously a way to punish your mother too? Maybe the reasoning behind your actions wasn't as singular as you thought."

A look of astonishment appeared on Alise's face before she said, "Honestly, no. Lynnie and I believed it was all about the siblings we'd lost, and not letting that happen to anyone else. At the time, we thought no cost was too high to pay."

"So you said the idea was yours. Did Lynnie not have any feelings about what your mother had done, that she shared prior to you revealing your plan?" asked Lorie.

"I don't know. We talked about our parents, mostly our mom, like normal teenagers did. We were perpetually pissed off at her, didn't want to be around her, blamed her for everything that was wrong in our lives from a stubbed toe, to a failed test, to a boyfriend breakup. We talked about what our lives would be like if she wasn't around anymore and how we didn't think we would miss her."

"Alise, that is not 'normal teenager talk' about parents, that sounds like children who despised a parent so much, they might wish them *dead*. And if Lynnie shared the same sentiment, my guess is she'd have come up with an equally destructive plan at some point, you just beat her to it."

"I guess I never thought about it that way before," said Alise. "After working so hard to change my thinking these past twelve years, I suppose a side effect of becoming a better person would be to put all the blame on me."

"It is also easy to misremember what someone was truly like after they have died. It is human nature to want to overlook all their faults and only think of their good qualities, and maybe even overinflate the good qualities. Is it possible that Lynnie was just as responsible for all that happened as you, but because you lived, you blame yourself?"

The question hung in the air for several seconds before Alise gave the response, "I suppose it's possible."

Lorie continued with her line of questioning, "Is it also possible that you are misremembering or exaggerating your role in everything? A group naturally seeks a leader, and you stepped up to that role. From what I understand, no members of that group were held against their will, were they?"

"They weren't," said Alise.

"Is it possible that, at eighteen, your naivety and ego had you taking credit for more than was deserved?"

"I suppose that is also a possibility."

"Okay, now that you concede that you might be willing to let up on yourself just a bit regarding your sister's death, and that of her unborn child, let's get back to what is going on with Sam, and why you felt you needed my files," said Lorie. "And I think we know what we have to unpack in our upcoming sessions together," Lorie added, then paused to see if the answer was as obvious to Alise as it was to Lorie.

Alise responded, "My mother issues?"

"Yes," said Lorie, "your mother *issues*," in a tone that indicated the word "issues" didn't encompass the magnitude of her mother's impact on her life.

CHAPTER 28

Tell me more about Sam and why he has you so worried," Lorie said to Alise, who seemed more at ease in the familiar setting after unburdening herself of a few major secrets.

"Until a few months ago, the last time I had spoken to—or even seen—Sam was at Lynnie's funeral. I know it's too 'new school' for you, but you know I use an online scheduling system for my clients, right?" Lorie nodded. "Well, there is a link on my website where people can request an appointment, my calendar pops up, and they can choose a time."

"Yes, I am familiar with the system," replied Lorie, "and you are correct, too new for me. I prefer the old fashioned way of scheduling appointments and they can call my assistant. Plus, I don't love the idea of someone knowing what my schedule is. It feels like an invasion of my privacy, but I digress. Go on."

"Anyway, it is not uncommon for me to have a name on my schedule that I don't recognize, so I thought nothing of it when a James Green was my last appointment for the day a few months back. With my office door open, I noticed someone entering the waiting room out of the corner of my eye. I needed to finish my session notes from my last client, so without looking up, I said, 'I'll be right with you.' I expected him to say 'okay' or 'no problem' but his response was, 'Hey, Allie-bug.' I froze. I hadn't been called that since I was a little girl.

I could still see him out of the corner of my eye, and by this point, he had taken a seat on the chaise across the room. Even though I was afraid to look up from my computer, I forced myself to turn my gaze toward the new client. But the person I saw wasn't who I was expecting. I was looking at a man whom I wouldn't have recognized if I passed him on the street. Hell, I wouldn't have recognized at all him if he hadn't used my childhood nickname.

Sam was older looking than I would have expected, like the years had been unkind to him. His hair was all gray and looked like it was about six months past a much-needed haircut. A messy, short beard, the kind that goes down a man's neck too, covered more of his face than was fashionable, and he was always clean shaven when I knew him before. Remnants of the chestnut brown hair he used to have on his head, that was the same color as Lynnie's, was peppered throughout the beard. There were crow's feet around his eyes and a deep crevice of a wrinkle that ran the length of his forehead. It reminded me of the same wrinkle that his father had too. For only being thirty-nine, he could have passed for twenty years older. We stared at each other in silence, without moving a muscle, for what seemed like too long. I felt what it must feel like to be a deer looking in the eye of a hunter with the sight of his gun trained squarely on its center mass.

I opened my mouth to speak, and nothing came out. I didn't know what to say, but even if I did, I doubt the words would have been able to escape my dry throat. Sam broke the silence first and with a devious half-smile, said 'You don't seem thrilled to see me.' He was right, I wasn't. Sam and I did not leave on good terms. The last time we spoke, at the funeral, was less speaking and more shouting. I was trying to be discreet, as it would be best the topic of our conversation not be overheard, but Sam obviously wanted people to hear. In the basement of the church, at the funeral reception, we stood around a bend in the hallway that I hoped was out of earshot of the many others in attendance. One of the older ladies who volunteered to serve food at the reception—as if she wielded any actual power—found us and said that if we didn't keep it down, we would be forced to leave. I knew our discussion was not appropriate considering the setting, and that we just buried our sister, but Sam didn't care.

He said to me, 'You know you're the reason she's dead, don't you? She told me *everything* before she died. I know why she was at that clinic and I know there is no way in Hell that she killed herself!' Even without going into further detail, it was clear that Lynnie had shared at least some of our plans with her older brother, and from the sound of it, she likely told him that she was with child. It shouldn't have surprised me as the two had always been close, even though there was a decent age gap. Sam looked after Lynnie as any protective older brother would, even after she was old enough to take care of herself. As kids, he and I had gotten along all right, but looking back, I'm sure that was at Henry's behest. Soon enough it became obvious that blood was thicker than water, and he more tolerated me than loved me because I wasn't his real sister. I think his increasing disdain for my mother over the years correlated directly to how he seemed to have a growing dislike for me as I got older. I never had a problem with Sam, but I don't think I really ever had a chance with him. All that made it much easier for him to blame me for Lynnie's death. As much as I denied having anything to do with the bombings and, Lynnie's death, he had no idea that I was secretly blaming myself more than he ever could."

Lorie interjected, more to give Alise a little break to catch her breath than anything.

"Well, it certainly makes sense why the two of you parted ways after Lynnie's funeral. But were there no family gatherings over the years that either of you were to attend together?"

Alise let out what almost sounded like a quiet half laugh.

"Not to be rude, but after everything that went down, do you really think my family wanted anything to do with me? And even if they did, they would have had to move with me in order for us to have a relationship. No one in the state of Arizona seemed to have an ounce of sympathy for me. It's possible they hated me even more than the rest of the group, because I got off with barely a slap on the wrist. So to answer your question, no. No obligatory family functions to attend for me. My life is here now, and I have a very select group of people with whom I associate, and you know me better than anyone."

The thought of Alise not having family, and likely not celebrating holidays or birthdays with anyone, made Lorie momentarily sad. But in reality, if she was going to feel sad for Alise, she should also feel sad for herself. Lorie couldn't remember the last holiday or special occasion she'd spent with anyone besides Freud, but the thought that might be changing for her is what caused her to empathize with her friend.

"After the trial, I truly thought I would never see Sam again, but there he was sitting across from me, looking like a ragged shell of his former self. I was finally able to get out the words, 'What are you doing here?'

'I am this close to having all the proof I need to show that you were just as guilty, if not more, than the rest of your fucked-in-the-head group,' he said to me as he put a paper-thin space between his thumb and index finger.

Torn between thinking it was bullshit and thinking he wouldn't have sought me out if he didn't have something, I took a chance and said, 'What proof could you possibly have? And why now?'

He replied, 'I have been talking to some of your old friends, you know, members of the *Righteous and Just.*'

His statement hit me like a punch to the gut. As far as I knew, the group's name had never been discussed with anyone outside the group. I knew that it couldn't have been Lynnie who told him either—she died before we came up with the name. He had to have been talking to one of the other members, and my guess was Marcus. Even though Marcus agreed to let me go free while they took the fall, I know he loved me. He hated the idea of people thinking he treated me poorly. Let that fester in a prison cell for over a decade and he might've been eager to talk. I should have been more prepared for the whole interaction, as I knew it was inevitable that my past would catch up with me someday. I have worked so hard to build a good life, and do good, that it hurt and surprised me more than I would have imagined. I told him to get out of my office, and if he came back again, I would call the police.

As he walked out, he said to me, 'With what I have on you, I welcome you to make that phone call. And if they don't do anything, I'm sure *karma* will. If not for Lynnie's sake, for our niece or nephew who should be thirteen now.'"

As Alise seemed to bring her story of Sam's reappearance in her life to a close, Lorie asked, "Did you think I had something in my records that might link you to the truth you shared with me about what really happened?"

"Yes. I keep *all* my files for all my patients, so naturally I assumed that you still had mine from when I was Allison. I knew where you stored them, and I was so afraid that Sam would be able to get access to them. I am sure somewhere it is listed that you were my court-appointed psychiatrist, and there is no doubt in my mind that he would eventually figure it out, if he hasn't already. I mean he figured out I am not Alise Jenks. I was quite surprised when I found that there were only about five years worth of patient files there. I thought about putting them back, but a thief breaking in twice, once to steal and once to *return*, seemed like it would narrow down the suspect pool a little too much for my comfort," said Alise, realizing that her thought process let her "criminal" show through just a bit. "I am so sorry, Lorie. I should have come to you with all of this when Sam showed up, but as you know, I haven't always had such a stellar record for decision making."

Lorie said, "Alise, while I do wish you would have come to me, I am relieved it was you who took my patient data. You and I have consulted on patients before, and I am so thankful that their sensitive information isn't in the hands of some random, untrustworthy person I don't know, but rather in the hands of an untrustworthy person that I *do* know."

Lorie felt like a little joke would bring a much needed bit of levity to the room. It did not.

"Lorie, I know I messed up, but *please* know that you can still trust me!"

"Oh, I am so sorry! That joke was in poor taste and on the contrary, Alise, you are one of the few people in the world who I think I can trust. You have bared your soul to me, I believe now in its entirety, correct? And what makes a person more trustworthy than that?" The question hung in the air for a moment before anyone spoke. "There's nothing *else* you need to tell me, right Alise?"

"No, I swear, this is everything, and I promise I won't withhold anything going forward," said Alise.

When Lorie glanced at her watch, she was surprised to see that her next session was scheduled to start in eight minutes. The two women had gotten so lost in their conversation, keeping track of time was not a priority, nor was eating lunch.

"Alise, I have a patient due to arrive shortly. Let's get another session on the calendar and we can discuss this business with Sam, and your mother, at that time."

"Okay thank you so much, Lorie. I appreciate you more than you know and I don't know where I would be without you."

The women stood, embraced, and Alise left Lorie's office in a rush.

While there was still the matter of who was killing Lorie's patients, which was deeply upsetting, Lorie felt oddly calm about the whole interaction with Alise. Knowing the whole truth about Alise gave her the satisfaction of putting in the last, temporarily lost piece, of a thousand-piece puzzle, and she could finally see the full picture. In Lorie's mind, there is no way her friend was guilty of the awful acts Chris suspected, which eased her overworked mind. She knew that Alise's upcoming sessions would be extremely beneficial, because unraveling a tangled knot of one's painful past must be done before one can properly knit a sweater. It was a metaphor Lorie had once heard that had always stuck with her.

CHAPTER 29

M ischa Taylor was another young woman, in the prime of her life, with seemingly everything going for her. Looks... check. Money... check. Handsome husband... check. Status... check. A darling daughter... check, check, check... It was the latter that bothered me most—yet another mother who shouldn't have been. And this time, well there was an additional challenge: the husband. Trenton Taylor was a real piece of work. The embodiment of someone who had been handed the perfect life, Trenton Taylor was three things: arrogant, impatient, and ignorant—three characteristics I despised. I almost felt sorry for Mischa having to deal with this man on a daily basis... almost.

I needed to move on to my next point faster than I had anticipated, so focusing my sights on the Taylors might not have been the best decision. They could have been more than I could handle, but they would undoubtedly make news. I knew I needed to deal with Trenton first as he was a presence, standing six feet, two inches tall and weighing, I would guess, close to two hundred pounds. It just made sense that he would have to be out of the way in order for me to take care of them both. I hated guns, and while I could have used one to deal with the husband from a distance, it wasn't an option I would have willingly chosen. I had to come up with something better suited to what I could handle. I own one gun, but I never wanted to incorporate it into my plans. I carried it only for extreme circumstances that I thought might have become out of my control, and due to my clever planning, I hadn't felt that any of my circumstances warranted the extra protection. Just as the thought entered my brain, I got the feeling that I might have just jinxed myself.

The plan for the Taylors came to me in my sleep, when my subconscious took over to help me right wrongs that I otherwise wouldn't have had the courage to. Although I liked to think my actions didn't reflect who I really was—that I was not a violent person, just someone forced to act—I was beginning to suspect there was something more sinister within me. This realization is becoming increasingly more difficult to ignore. I won't pretend to be disgusted with myself, because I'm not. I'm just not quite sure how I feel about unearthing this side of myself I never knew existed. I supposed that as long as I was able to keep the new part of myself under control—only doing the minimum of what needed to be done—then balancing the rest of my existence with the gentle nature I have grown accustomed to, I should be just fine. Just to be clear, there is no question that what I am doing was the right thing, it just wasn't easy.

As far as my next plan went, the big picture was I needed to get the couple together, along with their young child, and isolated from others. As a successful defense lawyer, I assumed Trenton had many very appreciative clients. I had no doubt he would question an enticing offer from a grateful person who is enjoying their time *not* behind bars. With some quick Googling, I found that Ritchie Santoro, an obvious "bad guy" client of Trenton's who he'd gotten off due to a technicality, was in the process of opening a restaurant. I figured an invitation to an exclusive party, for the most anticipated new restaurant in town, along with a night away from parenting duties, would entice the pair to go on a date.

The Butcher's Bolognese, an Italian steakhouse located a short drive out of town, was set to have its grand opening within a few weeks. It seemed logical that a private soft opening could be in order to toast the new owner. The name was a nod to a few things: obviously Ritchie was Italian, so the bolognese part made sense. What disgusted me enough to want to rid the world of that vile person too, was the reason he earned his nickname. "The Butcher" was given to Ritchie because of all the "alleged" killings he had done where the body was unidentifiable except using DNA because it was cut into so many tiny pieces.

The irony of hating a killer was not lost on me, though our missions were very different. Still, I could *almost* not believe people would patronize a restaurant owned by such a man, especially one that poked fun at a well-deserved yet disgusting nickname. However, I also knew that most people liked a brush with fame whenever possible, and fame came in many forms... including infamy. I could just imagine the selfies customers would be taking with the restaurateur holding a cleaver and all parties smiling, hoping the image might go viral. Ridding the world of all scum was not part of my mission, and Ritchie would live to see another day. He would also be an unwitting secondary participant in my plan, so I guess, *Thanks, Ritchie.*

I created the invitation on metallic gold cardstock with a scrolling black font, and it looked legit. It was amazing what technology allowed to be designed and printed at home. I was also concerned that if I farmed the job out to a drugstore printing service there might be something traceable back to me. The note invited the Taylors to the premier event to be wined, dined, and rub elbows with some of the area's wealthy, yet notorious, citizens. Five days after I mailed it, I received the corresponding RSVP stating the couple would be in attendance. I knew the next week we'd all be busy: The Taylors choosing attire and a babysitter, while I fine-tuned my plan.

CHAPTER 30

J ust over two weeks after I mailed the invitation, I stood next to an unremarkable and old Toyota SUV on an isolated patch of highway flanked only by trees. The car was maybe worth a few hundred dollars, but I had purposely overpaid by at least a few hundred more to make sure the transaction would stay private and the registration would not be in my name. Although I had been at my post for over two hours, I only saw two cars drive down that part of the road, neither of which stopped for me. It was better not to be noticed, but it was a disheartening microcosm of how humanity treated people in need, especially because it was unseasonably chilly on that early June evening and growing darker by the minute. While the highway was still in use, a bypass that was newly finished took the brunt of the traffic. There was part of me that was concerned the couple might take the new way, but the most direct route to the restaurant was down this road. Leaving as little to chance as possible, I had made sure to include a map with directions in the invitation that specifically stated the older road would be the best route.

I was more nervous with the Taylors than with Juliana because their plan relied on several educated guesses I made along with some luck, whereas Juliana's plan had fewer uncertainties. Plus, there was a lot more that could go wrong with *two* adults. I didn't like the idea of a plan not being flawless in its developmental stages, let alone when in action, but I felt some guesswork was necessary for Mischa and Trenton. Watching the pink glow of the setting sun had been so distracting, I nearly missed seeing the Taylors drive past. I saw their charcoal gray Range Rover SUV as it went by where I stood, and thankfully pulled over a ways ahead of me. I briefly panicked when I thought they had missed my overexaggerated wave, or possibly that it had been too late, but when I saw their brake lights, I felt more at ease. The pair sat in their SUV for what felt like an eternity, but was probably less than two minutes. No doubt they were discussing the merits of the heroic story of them rescuing a stranded person they would tell versus their inevitable tardiness to the party should they decide to help.

After another minute, I was surprised the passenger door opened because that meant it was Mischa who got out of the vehicle first. I did my best to hide my shock behind a smile and gave another wave as Mrs. Taylor began walking toward me, and as it turned out, she seemed a bit surprised herself.

"Hi there! Why are *you* here?" yelled Mischa, in an unexpectedly friendly tone, from about 100 feet away.

"*Oh*," I said as it wasn't what I was expecting from her. Not quite sure if she meant the obvious, like why was a person stranded on the side of the road, or something more. Still, I didn't want to give any inkling to my true motives, so I smiled big and just said, "Thank you very much for stopping. I am having some car trouble."

When she was closer to me she said, "*Oh*," just as I did, as if I was not who she was expecting either. After waiting a few more seconds, Mischa said, "I thought you… Never mind…" before trailing off.

It was an odd transaction and I felt uncomfortable because I couldn't read her thoughts.

Mischa continued, "I'm sorry, but I don't know much about cars. I'm not sure that I can be of any help."

"Well, you stopping is more help than anyone else has given me, so I kindly thank you," I responded.

"I can call someone for you, do you have roadside assistance or anything? If not, I can call ours. Do you know what the problem is?"

"That is a very kind offer, but it is just a flat tire. I don't have a jack, otherwise I think I could change it myself. Might you have a jack in your car?"

I extended my arm out to suggest she walk towards the rear passenger side of my car to show her the tire—that wasn't really flat. She understood the gesture and I followed behind her. When we were behind the open trunk, and out of sight of the SUV, I discreetly pulled a small syringe from my pocket and stuck it in her hip. Thank God the dress she was wearing was a silvery, almost sheer fabric, so I knew at first glance the needle would have no trouble piercing the material. I think she felt the pressure of my hand hitting her more than the pain of the prick since the needle was so tiny. Mischa spun around, and before she could question my action, I shoved her into the open trunk and closed it. She would be unconscious shortly, if she wasn't already.

Things were going well with my plan so far, and I almost wanted to give myself a pat on the back. It was still early though, and I was afraid I might curse myself if I got congratulatory too soon. Although, congratulatory might not be the right word, since what I was doing wasn't a game to be won. On the contrary, it usually felt like there was no winner. The troubled expression on my face as I approached the driver's side of the SUV was only half faked.

"Excuse me sir, but do you have—"

Trenton interrupted me with a tone of extreme irritation saying, "Do you *not* have a cell phone that you can use to call someone *you* know to come help? I mean I would like to help you, but my wife and I will be late to a party if we do. Plus, we have to drop our children off at the sitter first. We really just don't have time to help. You understand, right? Where is my wife by the way?"

Not really surprised by his response in general, but I was shocked by the *two* sleeping girls who were in the back seat. I only thought the couple had one child, but the second was a surprise that immediately created a greater sense of urgency for this plan to work. I composed myself as best I could as I glanced through the rear passenger-side window.

"Children are such blessings, aren't they?"

Trenton, undeniably becoming more irritated by the second, responded to my comment with a change back to the original subject.

"Where is your phone? Everyone has a phone these days."

What. An. Asshole.

I respond, "I do have a phone, it is just on my kitchen counter at home. I know, careless of me, but it is what it is at this point. I'd really appreciate some help. Your wife is assessing the damage of my very flat tire and said you might have a jack. I know how to change a flat, but it is just easier with two people, and a jack, ya know?" I said with a chuckle of feigned sheepish embarrassment.

During our conversation, I had been trying to act as casual as possible, while taking in all I could about the change in plans. The SUV was big, so I hoped it had a third row; I didn't want to leave those *kids* alone in the junker parked behind us.

"Wait, *my wife* is assessing the damage to your tire? What a joke! I don't think that woman knows how to change a lightbulb, let alone a tire," said Trenton with a laugh.

He paused before saying anything else, likely looking for a laugh from me too, which I begrudgingly provided before saying, "Women, right?"

Apparently, there was just enough misogyny within my remark to make him offer to call his roadside assistance to help me.

As he looked up the phone number, I said, "That is very nice of you, but I used to have roadside assistance and they would take *forever* every time I needed them. Plus, they would charge me an arm and a leg for the service. If you could just give me ten minutes, maybe less, you and I can get this tire changed."

Trenton rolled his eyes and aggressively exited his vehicle. The tall man looked even more unmanageable once he stood.

He looked down at his dress clothes—the suit no doubt cost more than my car— and rolled his eyes again.

"Honestly, I don't even know if I have a jack. If one came with the car, maybe, but I hire people to do this kind of shit. I can help as long as I don't get dirty. Not sure how much help I will be, but let's take a quick look and get this over with," said Trenton.

As I was starting to question my decision about knocking him out and having to *move him*, he did something that proved, once again, luck was on my side.

"Let me check the trunk to see if I have one," he said, but then paused, turned to me and said, "Actually can you? I really cannot get anything on this suit."

"No problem! It's the least I can do," I responded.

Happy that I would not have to move him from my car back to his, as this was something that would definitely prove difficult. As Trenton opened his trunk, I noticed it wasn't empty. A folded stroller was taking up some of the room, but there should still be enough space for him as well. And with the new addition of the children to my plan, I figured the stroller would come in handy. Next I took two more syringes out of my pocket and stuck them into his back, just left of his right scapula. I wasn't sure one would do the trick.

"The *fu*—" he said as he whipped around to hit me.

I winced as he yelled, hoping he would not wake the children. They were still very young, and while infantile amnesia was likely, I would hate to risk them having any memories of what was to come. Before he could make contact, he slumped down; his upper body landed in the trunk and his lower half draped over the rear bumper. Trenton was heavier than I anticipated and his body was cumbersome to move, but after a bit of time and struggling, I was able to lift his bottom half into the cargo area of the vehicle. Thankfully, the whole transaction went down without waking the small girls.

I got into the driver's seat of the Range Rover and backed it up to where my own rusty SUV sat, so the vehicles were as close trunk-to-trunk as I could get. It wasn't as difficult loading

Mischa into the vehicle. Even though she was like moving dead weight, she was still lighter than her husband. I climbed into the rear of the Range Rover and pulled her into her own car. It was no coincidence that I had chosen an SUV for this mission as I knew I might have to do some rearranging. I had planned to pull the rusty Toyota into the tall weeds beyond the edge of the road and leave it there. If found, it would have been completely inconsequential to me. However, with the tiny blonde and tinier redhead fast asleep in the back seat, I needed to revise my plan. I still moved the old car, but not as far out of sight as I originally hoped since I would definitely need it again. I got back in Taylors' luxury vehicle and drove the half mile to Shimmer Lake, where the final act of my scheme would commence. The plan was going even better than I had thought considering the last-minute changes. Just the universe confirming that I was doing what was necessary and just.

As I approached the lake, it was dark except for the moonlit water and it was obvious how the lake earned its name. I parked near the beach, got out of the car, and allowed myself a little time to bask in the perfection of the early summer's night, with the lake sparkling almost as much as the fireflies flitting around me. The zen allowed me to refocus on the task at hand and remember that it was no time for a vacation, even a momentary one. As far as resting places go, the lake was as picturesque as they come, although I was sure that was not where the couple would remain for eternity.

I got back into the borrowed auto and drove to a clearing at the top of the boat launch and assessed my surroundings. Shimmer Lake Park closed at dusk, so there was no one there but our quintet. Both Trenton and Mischa were still unconscious in the trunk of the car, and I needed to get them moved into the back seat, but first I had to get the girls out. From under the unconscious couple, I removed the stroller—built for two, *not one*—not an easy task considering they were heavy and limp. I gently took out the toddler first. As she began to rouse, I shushed her back to sleep and placed her in half of the buggy. Next, I carefully removed the car seat carrier that contained a soundly-sleeping infant. Moving swiftly, I snapped the carrier in the carriage next to the toddler. With the familiarity of the stroller, both sleeping girls seemed extremely content with the transition.

Next, I folded down the sixty side of the sixty/forty back-seat split then bent and pushed Mischa's body into a mid-dle-row seat. I underestimated how difficult to manipulate an unconscious adult could be. That fact gave me great concern for the part of my plan that required me to move Trenton. Once Mischa was in place, I buckled her in. I tried to get Trenton into the seat next to her, but with Mischa already seated, I couldn't fold the seat down. Trenton was too heavy and awkward for me to manage, so I had no choice but to leave him in the back of the car. I had one more syringe with me, so for good measure, I stuck him a third time to ensure he stayed put.

Since there would always be parts of my plans beyond my control, I tried maintain power over anything I could. Hind-sight always seemed to remind me that I could have planned better. I reminded myself that I was not a professional, and that I'd done a decent job thus far. Still, I couldn't help but think I should have brought a heavy rock to weigh down the vehicle's accelerator. Thankfully, as I looked around the area, there were many stones that appeared would do the job. I grabbed one, that as I lifted I could tell would work just fine, and carried it to the car. As I was putting the weight into place, I heard a small moan come from the rear seat. Her eyes were still closed, but Mischa Taylor's sedative was starting to wear off. I was ready to execute the final part of my plan, and it didn't matter to me if the Taylors were conscious or not when they entered the dark water. Either way, there would be enough sedation in their system to keep them in the vehicle.

Looking back at the pair once more, I said, "It has not been my pleasure and you left me no choice."

Mischa's eyes opened lazily and I thought, for a split second, there might have been a flicker of recognition in them—for a second time that evening. Even if she had known me, it wouldn't matter when she was dead. I slid the rock onto the accelerator and, in a risky move, reached in and bumped the gear shift from park to drive. I pulled my arm out just as the car lurched forward and sped down the ramp into the black glass of the lake.

Although I would have preferred to stay and make sure that the vehicle became fully submerged, and no passengers exited prematurely, I didn't know if there might be a ranger making after-hours rounds. So I began pushing the girls down the only paved entrance/exit to the park, while trying to think of a good excuse should I be seen. I was having trouble coming up with one, so I was relieved when we made it back to the main road without being approached. When we reached the highway, I couldn't stay hidden amongst the high grasses along the roadside since that would be impossible terrain to navigate with a stroller. I'd have much preferred the smooth pavement of the road, but that was not only dangerous in the dark, but would look much more out of place. I needed to stay in the middle of the two options—on the rocky berm. If someone saw me and asked what was going on, it would be easy to explain that I had car trouble.

It's always amazed me how children can sleep through a thunderstorm but wake at the sound of a door clicking shut as parents leave their room at night. I figured this would be the case here too, and sure enough, the fancy stroller's large wheels glided over the stones, while the white noise of grinding chunks of glass and blacktop kept them asleep. We reached the beat-up Toyota without being seen and I loaded the children into the vehicle. I strapped the infant's carrier in, but I did not have a seat for the older child. Again hindsight—I should have grabbed the toddler's seat out of the Taylor's car before I moved it, or even brought one of my own. I didn't feel comfortable simply buckling her in like an adult, but I had no other choice. We needed to get out of here before someone else decided they might want to be a good samaritan.

CHAPTER 31

It was now Tuesday morning, and Lorie had done her best to avoid Chris since their working meetup Saturday. Steering clear of the detective was unfamiliar to her, especially since she had spent the past few months wanting to do the opposite. Worried that in talking to him she might slip up and say the wrong thing about her involvement with the case—and her treatment of Alise—Lorie decided she needed to keep a low profile. Though the new information from the latest session with Alise did not seem relevant to Chris' case, Lorie still felt guilty for not sharing it with her detective partner. There did not appear to be enough separation between her career and her civic duty, and Lorie contemplated resigning from the case, as well as ending whatever had only just begun with Chris. Life for the psychiatrist was becoming more chaotic than she thought she could handle, and she wished things could go back to the way they were before Jules died.

As she reached for her phone to text Chris letting him know she was done with police work and likely also going to cancel their date that evening, her phone rang. Startled by the unexpected call—as though the quiet ringtone was blaring through a megaphone—she reflexively slid the decline button, so quickly as if it were hot to the touch. It was Chris, and she didn't want to say to him out loud what would be much easier over a text, but then her phone rang again, startling her just slightly this time. Chris was persistent. *Maybe it's an emergency?* she thought, and once a thought like was in her head, there was no way she could have ignored it.

"Hello?"

"Hi Lors!"

She couldn't help but smile; there was something endearing about the way he said her nickname.

"Chris, hello. What's going on?"

"Why the tone, and while we're at it, the cold shoulder lately too?" he said, not in a negative way, but more lightheartedly.

"Sorry, it's nothing you did; I've just had a lot going on. And I guess my tone is because, well, most of the times when you call me it's to let me know a patient is dead."

While she hadn't meant the statement to be a joke, the detective still laughed. Lorie had heard before how people working in law enforcement had twisted senses of humor...

"I'm serious, Chris."

"I'm sorry, dear, I know you are. Sometimes I can't help myself," said Chris. "But, *Lors*, this isn't a business call! Well, not one that involves you anyway. I have to apologize because I was so looking forward to our date tonight, but sadly to say, another detective called in sick and I have to work a double."

Relieved, but trying to sound at least a little disappointed—which, in a way, she still was—Lorie said, "Oh no, that is such a bummer!"

Lorie couldn't remember the last time she used the word "bummer," if ever.

Chris replied, "It is. But, do you happen to be free Saturday?"

"What time Saturday?" Lorie asked, like it mattered.

"All the time, Saturday! I want you to clear your schedule."

A whole day with Chris was something she'd been hoping for, but considering she was feeling the need for a little distance due to conflicts of interest, she wasn't sure how to respond. Apparently, she'd waited too long to answer, so Chris filled the silence.

"It's a date then!" Chris said, and Lorie could hear him clap his hands together on the other end of the line, like she'd seen him do before when he was excited. "I will pick you up at 8 a.m. sharp! Wear comfortable shoes, layers, sunglasses, and a hat. I can't wait!"

He hung up before Lorie could protest, if that was, in fact, what she was going to do. Either way, she had a date in a few days and had to use that short amount of time to figure out how to open up to Chris about Alise, or how to properly keep her mouth shut.

CHAPTER 32

The rest of her week was uneventful and typical. Her routine was on track and she was beginning to realize that, as much as she wanted to talk to the detective, no news from Chris was good news—at least when it came to the police work they were doing. At three-thirty Saturday morning, Lorie lay wide awake, tired of seeing that hour on her clock. At first glance, it might seem her early rising was due to the eighty-pound retriever lying on his back, snoring loudly with his head on her pillow. That was not the case since she was used to the nightly snorts and grunts that came from her companion, and found them comforting in their own way. She was awake with a nauseous mixture of both anxiety *for* and anxiety *about* her date with Chris. It was almost bad enough that she thought she might need to cancel, since a tentative tummy wasn't something to mess with on an all-day date, especially since she had no idea what their plans were. The desire to spend more time with Chris ultimately trumped all else, so she reached for a remedy in her nightstand drawer. Grabbing the bottle of chalky antacid tabs she kept in there for such an occasion, Lorie put four in her mouth, just to be safe, before trying her best to fall back asleep.

Though sleep didn't come, she hoped the adrenaline coursing through her body would mask how tired she really was when she met Chris in just a few hours. Finally giving up on sleep at six-thirty, Lorie got out of bed, made coffee, showered, and dressed in beige linen pants and a white boat-neck sweater. A pair of fresh, white Keds sneakers were on her feet. Lorie felt the outfit would transition well into any early-summer activity they might be doing, and looked dressy enough to show she cared, but without looking like she was trying too hard. Following the "rules of dating" had not been something she'd needed to do much in her life. As exciting as it was to go on a date at any age, the balance between trying too hard and not trying hard enough was exhausting. As the time neared eight o'clock, Lorie let Freud out one last time, gave him a treat, locked her door, and waited on the porch swing for her... *Friend? Boyfriend? Romantic companion? Whatever he was*, to arrive.

Eight o'clock came and went with no word from Chris. For a second, Lorie wondered if she had been stood up. She quickly shook off the momentary insecurity, reminding herself that *he* was the one who asked for the date—and hadn't given her the chance to say no.

"Where is he then?" she asked aloud.

Freud, seeing his favorite person sitting outside without him, scratched and whined at the door. Just as Lorie went to let him out, her phone rang—Chris was finally calling, *half an hour late*. Frustrated and disappointed, Lorie almost let the call go to voicemail. Instead, she decided to answer, irritation evident in her voice.

"What?" she said when she answered the call.

"Lorie, I am so sorry! I don't think I can put into words how sorry I am," said Chris.

"Okay. But you can try," replied Lorie.

Chris could recognize the sound of a woman scorned—it was actually quite familiar territory—and brought back some painful memories. Life in law enforcement had often been the cause of canceled dates, postponed dinners, and breakups.

"I swear I have a good reason. Well, the reason is valid, but I shouldn't say it's 'good.'"

This intrigued Lorie, and as it dawned on her that work was likely the reason for his tardiness, her voice softened.

"What happened?" she asked.

"Well, I'm almost certain it's related to our case. If you can be ready, I'll be there in about twenty minutes to pick you up and we'll still do our date, it'll just be less fun and less romantic than I had originally planned," he said with a bit of an nervous laugh.

"*If I can be ready?*" Lorie scoffed. "I have been ready for over an hour now."

Chris, realizing the error he had made, said, "I guess I mean to say if you still want to get together today, I can be there shortly."

Still feeling uneasy about seeing him and wanting to avoid all "shop talk," she replied, "I guess I'm ready as I'll ever be."

Lorie's snarky comment wasn't lost on him and Chris said with an unmistakably apologetic tone, "My sincerest apologies that I couldn't at least let you know before eight that I was going to be indeterminately late. I'll see you in twenty."

CHAPTER 33

I nstead of letting her anxiety over doing and saying the right—or wrong—thing consume her during the twenty-minute wait, Lorie decided to focus on what had Chris stuck at work this early on a Saturday. Hoping it had nothing to do with her two murdered patients proved futile, especially since Chris had hinted as much. If Chris was involving her in whatever this new development was, he knew it was connected. Lorie thought of calling Alise to put her own mind at ease as to whether or not she was involved, but then thought better of it. Further blurring the lines between being a friend, a professional, and an adjunct police detective wouldn't be in anyone's best interest. Besides, it was unlikely that Alise would readily admit guilt.

While Lorie hoped Chris was going to tell her he had a break in the case—like new evidence pointing to a killer she didn't know personally and who could be easily caught—a new thought bubbled to the surface in her mind, and it was terrifying. *What if it's the murder of another of my patients?* Unlikely as it seemed, it was still possible that the deaths of Jules and Brandie were purely coincidental. But the death of a third patient would solidify what everyone hoped was not true: a serial killer was targeting her patients. Lorie's knowledge of the limited people with access to her patient roster sent a chill through her body so strong she visibly shook. It was becoming clear that Alise was the prime suspect.

In his unmarked sedan, Chris pulled into Lorie's driveway. While he could have just waved, he got out of his car, met

Lorie halfway, and extended his elbow for her to grab. Though perfectly capable of walking to his car herself, the gentlemanly gesture was appreciated. Once at the car, as Lorie reached for the door handle, he beat her to it and, to her delight, chivalry was not dead. But the warm feelings of being cared for soon faded as Chris remained silent for the first several minutes of their drive. The silence provided the answer to her earlier question; she knew there was another murdered patient. To ease Chris' clear apprehension in divulging where they were going and why, Lorie spoke first.

"Chris, it's another one of my patients, isn't it?" she said in a somber tone.

Her question-like statement was met with a nod in response, and then Chris added, "Kind of."

Unsure what that might mean, Lorie paused for few seconds, hoping Chris would elaborate.

"This time it's a double homicide—Mischa Taylor and her husband, Trenton."

Lorie didn't respond right away; she just stared straight out the windshield.

She then said, "But since there were two victims, one male, and also not technically my patient—"

Knowing where she was going with her line of thinking, Chris cut her off before she could waste any more breath.

"Lorie, I know you don't want any of these deaths to be linked, but at this point, there's no way they *aren't*. On the surface, there are similarities, but when you look at all the facts, you will see the M.O.s are connecting."

"But—" said Lorie, when she was cut off again.

"Lorie, the Taylors' two children are missing now too."

"What?"

The word barely squeaked out of her mouth. Lorie should have known this is what was coming, but still something like that would never lose its shock value.

"I was already at the scene earlier today. An early morning runner saw a taillight sticking out of Shimmer Lake near the boat launch and called it in. I was there when the Taylors' car was pulled out of the water."

"Is it possible it was a murder–suicide? I hate to speak ill of the dead, but Trenton wasn't exactly kind to his wife," said Lorie.

"I know, I briefly looked over Mrs. Taylor's file. He was a real gem, but I really don't think it was a murder–suicide. Mr. and Mrs. Taylor were found deceased in the *back* seat of the vehicle. There was a large rock found on the floor of the driver's seat, likely used to depress the gas pedal."

The thought crossed Lorie's mind that she might need to close her practice to protect her patients, but would that even do anything? It appeared the damage was already done. She had tried to keep the nagging thoughts at bay, but again they crept into her mind. *Did the unknown reason have to do with me? Was their blood somehow on my hands?* The notions were absurd as Lorie had done nothing but her very best to help these people.

"The heat is being turned up on this investigation. This is a small town and four deaths in fewer than as many months is unheard of. Hell, we rarely have four murders in four *years*. There was only one other time I can recall where there were this many unnatural deaths in such a short period. Twenty years ago, Raymond Wilmer shot his wife, three children, two cats then himself because she had filed for divorce and was planning to move out of state with the kids. Sad situation, but it was an isolated, domestic incident. This doesn't appear random and I don't think our killer is done. On the contrary, they seem to be escalating. Two victims, one male, and kidnapping *two* children at once does not sound like they are slowing down. Also, some preliminary findings have come back in the Stevens and Amstell cases. Fibers that have yet to be identified, were found at Jules' apartment and on Brandie's body that connect the two women. It wouldn't surprise me if the same were found on one, or both, of the Taylors. Due to her lack of alibis and past behavior—I know this won't sit well with you—but as a courtesy, I'm informing you that we officially have our first person of interest—Alise Jenks."

CHAPTER 34

In her gut, Lorie felt that although all signs pointed to Alise, she hadn't committed the murders. Her history would indicate Alise was more than capable of murderous behavior, but Lorie just couldn't imagine her reformed friend and respected colleague had anything to do with what was happening. Maybe the fact that Lorie couldn't believe Alise still had evil in her was a problem all its own. But at the end of the day, it wasn't her call, and she would have to let Chris do his job, and the investigation run its course. If Alise was innocent, surely that would be proven—she hoped—and if she was, in fact, guilty, well then…

Lorie was so deep in thought—about Alise, the Taylors, Jules and Brandie, Chris, the investigation, and her profession—she hadn't noticed the awkward silence she'd created until Chris broke it.

"Lors? Are you okay? I mean I know *this* all is *not* okay, but… I am here for you if you want to talk about it, professionally, or personally speaking."

His offer brought a small smile to her lips, and Lorie said, "Thank you. I really appreciate that. It is all just a lot to process. I feel that I am responsible for everything somehow."

"Why would you think that?" Chris asked, but then followed up with, "That was a stupid question. I know why you would think that, but I guess what I meant to say was you shouldn't think that way."

"How can I not? I am the common denominator here, Chris. I am the thread that connects all these dead adults, missing children, and even Alise."

"I have become intimately acquainted with your patient records, and through them, have seen the good work you have done to help people. *You* are not *the problem.* You are not even part of the problem, Lors, you are part of the solution, I just know it," Chris said, trying to comfort his date.

"I am thankful I have you to pull me out of my thoughts, Chris," Lorie said as a tear began to form in the corner of her eye. "And so far this is the worst date I have ever been on."

After a brief pause, the pair began to laugh hysterically, so much so that Chris had to pull the car over. The comment was funny—given its truthfulness—but not as hilarious as their laughter indicated. The release of tension through their chortling was likely what kept it going. When they finally composed themselves and wiped away the sad-turned-happy tears, they both felt lighter and ready to proceed with their "hot date."

It seemed like the twenty-minute ride to the police station took more like twenty *hours*, but finally they were pulling into the underground parking garage reserved for employees.

"So what is the plan for the rest of the day?" Lorie inquired of Chris as they made their way to the elevator which would take them to the homicide department on the fourth floor.

"Crime scene techs are at Shimmer Lake, and will likely be there until at least this evening. If I stayed at the scene, I would just be in the way, plus I didn't think that was something you'd want to see."

"Correct," said Lorie, sounding down.

She pictured the pristine lake that she'd been to many times before, now tainted by images of the waterlogged bodies of Mischa and Trenton Taylor. Lorie felt sad because she would probably never be able to visit the serene setting again, or at least without being reminded of the Taylors and their fate. Then, she felt selfish, worrying about losing a scenic place to visit when there were people losing their *lives*.

Chris continued, "With any of the recent homicides, the first thing I do is compare the name against your files. My fellow detectives are calling them the 'death files.'" As soon as the words came out of his mouth, he wished he could take them back, quickly adding, "I'm sorry, that wasn't something you needed to hear. This isn't a joke, Lorie, it's just that cops tend to have a twisted sense of humor. It's often how we get through the tough stuff."

While the comment was insensitive, Lorie knew that was not Chris' intent.

"It's okay, I get it. There is a bit of that in my line of work too," she said.

"I figured while we are here, you could shed some light on your speculation as to why this time was different. Like why the husband was killed. I have a few theories, but don't want to taint your professional opinion," said Chris.

The elevator in the old building was slow, so the ride to the top gave Lorie a few minutes to think. Having met Trenton only a few times shouldn't be enough to make an informed decision as to why someone would want him, along with his wife, dead. But even with the limited interactions she had had with the man, she knew he was selfish, brash and inconsiderate, to put it nicely. While she wouldn't want to kill him, his personality might make someone else inclined to.

"Trenton Taylor was just such an inconsiderate, ignorant, rude..."

It was clear Lorie was trying to find the right words to covey her feelings about the man, but was also trying to maintain some professionalism.

Chris did not feel the need to hold back and finished her sentence saying, "Asshole?"

"Yes! That is exactly the word I was looking for, " said Lorie.

"Yeah, I got that impression too. Can you elaborate?" asked Chris.

"He sent Mischa to me because he wanted me to 'fix her,'" Lorie said, mimicking air quotes with her fingers. "And, yes, those were his actual words. Mischa was unquestionably depressed, and she would relay things he said to me. When he came to a session with her, he actually said them to my face. He said things like, 'Why the hell is she so damn unhappy? I've given her everything she could ever want.' 'Other people are so jealous of her life. She doesn't have to work, just take care of the children *she* wanted.' 'She drives a car worth more than some people's houses.' 'We live in damn near a mansion, our kids will go to the best schools. She wears designer clothes and shoes, and we eat at the best restaurants. How the hell can someone with so much be so ungrateful?' It was so hard not to show the disgust at his words on my face. I so wanted to show solidarity with Mischa, but I had to remain 'Switzerland,' at least somewhat, if I wanted even a chance to get through to Trenton. His poor wife was suffering from mental illness, yet he was calling her ungrateful, basically telling her to 'snap out of it.'"

One of Chris' longtime colleagues, Sergeant Arnold Alden, brought over two coffees to Chris' desk and said, "You two look like you could use these," as he handed the steaming styrofoam cups to Chris and Lorie.

Chris responded, smiling, "Thanks, jackass, for saying we look like shit."

Sgt. Alden smiled and gave him a slap on the back as he walked away saying, "Well, you certainly do."

"Got any frou-frou creamer here, or would the rest of the detectives make fun of you?" asked Lorie, further lightening the mood.

Chris held up a finger indicating he would be right back as he left his desk. He returned a minute later with a bottle of snickerdoodle-flavored creamer and placed it on the desk in front of Lorie with a pleased expression on his face.

"Oh, I am plenty strong enough with my masculinity to drink my coffee just the way I like it, no matter where I am!" said Chris as he poured more creamer into his cup than he likely wanted, to drive his point home. Then, without asking, he added a little to Lorie's cup and said, "Don't knock it till you've tried it!"

Lorie sipped her drink and stuck out her tongue, pretending to gag as she said, "Mmmmm, delicious!"

In reality, it was surprisingly good, but she didn't want to give Chris the satisfaction.

"So back to Trenton Taylor," said the detective.

Lorie was feeling better now, and had almost forgotten that they weren't *really* on a date.

"Mischa wasn't a bad person, but we hadn't yet gotten her depression under control, which meant that she wasn't functioning all that well. Trenton did not appear to be a good husband. He was maybe a little better father, but he wasn't very involved," said the doctor.

"In my professional opinion, these cases are undoubtedly connected, but there appear to be multiple motives. Are the killings the focus and the children a by-product left behind after their parents were murdered? Or are the kidnappings the focus and it's easier if the parents are out of the way first? It would definitely help if we knew where those kiddos were."

Chris hesitated a bit before expressing his next theory and Lorie noticed.

"Chris, what?"

"Or are *you* the focus?" he replied.

When that thought was just in her head, it seemed easier to dismiss. Hearing the words come out of someone else's mouth made the theory feel too real and impossible to ignore.

Chris said, "I know I have asked you this before, but now three of your patients are dead along with one on the periphery, and before we weren't sure there was a connection. Is there *anyone* you can think of who would want to hurt you for *any* reason? Unlike the first time he had asked Lorie the question, his tone was full of genuine concern for *her* and not just solving a case.

"Chris, I just cannot think of how or why I would be at the heart of what is causing someone to hurt others. If there was anything I could think of, I would have already told you."

While what she was saying was true, she felt guilty knowing what she withheld about Alise.

"Okay," he said, sounding a bit defeated, as if he was hoping she had been holding out on him, waiting for the perfect moment to share a revelation that would crack the case wide open. "I won't ask you that again, but please do not hold back if any detail, no matter how small, comes to mind."

Lorie nodded in agreement and took another sip of her coffee to avoid having to speak the confirmation.

"I need to do a few things that should take me maybe twenty minutes or so, and until the techs are done at Shimmer Lake, there isn't much more for me to do today regarding that case. Plus, it's supposed to be my day off, so Arny said he would handle notifications and interviews of the Taylors' next of kin. If you want to wait in the lounge, I will come get you when I'm ready and we can finish the date we haven't really even started. Sound good?"

"Works for me. What are we doing by the way?" Lorie asked.

"You'll see soon enough, my dear, but I can tell you it *will* involve food. There was no time for breakfast this morning and we've just about missed the lunch hour. Are you hungry?"

"I could eat," she said, but not sure she meant it.

She hadn't eaten breakfast either—or much of anything since murder entered her world, but she figured eating was necessary and part of any typical date, even though this date was far from typical.

"Great, I know this delish little Pad Thai place not far from here. We'll start there, if you like Asian food?"

She smiled big and said, "It's my favorite."

Chris led her to the detective's lounge, turned on the T.V. and handed her the remote. Before leaving, he reached down and gave her hand a little squeeze—unsure of what it was for, but nonetheless, Lorie liked it. As Chris left the lounge, Lorie assessed her seating options—a set of tan molded melamine chairs that were tucked under a matching table, or a worn sofa that looked like it was straight out of a frat house. Assuming that grown adults were cleaner than college boys, and tired from her lack of sleep, she almost chose to lie on the sofa, but instead opted for the safer choice and pulled out one of the chairs. The news was on television, and when she saw Mischa Taylor's face on the screen, she didn't know whether she should turn it off, or turn it up. She chose off, figuring she knew as much, if not more, than the news reports would be sharing anyway. Taking out her phone, she saw a text from Alise, inquiring if she'd heard about Mischa. Lorie then proceeded to turn her phone off too. She decided that in order for her to try to have as nice of an afternoon as possible, she'd go old school and read a magazine to pass the time. The cover of TIME Magazine had a date that was three years and two months prior, so she figured she was safe.

After twenty-two minutes—not that Lorie was counting—Chris came back in and said he was ready to go, and the two headed back down to the garage to retrieve Chris' vehicle and begin the date that was planned.

"I so appreciate your patience and understanding today, Lors. Not everyone would do the same."

"Of course," said Lorie, feeling like she didn't have a choice. "I'm in this as much as you are, if not more."

Chris' eyes widened as he said, "Oh *really?* You're in *this* more than I am?"

He waved his finger between them back and forth indicating that the "this" was whatever budding romance was unfolding.

Lorie blushed and said, "Sure, that's what I meant," as she playfully nudged him. They walked past the unmarked vehicle they arrived in and continued to Chris' personal vehicle, a shiny silver pickup truck. As she'd suspected he would, Chris darted in front of her so he could open her door. Once inside and buckled, Chris took Lorie's hand in his as the truck pulled out of the underground parking area and headed toward the restaurant.

CHAPTER 35

After a lunch of some of her favorites, Chris drove Lorie to a picturesque scene: a sparkling blue body of water at the base of a snow-capped mountain. The car went slowly around the winding road that led to a marina, and Lorie could see the masts of sailboats jutting so high they looked as though they could touch the clouds.

"Are we going sailing?" inquired Lorie.

"We are! Is that okay? I mean considering Shimmer Lake…"

"It's fine, Chris." Then abruptly changing the subject, she added, "I have never been on a sailboat before—or any boat for that matter."

"Wow!" Chris said with surprise. "Well then you're either in for a real treat, or a really upset stomach! And while that is the tamest confession I have ever elicited from someone, let's do our best not to talk shop for the rest of the day. I'd be willing to bet you could use a break from it as much as I could."

"Sounds like a good plan to me. And let's hope it is smooth sailing when it comes to my tummy today!" Lorie said with a laugh.

As the car pulled into the marina's parking lot, Lorie could see more details of the boats. There were ten slips and ten sailboats, not a speedboat in the bunch.

"Is this lake only for sailing?" she asked as they parked and began to get out of the car.

"It is. It's not as close as some other lakes I could sail, but it is more peaceful, and I think, more beautiful." Then, in a most sincere tone, he added, "But not as beautiful as you."

Lorie blushed for a second time that day, and stifled a giggle, as to not ruin the moment and the cheesy, yet well-placed, compliment. No one is immune to the butterflies of new love, Lorie included. Not knowing how to respond, she grabbed his hand and interlaced her fingers with his while making a visor to shield the sun from her eyes with her other hand. The sun sparkling on the tranquil water were like little blinding flashbulbs.

As they began to walk toward the docks she said, "Which boat is yours?"

He pointed to the one with the tallest mast. It was painted a shiny gray, like the color of smoke, with glossy wood trim and gold accents. It was the prettiest boat Lorie had ever seen and she was excited to take her own maiden voyage with the man holding her hand.

"Does it have a name?" Lorie asked.

"It does. *Grey's Sons,*" Chris responded in a sorrowful tone. "It was my dad's boat. Obviously, it's a play on our last name, but he also had three sons. He got the boat shortly after I was born, his third and final child. Knowing he'd be a father to all boys, he said the name was obvious. We spent a lot of time on this boat as kids, and even into our twenties."

"What happened after that? Did everyone just get too busy with life?"

"Not really. Beginning in my late twenties, then over the course of a handful of years, I guess you could say I became an only child and an orphan," Chris said, looking out with a mournful gaze over the lake.

It took a bit for Lorie to realize the weight of his statement and what it meant. When she understood, the psychiatrist in her wanted to continue the line of questioning, but the Lorie that was on an actual date wondered if it would be too painful for her companion. Wanting to show she cared—even at the risk of making him sad—felt like a better option than feigning apathy.

"So your brothers and your parents… they're all gone?" She asked gently, though she felt she already knew the answer.

Chris nodded, and Lorie gave him time to elaborate, should he want to. He didn't.

"So what do I need to know about being on a sailboat? Am I your first mate?"

The question brought Chris back to the present and his demeanor changed from forlorn to chipper again.

"Well, it should be smooth on the water today, but until you get your 'sea legs' I'd like you to pick a spot and plant yourself there. I will handle the rest! We will have you work up to first mate," he said as he did his signature wink.

The pair walked down the dock towards *Grey's Sons.* Chris boarded the boat first and extended his hand to help Lorie climb on. The boat was in pristine condition and Lorie could tell it had been well loved and cared for, and that it was important to Chris. Unsure of exactly what he was doing, Lorie still enjoyed watching him prepare the boat for departure. Within fifteen minutes, the budding couple was gliding across the clear water with a breathtakingly beautiful backdrop as Lorie was learning the meaning of "port," "starboard," and what it felt like to put herself first. Lorie felt like she was in a painting, and closed her eyes in hopes to preserve the memory. The date may have started off rather rocky, but was shaping up to be just about perfect.

After a few hours on the lake, snacks of charcuterie and wine, and even a brief attempt at fishing, they decided to head back. It had been a long day, and they were both starting to feel the exhaustion set in. As an added bonus, while en route to the dock, they were able to catch an awe-inspiring sunset, and just as the last sliver of the red sun slipped behind the horizon, Chris leaned in to kiss Lorie. So focused on the scenery, she was startled as she was not expecting the gesture. Once she realized what was happening, she embraced it, as it was something she had secretly been hoping would happen since their first encounter. It was an odd combination of feelings over the past few months; wanting to see Chris more often but knowing that each time she saw him it likely meant more bad things were happening. The deeper involved she became in both the cases and with him, the greater potential for messiness with both. All of it had been tearing her apart. The kiss was a much-needed confirmation that her feelings were not only real but were reciprocated.

As Chris pulled away, he looked at Lorie, her cheeks in his palms, and said, "So are you my girlfriend now?"

The question was so innocent, like he was passing a note to his middle school crush asking if she liked him. Lorie turned away because she was afraid she might laugh if she looked him in the eye any longer.

"Sure, I'll be your girlfriend."

"Wait," he said. "'Sure' like *whatever, fine?* Or 'sure' like *I'd love to be your girlfriend and I was hoping you'd ask me that since the moment I laid eyes on you?*" asked Chris.

Lorie loved how jovial he could be, but she also detected an undertone of insecurity in his voice.

"We can go with the latter," she said with a huge smile.

Chris brought so much levity and spontaneity to her life and she wasn't sure she'd ever been happier before. Prior to him, she hadn't felt particularly unhappy, or even like anything was missing from her life. Now that he was officially a part of her world, she realized how mistaken she'd been. But now that she had him, her happiness came with a shadow of fear: *What if she lost him?* Police work was dangerous. She was set in her ways. He wouldn't be able to discuss every case with her, nor she with him. *What if it didn't work out?* Was blissful ignorance better than vulnerability? No. She needed to push away the doubt and embrace joy. As much as she could enjoy considering what was happening to her patients, and what was likely to come for Alise.

CHAPTER 36

Thirty Years Before

It had been a few months since Theresa had been handcuffed to her bed, but there were many aspects of the mental hospital reminding her that, indeed, it was still a prison. Her room was locked from the outside at night and she wore a uniform which resembled off-white hospital scrubs. The clothing didn't fit well and Theresa felt like a marshmallow every day. Not that her wardrobe prior to her life there had ever been much, but the drearily dull ensemble added another layer to her punishment. The grounds were surrounded by a fifteen-foot-high wall made of concrete, painted white, topped with rusted razor wire—like a prison-yard scene straight out of the movies. Much like she assumed prison life would be, the days were long and the nights were longer.

It surprised Theresa that there were actually some things at the institution that were designed not to make one completely miserable. In a common area, there was a television, although it had only two stations—news and nature shows. There was also a library that had books she could check out. An arts and crafts room was available as a therapy, and there was an outside garden that could be tended. Some residents helped prepare food while others took care of cleaning the facilities. Theresa had not yet done any of these things… she didn't feel she deserved to not be completely miserable. As difficult as it was to call this place home, Theresa wished it was the only prison she had to cope with, because she could survive *that*. Nothing at WyldeWood compared to the prison Theresa had created within her own mind, where she relentlessly punished herself every day.

Walking freely around the facility, one of the privileges granted to well-behaved residents, Theresa made her way to yet another white-walled room. The Group Therapy Room was better than most because there were lots of windows that let in bright sunshine. At the top of each window was a small transom made of leaded glass. She punished herself every single day, depriving herself of little joys, but the simple pleasure of natural light shining through a window was unavoidable. An added bonus on sunny days was the way tiny rainbows of light danced across the floor as the sun's rays passed through the prismed bevels of the leaded glass. The small flickers of color were welcome in a place devoid of nearly all of it, and Theresa couldn't fight the tiniest bit of happiness she felt from seeing those colors dance across the floor. The momentary ability to forget where she was and why she was there made her feel slightly sick as she returned to reality from her daydreams.

Twelve residents were present in that day's group therapy session, but just like always, Theresa did not feel like talking. She listened to the other patients tell their stories, share their struggles, and discuss their plans for the future when they were well again. The problems these people had were nothing compared to Theresa's. She often wondered why they were ordered to be at the place, since nothing they talked about even seemed all that bad. None of those people had killed *their own child*, or at least not as far as they were letting on. There was no point in talking and sharing her own story because there was no way they would understand. When the group counselor called Theresa out and asked if today would be the day she would like to open up to her peers, she politely declined, resisting the urge to add, "these aren't my peers." In her continued silence, she pondered what WyldeWood would be like if these people truly were her peers, and had done what she had. Dark walls, dark uniforms and fiery coals for a floor were images that crossed her mind.

The initial months at the involuntary institution she spent punishing herself as much as possible but without any physical harm. Theresa did not allow herself any form of comfort or enjoyment, except for the light rainbows. Television was not watched and books were not read. Time spent outside was not in the garden amongst the fragrant blooms of colorful flowers but instead walking the perimeter and forcing herself to only look at the expanse of white concrete at the edge of the grounds. But while she still felt like she was the worst of the worst inmates—or *residents* as they were referred to by staff—in time Theresa began to see value in the treatment her peers were receiving. She had been a resident at WyldeWood for ten months at this point, and she could see the visible progress many of the patients had made in that amount of time. In addition to group therapy—which Theresa felt was effective only because she could see progress others were making—she had a psychiatrist she saw on her own. Appointments with Dr. Shaw were attended regularly and without argument.

Dr. Delores Shaw was a slender woman of average height, with hair the color of a Hershey bar and a light complexion. The tortoiseshell glasses she wore lent an air of authenticity to her role as a psychiatrist and were a subtle nod to her being a *real* person who also had imperfections just like everyone else. Since you never ask a woman her age, many of her colleagues and patients guessed the doctor to be in her early to mid-thirties. However, if one didn't know she was a well-respected doctor, and the amount of schooling and time required to achieve that status, one might think Dr. Shaw was in her mid-twenties. The trendy clothes peeking from under her white lab coat appeared to be the perfect balance of professional and chic. Initially, all of this was irrelevant and unnoticed by Theresa as she was in no mood or mindset to talk about her feelings with anyone, which often caused her to avoid acknowledging others were even there.

As time went on, Theresa grew to notice and love all of those little details about her doctor, who at times felt like a friend, or even more so, a mother figure. Another reason Dr.

Shaw intrigued Theresa was that she reminded her of someone. Theresa often felt like she was on the brink of remembering who, but the name remained elusive. The feeling was both comforting and a bit unsettling. *Did she look like the cashier at the market where I used to work? Was she related to my first grade teacher, Mrs. Norris? Was she the doppelgänger to the librarian in town?* The answer often felt like it was on the tip of her tongue, but Theresa was never able to identify the owner of the resemblance, and over time became distracted by the topics of their conversations and put the thought out of her mind.

At first, discussing what she had done with Dr. Shaw felt pointless, Dr. Shaw had a way of getting her patients to open up—even Theresa. Presumably to make Theresa feel more comfortable, Dr. Shaw wove bits and pieces of her own life into their sessions. That was one technique the doctor found to be especially effective when trying to connect with her patients, because it humanized her. Exposing her emotions was not something Theresa wanted to do, but she knew it was part of her mandatory life sentence in Hell. And while it took some time, Theresa came to realize if she had to be there, she might as well talk. Dr. Shaw didn't do anything wrong, so why punish her too? Not that she would admit this to anyone, but Theresa grew to enjoy her appointments with Dr. Shaw as they were a break from the monotony of her sterile, colorless existence. Dr. Shaw was also the only person Theresa discussed anything of value with and the only person she would even consider to be remotely like a friend.

Talking to her psychiatrist was the only time when Theresa felt like she could *breathe.* The doctor knew why Theresa was required to be there, but the resident did not feel judged. When Theresa talked, Dr. Shaw genuinely seemed to not only listen, but to care. *Was there a time when anyone cared about me like this?* Theresa asked herself. Her mother did care for Theresa, but it was in her own way. She was never the stereotypical "pancake breakfast before school, packed lunch with a sweet note, and warm cookies waiting after the bus dropped her off" kind of mother. Looking back, Theresa had never felt unloved by her somewhat unstable mother, but she also had never felt a connection quite like the one she had with Dr. Shaw either. Thinking about her childhood, Theresa recalled something she'd heard her mother say at least a handful of times, but it didn't make sense to her then. Lottie would say to her daughter, "You must first unravel the tangled knot of your past before you can knit a proper sweater." Now that Theresa was an adult, and considering the situation she was in, she began to understand and appreciate the metaphor—and also wonder about her mother's own past. Sharing the sentiment with Dr. Shaw, the two decided to embrace the idea and the twice-a-week appointments were increased to three times in order to further accelerate the "unraveling."

After just shy of a year with Dr. Shaw, and 102 sessions, Theresa began to feel the tiniest bit of weight lift. Not long after she awoke in that place, Theresa was told that because of what she had done, a judge had deemed it would be the best place for her—*for the rest of her life.* Now, with her nineteenth birthday just three months away, she knew it would feel like an eternity—because it *was.* But after experiencing that first small reprieve from the torment in her mind, Theresa thought maybe she should do more with her time at WyldeWood. She bared her soul to Dr. Shaw, who, in return, suggested ways she could create a meaningful existence. Over time, Dr. Shaw had achieved what felt, to Theresa, like a small miracle. Despite the terrors from her past, the life outside the white walls she would never experience, and the daughter she would never get the chance to know, she made Theresa see that her life might still have worth.

CHAPTER 37

T he following morning was Sunday and Lorie was still on a high from her date with her *boyfriend*. The couple agreed they would meet for dinner Sunday night, since Chris had some work to do on his day off, yet again. So consumed with the moment, and not wanting to think at all about anything dealing with police work, Lorie had not questioned why he was going into the office on a Sunday. After sleeping in, taking Freud on a lengthy walk and play session at the dog park, followed by a long bubble bath, she decided she would watch a home design show on television. Lately her tiny condo had been looking more shabby than chic, and with the prospect of "company" coming over more often, Lorie thought it could use a refresh—and she could use some inspiration. She turned on the TV, then grabbed her phone so she could take pictures of any remodels she liked. In the background, she could hear the local news report, but thought nothing of it. When she returned to her living room, Lorie's relaxing day came to a screeching halt when the first thing she saw on TV was Alise's face.

Alise was being filmed walking into the police station of her own accord, shielding her face from the cameras. Jack Eastman, a reporter for News 6 whom Lorie did not recognize, explained that the police said that they were going to speak with a "person of interest" regarding the cases of Juliana Stevens, Brandie Amstell, and the Taylor couple. News 6 received an exclusive, anonymous tip that the aforementioned *person* would be reporting for questioning at 11 a.m. Mr. Eastman clarified that Ms. Jenks was not under arrest, and likely only there for questioning, assuming she was indeed *the* person.

Lorie wondered if it was legal to release the name of a person of interest, or even imply someone was one by sharing a video of them under incriminating circumstances—like walking into a police station. Alise tried so hard to maintain a low profile for the past twelve years, and her appearance on the news would threaten the life she had built. If anyone recognized her face, it wouldn't take long for them to figure out her true identity. Lorie had always thought that while a name change was wise, Alise should have chosen one less similar to her real name. Allison Jenkins and Alise Jenks were close enough, and even more so now considering the current situation. Whether or not Alise was guilty felt irrelevant; now that people knew she was linked to the case, she would likely become a suspect soon. With the possibility of her past being brought to light, she would be convicted in the court of public opinion—*for a second time in her life*—before she would even get to trial.

Too focused on Alise, Lorie hadn't noticed who was escorting her into the police station. As the camera panned to follow Alise into the building, it became abundantly clear why Chris had gone into work that morning. *How would this affect their dinner plans? Was it okay for Lorie to inquire about the Q and A session with Alise? Did she even want to know the answer to that?* Calling Alise was out of the question—besides what would she even say? Overwhelmed by the situation and no idea what to do, Lorie decided that her only option was to let the evening play out. There were two balls in two courts, neither of which belonged to her. It would be up to Chris and/or Alise to bring up anything pertaining to the case, whether they realized that or not. And the confusing sports idiom, with too many balls and courts, confirmed that Lorie might just be playing a reckless game where there could be no winner.

CHAPTER 38

I just finished watching the news segment—a *full segment* and not just filler—about the tragic death of Mischa and Trenton Taylor. The couple's prominence within the community had been evident, likely due to their socioeconomic status, as suggested by the extensive coverage of their deaths. There was a call to action to comb the area to help find their daughters, whom everyone hoped were still alive. I rewound the program and watched again. I suppose I was wishing for something different—or rather something *more*. I realized that was just about the definition of insanity—doing the same thing and expecting different results—and while I was positive that I was saner than most, I wondered if all the work was even worth it. The media was missing the big picture. Instead of addressing the problem, they misrepresented the kind of people Juliana, Mischa and Trenton were—canonizing them instead of demonizing them—and brushing Brandie under the rug. I thought it might have been necessary to leave clearer messages, but something like a note or manifesto seemed too risky. Specific messages of any kind could leave behind evidence, no matter how careful I was. Damn the news, and damn society. I knew in my heart I was doing what was best for those families—for those *children*—and that was all I needed to know to keep going. After all, Rome wasn't built in a day.

I decided to stop watching the news and searching online for anything relating to my *point*. I would focus solely on saving one child from their parents—and one parent from themself—at a time... but who was next? There seemed to be so many competing for the title of "worst" that it was hard to choose, but it appeared that the universe helped me decide. While I had vowed to stop watching the news, I hadn't actually turned off the television. The news program faded into a sitcom, which was interrupted by breaking news that gave me an idea for my next target.

CHAPTER 39

I believe most would have wondered about my next choice, Eden Darrow, and why I trained my sights on her. She suffered no addictions, came from a good family, and wasn't even a mother. So why did I think she fit the bill? When Eden was twenty-four, she had the chance to become a mother, and she blew it. That fact was not necessarily a problem for me, but her actions over a period of a few years made it clear why she deserved to make my list.

As a newlywed, she and her husband, Marc, had not been trying to conceive, but they were the type of couple that didn't need to "try." While having children had never been formally discussed—because Eden hadn't let it get that far—she knew that Marc wanted a large family. Having been an only child, he had always wanted siblings. Eden, however, did not share his same feelings when it came to children. Not wanting to be a mom at that time—or maybe ever—was not something she had shared with her husband. Every time he tried to bring up the topic, she would smile, bat her eyelashes, and change the subject. Her tactic wasn't an issue while she was on birth control—which she never stopped taking—but she had never read the fine print on the medication. She often forgot to take her pill, or took it at inconsistent times, rendering the medication ineffective. Eventually she found herself "changing the subject" often, and her strategy had backfired as she had gotten pregnant. Knowing Marc would be overjoyed with the news, Eden chose to keep it a secret and unilaterally decided to terminate it.

Less than a year after her abortion, Eden found herself pregnant again—this time, surprisingly while using an IUD, another form of birth control that Marc was unaware of. It turned out she was extremely fertile—something that many women, especially those facing fertility issues, would consider a blessing. Around that same time, she realized she had lost interest in being a wife, and not long after her next abortion, Eden filed for divorce from Marc. It was her right to terminate the pregnancies—all four of them—and if she had left it at that, she would not have been on my radar.

In college, Eden dated a guy named Drew and they just weren't as careful as they should have been. As young people often do, the couple believed that unwanted pregnancies were a thing that happened to other people, not them. Like Marc, Drew never knew that he could have been a father—two times over. While I am not fundamentally pro-life, and I believe there is a place and time that could warrant the termination of a pregnancy, I don't feel that abortion should be used as a form of birth control, especially since Eden has decided that she does, in fact, now want to be a mom. Why should she have that right when she so prematurely ended the lives of her previous children? In light of recent events, Eden Darrow was the perfect choice for more reasons than one.

CHAPTER 40

Lorie's personal life felt a lot like a rollercoaster ride as of late, which made work difficult as well. Previously, she had taken for granted how easy it was to keep her personal life from affecting her counseling—that was before she *had* a personal life. But faking it was often required for a psychiatrist—pretending you weren't judging, lying about having no opinion, and more—so Lorie did her best to put on a good front with her patients and go through the expected motions. After the murders of three of her patients, and Trenton, it became increasingly difficult not to treat every session like it might be each patient's last. In truth, she hadn't even realized she was doing that until her patient, Eloise Rosenbaum, brought it to her attention.

Eloise said, "Why do you keep talking to me like I have one foot in the grave? 'Oh Eloise, make the most of your time on this Earth. Oh Eloise, you know how much I have enjoyed helping you heal, right? Oh Eloise *this* and Oh Eloise *that*.' You look at me as if this might be the last time you'll ever see me. I am not *that old* you know!"

Embarrassed to have let her concerns creep into her sessions, Lorie apologized to her patient and excused it away by saying she had been feeling sentimental lately, and Eloise reminded her so much of her mother. Lorie was constantly forgetting that unless they passed in the waiting room, none of her patients knew who else she was treating. It was likely that not one of her current patients knew Jules, Brandie or Mischa had also been her patients, and they could be at an at increased risk. Lorie kept trying to convince herself that their ignorance was for the best, given that none of her patients needed more on their plate to worry about, but then again, *should they be worried?*

At least the time she spent with Chris was moving in the right direction. Outside of work, Chris and Lorie spent most of their time together, which made life better and also more stressful. Lorie was thankful for the opportunity to work together, otherwise they may never have gotten further than their first interaction, but she often wished that his job, these cases, and her patients were not interwoven. Lorie reviewed her two familiar options: keep the forward momentum going with her new beau and compartmentalize the rest; or end her relationship with him and take herself off the case. She chose the former. For the first time in her life, a big part of her felt rejuvenated and excited, like she was really *living* and not just simply existing.

While Lorie never openly discussed with Chris that she would have preferred to sever their working relationship and keep it strictly personal, she had begun to notice that the less he talked about the cases with her, the happier she felt. She assumed that when he had asked her on as a consultant, Chris' only focus had been to solve the murders. He probably hadn't considered the impact it might have on the doctor at the time, and in all honesty, he didn't know her well enough to care. However, now that Lorie was more than just a consultant to Chris, she could tell he did care about the implications of how intertwined she was with all parts of the cases. While solving the murders remained a priority, Lorie was on a mission to phase herself out of police work—which would be much easier to do if they could stop the killer and preserve her clientele.

CHAPTER 41

Once I chose Eden Darrow, I knew time was of the essence. She was scheduled to begin IVF in a matter of weeks and if she became pregnant, my window to act would have closed. After a quick social media search, I was able to ascertain that Eden was part of a few Facebook groups pertaining to infertility. Interestingly enough, the group wasn't exclusively women; many men were members as well. I chose a group for Colorado residents, asked to join, agreed to the rules, and was able to connect with Eden over messenger within a few minutes. Just before I was sent my first message, it occurred to me that I should make my presence known within the group, as this would add to the authenticity of my story. Of course I didn't use my real name or photo, so I was able to participate freely without worrying about revealing my identity.

Cam Smith

> Hello everyone. I'm new to this group. My wife of seven years is beginning the IVF process for a third time and I am really scared for our mental health and her physical wellbeing. I am also afraid I might not be able to hide my disappointment should it not work… again. Hoping to find some support from this group.

Within seconds, I received a notification that someone had already commented on my post. It should not have been surprising, considering the group had over nine hundred members, that someone would see my post almost immediately. Over the next few hours, I received a total of fifty-seven replies, all welcoming me to the group and offering support and advice. I only skimmed the comments, as I was more concerned with the names of those who responded. The next morning, I was disappointed to see that Eden apparently hadn't found my post comment worthy, until I noticed the telltale gray dots indicating a comment was in progress. As luck would have it, Eden did find my post compelling enough to respond.

Eden Darrow

I feel your pain.

To avoid drawing attention to myself by responding to just one comment, I blended in by replying to a few others first.

Greta Mason

We are all here for you, Cam.

Cam Smith

Thanks, Greta. That means a lot.

Joseph Tillman

It's good to see that you realize it can affect you, too. The more you are able to take care of yourself, the more you will be able to be a support for your wife.

Cam Smith

Good tip. Thank you!

Gayle Blankenship

> You are doing the right thing by joining this group and getting support from those who have been there, and are still there…

Cam Smith

> I am trying to do the best I can. Thanks for the reassurance, Gayle.

When I thought I had sufficiently interacted with the kind commenters, I responded to Eden's remark.

Eden Darrow

> I feel your pain.

Cam Smith

> It really is painful, isn't it? How would you describe yours?

The probing question worked, and not long after, I had a direct message from Eden. Her response—had I not known better—would have been heartbreaking to read.

Eden Darrow

> Hi Cam. You asked me to describe my pain. Here goes… I feel like I was put on this Earth to do one thing, yet my body won't let me. It's like the universe not allowing me to be a mother has made everything else look dull, pointless. I feel so alone without a child, but with the help of people like you, who understand how hard it all is, makes me feel a little less… solitary.

While I would reply with something that perfectly fed into my new online persona, I was disgusted by the thought of Eden saying such things to the other people in the group. They were people who had never been given even *one* chance to have a child, let alone *four*. I took a little comfort in the fact that it was highly unlikely that anyone else knew the truth about Ms. Darrow. I was quite sure they thought Eden and I were both just "one of them" too, so they wouldn't be hurt by her comments. After a handful of messages back and forth, I decided to push the envelope.

Cam Smith

> Would you be willing to meet and discuss the highs and lows, and support each other over coffee or tea, decaf of course?

Eden Darrow

> Would your wife be okay with that?

Shit, I thought. *Right. In this scenario, I have a wife.* But the way she worded the question led me to believe that as long as I said all the right things, she was amenable to our meet up.

Cam Smith

> Oh, yes. And she would like to join us as well, if that is okay? I know she could use the support, too.

Eden Darrow

> Well then, that would be just fine. How far are you from Wyndisburg?

Cam Smith

> Only about a half hour. We can meet where ever you like.

Eden Darrow

> Let's meet at a coffee shop not far from my house. It's called Pour Over. They have great coffee and other specialty drinks, and the best scones around.

Cam Smith

> Perfect.

I wanted to do some research on the location of the coffee shop to make sure it would be conducive to getting some much needed alone time with Ms. Darrow. A quick Google Earth street view search showed that, as it turned out, Pour Over would be the perfect spot to meet. While I had assumed that a trendy java establishment such as that would likely be located in a strip mall in a populated area, it was quite the opposite. Situated all on its own, in a freestanding building that looked like a tiny log cabin, on the very outskirts of a state park, sat the quaint coffee shop. I replied to Eden that it sounded like a good plan, and we decided to meet six days from then, next Saturday. That provided me enough time to determine how I would work out all the details.

Since I had never been to Pour Over, and wasn't familiar with the area, I figured I should arrive extra early so I could scope it out. Just a few days later, I found myself driving down the winding road that ended at the parking lot in front of the establishment. It was a larger, and more full, lot than I expected, but then realized it was also one of the lots people used when parking at the state park. I pulled my rental vehicle in a corner space, and passed not one, not two, but three Vespa scooters on my way to the building. It seemed typical of such an place; they fit right in. Once inside, the cozy shop was bustling with patrons, nearly all appeared to be young-adult hipsters in beanies, again not surprising.

Looking over a handmade paper menu that listed all sorts of artisanal coffee and tea beverages, I found myself having trouble deciding what to order, mostly because I didn't know what the majority of the menu items were. I decided to try a protein coffee concentrate with pea milk and a whipped honey sweetener. While I understood all the words independently, I had absolutely no idea what I had ordered, but I did so with such confidence that no one seemed to question I was clueless.

I took my beverage, which was actually not terrible, outside to check out the grounds. There was a grassy yard that surrounded the coffee shop on three sides, with the parking lot covering the fourth. Beyond the grass the entire property was surrounded by trees, with the exception of a sliver of a mountain view from the small festival-light-strewn patio. It really was a cool little spot, and kind of a shame how tainted it would soon become for many of the current patrons. Oddly enough though, after Eden's death, it might draw in a new kind of group, one of the "dark tourist" kind.

I became somewhat concerned that the semi-remote location was now too populated to be able to take care of business. But as I was surveying the property, I noticed the mouth of a walking path that led into the dense pine forest maybe thirty yards from the edge of the patio. I ventured into the woods, and it didn't take me long to realize that the spot would do just fine. As I walked through the peaceful scene, I was able to fine tune the details of the duty I needed to perform a few days from then. The path was long enough to get a safe distance from the coffee shop, assuming no one else would be wanting to wander. I walked at least a mile before the canopy of foliage that significantly darkened the trail—even during the day—began to open and illuminate the ground.

When I reached the clearing, I noticed another parking lot not far away, which must also be a part of the state park system and thought, *This would be even better.* I would park *there*, walk to the coffee shop, then after I was done, could head back that way and no one would be the wiser. All I had to do was make sure Eden and I avoided drawing any attention to ourselves while we ordered, and hopefully she would be agreeable to the walk in the woods.

Eden's striking appearance, with her almost black hair, green eyes, and porcelain skin, would likely make her stand out. In order to offset the attention she might naturally draw, I would have to blend in even more. Not that I typically was someone who would stand out in a crowd, but I felt like I looked a bit out of place considering that particular crowd. It would appear I had a little shopping to do in my very near future.

On my way back towards Pour Over, I noticed a handful of offshoots from the main trail that I had overlooked on my initial pass through the area. The little paths, just wide enough for two people to walk side-by-side, led deeper into the wooded park. Arbitrarily choosing one of the branches off the primary footpath, I ventured farther into more secluded territory. Lucky guess that the first path I chose led to the perfect spot where, if all went as planned, I would be able to save Eden's future children. Or maybe it wasn't luck at all… Quite possibly the universe could be aiding my cause, and I prefer to think of it that way. I headed back to the coffee house, tempted to try another strange but oddly satisfying concoction. However, I decided against it, thinking it was better to avoid being seen as much as possible.

I maintained a low profile the next few days as there was no reason anyone should see more of my face than necessary. There was no further planning to do, other than virtually over social media messaging, with my new friend and pseudo support system, Eden. She reached out to me first, to confirm that we were still on for Saturday, and we set a time to meet for two o'clock that afternoon.

I worried for a moment that having a record of our messages might prove problematic for me in the future. But everything about my profile was falsified, so I let the worry dissolve and channeled all my focus into making sure I could control all the controllable aspects of my plan. I knew what I was doing needed to be done, but I also knew that each time I rid the world of someone who didn't deserve to be there, the risk I was taking became greater. Fine tuning the details was more important than ever.

I decided it would be best to stay a safe distance from the soon-to-be scene of the crime, but not so far that I would be on the road, or out in the open too long. On the day of, I got up earlier than necessary to make sure I had more than enough time to get ready. It was essential that I arrive at Pour Over prior to Eden, and I had to also take into consideration the mile walk ahead of me once I arrived at my parking destination.

The fifteen-minute drive to the state park had me considering an important possibility that I hadn't previously. Would Eden be turned off and cancel our meet up once she realized that I had arrived without a spouse? Even if she felt uncomfortable, I shook off the thought that she would leave and replaced it with the confidence I had that I could win her over nonetheless. Once at the park, I found a parking spot at the corner of the lot that wouldn't immediately be noticeable if others wanted to utilize the area as well. Donning the marled gray stocking cap worn just slightly too high on my head, I made my way to the trail that would lead to the rear entrance of the coffee shop.

CHAPTER 42

After my walk from the state park parking lot, I arrived at Pour Over at just shy of one-thirty that afternoon. I didn't want to look as though I was waiting for someone, so I brought a tablet with me to look busy. Turns out, no one would have noticed as everyone's nose was either in a device, a book, or they were extremely consumed with their own conversations. Even so, I powered up the tablet and started scrolling to settle my nerves a bit. Originally, I was going to wait until Eden arrived so we could order together, but I decided it would be better if we were not seen at the register together. One more layer of security for me. After I ordered the same drink as before, I checked Eden's Facebook profile, hoping she hadn't "checked in" or otherwise indicated that she would be at Pour Over that day, and up to that point, she had not.

At 2:19, she walked in the door and began scanning the crowd, looking like someone who was looking for someone. She didn't have any photo to go from, as I just had images of nature set as my profile pictures. Thinking about it now, I was kind of surprised she hadn't asked me for a photo of my wife and me to make identifying us easier. I, however, recognized her straight away, and to my disappointment, while it seemed no one noticed me whatsoever when I walked in, several eyes were on Eden. I rose from my seat in an upholstered chair in the corner of the room and gave a little wave accompanied by a friendly smile.

As I walked nearer, I said, "Eden?"

With a confused look on her face, Eden said, "Cam?"

It was clear that me being alone, maybe just *me* in general, wasn't quite what she had been expecting. Without a change in my smile, I extended my hand to shake hers.

"Pleased to meet you! Thank you so much for meeting me. I am sorry that my wife was not able to join us today. We think she might have gotten food poisoning last night at dinner, and was in no shape to leave the house today. I told her she shouldn't have ordered the carpaccio, but..." I said with a shrug.

"Oh, I am sorry to hear that. Food poisoning is no joke. Once I ate a batch of bad clams, and..." she trailed off.

As if telling me about her experience with food-borne illness was somehow too personal; odd considering the conversation she went there to have.

"Have you ordered yet?" Eden asked me in an abrupt subject change.

"I did. I hope you don't mind. I was feeling a little apprehensive about our meet up and oddly enough, coffee settles my nerves."

"Totally fine! Plus, I was late anyway. My apologies!" Eden said.

I suggested she order and meet me outside, since it was such a lovely day. Once Eden had her decaffeinated nitro cold brew in hand, she met me on the patio. I asked if she wanted to walk the grounds while we talked, and she thought it was a nice idea. When we reached the start of the wooded path, I paused, hoping she might suggest we explore the trail, but she just kept talking about herself. In fact, she didn't even notice I had stopped walking, and was about ten steps ahead.

Once she realized she had been talking to herself, she quickly walked back toward where I was standing.

"Have you been down this trail before? It really is so peaceful," I said as I took a few steps in the direction I wanted her to follow.

"I never have. I have been to this place at least ten times, and never even noticed the trail," Eden replied.

"Would you like to check it out? I asked.

Hesitantly, after a pause, she replied, "Sure."

It didn't hurt that she likely felt she owed me one for not realizing she had commandeered the conversation, so we headed down the trail. I found myself hoping she was enjoying the scenery as those would be some of the last images she saw, and because after all, I'm not a monster. I noticed less of the beauty in the trees than I did on my last visit and it certainly wasn't enjoyable for me. This trip was strictly business and who liked work, anyway? When we came to the first smaller pathway, I stopped for a moment to look down the path, and the universe again provided its approval of my actions. A lone ray of sun shone down illuminating a patch of brightly colored red and white mushrooms on the forest floor. Eden saw them too, and when I pointed towards them, she nodded. We walked down the path to check out the grouping of fungi, then moved deeper into the trees.

We hadn't said much as we walked through the woods, and I was concerned that Eden might have found it odd—but then she spoke.

"You know, it's nice to be around someone who doesn't pressure me to rehash all the details of my IVF journey. You know, someone who just *understands?*"

"I do know. Talking about it with people who have never been through it is just... well, it's exhausting."

While I personally have never experienced these kinds of troubles, I was able to empathize and deliver a very convincing performance.

"Right," said Eden.

We walked a bit farther and then I started having pangs of second thoughts. I had felt this way before, and I was used to it by now. If I didn't question my behavior I would be concerned that maybe I was turning into a monster after all. If I was going to be able to go through with the plan, I thought, I *need* Eden to start talking, to say something that validated that what I was doing is what needed to be done.

I tried to get the ball rolling by saying, "Can you share with me some of your background, like what led you on your road to IVF? I mean, if you feel comfortable, that is."

"Oh, yes of course," Eden replied. "I have always known that I would have trouble conceiving. My doctors told me as a teen that cysts on my ovaries would likely prevent me from ovulating properly, if at all."

My lips said, "Wow, that must have been hard to grasp at such a young age, that you may never be able to have children," but my mind said, *There it is.*

Bring on the lies.

"I was married before, and when my husband found out that I couldn't likely have children, the traditional way, it hurt our relationship."

More bullshit.

Eden continued, "When I mentioned IVF, he said that was too much money and it was a 'me' problem that caused an 'us' problem. His exact words."

Wow, she was good. Believable too, with a tear running down her cheek as she told more of her "story."

"That is just unbelievable," I said, shaking my head in faux disbelief but meaning my words this time. "I don't know how anyone could be so cruel and insensitive." *Actually, I do. And so do you, Eden.*

"I know there are no guarantees with IVF, but I just want to give it all I have to try to have a baby before I give up. I just want *one chance* to be a mother, because I know I would be a great one, and that baby would be so loved and so wanted."

And with that, the deal was sealed. Did she really believe what she was saying? Eden had her chance, or *chances*, and she didn't deserve another. I let her walk ahead of me a few paces as I bent down and pretended to tie my shoe. I could tell she was either distracted in thought, or with the allure of the surrounding nature. Either way, this was the end for Eden Darrow. I walked up behind her, the leaves and twigs cracking under my feet didn't even cause her to turn around since she was expecting me to catch up. Without hesitation, I reached forward and wrapped my hands around the neck of the undeserving, never-would-be mother.

CHAPTER 43

As much as Lorie hated when Chris had to bring work home, sometimes it was unavoidable. The fact that Chris had moved in with Lorie meant that when he took work home, he was bringing it home to *her*, too. It was the only thing she hadn't loved about their new living arrangement, but other than working ridiculously long hours at the station, she knew he didn't have much of a choice. On that particular night, it was doubly hard because Lorie could tell he wanted to loop her in on something—likely related to her patients' cases—but was hesitant to ask her. She could almost feel his eyes on her as she watched her programs on television, and out of her periphery, she could see him glancing her way. It had been almost a month since the Taylor deaths, and since the two hadn't discussed the case in that time, she was afraid it might begin to reopen wounds that had barely just scabbed over.

Lorie had given up watching the news and most live television, hoping to avoid hearing anything she didn't want to think about. She knew Chris would inform her of any pertinent details, and beyond that, she was content burying her head in the sand. To fill her newly found free time, Lorie had taken up cooking. The once dreadful task when cooking for one had morphed into something she really enjoyed—especially with her favorite sous chef. When Chris arrived home, he kissed Lorie on the cheek and handed her a bouquet of roses.

"What a nice surprise," she exclaimed, with a big smile. Then, noticing the look on his face didn't match his gesture, she said, "What's wrong?"

"Tough day, but it can wait a bit. Let's enjoy a nice meal first, then we can talk about work."

She and Chris proceeded to cook a meal of chicken cordon bleu over orzo pasta with a blue-cheese wedge salad. It was one of Lorie's favorite meals to order when dining out, and she was thrilled that it was now part of their culinary repertoire at home. She was having a good evening, preparing food, sipping wine, listening to good music, and moving about the kitchen with Chris. Lack of awareness of current events meant she was oblivious to what Chris would soon be sharing with her, and would dampen her high spirits.

After the plates were clean and the dishes had been cleared, Chris refilled her glass of chardonnay.

"Wow, you definitely utilized the full capabilities of my wine glass!" Lorie said as Chris filled it just shy of the brim. "Are you trying to make me tipsy?" she asked with a grin that implied his motives weren't so innocent.

"Well, yeah, um… I have something I need your help with… and… sorry in advance, Lors."

Even though he left out the specifics of his request, Lorie knew it had something to do with her murdered patients, and could tell he was trying to butter her up with the flowers and extra wine first.

With a sigh, she said, "Sure, hun. You know I am always happy to help you if I can."

Chris winced as if the somber tone of her voice actually hurt his ears. He hated doing this, but his hunches usually weren't too far off base, if not spot on. He just couldn't see the full picture without the clarity he was hoping Lorie could provide.

"Okay, thank you very much, dear. When would be a good time for you?" he asked tentatively.

"Oh now is as good a time as any, I suppose," said Lorie. "Whatcha got for me?"

Chris, as if he had anticipating her response, was already prepared with what he wanted to show her.

"I have the documents right here," he said as he reached for the stack of folders on the buffet table.

Chris explained the newest death, even though on the surface, it appeared unrelated.

"There was another murder two nights ago, and while it doesn't appear there is a connection to your deceased patients, my gut is saying otherwise. At least, for once, I am able to tell you that she was not on your patient list."

Lorie's relief was plainly visible and she let out an audible breath, one she was likely holding since he grabbed for the folder containing information about the latest homicide. But her comfort was short-lived when she learned the name of the victim. Opening the folder, Chris pulled out a photograph of Eden Darrow and handed it to Lorie. Immediately, her eyes widened and then her head bowed towards the floor. Chris didn't need to ask Lorie what she was thinking; her reaction made it clear he had been right to involve her.

"Eden Darrow," said Lorie.

Chris nodded, "So you know her, too."

Lorie nodded.

"But she wasn't a patient of yours, right? I mean she wasn't on your roster, so..." Then, in a mildly accusatory tone, he said, "Unless she's one of those secret patients you don't keep files for, like Alise Jenks?"

At his comment, Lorie looked at him and her eyes narrowed, one of her telltale signs that she was displeased with him. But truthfully, if she had more classified records for confidential patients, he would be displeased with *her*.

"I'm sorry, that came out wrong. Let me try again. How do you know Ms. Darrow?" inquired Chris.

"Eden was not on my list of patients, but I have treated her. Remember when I told you that sometimes Alise refers her patients to me who need medication? Well, Eden was one of those referrals. I do not take any notes on our sessions, because they are brief and never extend beyond ten minutes. I speak with Alise about each referral and rely on her notes and expertise to make my medical recommendations and write prescriptions. I follow up with patients, but put any notes that may be pertinent in *Alise's* file for them. I have no handwritten documents on any referral, they are all electronic and are considered Alise's property, not mine. I hadn't thought about the referral patients since they weren't in the stolen files and no one from that list had been harmed until now. Honestly, Chris, it didn't even cross my mind that I should share them with you."

"Well, that makes perfect sense. Thank you for explaining it to me. This may be the break in the case we need, Lors, since this homicide is related, but also seems very different from the others. As far as I can tell, Ms. Darrow was not a parent and she was not directly one of your patients. Those seem to be some compelling inconsistencies when looking at all five murders. I was starting to think it was more about the children, and less about the adults, but Eden Darrow blows that theory right out of the water."

"Maybe not," Lorie said as she got up from the table and walked out of the room.

Returning in less than a minute, laptop in hand, she powered it on and logged in to her patient portal. Lorie quickly located Eden's file from the drive she shared with Alise.

"You need to look through Eden's records. I think what is in there might help clear up your quandary," insisted Lorie.

CHAPTER 44

Twenty-Seven Years Before

Nearly three years had passed since Theresa first opened her eyes at WyldeWood. Her daily routine had been established long ago, and she took comfort in the familiar. Life was predictable and she liked it that way. Dr. Shaw explained the healing powers of routine, procedure, and predictability, and Theresa did her best to follow her doctor's advice. It was clear that Dr. Shaw also practiced what she preached because her office was a picture of tidiness and order, and the appointments always followed the same arrangement: greetings, light conversation, deep conversation, homework, goodbyes.

Appointments with Dr. Shaw varied between two to three per week, depending on the doctor's availability. Group sessions were once each week and occasionally, Theresa shared something small about her day, but she still never discussed why she was there. Over the years, she came to realize that there were some inexcusable things that others there had done, and one might argue that she wasn't even the worst resident. Yet still, she remained silent about what *she* had done. Initially, Dr. Shaw helped her realize that shame likely kept her from speaking about what earned her a stay at WyldeWood. However, at this point, Theresa felt that sharing with anyone other than Dr. Shaw would feel as though she was reopening a wound that was just now finally beginning to show the faintest signs of healing. To her own surprise, Theresa started to believe that she might even deserve to feel better, at least a little. Theresa had recently begun to allow herself some small pleasures, which Dr. Shaw assured her was a part of the healing process. There was a book about flowers in the library that she would frequently borrow and study so she could learn how to identify the blossoms and blooms in the garden. She took it upon herself to create little plaques, made from plastic cafeteria spoons she'd asked permission to take, to label each type of flora. Theresa had grown used to keeping her hands busy and her mind occupied during the day, and she welcomed the distraction. Yet each day, as the light faded into darkness, and Theresa found herself alone with nothing but her thoughts, she could feel the relentless grip of the nighttime torment begin to tighten.

One Monday morning Theresa awoke in the usual way: sweaty, breathing heavily, and scared. Once she oriented herself and knew she was waking from her typical nightmare, she used the breathing techniques her doctor had taught her in some of her earlier sessions: *breathe in 2-3-4-5-6-7-8, hold 2-3-4-5-6-7-8, breathe out 2-3-4-5-6-7-8.* This had been her morning routine while at WyldeWood for as long as she could remember, and her recovery back to reality seemed to go just a bit quicker each time. It was always better on days when an appointment with Dr. Shaw was on the agenda, and mercifully today one was scheduled. Theresa showered, slipped into fresh marshmallow scrubs, tied her wet hair into a low ponytail, and made her way to Dr. Shaw's office.

The appointment went just like any other. They exchanged pleasantries, Theresa asked Dr. Shaw about her weekend and Dr. Shaw reciprocated, questioning if there were any new flowers about which Theresa had learned. The doctor asked how Theresa was feeling and the patient shared about her nightmare and that the breathing exercise she had learned had helped. There was further discussion on how to address Theresa's night terrors and how inadequate sleep could lead to various issues, including diabetes, stroke, heart problems, high blood pressure, and worsening depression. Dr. Shaw asked if Theresa had made any progress towards forgiving herself and if she had completed her homework from the last session: a letter to her daughter.

Wanting to avoid discussing the letter assignment, and hoping to be "saved by the bell," Theresa looked at the clock on the wall because her hour-long session must be close to over. The clock read 10:03 a.m. Theresa blinked and squinted at the clock because that couldn't be correct because she couldn't think of one time when her appointment went over, by even one minute. She liked order and routine, so Dr. Shaw was *always* on time. Three minutes may not seem like much to most, but the 180 seconds of overage made Theresa start to sweat. Something was amiss but she didn't know what. After a long pause, not totally out of character for her, Dr. Shaw spoke. What Theresa was told was something that threatened her years of progress to come to a screeching halt: Dr. Shaw was leaving WyldeWood.

Dr. Delores Shaw had made the decision to open her own private practice. While undoubtedly an exciting new venture for the psychiatrist, her patient didn't share the sentiment. Theresa viewed her doctor's endeavor as a child might view a parent abandoning them. Even though Dr. Shaw was not even close to being old enough to be Theresa's mother, she had become somewhat of a mother figure to Theresa. The guidance, attention and support that Dr. Shaw had shown Theresa resembled that of a parent, or at least how Theresa thought a normal, loving parent would behave. Dr. Shaw assured Theresa that the next psychiatrist she would be seeing would be just as qualified and would be sufficiently briefed on her therapy plan, but Theresa knew WyldeWood would never be the same for her. It was as if all the work and progress the pair had accomplished in the past three years was undone in a matter of three minutes.

Four short weeks later, during Dr. Shaw's last week at WyldeWood, the staff threw her a going-away party. In addition to the other psychiatrists and hospital staff, any patient of Dr. Shaw was invited too. Although she had wanted to decline the invitation, it was strongly recommended by her new psychiatrist, Dr. Ernest Castaneda, that she attend. Theresa had trouble enjoying herself for all the usual reasons, but also because the person who had been her rock for the past three years was leaving. While Dr. Shaw had given double the standard departure notice in order to help her patients transition—as well as sitting in on all patient appointments with their newly assigned psychiatrists—it did nothing to help Theresa. It was like a long and slow pulling of a band aid when it would have been better if she'd just ripped it off; informing Theresa of her departure the day before leaving.

Wanting her former doctor to know how hurt she was, Theresa did her fair share of sulking and ignoring Dr. Shaw at the party she was forced to attend. About halfway through the gathering, Theresa began to realize that whether Dr. Shaw was at WyldeWood or not, Theresa still wanted to get the hell out, and the antisocial, angry behavior would get her nowhere. Changing her demeanor, albeit a mediocre attempt, allowed her to fit in at the soiree, at least better than she had been up to that point. She pushed cake around on her plate and put a flower lei around her neck to fit with the Hawaiian theme. The motif made no sense to her as Dr. Shaw was moving to South Carolina, not a tropical island. While she sat a table decorated with grass skirting alongside other patients, Theresa did her best to look involved with the conversations, even smiling at fellow residents. Maybe what would hurt Dr. Shaw more than knowing Theresa was hurting, was to see that she would be perfectly fine without her..

At the end of the party, she agonized over whether or not to say goodbye to Dr. Shaw. Part of her really wanted to because she remembered how difficult it was that she didn't get to say goodbye to her mother. Plus, if she wanted to keep up the impression that she was just fine without Dr. Shaw, Theresa would have to make an up close and personal appearance. Finally, getting up the courage to say a last farewell to her confidante, Theresa searched the room for Dr. Shaw but couldn't locate her. It was easy to tell she wasn't in the hall as it was now empty except for Theresa. It was not uncommon for Theresa to be so lost in thought that she barely noticed the world moving around her, but it was surprising that she hadn't noticed a roomful of people had left. As she wandered around the facility looking for the doctor, she heard voices coming from the staff lounge. Typically, patients were not allowed in that area, but the rules had been lax today due to the party and Theresa was able to move about more freely than she normally would. Not wanting to interrupt the conversation, Theresa waited silently in the hallway, listening through a cracked door.

Theresa knew the sound of Dr. Shaw's voice like she knew her own, so it was unmistakable. Two other voices congratulated Dr. Shaw on opening her own practice and expressed how much she would be missed. Theresa almost walked away as it felt wrong to listen in, plus the conversation was frustrating to hear because she had been feeling the same congratulatory vibe. As Theresa headed back toward her room, she heard something that piqued her interest: the mention of her name. So she turned around and tiptoed as close to the door's opening as she could without being noticed.

A male voice said, "So Delores, you have to tell us, how did you do it? I know we're all trained to keep our emotions hidden, especially from patients at a place like this, but I need some guidance on how to do it as flawlessly as you did."

Though she had not known him for long, Theresa recognized the voice belonged to Dr. Castaneda.

A female voice that she could not place then added, "I mean, seriously impressive, Lorie."

"Honestly, I think it was some of my best work, but it sure was difficult," replied Dr. Shaw. "I didn't realize she would be my patient for *three years*. I was prepared to treat Theresa in a temporary capacity, maybe for just a few months, six tops. Then Theresa requested to see more of me, and Director Hall shared that he thought it would be best for me to continue seeing her as my patient. Plus, he added that it would likely be a resume builder because 'not everyone gets to work with a person who has done what Ms. Miller has.'"

While Theresa couldn't see the doctors, she could hear their "mmm hmms" in agreement. Then the unknown female voice excused herself from the discussion because she had a patient appointment to attend. As the psychiatrist left the room, Theresa hid behind a display case that stood in the hallway housing patient art. After she peeked out from her hiding spot, Theresa could see the woman was Dr. Johnston; not someone Theresa knew personally, but she recognized her from around the facility. After Dr. Johnston left, Dr. Castaneda could again be heard.

"As you are aware, I will soon be treating Ms. Miller without your helpful presence. I am concerned I will struggle with feigned acceptance of what she has done. I have children of my own and even with all of my training, I cannot fathom what she did. How did you do it, especially being so new to the profession?"

The hallway she was standing in felt like it was being drained of oxygen and the hum of the fluorescent lights grew louder with each passing second. Theresa's senses were overloading, desperately overcompensating for a brain that refused to process what she was hearing. The effect was dizzying and it was at this point that Theresa couldn't stand to listen to any more of their conversation. She felt so stupid to think that Dr. Shaw had cared about her—as a person, not a monster. As much as she had come to trust, respect and even love her psychiatrist, she now knew how two-faced psychiatrists could be. The walls felt as though they were closing in around her squeezing her chest in a vice of claustrophobia and made it even harder to breathe. WyldeWood was no longer the Hell she thought. Instead, it was much worse… It was *purgatory* and she *had* to get out.

With their eavesdropper now gone, the doctors' tête-à-tête continued.

"Delores," said Dr. Castaneda, "I know you have not shared this fact with Ms. Miller, but do you feel that it would help or hinder her recovery to let her know that her child *lived*?"

Dr. Shaw responded, "I believe by telling her that her child not only survived, but is thriving with another family, could have a few serious consequences. Firstly, I fear she would want to get custody of her child. In fact, I think it would become an all-consuming goal. She could become very unstable when denied that privilege, potentially devolving and even becoming violent, as we already know she has a propensity for. Secondly, I am not sure she deserves the luxury of knowing at this point. Ms. Miller committed an unthinkable act, and by the grace of God, the child survived without any long-term consequences to her health. It would potentially diminish the way she feels about what she has done, and might allow her to completely forgive herself without putting in the time and effort necessary to fully understand what she did and why she did it. And none of that takes *the child* into consideration. What would it do to her daughter to find out what her biological mother had done? As far as I know, her adoptive parents are not even aware of what happened."

"I understand your line of thinking Delores, and I would like to do my best to steer the same course you have charted for the past three years. I greatly admire you as a colleague and person, and I hope to do you justice in continuing with Ms. Miller for many years to come. I do have a few of my own methods I will add in, and of course my disposition is not as sunny as yours."

Both doctors had a little chuckle at the comment since it was common knowledge how dry Dr. Castaneda's personality was.

"Feel free to reach out to me if you ever have questions about any of my patients who will now be in your charge. I am looking forward to this next adventure, but I fear I may miss the structure of this place," said Dr. Shaw.

"Thank you for the offer, but I know you'll be busy since you will be both the psychiatrist *and* the boss," replied Dr. Castaneda.

With a clink of their glasses filled with sparkling grape juice, and one sip each, they shook hands and parted ways down the hall.

CHAPTER 45

C hris studied the file of Eden Darrow intently, scrutinizing each word to ensure no detail was overlooked. Lorie hadn't wanted to explain, believing it would be better if she and Chris each reached the same conclusion independently.

When he was done reading, Chris spoke, "We may be in for a long night, but I think we need to look at everything we know about each victim and how they were killed, then maybe we can solidify the *why*. I appreciate your help with this more than you know. I understand how difficult it has all been for you."

"You're welcome," was all Lorie could say.

With the team back together, they retrieved the copy of Lorie's handwritten patient notes and printed Alise's file on Eden Darrow. Chris took out the post-mortem data he had gathered, and they organized all the information into piles by individual victim. Chris began by looking at Jules' patient notes, and Lorie reviewed Brandie's, then they moved on to each person's police file, respectively.

Chris said, "Ms. Stevens was twenty-one at the time of her death. Her family was well-off financially and both her parents were involved, however she was raised primarily by nannies it appears. She attended private school as a child and graduated with a degree in art history from Colorado University. Unmarried, her child's father was a sperm donor. One son, missing since he was thirteen months old, who would be..." Chris paused thoughtfully before saying, "...about a year and a half now, or a little older, right?" He knew he was close enough, so he didn't wait for a response from Lorie before continuing on. "She seemed rather detached from her son. Ms. Stevens' manner of death was, as you know, homicide and the cause was drowning, which occurred in her bathtub."

Lorie spoke next, in reply to Chris, but in a fragmented way, as if the couple was having two separate conversations within one.

"Brandie was twenty-eight and also had one child, Corie, taken at age fifteen months, who would be twenty months now. Father is in the picture-ish. He is currently in jail, and was at the time of the murder. Brandie graduated from West High School. No post-secondary education. Raised by her single grandmother, who had trouble providing for all Brandie's needs. Brandie was an addict, and her addiction made it hard for her to be a suitable mother to her child. Manner of death, homicide, cause of death was due to stab wounds that caused major blood loss which was secondary to the penetration of the heart muscle."

Chris paraphrased the cause of death for Jules, but reading the intricate details of Brandie's death allowed Lorie's mind to paint a vivid picture of what her patient's last moments might have been like. It was almost as if Lorie had been there to witness the butchery. Trying to redirect her focus to the task at hand proved difficult as images of gaping wounds, spraying blood, and the color draining from Brandie's face refused to leave her thoughts. Then, in the back of her mind, she heard a quiet voice saying her name: *Lorie. Lorie.*

"Lorie!" Chris said as he shook the shoulders of his partner and girlfriend to bring her back to reality. Once she was back with him he said, "You okay? Where'd you go?"

Lorie shook off the brief departure from the present and apologized for zoning out, saying, "Sorry, just lost in thought about what happened to Brandie. Thanks for pulling me out of that nightmare," she said, tentatively, since she was afraid the nightmares would ever end.

Going through each victim's pile of information was taking a long time, and when they finished one and started filling their brains with the material from the next, it began to feel overwhelming and become a bit jumbled. Reevaluating what they were trying to discern, Lorie suggested that creating a chart was the best way to help them see the similarities and differences between the five homicides and four kidnappings. If they weren't able to figure it out, who knows how many more would die? So far, the differences seemed to outweigh the similarities when it came to the categories of: upbringing, socioeconomic status, relationship status, educational background, and causes of death. However, the following boxes were able to be checked: gender—assuming Trenton Taylor's death was a by-product of Mischa's, same general age bracket, manner of death, and what both Lorie and Chris thought to be most important: their connection to Lorie *and Alise.*

Using the chart to help sift through the rest of the victims' information proved to be very useful.

Chris thought out loud, "Why didn't I do this months ago? I fear I might have lost my edge."

"Or maybe you have just been a little distracted over the past several months," Lorie said with a flirtatious smile.

Chris returned the smile and nodded in agreement. The comment brought a little light to their very intense day. As dawn broke outside the kitchen window, the two detectives—one official and one honorary—were examining a chart that resembled a riddle. As they delved deeper, the pieces began coming together forming a grim, yet clearer picture. From their hard work and long night, they were able to ascertain that, while there were some similarities between individuals in the group, there was one thing that became glaringly obvious. In tandem, the pair looked at each other and verbalized their same thought.

"It's about the kids."

Lorie added, "It's ironic that Eden's lack of children makes it very apparent that whoever is doing this is doing it for the children."

Chris contributed, "If Ms. Darrow hadn't decided that she wanted to finally become a mother, I doubt she would have been a target."

"I agree. As you have wondered before who the real targets are, the kids or the adults, and until now, we didn't know which was the 'chicken' and which was the 'egg,'" said Lorie.

"So these people were killed because they were bad parents, is what we are saying, correct?" asked Chris.

"It would appear so. Although, as I mentioned before, Trenton Taylor wasn't a fundamentally terrible parent, but the way he treated his wife was deplorable, especially regarding her mental health. That detail was in Mischa's file, so assuming that is what the killer is using as a tool to determine the 'worthiness'—for lack of a better word—for their victims, Trenton's murder still somewhat fits the motive."

"See, this is why I knew I needed your eyes and mind on this case with me," replied Chris as he squeezed Lorie's hand.

"You know, for a while I was afraid for the lives of the children too. Waiting with bated breath to hear from you that they turned up alive, or *dead*, but that hasn't happened."

"Just being a morbid devil's advocate here, since we have to consider all possibilities, but we haven't found them, so they could still be dead," said Chris.

The fact that Lorie didn't want to believe that to be true might have tainted her judgment a little, or a lot.

"I really don't think so. Assuming our theory is correct, if the killer wanted to protect the children by killing their parents, why would they want to harm the children afterward?" asked Lorie.

"That is an excellent point, but the mind of a serial killer is something that often can't be explained in a reasonable way. The killer may be justifying that they are saving the children from a worse fate than life. Think about those women you hear about on the news—mothers suffering from postpartum psychosis that end up killing their children because they believe life would be too hard, or something like that," said Chris.

Lorie didn't respond and she sat for a few minutes deep in thought. This was not a concept she was unfamiliar with, but it hadn't been something she had thought about for a long time. Then a light touch of her shoulder from Chris brought her back to the present.

"I'm fine, I'm just thinking. Give me a sec to check a theory."

Lorie then began frantically searching for something on her laptop. About ten minutes later, she was ready to reveal her hypothesis to Chris.

"So what you said about mothers with PPD sparked a thought that I just couldn't quite place. I believe Jules had suffered from postpartum depression, and likely Mischa. But obviously Trenton didn't, and I do not feel that Brandie did. *But...* look at their causes of death," she explained as she handed her laptop over to Chris. "While we thought that, although unlikely, it could be possible the cases weren't linked because the causes of death appeared so different, I think they might actually have an M.O. that's the *same.* Take a look at *this...*"

Lorie pointed at her computer screen so he could see there were a handful of news articles, each with its own tab across her browser. The first one was about a mother who drowned her five children in the bathtub of their home, in part, she said, due to a diagnosis of postpartum psychosis. The next tab showed a story about a mother who killed her three small daughters by stabbing them in the heart. It was becoming clear to Chris where Lorie's train of thought was going. If there was any doubt, the next headline solidified that Lorie was right; the causes of death, while they appeared to be different, really were *the same*. The third article explained how a mother had strapped her two young sons in the back of her car and let it roll into a lake, drowning them. At that, Chris had seen enough.

"Lors, you are a genius," said Chris with understated enthusiasm, considering he was both excited *and* horrified by the heavy revelation. "These murders were committed in the same fashion as these parents who committed filicide."

"It just wasn't adding up, all the different ways they were murdered. These articles provide the answer to that question. I think the person responsible saw some 'writing on the wall,' or at least *thought* they did, that my patients were likely going to do something similar to their own children. In Eden's case, and in the killer's mind, I would guess they thought she had already killed previous children, and they wanted to stop her from doing so again with the next one."

Not that any of these discoveries were leaving anything but a queasy feeling in her gut, but a new thought entered her mind made her want to vomit. She gagged back the burning bile as it entered her throat, something that was noticeable to Chris.

"Lorie, what's wrong? Are you going to be sick?" he asked as he rubbed her back and, in a natural response, started to pull back her hair.

It took a moment for Lorie to feel like she could safely open her mouth to speak, but when she did, all that came out was a hushed, "Alise..."

"What is it? What do you want to tell me?"

She couldn't believe the words that began to come out of her mouth.

"I think Eden Darrow's murder is more significant than we originally thought. She wasn't one of my patients, and she wasn't in with my other files. At first I thought I was the connection, but if you look at who stole my files, and whose patient Eden was, and considering her past involvement with the anti-abortion group..."

Tears began to run down her cheeks as she trailed off. Lorie couldn't bring herself to say any more, she already felt like she was betraying Alise's trust as it was, but it would appear that she didn't know Alise as well as she thought.

"Wait, we *know* Alise stole your files?" asked Chris with surprise.

Dammit. Lorie thought to herself. She hadn't disclosed Alise's file-stealing confession to Chris, and it was too late to do so now.

"Well, I mean we *assume* that Alise stole the files, right?" she said, trying to backtrack.

"Well, right," Chris replied. "It appears I need to request an arrest warrant for Alise Jenks. At least the sun is up, so I'm sure the judge won't mind the early call."

Chris hadn't paused to think about her slip up which made Lorie feel better about the misstep—but also worse. If it happened once, it was bound to happen again.

CHAPTER 46

Twenty-Seven Years Before

D r. Ernest Castaneda was not the same as Dr. Delores Shaw. His crotchety old-man demeanor was a stark contrast to the cool, older-sister vibe that Dr. Shaw gave off. Dr. Shaw looked Theresa in the eye when they were speaking to each other. She would respond with kind words, head nods, probing questions. He wore reading glasses at the tip of his nose, and when he occasionally looked up at Theresa, it would be over the top of the glasses giving the effect that Theresa was in trouble. His responses did not vary and did not provide any meaningful feedback as they were almost exclusively just an occasional "mmm hmm." Dr. Shaw would offer suggestions as to why Theresa might be feeling or acting a certain way. Dr. Castaneda would always ask his patients, "why do *you* think you feel this way?" *I don't know, you're the damn doctor, you tell me!* Theresa would scream in her own head. However, Theresa would never voice those thoughts, as it would be counterproductive to her goal of appearing like a model resident. If she could be fooled by Dr. Shaw, she could figure out how to do the same to Dr. Castaneda.

Appointments with her new doctor began on the same schedule that she saw Dr. Shaw, at least twice a week. After months of torture pretending everything Dr. Castaneda said was like the gospel, Theresa requested a reduction in the frequency in which she saw her new provider. The request was reviewed by Dr. Castaneda and Director Hall, and was subsequently approved. The request served two purposes. First, it allowed her to avoid tamping down the rage she felt when she was in the same room as Dr. Castaneda—faking it was tough. Second, the approval confirmed to Theresa that both her doctor and the director felt she was making good progress. Though the possibility of getting out of WyldeWood was slim, she would have no chance without evidence of continual progress.

Settled into her new routine, Theresa was no less frustrated or angry, but she was accepting the feelings as part of her new normal. On her way to the cafeteria one morning, she passed a custodian, Hank, who must have been working at WyldeWood since the dinosaurs roamed. He was probably eighty years old, working hard as he mopped the floors at a snail's pace. The poor man probably didn't have much to go home to, and the job likely was his life. While Theresa found her own time at WyldeWood to be quite depressing, she found it even more sad that someone who has the choice to leave has willingly stayed so long. When she saw him around the facility, Theresa greeted Hank as warmly as she could manage. Other than Dr. Shaw—pre going away party—Hank might have been the only person who seemed not to judge her.

"Good morning, Hank."

"Good morning, Miss Lottie."

Theresa stopped in her tracks, pivoted and headed the few steps back toward Hank.

"What did you call me?"

"I'm so sorry Miss Theresa. My mind ain't what it used to be and I've been messin' up peoples' names lately. You just look so much like her."

"I look like *who*, Hank?"

Theresa said with more vinegar in her voice than she meant to spew at the sweet, elderly man, then did her best to change her tone.

"I mean, is there a resident here by that name?" she asked.

Theresa knew the name of each of the sixty-four residents at WyldeWood and none were named Lottie. She hoped it was someone new she hadn't met.

"Well, wasn't your momma Lottie Miller? I do apologize. I will do my best not to make that mistake again, Miss Theresa. You have a nice day, okay?"

"You have a nice day too, Hank."

Theresa instinctively replied to the frail custodian, but her mind was reeling. She had heard the name, in its variations, many times over the years when overhearing someone else's conversation referring to someone Theresa didn't know. Anytime she heard it, it would strike a painful chord, but another Lottie Miller, *here? That I resembled?* That couldn't be a coincidence. Abandoning her original plan of a grapefruit and cottage cheese breakfast in the cafeteria, she instead opted for the fastest route to Dr. Castaneda's office.

Upon her arrival, knocking wasn't even a fleeting thought in her rage-filled mind as she turned the knob and burst through the office door, interrupting another patient's session. She slammed the door shut so hard, the framed credentials on the wall rattled.

"*Theresa what are you doing?*" shrieked Dr. Castaneda with more emotion than she had ever before seen on the man.

"Was my mother a patient here!?" Theresa said so loudly and forcefully that spit flew from her mouth hitting the other patient, the desk, and anything else in its path.

In a slightly calmer voice, her psychiatrist replied, "Theresa, calm down. This is not your time, this is *Peter's* time," as he gestured toward the stunned patient sitting across from him.

Looking at Peter, Theresa said, "Pete, I'm afraid your session is being cut short today. That okay with you?"

The visibly rattled Peter shook his head in agreement and quickly exited the office.

"Peter, wait! You don't have to—" Dr. Castaneda was cut off by Theresa.

"See, you have time now," she said with a wild look in her eyes. In a quieter, less excited voice that did not match her demeanor—which was more disconcerting than when she yelled—the disgruntled patient repeated her original question.

"Was. My. Mother. A. Patient. Here?"

"Now why would you ask me that, Theresa?"

Don't fuck with me doc! was what she wanted to say, as she swept everything off his desk with one arm. But remembering how badly she wanted out—no, *needed* out—of WyldeWood brought her back to the reality where she pretended to be calm and rational. Composing herself, she sat down in the chair across from her doctor, and with all the sugar she could muster, she explained the reasoning behind her question.

"I apologize for my outburst, Dr. Castaneda. It won't happen again. About five minutes ago, Hank—do you know Hank the custodian?" The doctor nodded in agreement. "Well, he called me Lottie as I walked past him. When I inquired as to whom he was referring, he apologized and said I look so much like *her.* He knew my mother, he called her 'Lottie Miller' and that *cannot* be a coincidence. I know so little about what happened to her. Did she end up here?"

"Sit tight, I will be right back. *Do not* leave this office, or I will have you confined to your room for the next forty-eight hours. Do you understand, Theresa?"

"I am not going anywhere until I have some answers, you have my word."

It didn't appear he liked the sound of that by the look on his face, or at least not in its entirety, but he nodded and shut his office door as he exited. Theresa watched the time pass on the cuckoo clock hanging on the wall behind the desk, and by the time he returned, she swore her eyes had deceived her. There was no way he was only gone for six minutes. But when you are awaiting knowledge that you have wondered about daily for the past three years, each second feels endless. As he sat at his desk, Dr. Castaneda slid a thin file in front of Theresa.

"You may open it," he said to his patient.

Carefully, as if the file was made of thin glass, Theresa unlocked the mystery of what happened to her mother. It was jarring at first, seeing the familiar yet foreign face staring back at her; a ghost of the mother she once knew. She recognized the lines at the corners of her mother's eyes and the small birthmark above her right eyebrow, but the woman in the photo could have been someone else if Theresa hadn't noticed the small details. The wild hair, dry cracked lips, and soulless eyes look as though they belonged to a stranger. She looked pale and frail and not at all like the woman she remembered leaving behind when she was just seventeen years old. Tracing the edges of the photo, Theresa thought of her own intake picture and imagined it didn't look much better.

Not really able to process what she was reading, she kindly asked her psychiatrist, "Can you please just tell me what happened?"

Dr. Castaneda massaged his temples as if the mere thought of what he had to tell her physically hurt. Before responding, he let out a groan. Theresa wasn't sure if the noise was out of exhaustion, annoyance or pity—she supposed it could be a combination of all three.

"I don't know if this will help or hurt you, but you deserve to know the truth. Your mother was a patient here. She arrived as the result of a judge's determination that she was not mentally sound enough to stand trial for... ahem..."

He cleared his throat, hoping to buy a little time to consider whether telling his patient about her mother would hinder all the great success he was having with her. He was not a bad psychiatrist, but he was guilty of weighing his options to make sure they suited his needs before making sure they were best practices for his patients. Realizing enough of the cat was out of the bag to make turning back possible, he continued on.

"Theresa, your mother was guilty of murder."

The word hung in the air. Theresa was not sure what she was expecting to hear come out of the doctor's mouth, but she knew *murder* was not even on her radar.

"*Murder?*"

The word squeaked past her lips as a sound just above a whisper. Her throat felt beyond parched, she had a dull ringing in her ears and she noticed the beginnings of tunnel vision around the corners of her eyes. Fighting her body's desire to pass out because she *needed* to hear what he had to say, she thought back to what Dr. Shaw would do to help her through this. *Breathe in 2-3-4-5-6-7-8, hold 2-3-4-5-6-7-8, breathe out 2-3-4-5-6-7-8.*

"Are you sure my mother *murdered* someone?"

The breathing exercises helped pull her from the looming darkness, but the word *murder* still didn't sound right coming out of her mouth when it came to her mother.

"I am afraid so. She was caught in the act of beating a local man, Caleb Nixon, with a baseball bat. A couple walking in the park, where she and Caleb had their altercation, saw what was happening and intervened. As far as I could tell from the police report, she stopped when the couple began to yell at her, tossed the bat, and just stood there. The man ran to where the bat lay and grabbed it, while his female companion went to Mr. Nixon's aid, but found no pulse. The woman ran to get help, and the police soon arrived on the scene. Your mother was arrested without incident. Lottie never provided a reason for her actions, and stopped talking altogether from that point on. I surmise that is how she ended up here. The authorities were never able to find a motive for why she had such rage for a person she seemed to have no connection with, other than he was a teacher at your school."

A lone tear, no doubt an indication of a leak in the flood-gates, ran down Theresa's face and dripped onto the desk. While others may have sought a motive from Lottie Miller, her own daughter needed no explanation. *Her mother killed that man for her.* Only three people knew the identity of Theresa's baby's father: Theresa, her mother and the father… *Mr. Nixon.* Not sure who he might have told about it, but Theresa guessed no one, considering the circumstances. Theresa thought she could trust Mr. Nixon, and she even believed he loved her… Next thing she knew, Theresa was pregnant with her teacher's baby and he wanted nothing to do with her. It wasn't until she was in therapy that she realized their relationship was not only inappropriate, it was also illegal. It was clear her mother knew how wrong it had been much sooner. Only just a few years older now, Theresa felt like she had gained a lifetime's worth of perspective. *How could I have been so stupid and naïve?*

The frustration and anger with her slightly younger self was amplified by her next thought, *I'm responsible for what my mother did, and anything that happened to her.* Even though she knew she was a child at the time she became pregnant, she still felt liable.

Dr. Castaneda let Theresa process what she had just learned, giving her ample time to think. Theresa was, in fact, processing, however she was dealing with more than he knew. Letting her doctor know there were more layers to the tale, and to her own life's story, would do her no good in advancing her quest to leave WyldeWood, it would likely do the opposite.

Theresa asked the next logical question, "But how did she die?"

"I didn't treat your mother, but I was a doctor here during that time, so I'm aware of her actions. As far as I know, she never spoke a word while here. Silence was her constant companion; when that wasn't enough, she added hunger. About three months into her stay, your mother stopped eating. Since I have become your doctor, I have reviewed your mother's file and I know that she was not well. It appears that for much of her adult life, she was in and out of hospitals for treatments that all seemed to stem from mental instabilities. Do you remember there being periods of time, some short, some lengthy, when she would not be around?"

With wide eyes trained squarely on Dr. Castaneda, Theresa nodded her head.

He continued, "No one knows why she wouldn't speak or eat, but I don't believe her decision making was coming from a rational place. Lottie began to wither away, and when she was a shell of a person, not likely long for death, she decided she had had enough and took her own life."

Allowing for more processing time, Theresa first said in her head what she wanted to say aloud, but again realized it would be counter productive to her ultimate goal. *Why wouldn't she have called me? She had next of kin, why wasn't I notified? How'd she do it? I wasn't even able to give her a proper burial!* But her mother was dead, and there was nothing she could do about it. The pain she'd harbored from her mother's previously unexplained death was eased by what Dr. Castaneda shared with her. Unfortunately for Theresa, it was replaced with pangs of guilt and feelings of agony from old wounds that had never healed. Conflicted between wanting to know more and wishing she knew less, Theresa thanked the doctor for the information and apologized a second time for her outburst.

Dr. Castaneda nodded in acceptance of her apology, and as she got up from her seat, said, "Theresa, I assume we should weave the topic of your mother and this new information into your upcoming sessions?"

It was said as a question, but meant as a statement, which was a trick he often employed when he wanted to elicit a certain response. As far as Theresa was concerned, there was nothing further to discuss on a matter that would surely create more issues to fix. But appeasing him, as difficult as it was, played better into her hand than if she argued the point.

"If you think we should, Dr. Castaneda, that is fine with me. But just knowing what happened feels like a weight has been lifted."

And with that, she headed back to her room. The plain white walls flanking her on either side provided no escape from her thoughts as she made her way back to her personal space. She would have preferred to look at some of the residents' ugly paintings or at the hall lined with photos of the stuffy, old white men who were former directors. To her dismay, the path from her psychiatrist's office to her room provided nothing to look at but unadorned, alabaster-colored cinder block. Her mind snarled with unanswerable questions about nature and nurture, and she feared they might drive her insane. *Is it genetic? Was she born that way? Was I? Did I ruin her life? Did she ruin mine? Did I ever even have a chance?* She had never been so glad to be back in her own private space, because it was there she could let herself sob hysterically.

CHAPTER 47

For the second time in as many weeks, Lorie saw Alise's face on the television screen, and fortunately—or *unfortunately*—it did not come as a shock this. Unlike last time, there were several media outlets from around the state, and even other states, covering the arrest of the "C.R.K.," or the "Cradle Robbing Killer" as she'd been dubbed. What made things worse was that somehow the media had figured out her past identity. In a way, she felt pity for Alise; she had done so much to turn her life around but, in the end, couldn't outrun her past. *Could Alise's mental state be the same as it was when she began treatment twelve years ago? Had Alise—or Allison—been pulling the wool over her eyes this entire time? What kind of mental health professional could fall for something like that?* The thoughts made Lorie question whether she could continue with her profession.

As Alise Jenks was paraded from the back of the police cruiser in which she arrived to the front entrance of the police station, hands cuffed behind her back, she looked towards the ground. One might assume her defeated look perfectly matched her alleged guilt. But if the right person had been caught, Lorie imagined a more satisfied expression would have been on their face. For a second, Lorie questioned whether Chris had arrested the right suspect. Then, just before she entered the double doors to the hall, Alise looked directly into one of the cameras, as if she was staring directly into Lorie's soul. While no sound could be heard coming from her mouth since no microphone was in front of her, Lorie could still read the word that crossed Alise's lips: *Karma*. And she wasn't wrong. The conversation Lorie and Alise had not long ago about Sam's visit came to mind. Sam had threatened Alise that if he couldn't get her, karma would. Turns out, he was right.

The notion of Sam caused Lorie to have an epiphanic thought: *Is it possible that Sam is framing Alise?* From the sound of it, Sam was deeply scorned and out for metaphorical blood when it came to Alise, so it was well within reasonable thinking that he might be manufacturing the "karma" he threatened. But since Lorie didn't know the man, she knew she really shouldn't further speculate on his intentions. Sam was angry at Alise—rightfully so—but Lorie had only heard Alise's side of the story. As much as Lynnie was likely responsible for her own death, Alise was not without fault in the matter. Rational thought soon took over, leading Lorie to conclude her mind was searching for any answer that did not involve Alise's guilt. In reality, it was probably an Occam's razor situation—the simplest explanation is most likely the correct one.

Once the conclusion was reached, Lorie felt she had enough justification to share with Chris what she had known about Alise all along. While she couldn't be retried for the bombings, the information might still be useful in convicting her of these most recent crimes. In fact, she was almost certain that Alise's past confidential confessions would be more damning in the "C.R.K." case—as it was also being referred to around the police station—than the combined power of all the circumstantial evidence actually related to the case. Yet something nagged at the back of her mind, an insistent voice urging her to stay quiet.

Lorie wondered if it was her selfishness forcing her silence; she assumed that Chris would likely be angry for the tardy sharing of extremely important facts. It could also be her loyalty to the friendship she had with Alise for the past several years, and fearing it coming to an end. Maybe it was because she was embarrassed that she had trusted someone who, admittedly, was a dangerous criminal. As a psychiatrist, she should be able to see through the lies and manipulations, just as she had when first treating Alise. There was also a chance it could make things worse for Chris and the District Attorney's case against Alise. Relying on her knowledge of television legal dramas, and the bits and pieces she heard Chris say over the past few months, it is possible that anything related to the bombings would be inadmissible in court. Revealing the information might only frustrate the prosecution.

Lorie was even more seriously considering switching professions at this point because all of this was getting out of hand, and almost becoming not worth it. But changing careers at her age would be a daunting process, and you know what they say about old dogs and new tricks. Indecision once again shackled her in place, and Lorie grew envious of the ignorance shared by those around her. With so many forks in her metaphorical road, and no path ending with the guarantee of making the right decision, Lorie pondered what to do. Finally, she determined that silence was her best option.

CHAPTER 48

I t had been two months since the arrest of Alise Jenks and there had been no additional murders. While that should have been good news for Lorie—and for the most part, it was—each passing day without additional evidence pointing another direction made it abundantly clear that they had arrested the right person. Good news, *bad news*. Lorie was still in disbelief that Alise was responsible and that she hid it so well. Then a thought made the hair on the back of Lorie's neck stand straight: *How many of my other patients could be murderers too?* Though the statistics were reassuring, Lorie couldn't help but wonder what other deviant behavior she'd missed that had been right under her nose. While initially she had felt her knowledge would be an asset when it came to solving the cases of her murdered patients, she was now thinking that she was not at all qualified to help.

During this time, Lorie and Chris' connection progressed quickly due to emotions running high and the close intertwining of their professional and personal lives. Plus, no new deaths gave them the time and space they needed to relax and enjoy each other's company without weighty distractions. Going through something so difficult at the start of a relationship was challenging, but the bond forged from their experiences only seemed to make them stronger. Their time together was mostly wonderful, though it could get a little strained. Still, she believed him when he used the old cliché, "It's me, not you," to explain the moments when he wasn't fully present. While her brain understood this, it was tough on her heart, and at times, she, too, was guilty of her thoughts pulling her away from him. Since she felt there wasn't much she could do to help, she did the best thing she could do to occupy her time… she worked.

One particularly slow day at the office, she found herself in the mood to declutter and rearrange. Not that her office was *cluttered*, since she was a very orderly person, but there were indeed some things she could purge, reorganize, and revamp. She began with the shelves of books, many of them scholarly dealing with her field. Instead of grouping them alphabetically by title, she thought it might be more pleasing to her clients' eyes if they were organized by cover color. She had seen this done at her local library in the "new titles" section and it was visually satisfying. After the books, she took down all credentials and artwork from the walls, and using painters tape, mapped out the new layout.

The last thing she tackled was her desk. She did the opposite of what she preaches to her patients and saved the most dreaded task for last. For whatever reason, her desk was not as neat as the rest of her office—or her life. It was a black hole where rubber bands, pen caps, spare change, and hard candy went to die. Often, there wasn't much time between appointments, just a few minutes, and that meant that a lot got shoved into the desk. In anticipation of the job needing done sooner than later, she had purchased decorative drawer organizers, pencil cups, and sticky note holders. They were in coordinating shades of rose gold, light gray, and pink. The receipt found with the items showed they were purchased more than two years ago, which emphasized how much she did not look forward to tackling her desk. If she only knew what was to come, she might have never taken on the challenge.

Working from top to bottom, she grouped paper clips, tossed brittle rubber bands, and tested pens for efficacy. Many, many papers were thrown out and file folders were given fresh, unfaded labels. Nearing the end of her arduous task, at the very bottom of her lowest desk drawer was a sealed manilla envelope that was addressed to her. Fleetingly, she glanced at the address label, it was from WYGITG. When she didn't recognize the sender, she tossed it into the trash. After a few moments, recognition flashed in her mind and she recalled whom the letter was from, and what the initials stood for.

About a year and a half ago, Lorie attended a conference for mental health professionals about the topic of genetic genealogy and how it could potentially help with the diagnosis and treatment of people dealing with varying mental illnesses. One of the presenters at the conference was a brand new genetic testing company called *What You Got In Them Genes?* A ridiculous name for a company, no surprise run by a cohort of gen Z'ers, but they had an unexpectedly good pitch, and the science backing it seemed sound. As part of getting the medical professionals on board with using their company, WYGITG asked that each person in attendance submit their DNA. Everyone was excited about the breakthrough idea, so there were no reservations about completing the kits they were given, with the exception of Lorie. While she thought the concept was a good one, she just didn't love the idea of sending such personal information, like her DNA, into uncharted waters. Finally she gave in—after being the only holdout at the conference—due to peer pressure and curiosity.

The results were mailed a few weeks later, in the manilla envelope. Lorie had received the results, but, with her busy schedule and thinking they wouldn't be of much benefit to her personally, had shoved them into the bottom drawer. It was not until that moment that she'd given the results a second thought. The parcel had been collecting dust for over a year; surely its contents wouldn't hold anything of importance. Still, something urged her to open it. Dr. Shaw slid her letter opener across the top of the pouch and pulled out the documents.

Inside were several papers with borders that looked like faded denim, each containing a multitude of data. There was information about her ancestral heritage, and with her fair skin and blue eyes, it wasn't surprising that she was 72.3% Northwestern European. Amongst her genes was also a smattering of Southern European, Native American and even a trace of Ashkenazi Jewish—which was a surprise. There were also several genetic-related health conditions that were tested for, such as the BRCA1/BRCA2 genes for breast cancer, Alzheimer's, diabetes, Huntington's disease and muscular dystrophy—for none of which Lorie had indicators. Her cancer risks were somewhat elevated. Utterly unexpected genetic predictions included that Lorie's favorite ice cream flavor was likely coconut and her feet were 66% more likely to develop bunions than others who submitted their DNA. *Had I known I could learn about my potential bunions through this report, I would have taken it more seriously when I received it*, she thought with a chuckle. *This will certainly make for some interesting dinner conversation this evening.*

The real "meat" of the report, based on the conference she attended, was the possible genetic links when it came to the health conditions often treated in the world of psychiatry. A myriad of disorders and syndromes were listed in hopes that a provider could help prevent the onset of symptoms if their patient had a higher likelihood to develop them due to genetics. Substance abuse disorders, obsessive compulsive disorder, depression, anxiety, ADHD, bipolar disorder, autism spectrum disorders, schizophrenia, and paranoia were a few of the major areas of treatment for psychiatric patients contained within the report. Lorie was within the normal ranges for most, with some slight elevations that were of no concern. Lorie was a full-fledged adult and would have likely seen some indication of any issues arising by that point, so she was uncensored with the results.

The last page of the report was Lorie's family tree. Most of the familial placeholders were gray circles with white question marks in the center, since the generations older than she were virtually all deceased or had not submitted DNA samples. There were, however, a few faces and names in the report. Lorie had a third cousin on her father's side, Hallie Robinson, just a few years younger, along with her husband Bryant and their three children: William, Lauren and Olivia. Olivia's branch extended further to show she had a husband, Mike and one young son, Aidan. On her mother's side of the tree, there was a great aunt,

Aggie Johnson, who was closer to her mother's age than her grandmother's age. Lorie had never met, nor even heard of, any of these relatives, but it was interesting to know they existed.

Then there it was. How was it not what Lorie's eyes made a beeline for first? Maybe because she knew there should be *nothing* below her name, no one on *her branch.* Encased within a small pink bubble was a tiny picture of a woman with blonde hair and blue eyes. Squinting in disbelief at the document, Lorie moved it closer to her face. Even with the image as small as it was, other than hair color and age, Lorie could swear she was looking in a tiny mirror. There had to be a mistake because it was not possible. But as a doctor, she knew that genetics didn't lie. However, human error could be responsible for the mistake. There was just no way Charlotte Whitman-Sanchez was her daughter.

CHAPTER 49

The sound of a phone ringing at 7:42 p.m. broke Lorie out of what felt like a trance. Although she wasn't sure exactly what time she had looked at the familial part of her genetic report, she knew it had still been light outside. Now it was dark, and Lorie felt like a few hours from her day were missing. The ring of the phone startled her, and she let it go to her voicemail since she was in no condition to talk to anyone, especially Chris. After careful consideration, Lorie decided the only explanation was that it had to be a clerical error or a swapped sample. She was going to call the company's customer service to file a complaint the following morning. Now she needed to figure out how to put the confusion out of her mind so she could act "normal" around Chris that night. The genetic report would definitely *not* be a topic of dinner conversation.

When she arrived home, she told Chris she was exhausted—which wasn't a lie—so, she kissed him and went right to bed. The following morning, after feeling as though she didn't get a wink of sleep, Lorie was anxious to get to the bottom of the error on her report. Not wanting to be overheard in case Chris was still around the house, she headed to her office early, where she called WYGITG as soon as they opened. The number on the company's website led her to a recording, each option redirecting her to another recording, and she felt as though she might never get to speak with a real live human. After navigating through at least ten menu items, she finally spoke with Tenley, whose high-pitched voice reminded Lorie of an excited eight-year-old girl.

"Good morning! Thank you for contacting ITG! My name is Tenley, how may I help you?"

Lorie was skeptical that *Tenley* would be able to help her since she sounded too chipper and too young to know much of anything, but she was all Lorie had.

"Hi Tenley. My name is Lorie Shaw. A few years ago, I participated in a free DNA sampling with your company, when they were first getting started."

"Oh that is wonderful! We sincerely hope you enjoyed the experience!" said Tenley.

Not knowing how to respond to that, Lorie continued on her course, "I am calling because I just, today, opened my results, and I believe they are incorrect."

"OMG, I am so sorry to hear that, Lorie! Might I ask why you think there is a problem with your results?"

"Well, it matched me up with a child, and I don't have any children."

"Oh gosh, that is very odd! We have never had anyone complain about invalid results. Give me one quick sec, and I will see if there is anything we can do to remedy the situation."

As trendy music played through the phone, Lorie wondered what they could do to make it right and if Tenley had the clearance to speak to someone who could help. About two minutes later, the shrill voice returned to the line and startled Lorie who was lost deep in thought.

"Lorie? I spoke with our chief geneticist and he said the only thing we can do is run your profile again. Would you be willing to submit another test?" Probably assuming Lorie's response would be "yes," Tenley continued, "He said he would oversee your testing himself to make sure nothing is out of order. We will put a rush on your results, and should have them to you within a week of receiving your genetic sample. I will send you another collection kit in the overnight mail. Of course this will all be at no cost to you. We want everyone to be beyond satisfied with their experience!"

It was apparent that Tenley did not understand the seriousness of Lorie's concern, but it wasn't the employee's fault, either.

Lorie replied with the distinct sound of defeat in her voice, "Okay thank you."

"You are so very welcome, Lorie! And thank you for reaching out to ITG! We greatly appreciate your patronage and feedback, and sincerely hope you recommend us to all your friends!"

Lorie heard the telltale click of Tenley hanging up, again without waiting for a response from Lorie. Anxious about the week-long wait for her results, Lorie calmed herself by believing the new data would reveal an the mistake and the egregious error would be corrected. There was just absolutely no way she had a child. As a woman, she couldn't have had a child without knowing. Only men could be unaware of biological parenthood. Even with her renewed confidence that the test was wrong, she still was not able to focus as well as she needed to while at work. Lorie asked Eddie to cancel the three appointments she had scheduled for the afternoon, and sent him home early to enjoy another partial day off. Freud would be happy to see her home early, and Chris wouldn't be be there until later in the evening, giving her some breathing room to compose herself. A part of her wanted to share the odd findings with her boyfriend. She felt a little silly thinking of him as her boyfriend; the term seemed better suited for teenagers. However, she decided to wait until she had the second set of results confirming the mix up. Only then would the strange outcome become just a funny little anecdote.

At six o'clock that evening, Lorie received a call from Chris saying that he might have to pull an all-nighter at work. One of the other cases he was working on, something about college kids, was heating up and all hands were on deck. Partly sad about not getting to see him and partly relieved because she wasn't sure she could hide her agitation, Lorie found the conflicting emotions unsettling, and the whole situation was nagging at her. Just like old times, she ordered takeout and ate it on the couch while watching mid-evening television, drinking a glass of wine. Freud pawed at her for the occasional bite if she wasn't fast enough to share, and she happily obliged. Nearly a bottle of wine later, she decided to turn in early as sleep would at least free her mind from so many of the consuming thoughts she had. The genetic testing report. Five dead patients. Four missing children. Alise. Chris and all his unsolved cases. It was all too much to handle.

Needless to say, sleep did not provide the mental sanctuary Lorie hoped for as her mind was still a tornado of faces, places, and emotions that her subconscious was trying to process at a feverish pace. She awoke at 4:07 a.m. in a cold sweat, hair plastered around her face, and sheets soaked. Somewhat disoriented, and with an overwhelming sense of déjà vu, Lorie made her way to the bathroom to splash water on her face and try to make sense of the dream she just had. She grabbed a towel and dried her face, then looked at herself in the mirror. She assumed it must be the dim lighting of the bathroom's nightlight, but for a moment, Lorie didn't recognize the face staring back at her. She blinked several times, rubbed the sleep out of her eyes, and looked again. It was her reflection, but at the same time, it wasn't.

The face she saw looking back at her in the mirror was familiar, but hadn't been seen since long ago, and suddenly the images from her fitful sleep began coming back to her with clearer focus: Jules, Brandie, Mischa, and Eden in various states of life and death. Yet there were still other snapshots she couldn't quite discern: a tiny sleeping infant, an all white room, a rundown little house, a tattered bedspread, an older man with glasses, a handsome younger man... The images seemed so vivid, like memories, but whose memories were they?

Moving closer to the mirror, turning her head left and then right, something was just... off. She turned on the bathroom light and looked again, gasped at what she saw, and screamed.

"NO!"

In a knee-jerk reaction, Lorie hit the mirror so hard with the palm of her hand that it shattered into hundreds of pieces.

Staggering backward and catching herself just before she fell into the bathtub, Lorie couldn't believe her eyes. So distraught with what she saw, she didn't feel the pain of the deep cuts on her hand and wrist or the streams of blood running down her arm.

Through quick, shallow breaths, almost on the verge of hyperventilation, she yelled, "GO! GO AWAY!"

Lorie had heard of people claiming they had out-of-body, or as the medical world called them "dissociative," experiences before, but she had never felt something like that herself... until now. *Is that what this is?* Lorie thought to herself. It was like she was watching a disjointed movie from the point of view of the main character, and it was profoundly unsettling. *This had to be a dream, or more accurately, a nightmare,* she thought, and willed herself to wake up. But there was no waking from it, as she was already awake.

Just like in the past, her senses tried to protect her mind. Her chest felt tight and the running water from the sink sounded more like a hurricane than a trickle. The realization of what was going on made Lorie's head spin, and she felt very nauseous. Vomit was swiftly making its way up her throat and on her hurried way to the toilet bowl, she dripped and smeared blood all over the small bathroom. After Lorie emptied her stomach to the point of dry heaves, she stood on shaky legs and noticed the bathroom looked like a crime scene. With blood and broken glass everywhere, Lorie wasn't sure she'd be able to think of a plausible explanation to tell Chris. It all was too much; dizzy from the loss of blood and realization of what had happened, Lorie's body took over. Looking into what was left of the shattered mirror, the last thing she saw before her world went black was the surreal, fractured face of Theresa Miller.

CHAPTER 50

L orie began regaining consciousness, and with her eyes still closed, she heard beeps and whirs. Confused by the unfamiliar sounds, she slowly and tentatively opened her eyes. It took a moment for her eyes to adjust to the fluorescent lights, even though they had been dimmed, and took in her surroundings: bed rails, machines, a blue and white striped curtain that hung from the ceiling. She could have sworn she'd been there before, but then again, couldn't think of a time when she had. She couldn't trust her mind because it felt like it had been playing tricks on her. She shut her eyes tight, hoping when they opened again, she would be back at her house. Then she heard a familiar masculine voice above the hospital noises.

"Miss Miller, please… I have some questions."

Lorie couldn't believe what she was hearing. She now recognized Chris' voice, but how did he figure out about Theresa? As her two worlds collided, a rush of fear coursed through her body and she jerked her arms up, expecting to be met with the resistance of handcuffs strapping her wrists to the bed—but there were no restraints. The lack of resistance, however, meant her arms went flying above her head. The pain from the aggressive movement of her right hand shot down her arm like a lightning bolt and she began to understand why she was in the hospital room. Overwhelmed by both physical and emotional pain, she couldn't keep her eyes shut any longer.

"Whoa, Lors! Calm down, it's okay!" Chris said as he hurried to her bedside. "You're at the hospital. Do you remember what happened?"

Lorie wanted to be happy to see Chris, but considering the circumstances, she didn't know how she felt, or how *he* felt, and she could not yet bring herself to look into his eyes.

"Lors?" Chris asked tentatively. Instead of repeating his original question, he decided there was a more pressing question he needed the answer to. "Lors?" he said again. "Do you know who *I am*?"

The fog in her head from pain, disbelief, and reality lifted just enough to realize Chris had called her Lors, not Theresa or Ms. Miller. Still, she did not respond.

Lorie's silence caused Chris to turn to the nurse with a look of great concern. Ms. Miller, what is going on with Lorie?"

Then Lorie understood—quite the coincidence—her nurse's last name was also Miller. *What are the chances?* she thought. The situation felt much safer than it had just moments before, but Lorie still was not sure what to say.

"Lorie hit her head pretty hard, Detective. It's difficult to predict the effects of a head injury until a patient is conscious, and even then it could take much longer," the nurse said, placing a comforting hand on Chris' shoulder.

Giving Chris the form of silent treatment didn't feel good, but Lorie needed all the time she could squeeze out of the situation to figure out what to do—and also *who she was*. At first, she almost wanted to play up the amnesia angle, but she couldn't stand the thought of putting Chris through any more pain than he had already been feeling. While she wanted to reassure Chris that she knew and loved him, even more than she wanted the pain in her hand to cease, she wasn't sure how to go about telling him. What would *Lorie* do right now? What would she say?

There had been a time, a very long time ago, when Theresa had to pretend to be Lorie. Every word she spoke, each movement and decision, had to be carefully calculated and rehearsed to match the real Delores Shaw and how she would act. Back at the beginning, when she was intertwining her life with Dr. Shaw's, Theresa's identity clung to her like a shadow—unshakable, always reminding her who she really was. But over time, the shadow faded away. Her life depended on the impersonation and eventually became flawless—Theresa was able to stop pretending. Every fragment of Theresa Miller had vanished. Each thing she did no longer required effort to make sure it was what Lorie would do—because she *was Lorie.*

Now, in this sterile hospital room, the shadow returned, darker than ever and looming large. For the first time in years, Theresa realized she couldn't shake it. She would have to choose—Lorie or Theresa. But each path carried consequences. The truth would unravel everything she had built, exposing the lies that formed her life. Yet the alternative—continuing to live as Lorie, knowing it was all a façade—might drive her to madness.

The return of who she truly was cast her mind into chaos, a fog clouding every thought. For so many years, there had only been one—Lorie. Now, there were two. Two voices, two selves, pulling her in opposite directions. Taking a deep breath and thinking to herself, *Well, this is either going to work, or it isn't,* she resolved to maintain the course as Dr. Delores Shaw. It was the only choice she could live with. For now…

In a raspy, quiet voice Lorie said, "Yes."

Chris jerked his head up from looking at the floor in defeat to looking at Lorie.

"'Yes' what, my love?"

"Yes, I know who you are, Detective Greyson," Lorie said with a little smile.

She could tell by the happiness and relief that spread across his face that she was either a convincing "Lorie," or at that time, Chris didn't care that she was a bit off.

"How long was I out?" she inquired.

Gingerly taking her unbandaged hand in his, Chris began recounting what he'd experienced upon finding her hours earlier.

"For the last eighteen hours. At least that's all I'm certain of, though it was likely longer. I found you unconscious in the bathroom of the condo when I arrived around seven yesterday morning. I was so terrified that I had lost you. There was blood everywhere—on the walls, the floor, your clothes, your hair, your hands—and I couldn't tell where it was coming from. Not to mention the bloody paw prints of Freud trying to navigate his way to you so he could lay by your side, which is where I found him."

"Such a good boy," she said in a quiet voice.

"I thanked God when I was able to locate your pulse, then called 9-1-1, and the paramedics arrived a few minutes later. Not knowing where you were injured, they brought you to the E.R. and did an eval. Looks like you have a nasty cut on your right hand and a good sized bump on your head."

Then the detective in Chris took over, and the interrogation began.

"What happened? Did someone break in? Did someone hurt you? Hun, *what happened?!*"

Before Lorie had a chance to respond, the nurse said she needed to check on her patient.

"All vitals look good. Ma'am, are you in pain?"

Lorie nodded.

The nurse then asked, "What is your pain level, with one being very little pain and ten being unbearable?"

Lorie responded with, "A seven?" said more as a question and not a statement.

This was always something that Lorie found was hard to answer as it was such a subjective question. The nurse pushed a syringe of something—Lorie guessed to be morphine or hydromorphone—into her IV tube. Happy to have the relief from physical pain, she was also glad there would be some emotional relief too. Years of prescribing medicine told her she'd soon be drowsy, and could avoid answering Chris' questions until she had time to come up with suitable responses.

Chris repeated his questions in rapid-fire succession, and Lorie had trouble processing them all at once.

Responding to what she could, she said, "No one broke in."

As soon as the words were out of her mouth, she wished that was the story she went with. It would have been so much easier than trying to come up with something plausible on the spot. Instead she tried to stay as close to the truth as possible, simplifying it and leaving out the important details.

"I woke up in the middle of the night feeling very nauseous and dizzy. I remember vomiting, and almost falling, and that is when I hit the mirror with my hand. I tried to stand up but stumbled, and must have hit my head."

The nurse, still in the room, was writing notes on her chart.

"Due to the head trauma, we are sending her for some neurological scans when the doctor arrives," said nurse Miller.

This was addressed to Chris, as if Lorie was already unable to process the information, which further helped her buy time.

"I know you are excited that your wife is conscious—"

"She's not my—" Chris started to interrupt the nurse, but then decided against it, and motioned with his hand for the nurse to finish her thought. He only half listened to what the nurse said next, as his mind was preoccupied with an idea.

"As I was *saying*, she is still in pain and requires more tests, and most of all *rest,* especially *mental,*" said the nurse in a very motherlike tone. "The twenty questions will have to wait a bit, and visiting hours are over in ten minutes."

Chris agreed reluctantly, and after the nurse walked out, he said to Lorie, "Have your meds kicked in yet?"

Lorie responded, "not yet."

"Okay, good. I will be *right back.* Don't go anywhere," he said with a wink.

He then exited the room in a hurry, and Lorie felt puzzled. It was odd that he was happy her pain medication was not yet providing her relief, and that he was wasting the few minutes of visiting time they had left. She then thought maybe it was a good thing, as time apart meant time she couldn't say the wrong thing.

Four minutes later, Chris returned with a huge smile on his face.

Having no idea what the grin was for, Lorie asked, "What's got you so smiley? A look of grave concern is all I have seen on your face so far today."

"I was so scared when I found you unconscious on the floor and covered in blood. I thought you were dead, and my world felt like it could have ended right then. It made me realize that I've been worried about you since the first time we met; that whoever was after your patients, would eventually come for you. And by the looks of things yesterday, I thought my worst nightmare had come to fruition."

"But Chris, why are—"

"Please, hun, let me finish. You'll see…" said Chris as he removed an expandable butterfly ring from his pocket. Lorie nodded and he continued, "While you were unconscious, I had time to reflect. Something I think I've known for a while now, came to the front of my mind, competing with the worry over your condition and wondering what the hell happened. Frankly, I'm not sure why I haven't done anything about it yet. I guess I've just been so consumed with the C.R.K., and all my cases for that matter, and I thought I had more time… until yesterday morning. When the nurse just referred to you as my wife, and I realized how much I loved the way that sounded, it was the last nudge I needed. Delores Ann Shaw, you are the most amazing person I have ever met, and my perfect match. Will you do me the honor of marrying me?"

Chris dropped to one knee and held up the ring—it's playful design resembling a child's mood ring—beside Lorie's hospital bed.

"This isn't the ring I want to give you, but I hope you accept it as it is all I could get on short notice."

Though she wanted to give Chris a resounding "yes," she needed some time to think. The weight of her hidden truths made her hesitate, and she didn't feel it was right to make the decision quickly. However, the "some time" she was allotted was only two minutes. Chris was looking intently at Lorie anxiously awaiting her answer, but it wasn't enough time to thoroughly consider the weight she would bring with her to the marriage—unbeknownst to Chris. Lorie really did not want to hurt him, but again, it would hurt him if she said "no" to his proposal too. With one minute left of visiting hours, Lorie made her decision, going with her heart rather than her head.

"Yes of course I will marry you."

Chris gave her the biggest, yet most gentle, hug as it was clear he was thrilled with her reply. Although she, too, was overjoyed, there was a quiet voice in the back of her brain that whispered to her, *"You fool. You have just made life so much harder on us."*

CHAPTER 51

A baby with the faintest wisps of white-blonde hair was asleep in Lorie's arms. Rocking in a chair in the corner of a pale pink nursery next to a white crib and matching dresser, Lorie slowly brought the baby's head to her face, careful not to wake her. With a deep inhale, Lorie took in the wonderful scent of the tiny, young human. It was the comforting smell of innocence, promising that as long as they had each other, everything would be okay. When the baby started to rouse, Lorie stood, gently bouncing and swaying as she shushed the baby back to sleep. Not wanting to put the child down for fear she'd wake, Lorie returned to the rocking chair. Positioning the infant girl on her chest, Lorie remained seated for the remainder of the baby's nap. The rocking chair was uncomfortable, causing pins and needles in her legs, however, the joy of holding the baby and keeping her safe helped ease the discomfort.

Like a "jump cut" of a TV show, the scene shifted, and Lorie found herself walking through a field of wildflowers as the warm sun shone on her face. Looking down, she saw she was holding the hand of a towheaded child. The girl, no more than five years old, was looking up at her smiling widely, her bright blue eyes shining. The little one picked a yellow flower and held it up for Lorie to smell. Leaning down, she breathed in the sweet floral aroma of the bloom and then kissed the girl on the top of her head. The girl let go of Lorie's hand and ran toward a large tree with a wooden rope swing. The child motioned for Lorie to come too, so she followed along. As

Lorie pushed the little girl higher on the swing, her smile grew wide and toothy, radiating pure delight.

Abruptly, the setting changed again and Lorie was in the stands of a high school gymnasium. Wearing a purple sweat-shirt emblazoned with a large tiger mascot, Lorie was watching teenage girls play volleyball. A blonde young woman, not the tallest on the team, spiked the ball and scored the winning point. Lorie didn't react right away, but everyone around her was giving high fives and hugs, and Lorie soon felt compelled to cheer. The winning scorer ran up to Lorie and threw her arms around her in a huge, tight hug that Lorie reciprocated.

Next on the reel was a young woman wearing a black robe and matching mortarboard, looking so small from a distance. She walked across the stage as her name was called over a microphone. The woman shook hands with each person she passed, then paused at the end of the line to pose for a pho-tograph. Somehow, Lorie knew to clap and cheer as loudly as ever for this particular small figure, even though she was in a sea of several hundred others who looked the same. Unable to make out the expression on the young woman's face, still she could guess it matched that of her own; one full of pride, relief, and excitement. Even with all the happiness in the room, Lorie also felt a twinge of sadness as she watched the girl become an adult before her eyes.

Then suddenly Lorie was in a room with high ceilings, many windows, and lots of natural light. Looking around, she realized there weren't all that many windows, just a grouping of mirrors reflecting the light of the few windows in the room. Out from a side door stepped a beautiful woman dressed in a simple, flowing, ivory-colored gown. The woman walked over to Lorie and turned her back to her, showing the all-lace back of the dress was open. Without hesitation, Lorie began to fasten the twenty satin-covered buttons to close the dress. The woman, with the baby's breath in her hair, motioned for Lorie to follow her through the door and down the hall. When they reached a closed set of double doors with small, arched-shaped stained glass windows, the woman interlaced her right arm into

Lorie's left. The double doors opened shortly after, and the two women began walking down the aisle toward the handsome man in a tuxedo, tears beginning to well in his eyes. As she let go of the young woman and embraced the young man, Lorie faded from the beautiful scene, drawn back by the sounds of beeps and whirs.

CHAPTER 52

L orie awoke, groggy but filled with a joy deeper than she'd ever felt. Not wanting to open her eyes and risk losing the vivid memories that had played in her mind like a fragmented movie reel, she kept them shut just a few moments longer. Seconds after opening her eyes, she realized that everything had just been a medicated dream. She had never been there for any child's, well... *anything.*

As she became fully conscious, a jolt of pain in her hand indicated the medication had worn off, and bits and pieces of the previous day's events started to return: Waking in a pool of sweat, the confusing images from her dream, the off putting conversation with Tenley... And then her heart began to race so fast she was sure it would explode. Lorie remembered hitting the mirror and cutting her hand, but more importantly, she remembered *why* she had done it. For the second time in as many days, the realization that she was not Dr. Delores Shaw was as confusing as it was painful.

Now, with piercing clarity, Lorie remembered her true identity. She didn't doubt it, but she could hardly believe how she'd convinced herself otherwise for so many years. Though well-versed in mental health and the complexities of the human brain—*this*, this new development about her own mental state—was beyond troubling. Concern grew as she wondered, If she, *Lorie*, was really *Theresa*, were there other implications that accompanied that knowledge? The images her mind had conjured over the past few days started coming into focus and she began to recognize some of the people and places:

the bed in her childhood home... her patients' faces... her room at WyldeWood... her own daughter...

"Oh my God," she said aloud. "*My daughter.*"

The genetic genealogy report now made perfect sense. Her blood couldn't lie and couldn't pretend to be someone else. The genetic material submitted to WYGITG belonged to Theresa, not Lorie—and Theresa *did* have a child. As if grappling with the knowledge that Theresa's child—*her child*—survived wasn't enough, a new and disturbing notion seized her mind. Because her patients had appeared in her subconscious, she wondered if it was possible she had been the one to hurt them. Her initial thought was no—that would be an impossibility—but then she would have thought her having a living, breathing, adult child would be an impossibility too. *If I could convince myself that I was Dr. Delores Shaw for so long, what else am I capable of?*

The motive, should she have committed the crimes Alise was accused of, was evident: she was protecting her patient's children from a fate she thought she had imposed on her own child. If Lorie thought the wave of emotions she had felt over the past few months was too much for her circuits, she definitely wasn't equipped to handle the tsunami she was feeling now. Terrified that Theresa was no longer dormant and fearing her strength, it suddenly seemed plausible that Theresa could be a killer... Which meant Lorie could be one too.

It was all too much. Theresa's reentry into her world would have been more than enough to deal with, let alone finding out her child was alive. And now she, *Theresa*, might be doing the unimaginable... again. Hurting people is not something Lorie could have *ever* done, but as it turned out, Lorie had been hosting an invisible parasite for years. Her whole body shuddered as she remembered all too well what that parasite was capable of. Or was it the other way around? Was Theresa more like a sponge who absorbed all the good from Dr. Delores Shaw? Either way, the fact that Theresa was back, Lorie knew, was not a good thing.

Nauseous didn't seem a strong enough word to describe how she felt, but because she couldn't think of something stronger, it would have to do. As she heaved the little she had in her stomach into the bedpan she'd grabbed from the side table, Lorie hoped she was expelling the demon inside her, a desperate attempt at a self-performed exorcism. But when she'd vomited all she could, she found herself left with a splitting headache, more questions than answers, and a sinking feeling that her life was over. Mercifully, Chris—her *fiancé*—wasn't there yet to see her because she still had some major figuring out to do.

CHAPTER 53

Twenty Five Years Before

She couldn't believe it, but her hard work and deception had finally paid off. Theresa had portrayed a healed patient as though it were the role of a lifetime, not realizing then that Oscar-worthy believability would be useful for the rest of her life. Deemed "well enough," and aided by overcrowding and her good behavior, Theresa was told she would be released back into society within the next few weeks. Unbeknownst to her, it was also because she had committed *attempted* murder, which was a lesser crime than those who had completed the act.

Anger and guilt had been her constant companions for as long as she could remember, so the feelings associated with being released from WyldeWood felt foreign. After just five years of what should have been a more permanent stay, Theresa struggled to describe how she felt. Was it happiness? Freedom? Dread? Without being able to identify the emotions, Theresa thought she would humor her psychiatrist one last time, and during their final session, she asked Dr. Castaneda to help her put words to her feelings. The doctor decided it was a combination of joy and relief, all under an umbrella of guilt. After hearing the doctor's reasoning for each emotion, Theresa was in agreement.

Dr. Castaneda was actually quite supportive of her release, much to Theresa's surprise. She had assumed that he'd agreed with everyone else, that she should be locked up indefinitely because of the crime she had committed. Over their last few sessions, the pair discussed how to behave appropriately in society, where she might live, and what she could do for work. The psychiatrist gave her pointers on phrases that "normal" people used. For example, when someone said, "How are you?" they didn't really care how she was doing—it was just another way of saying, "Hi." The appropriate response would be, "Good! How are you?" He informed her that it was not necessary to wait for a response from the other person, as again, it wasn't truly about knowing what another person felt. At WyldeWood, when someone asked, "How are you?" they genuinely wanted to know—because the answer could mean the difference between life and death.

Theresa had only been away from the "real world" for five years, but the world behind the white walls was vastly different from what lay beyond. It was long forgotten by most, if not all, of the residents what it was like to wake up and decide what to eat, wear, and do for the day. Regimented routines and structures were in place at the mental facility to help people recover and rewire, and decision-making was not something the residents did much of their own. As happy as she was to be getting out, until her exit was imminent, Theresa hadn't thought of the ramifications that would likely accompany her leaving WyldeWood... Her purgatory... Her protective cocoon.

In order to prepare his patient for assimilation back into society, Dr. Castaneda did simulations with Theresa, what he called "A Day in the Life of Theresa Miller." He would have her set an alarm clock for her desired time, then pretend to sleep for a few minutes. When the alarm sounded, she would "wake," *if* she chose to do so. Once "awake," her first decision would be between three sample outfits that he had laid out for her. After her clothes were chosen, Theresa would move on to other decisions that she would likely encounter in a typical day such as: what to eat for each meal, what to do for fun, and what bills to pay. A pretend salary was given to her as well, so she could practice budgeting. Theresa went through the motions and showed her psychiatrist that she appreciated everything he was doing for her, because that was what she trained herself to do. But if she was being completely honest with herself, she did appreciate it because the transition back into society would likely be extremely difficult, and she wasn't sure it was something she even deserved.

Although on the surface it would seem that Theresa had adequately prepared for her rebirth into the world, when the day to leave came, she was terrified. All the recreations Dr. Castaneda could think up couldn't adequately prepare a person for becoming an adult overnight. Growing up, Theresa didn't have any role models to show her what it was like to be a productive member of society, and considering her past, feared she might fail.

She had no recollection of her father before he died. Her mother, who, in hindsight, was likely an unmedicated bipolar or manic depressive, was not the embodiment of what a successful adult should be. While she usually had a source of income, her mother rarely kept the same job for long. There would be periods of time where her mother wouldn't leave the house and they ate tomato soup and saltine crackers for a few weeks at a time. Other times, she would have worked long hours on end, earned extra money, and they would "splurge" on ice cream and donuts for breakfast, lunch and dinner. Theresa had no memories of her mother having friends, or even seeing her interact with other adults much. As she recalled memories of her childhood with her mother, Theresa wondered what kind of mother she would have been, an abhorrent thought she had never let herself think before.

Not wanting to articulate those feelings of apprehension to anyone, let alone Dr. Castaneda, for fear she would not be released, Theresa kept them to herself and put on a brave face, or so she thought. Apparently, she was so focused at first on her anger with Dr. Shaw, and then on her singular goal of getting out of WyldeWood, she hadn't noticed that her psychiatrist wasn't half bad. Dr. Castaneda observed something was amiss with his patient and guessed that she was nervous about leaving, and that quite possibly WyldeWood was more of a safe haven than a prison. There wasn't much he could do to help her outside of WyldeWood, largely because he believed it was unlikely she would stay in the area, so he did what little he could with the time they had left.

At the end of their last session, Dr. Castaneda pulled out his wallet and gave her all the cash he had—a total of $327, a small fortune to Theresa. After handing over the money to his very surprised patient, he did something he rarely did, in either his professional or personal life—he embraced her. Hesitating for a moment at the second surprise of the session, she slowly wrapped her arms around her doctor. Not remembering the last time she had given or received a hug, it felt both foreign and comforting, much like a hug from her father might have felt. Releasing his arms from around Theresa, he stepped back and placed his hands on her shoulders and looked her straight in the eyes.

"You can do this. I know it," he said.

At at that, Theresa gave him another quick hug, and walked out of the office before he could see her start to tear up. Walking back to her room for the last time, she questioned her judgment of character when it came to the two most important people in her life over the past five years—Dr. Shaw and Dr. Castaneda. The fact that she had gotten it so wrong did not make her feel any better about leaving, it did the opposite. How was she supposed to know who to trust *outside* when she had so horribly misjudged both her doctors *inside.* But what she thought didn't matter at that point—either way, she was leaving WyldeWood.

With no thoughts about where to go, she headed to the only place she'd known besides the institution… home. Bus fare wasn't an issue since funds had been provided by her former doctor, so Theresa purchased a ticket and took the few-hour bus ride back to Roseville. Her return to her hometown was not like the return of the prodigal son; she wasn't forgiven her mistakes or welcomed with open arms. Instead, she was shunned by those who recognized her and ignored by those who didn't. Her childhood house, the only place she had to stay, wasn't welcoming either—it was gone. Uninhabited for the past five years, and rundown at best before that, it had been condemned and torn down. Not that she wanted to return to the scene of her biggest regret, but she felt she had no other option. Dr. Castaneda had done his best to prepare her for a life where she would again get to make her own decisions, but it might have been for naught. Life still seemed to be making decisions for her and Theresa might not have been as free as she thought.

Lacking a better idea, she decided to get back on a bus and ride until she could figure out what to do. The money she received from Dr. Castaneda, while very generous, would not last long and she had to use it sparingly. A bus was a relatively inexpensive form of shelter and safety, and she could use the ride to prepare for her next move. Before she knew it, she began to recognize familiar scenery and realized she was back in Kellerton, Georgia, home of WyldeWood. Had her subconscious put her on the same bus back to WyldeWood for a reason? Was it her destiny to be a resident at the facility forever? That couldn't be, but again, what other option did she have?

As the bus stop that was just a five-minute walk from the institution approached, Theresa remained in her seat and watched it pass by through the large window. WyldeWood was *not* the solution, but she was starting to get an idea of where she could begin. If she had some answers, from someone who owed at least that much to her, she might be able to move forward. Remembering hearing someone mention the location of her new private practice, Theresa switched buses at the next station and proceeded farther North in search of Dr. Delores Shaw.

CHAPTER 54

Lorie sat on the couch in the living room of the new home that she and Chris recently purchased. The reminder of life's fragility seemed to be around every corner over the past year, so the couple decided to move forward at full speed. With their forever home purchased and wedding plans well underway, a mostly-content Lorie was curled up under Chris's arm, with a hot cup of tea in her hand and a warm, furry boy lying across her feet. As they watched the nightly news, something she could now do without wincing, she could feel that contentment also radiated from Chris. While his ignorance was bliss during this happy time, Lorie had to work much harder to find her own version of bliss—or at least something close to it.

It had been two months since Lorie discovered the truth about herself, and she had made the decision to keep that information private. She had taken a sabbatical from her practice for an indeterminate amount of time to do some soul searching, and figured that, no matter how terrified she was of Theresa, it was improbable that Theresa had hurt her patients. This was what she chose to believe anyway. And since Alise had been behind bars awaiting her trial, no additional murders of anyone Lorie knew had occurred. Chris was convinced he had the right person, and Lorie found herself believing it more with each passing day. Believing in karma had helped ease the pain of what Alise was going through, however, the notion of karma also filled Lorie with fear and worry. If there was such a thing as karma, would it come for her too? *Had it already?* As long as she could keep Theresa and her *other* life story at bay, Lorie knew, deep down, her life would likely be what she had always hoped it would—with one exception—Charlotte.

Lorie wasn't sure how she could continue on the path that was laid out so many years ago—when she had somehow convinced herself that she was Dr. Delores Shaw—now that she knew her child was *alive*. She had come to terms with the fact that she would have to share her existence with Theresa, but she couldn't stop thinking about her daughter, and had so many questions. *Would her daughter want to get to know her biological mother? Did she even know that she was adopted? Did she know what Theresa had done to her? Would she have to be Theresa in order to get to know her child? Would she have to risk trading Chris for Charlotte?* As upsetting as it was to find out that she was not, in fact, Delores Shaw, and that her true identity, Theresa Miller, was not who she wanted to be, Lorie wouldn't change a thing. Knowing all of this meant she had discovered that her baby hadn't died by her hand… that she hadn't died at all.

An idea popped into Lorie's head that she had not seen coming. Sharing her mind with another person meant it was bound to happen occasionally, but Lorie had yet to experience it.

"Chris, dear…" she said to her fiancé, before she could second guess her thoughts.

"Yeah, Lors?" Chris said, as he looked lovingly in Lorie's direction.

"I think I am ready to restart treating patients again."

In truth, after realizing how precarious her mental state had actually been over the past thirty years, Lorie seriously doubted whether she should be treating patients at all. However, she needed to have an excuse to be out of the house, and one that Chris knew she couldn't talk much about would be perfect.

"Oh yeah? Well, I think that's great! You are so good at helping others, I was hoping you weren't going to tell me you were ready to hang up your hat," replied Chris. "When do you think you will start taking appointments?"

"I think I will head into the office sometime in the next few days and start contacting former patients to see if they would like to return to working with me."

"Will you try to rehire Eddie?" Chris asked.

"Oh, I would love to, but I know he has already found other employment, and it wouldn't be fair to him if I decide I want to retire sooner rather than later."

She didn't love the idea of being less than truthful with her soon-to-be husband, but did that really matter? She was already lying to him about Theresa and Charlotte—albeit they were lies of omission—so what would a few more hurt?

"I plan on attending more conferences than before, and with managing my own appointments and paperwork, I don't even think an assistant will be needed," replied Lorie.

Each lie became a little easier to tell than the one before—a skill that was a blessing in the moment, but in reality, was also a curse. But if she was going to figure it all out, she needed to buy some time before she committed to a major identity change. Lorie could tell that while the web was being woven, Theresa was present and responsible, and there was nothing she could do about it. She smiled at Chris—a smile he recognized as his Lorie—but she was concerned that when he looked at her, he might see Theresa in her eyes. But it was not like Theresa's existence within Lorie was something new. Theresa had been there all along, and Lorie took solace in the fact that she never saw a glimpse of Theresa, so why would Chris? If Chris truly loved her, she hoped he'd love *all* of her if he ever found out. And with that, the stage was set for what she knew she had to do… as a mother.

PART 3 ~ REQUIEM
25 YEARS LATER

CHAPTER 55

L orie heard a soft knock on her door.

"Come in," she said cheerfully.

The door opened enough for Ruth, the nurse Lorie had been working with for a while now, to pop her head in.

"Good morning, Dr. Shaw?" said Ruth tentatively.

"Yes? What can I help you with?" replied Lorie.

"Oh, okay! Hi! It's a lovely day today, isn't it?" Ruth said with a smile, as she entered the room.

"It is! But I'm assuming you didn't come in here just to discuss the weather?" said Lorie.

"Right. So, I was wondering if you would be willing to see a new patient soon? Sorry for the short notice. He just won't speak with anyone. We thought since you are so good at your job, you might be able to make him feel comfortable enough to open up?"

"Well, of course! I am happy to be of service. As you know, helping others has been my life's work," Lorie said enthusiastically. "You may bring him by anytime."

"Wonderful. I will bring him to see you tomorrow morning. Are you available at 9?"

"Let me check my schedule," Lorie said with a chuckle.

She flipped through the pages of the notebook on her desk, and without even looking, said, "I just so happen to be free."

The prospect of a new patient gave Lorie a rejuvenated disposition for the rest of the day. She could not wait to get back to work.

Waking up early had not been part of Lorie's routine for quite some time now, and her appointments were few and far between. However, due to the new patient, she was up before the sun as she could not contain her excitement. It was almost as if he was Santa Claus and she an eager child awaiting the perfect present on Christmas morning.

Promptly at nine o'clock, Ruth arrived with the new patient and pushed his wheelchair to where he was within arm's reach of Lorie's desk and locked it in place. Unsure if the wheelchair was due to disability or simply a reluctance to walk himself to the appointment, Lorie knew there was no need to ask because that information would reveal itself in due time.

"I will be just outside if you need anything, Dr. Shaw."

"Thank you, Ruth, but I am sure we will be just fine, won't we?" Lorie said, smiling at the patient.

Now directing her attention at the visitor in her room, she said, "Good morning. My name is Dr. Delores Shaw. You may call me Lorie or Dr. Shaw or even Delores, whatever you find most comfortable. What is your name?"

Her question was met with silence as the patient stared at the floor.

"Okay, I will refer to you as 'Sir' until you feel like sharing your name with me, if that is all right?"

The question was somewhat rhetorical since Lorie knew she was unlikely to get a response.

"How about I tell you a few things about me?"

And with the second question for which no answer was expected, she began modeling the type of behavior she wanted to see in him—a classic psychiatrist move.

"I already told you my name. It's ironic that as a child I hated the name Delores because I thought it was a name for an old lady. Now that I am an old lady, I feel like Lorie almost seems like too young a name for me. It's as if my name has taken on a 'Benjamin Button' quality all its own. I have been a psychiatrist for a very long time, and I am good at what I do. You will come to know that, should we make these appointments together a regular thing. Is that something you think you might like, Sir?"

Eye contact was given briefly, but the pause to wait for a response was truncated, as she knew that, again, there was not likely to be one.

"I have always loved dogs. I have had several throughout my life, mostly golden retrievers, but I have had a few mutts too. Here is a photo of me with my most favorite from many years ago," Lorie said as she held up a framed photo of her younger self with Freud. "His name was Freud and he embodied the true meaning of unconditional love. If you like dogs, there is a therapy dog that is here on Tuesdays and Fridays. He is a labradoodle named Stanley," said Lorie.

"Then there is the other love of my life, Christopher. Chris and I met in the unlikeliest of places. He was a police detective, and our paths crossed while he was working on a case. He knew of my prominence as a psychiatrist, so he enlisted my help as a consultant on a case. The details of the case don't matter much anymore, but our love grew from the depths of others' misfortunes, much like a phoenix rising from the ashes. I felt like a new person when I met Chris, like life had finally just begun. Have you ever been in love, Sir?"

Again, no pregnant pause was needed, but this time the patient did look in Lorie's direction. He mildly intrigued by her story, so she continued.

"We started spending more and more time together, at all hours of the day, to try to solve the case. Neither he nor I could deny that there was more than just a working relationship happening, since we had an obvious chemistry. The first time Chris came to my house, Freud was there at the door, protective of me as always. Chris reached his hand out to let Freud sniff it, then Freud let Chris give him a pat on the head and a scratch behind the ears. Once I had the approval of my best boy, I knew my gut had been right about that man. Chris and I became inseparable. Neither of us entered the relationship with children, and by the time we officially started dating, we were both too old to start a family, but that was not an issue. We used the time to travel, eat good food, try new things and just enjoy life. We had some excellent years together, and I am so grateful for that. Do you have anyone in your life you are grateful for?"

Much to her surprise, he nodded. She was making progress because *she was good.*

CHAPTER 56

L orie was so engrossed in her storytelling that she didn't notice the second visitor standing in the doorway, listening almost since the beginning.

She continued, "Twenty-five years in love with the same man has been quite a blessing, and I know he never ceased to be amazed by me. I have no doubt I have always been the only woman on his mind."

With that, the doorway eavesdropper spoke, "That's true, you have never left my mind."

Lorie turned towards the door and her face beamed with an ear-to-ear grin.

"Christopher, dear! I wasn't expecting you! Do come in! Sorry for the interruption, Sir. *This* is my Chris. He's a bit shy at the moment so I haven't yet gotten his name, but he is my newest patient," Lorie said, referring to Sir.

"How do you do?" Chris said, nodding towards the stranger. Turning his gaze back to Lorie, he said skeptically, "Patient, huh? Well, that's an interesting tale you're telling him. Mind if I add my own twist to it?"

In a feeble attempt to protest, Lorie squeaked out a, "But—"

Chris cut her off and continued with his story as if he hadn't heard her objection.

"Dr. Lorie Shaw and I did meet while working on a case, many years ago. She was a well respected and brilliant doctor who helped many people over the course of her career. While I did find her attractive right away, I fell in love first with her mind and her passion for healing others. We began our relationship at work, and it blossomed into something beautiful."

The new patient looked as though he couldn't care less about the story, but Lorie was thrilled with his additions to her monologue.

"Oh, Chris, that's the way I remember it all starting too," said Lorie beaming.

Without acknowledging her comment, Chris continued, "As our working relationship dwindled and our romantic relationship heated up, we decided it was time to move in together. Wanting a fresh start, Lorie and I purchased a small mountain cabin with a nice big yard for Freud, our dog. Our lives felt damn near idyllic for almost a year or so. I was so happy, and I could tell Lorie was happy too."

The look on Chris' face was one of anguish, and clashed with the happy love story that he told.

"After a while, I began to notice that Lorie would leave often to 'run errands' or to attend 'appointments,' which in and of itself is not that odd. But when she said she had a dentist appointment, and I remembered she had said she went to the dentist two weeks prior, that didn't track. I started to grow suspicious of what she was doing. Our lives were great, but I had been a cop long enough to know that many domestic disputes arise from a scorned lover who was shocked to discover their partner was cheating. I felt sad and scared that I was losing her. I could not get my mind off where she was going and who she might be with, and it became all-consuming. I couldn't focus at work; at home, my mind wandered every time she received a text, got a phone call that she let go unanswered, or arrived home later than expected.

"One morning, I stopped by her office. I thought I would surprise her and take her to lunch, bringing back some of the spontaneity that was there when we first met. I was shocked to find that she was not only not at the office, but the practice was closed—permanently, and there was a 'for lease' sign in the yard. That revelation sent my mind reeling. I had thought she returned to work—she said she was treating some new patients, she left for work each morning, and she seemed very happy. After over a month of feeling torn between giving the woman I loved her privacy, and easing my pain of wondering, I knew I had to do something."

As the interest the new patient had in Chris' story seemed to increase, the smile on Lorie's face began to fade.

Chris continued, "On a day she said she was heading into her office to catch up on work, I decided that would be the day I took action. I tailed her—expertly, I might add—to her destination. It wasn't her office—no surprise there—since I already knew she no longer had one. I followed her to a local coffee shop and watched from my car as she sat in the front window. No coffee was drunk, no pastries eaten, and no lover arrived to join her. The only two things out of the ordinary were that she pulled out a phone I did not recognize and was intently focused on it, and she was not at the location she had said she'd be heading to. I felt relieved she was alone but uneasy because it was apparent she'd been hiding *something*. Being right never felt so *wrong*. I tried to convince myself that maybe it was a good surprise she was hiding from me, and I chose to drop it."

The patient was now intently listening to Chris' story while Lorie was looking out the window, trying to ignore his recollection of events.

"A few months passed but unfortunately the disingenuous behavior did not go away, nor did any fun surprises come about for me, and I just couldn't let it go. Lying to me about something so big as her career, or lack thereof, almost felt as bad as if she actually was cheating on me. As someone who was in law enforcement for years, it was ingrained in me not to trust. But when I met Lorie, there was just something about her that I couldn't help but believe. Not only did I feel betrayed by her dishonesty, I questioned my abilities as a detective.

"A day came when Lorie casually informed me she was attending a conference on child psychology in San Diego, California. I suggested that I go with her, and we stay a few extra days to make a vacation out of it. She responded a little too quickly with, 'Oh no, that's all right. It will be boring for you while I am at the conference, and what will we do with Freud? I don't want to be out of work too long either.' This was very out of character for my love, as we enjoyed traveling together, and our neighbor had never said 'no' to watching our dog. That night, after Lorie had fallen asleep, I looked to see if any child psychology conferences were being held in San Diego at that time. Not only were there none there, but there weren't any being held anywhere in Southern California—or the United States, for that matter. I decided then that I would be taking a trip to sunny SoCal after all."

"Sir" was now hanging on Chris' every word while Lorie was doing her best to pretend Chris hadn't shown up at all.

"I asked our neighbor to look after Freud and I booked on the same flight to San Diego as Lorie, which I knew because she shared her flight info with me. A risky move, but I bought first class, and asked to board the plane last hoping that she wouldn't see me. If she happened to notice my presence, my cover story was that I wanted to surprise her; however, I successfully made it to California undetected. In my unmemorable rental car, I followed Lorie to a small house in a quaint suburb of the city. My police training taught me how to stay undetected while performing surveillance, but what they don't tell you is that it's about a million times harder when you are surveilling someone you know.

"Lorie knocked on the front door and was greeted by a blonde-haired, blue-eyed woman, who, apart from the hair color, looked a whole lot like Lorie. I thought maybe it was her niece, or younger sister, although Lorie had never mentioned that she had any, in fact, she had said she was an only child. Doubting that this younger version of Lorie could be her lover, I grew increasingly intrigued more than afraid. I sat outside the house until the veil of night fell over the neighborhood. I was settling in for what could be an overnighter, glad I brought snacks, water, and a thermos of coffee. Just after 10 p.m., Lorie left the house. Not wanting to miss her next destination, I followed her, making sure to first mark my location in GPS so I could return later."

"Ruth? Ruth!" Lorie called out, but there was no response. The new patient shushed her and nodded at Chris to continue.

"Lorie's next stop was her hotel, a little boutique B&B with ocean views. She was always a sucker for the picturesque and cozy, and if there was a water vista to be seen from a room, that was the room in which she'd stay. I had not made any accommodations for the evening, not knowing where the day would take me, so I pulled onto a perpendicular street, parked, and slept. I set my alarm for 4:30 a.m. in hopes that I would not miss her departure. I woke up with a sore neck, stiff back, and drank cold coffee, both thankful and cursing my stakeout abilities and experience. I couldn't unsee what I was seeing, but putting blinders on could have had its own consequences, and I had to see where it was going.

"I didn't let the lack of creature comforts bother me because I could still see Lorie's rental car parked in front of where she was staying. I noticed I had missed a text from her the night before: she said she missed and loved me. I waited until the first sign of the sun's rays pierced the navy sky, then I responded, 'I miss and love you too. I hope the conference is going well.' As she is not typically an early riser, I was surprised when Lorie promptly texted me back, 'It went great yesterday. A really full day of learning all about the mind of a child. I think I might expand my practice to include seeing a few children.' Knowing the majority of what she was saying was bullshit made my stomach turn, but still I forced myself to eat a breakfast of peanut butter cheese cracker sandwiches while I continued to watch and wait. At 9:30 that morning, Lorie emerged, got in her vehicle, and began driving in the direction from which she came yesterday. If my gut feeling was correct, she was heading back to see the younger woman.

"The two women meeting for a second time in two days was causing my brain to go into overdrive. I just couldn't work out a logical explanation for what was going on. My lack of sleep and sustenance wasn't helping matters, so I got myself a hotel for the night. Since she was supposed to be at a conference, I didn't want to call her, so I sent a text letting her know that I, too, would be traveling for work. I made up a plausible story as a cover to allow me to stay in California until *after* Lorie had left. I managed to follow her undetected for the rest of her time in and around San Diego, with nothing else to report except one more visit with the other woman. Once I was sure Lorie was at the airport, I headed back to the small house in the suburbs.

"I was taken aback when a man answered the door of the house Lorie had been frequenting, and instantly went from boyfriend mode to detective mode. Even though I knew it was unethical, I used my badge to help me figure out the mystery of Lorie. I introduced myself to a man who said he was Matteo Sanchez and explained that I was investigating a case and needed help. After asking if a woman also lived at the residence, I told Mr. Sanchez that I didn't know her name, but I had received a tip that she might have information. He told me that his wife, Charlotte, was home, so I asked if I could speak with her. I was not yet invited in the home, but Charlotte Whitman-Sanchez met me at the door. Up close, the woman was the spitting image of Lorie—they just *had* to be related, but how? Sounding as professional a detective as I could manage under the unsettling circumstances, I began my line of questions."

Lorie got up to leave the room, but Chris said to her, "Why don't you stay, *Dr. Shaw*? It really is a good *story*."

She was on her way out the door when the new patient said, "Well who was the woman?"

This made the psychiatrist stop in her tracks. She was torn—she didn't want to hear any more of Chris' account, but seeing the progress being made with the new patient was too rewarding to resist. *She* was the reason he was speaking now, and she wanted to see how far she could take him on his first visit. It was important for her to demonstrate to the other psychiatrists that she was still the best. So, Lorie did an about-face and returned to her desk chair.

Looking at Chris with measured calm, she said, "Well, go on, Chris. Who *was* she?"

CHAPTER 57

Lorie's interest in his version of events both surprised and annoyed Chris, but he continued, "I explained to Charlotte Whitman-Sanchez who I was and that I was working on a case in which she might be able to help. Although I couldn't disclose much, I was able to say that it had to do with the woman she'd seen a few times recently. She told me that Dr. Delores Shaw was her biological mother. Charlotte had been given up for adoption shortly after birth and was adopted by Lawrence and Catherine Whitman soon thereafter. I did my best to hide my surprise at learning the woman I planned to marry had a secret child—no easy feat considering the magnitude of the revelation—so I could continue the conversation with Mrs. Whitman-Sanchez.

"Charlotte said that for a fun family Christmas present a few years prior, her adopted brother, Kevin, had purchased genotyping kits for the family. It was no surprise to Charlotte that there weren't any matches in her familial tree to any of her current family members, but there were people she was related to by blood whom she'd never met. A few distant cousins showed up, but that was it. Kevin apologized after the results were in, regretting the gift since she wouldn't show up with the rest of the Whitman clan. He could have had no idea how this seemingly small gift would change his sister's life forever. It didn't bother Charlotte; she obviously knew she was adopted. It made her feel good that Kevin viewed her just like his biological sister, even if they wouldn't technically be on the same family tree.

"A few months after she'd received her DNA results, Charlotte got an unexpected surprise. She received an email from the testing company stating that a new member of her family had been added to her tree. Intrigued by the notification, because she knew that person had to be a blood relative, she promptly signed into her account to view the new addition. Another distant cousin was what she expected, but not what she got. The name and image of the new addition to her tree was there, but something stood out. Except for the dark hair, it was like looking at a future version of herself. Blinking several times to make sure her eyes weren't being deceptive, Charlotte confirmed she was looking at the name and image of her biological mother.

"After doing some research on Delores Shaw, and discussing it with her husband, they made a plan for Charlotte to meet her biological mother. Not wanting to upset her mother or risk rejection herself, she and Matteo decided that she should schedule an appointment with the psychiatrist. After meeting with her, Charlotte could decide for herself whether to reveal her true identity. The appointment with the mother she'd never known went okay. It wasn't what Charlotte had expected, but then again, she didn't know what her expectations of the reunion even were. Charlotte talked, the doctor listened, and then it was over. Though she was glad she made the trip, Charlotte was left with a hole inside her that was not there before she knew Delores Shaw existed.

"Charlotte told Catie and Lawrence about the exchange, and they were understandably skeptical. She had never asked questions before about the topic, so with this sudden interest, even as an adult, it was understandable that her parents were protective of their child. Hoping they could tell her more, Charlotte was a bit disappointed when all they could provide was that her name was Charlotte Miller and that they had to travel to Florida for the adoption. Charlotte assumed her biological father's surname was Miller, unless Delores Shaw had been married and changed her last name."

"Is any of this sounding familiar, *Lorie?*" Chris said, looking at her with an inquisitive expression.

Ignoring him, Lorie turned to the new patient and said, "Sir, are you enjoying this story?"

The patient looked at Lorie and replied, "I am."

"Well then, Chris has been generous enough to provide you with so much, the least you can do is tell us your name."

The new patient nodded and said, "Okay, that's fair. My name is Cole. Cole Beeman."

Lorie's face lit up with a Cheshire-Cat grin, clearly pleased with herself. The irony was that *Chris* was the one making the progress with Cole. Chris hesitated, reluctant to contribute to the psychiatrist's satisfaction, but a small part of him was glad to see her happy. No matter how his mind felt about it, his heart would always love *Lorie*.

He continued, "The information provided by Charlotte's parents was enough for Charlotte to put the issue to rest for the time being, and she continued on with her life. Until one day she received an email from Delores Shaw asking if they could meet. I observed their first official meeting when I watched Lorie knock on Charlotte's door. The information that Charlotte Whitman-Sanchez had just provided me gave me something I could run with."

CHAPTER 58

"I went back to Wyndisburg and started researching birth records under the last name Shaw. I knew that Lorie had never been married, at least that was what she told me. While I wasn't confident, I was hopeful that my guesswork would pay off and that Charlotte's given last name would have been Shaw. After an exhaustive, unsuccessful search, I was about to give up. Then I decided I would look at birth records under the last name Miller. If Lorie had hidden so much from me already, maybe she had changed her name at some point too. Thankful that the internet saved me a trip to Florida, it hadn't taken me long to locate a comprehensive list of births, with the last name Miller, on the same date Charlotte had been born.

"Fact-checking each Miller baby against the information I had was a more arduous task. The vast majority of the Millers in question had never given a child up for adoption and a few of the children had died at a young age. I searched through databases, yearbooks, archives, registries, and any documentation I could access. I felt as though I had hit a dead end. I had almost given up the taxing search when I found what I was looking for. A black and white yearbook photo from Rose Senior High School in Roseville, Florida, on my computer screen, showed a group of young girls wearing choir robes. The girl on the far right end of the front row looked very much like a teenage Charlotte, *and a teenage Lorie,* but due to the graininess of the image, I couldn't be sure exactly who she was."

Chris pulled a folded piece of paper out of his wallet and handed it to Cole. It was a printout of the yearbook photo.

There was a list of names in the caption from left to right: Rose High School Girls' Choir, from top left: Mary Turner, Emily Perkins, Patty Jones, Winnie Sullivan. From bottom left: Eileen Stover, Deborah Mears, Iris Rosencrantz, Theresa Miller.

Lorie scrunched up her face at the nails-on-a-chalkboard way the name "Theresa" sounded when it hit her ears. Cole's eyes widened slightly, a reaction Chris might have missed if he hadn't expected it. Chris was looking for the same flicker of recognition in Cole that he himself had felt when first seeing the image.

"Theresa Miller... You found Charlotte's mother?" Cole said, with great interest.

"I had my suspicions that I had found her, but I needed to confirm. I researched the Theresa Miller from the photo and discovered that she had not put her child up for adoption. Not *technically*. Nor had that child died. *Not technically*. Theresa Miller had been ordered to spend her life at a WyldeWood Mental Hospital for the attempted murder of her six-week-old daughter, Charlotte Miller. The lifetime of confinement for her mother, combined with the fact that her father was unknown and no other family could be located, meant that Charlotte was placed in the care of the state of Florida.

"Baby Charlotte was not in the system for long, and was adopted shortly thereafter by the Whitman family. It became clear to me that Mr. and Mrs. Whitman had likely known about Charlotte's abysmal first weeks of life and the trauma she endured as an infant. After their slightly cagey behavior when their daughter broached the subject of her birth mother, they probably wanted to protect her from the damaging effects knowing the truth could cause. What I had discovered was a big break, and I was hoping to be able to find out more now that I had names and faces. At least by this point, I knew three things to be true: Theresa Miller was Charlotte's biological mother, Theresa Miller was a convicted criminal, and Theresa Miller was *Delores Shaw*."

Cole's eyes were as wide as saucers as he slowly turned his head to look squarely at Lorie, whose own eyes were looking down at the floor.

Cole questioned Chris, "How did Theresa become Delores?" He then looked back at Lorie and said, "How did you become... *you?*"

"Don't you want to field that question, *doctor?*" Chris asked.

In a role reversal, Cole was doing the talking and Lorie had become the mute. Just then, Ruth returned to the hallway outside the room. Having worked with Lorie for many years without incident, Ruth felt there was no reason to eavesdrop. But when she heard the familiar voice of a third party in the room, she started to panic.

Ruth had seen Chris around the building before and knew who he was. She also knew that Lorie had unpredictable reactions to his presence. If Chris reported that Lorie and the patient were unsupervised, or if something went wrong, Ruth could lose her job—or face legal consequences. Just when she was about to rush into the room to grab the new patient, she saw that not only was Chris talking, but Cole had been talking back to him. Pausing to weigh her options, Ruth thought it might be in her best interest to let the "group session" continue, hoping her initial carelessness didn't cost her her job, or more. She might even be rewarded with a promotion if she could be the one who got the new patient talking. Ruth decided to remain outside the room, and take a gamble by letting the conversation carry on.

"How did Theresa Miller become Delores Shaw was the $25,000 question," Chris continued. "I was able to obtain records that showed Theresa Miller was released from her life sentence at the involuntary mental facility just five years into her stay. Her exemplary behavior, remorse, and commitment to improvement—combined with the institution's overcrowding—made her an ideal candidate for early release.

"As I pored over everything I could find about Ms. Miller, I came across her patient file that listed Dr. Delores Shaw as her primary provider for the first three years of her stay. I have a guess as to what happened to Dr. Shaw, but I have never been able to prove it. Lorie, do you care to elaborate on this? And while we're on the subject of elaboration, *what happened to the babies?*"

Theresa, responding as Lorie, replied innocently, "Chris, you know *I* didn't harm anyone. I'm sorry I can't tell you what you want to know."

"I know the answers are in there. *Theresa, tell me!*" Chris said with an angry and loud voice, startling Cole.

Outside, Ruth was beginning to question the bet she'd taken letting the three remain unsupervised. Still, she decided to give it just a few more minutes...

Lorie had disappeared, replaced by Theresa. As her expression hardened and her eyes darkened, she responded in a calm, deep voice.

"No."

Although she looked the same, she was different and it was hard for Chris to recognize the woman sitting in front of him who he'd known for so many years.

"You belong in Hell, Theresa Miller, but I guess this place will have to do until then," Chris said, as he got up to leave.

As he left the small, white hospital room, he tapped on the plaque by the door, which read:

Dr. E. David Castaneda, Jr., Director
WyldeWood Mental Institution

CHAPTER 59

D r. Delores Shaw—or rather the second iteration of her—disappeared completely after her final visit with Chris. She had made a life for herself at WyldeWood under the delusion that she was still Delores Shaw, practicing psychiatry, and in a relationship with Chris Greyson. A gifted psychiatrist, or pseudo-psychiatrist as it were, the staff at WyldeWood often played into her fantasies of a life she stole, but believed was hers all along. Letting the pretend Dr. Shaw treat patients off the books had its benefits, as Nurse Ruth knew. Cole Beeman was not the first patient brought to her, and it was not the first time someone who worked at the facility relied on Dr. Shaw's expertise.

The departure of the respected and loved Lorie, and the return of Theresa as a lone person, was more than the woman could bear. Once the doctor was *out*, and only Theresa remained, no more patients were sent her way. Theresa was not equipped to treat anyone, and her delusions had begun to crumble. She clung to her memories—memories of a false life she didn't deserve—as best she could, but eventually they were just not enough.

For the past twenty-five years, Delores Shaw had only two visitors during her second stay at the institution—two more than her first—Chris Greyson and Alise Jenks. Chris never went to the facility specifically to see Lorie; he had other business to attend to at there over the years. He would just stop in to see her, but he wasn't quite sure why. Undoubtedly a combination of reasons he didn't want to admit were what led to the visit—surely he had been searching for answers. Possibly, he wanted to open her old wounds. Perhaps he missed her. While she was never quite sure if he'd return after each visit, and years might have gone by in between, he had always come back. But after their last encounter, Theresa could tell he was just… done, and her time with Chris had come to a close.

Unlike Chris, Alise had deliberately made the journey to visit Theresa. Once Chris discovered Lorie's true identity, he quickly connected the dots, suspecting Theresa was behind the murders of her patients. Alise, who was released around the same time Lorie was being taken into custody, spent a few years being angry, and rightfully so. Of course Alise was happy to have her name cleared, but for a long time she was in disbelief about Lorie's true identity and past.

After the situation cooled off and a few years had passed, the irony was not lost on her that their lives were so similar, and she realized she owed Theresa more than passive forgiveness. Drawing upon her understanding of mental health and dissociative identity disorder, and knowing that Lorie—or Theresa—had never shared the truth about her, Alise realized her friend and confidante had not wronged her on purpose. Alise Jenks was also acutely aware of how lonely life could be when people believed the horrible things about you, even if they were true.

At first, Alise was unsure how to address her old friend because she didn't know if she was Lorie, Theresa, or both. It soon became apparent to Alise that she would only be dealing with the Lorie she once knew, which made things both easier and harder for her. It was like old times in a way, talking like they used to, and it was like nothing had changed with Lorie. The difficult part was that the more Lorie clung to *Lorie*, the more detached from reality Alise knew she had become. While Alise had assumed a new identity to try to leave her past behind, she had never forgotten—or rather blocked out—what she had done. It was hard to watch as someone believed something that was so unbelievable, especially about themself. In all the years they knew each other, Alise never got to officially meet Theresa.

Noticeably absent from Theresa's list of visitors was her daughter. Once Charlotte learned of her mother's true identity, and what had happened to her as an infant, she cut all ties with Lorie, or Theresa, or "*whoever the hell you are,*" were her words. The short time that Theresa, as Lorie, got to spend with her daughter, son-in-law, and grandchildren had become such an important and special part of her life, that she was torn apart when it was ripped away. Deep down, Theresa knew it couldn't last forever—that was keeping her life with Chris separate from her life with Charlotte. She also knew that merging the two worlds probably wouldn't end well either. Again, she had found herself in purgatory with a crippling decision to make. In the end, the universe chose for her, severing all the relationships in Theresa's life—something she ultimately felt she deserved.

One week after her last visit with Chris—although "visit" might be too soft a word for the encounter—Theresa took out her one pen and two sheets of blank paper. Pens were not something handed out often at the facility due to their ability to double as a weapon, however, she had earned the writing utensil as a reward for years of good behavior. Theresa sat down to write two letters, one for Chris and one for Charlotte. It didn't take her long to scribe as the thoughts had been in the back of her mind for the majority of her life.

When she finished, she put the letters in two envelopes labeled with the corresponding names, sealed them, and placed them on the center of her desk. A few items in her room were out of place, so she took a moment to tidy up, restoring the impeccable order she loved. From a small hole in the side of her mattress, she pulled a crumpled tissue. Opening the wad revealed the store of pills she had been saving for quite some time, at least a year, just in case. Unlike her first attempt when she was young, she swallowed each pill calmly, one by one, finishing the job she had failed to complete so many years before.

CHAPTER 60

Nurse Ruth knocked on Theresa's door, but there was no response. This was not unusual, since for the past week, there had been no more Dr. Shaw—only a severely depressed Theresa. Gone were the chipper morning welcomes Ruth had received for most of the ten years she had been working at WyldeWood in Theresa Miller's wing. There were no more real patients sent to the pretend doctor, not even Cole Beeman. Theresa had nearly stopped eating, showering, and caring, and there were no more delusions of hers that needed feeding.

Since doors to patient rooms couldn't be locked internally, Ruth opened the door slowly, not wanting to startle her patient. At first glance, Ruth believed her patient to be asleep, but when trying to rouse her, the nurse got no response. When checking for a pulse, Ruth felt none. Just as the nurse went to press the emergency button on the wall—there was one present in each room, more for staff safety than for patients—she paused. She had noticed the envelopes on the desk when she entered the room, but they hadn't really registered with her. Quickly grabbing the white papers and putting them inside the pocket of her scrubs, Ruth then pushed the button to call for help.

Theresa Miller, true age of seventy-two, passed away after a week in a coma, just four days shy of her twenty-fourth anniversary of her return to WyldeWood. Charlotte and Chris were notified, but neither wanted to claim her cremated ashes. Only Ruth, Alise Jenks, and the institution's chaplain attended the small service when they buried her remains on the grounds. Ruth thought it seemed so sad, but it happened fairly often when patients died there. WyldeWood was not a place where residents had many left who still cared about them, especially after a lifetime there. Attending her patient's funeral was the least Ruth could do as a final "thank you," as Theresa had provided more for Ruth than she would ever know.

Chris and Charlotte never received their letters, but they would have the opportunity to learn what Theresa had written through Ruth A. Carpenter's unauthorized biography, *Break*. It turned out Ruth had a knack for writing, and, when combined with her eye for opportunity, it paid off. Shortly after Theresa's passing, Ruth Carpenter retired from the medical field a wealthy woman. She received a slap on the wrist for stealing the letters, but due to her resignation, and no one to fight on Theresa's behalf, the issue was dropped. Royalties Ruth earned from her best-selling book would continue in perpetuity, all thanks to the twisted mind and actions of Theresa Miller.

CHAPTER 61

D earest Charlotte,

My daughter. My own flesh and blood. I am hoping that you have opened this letter and not just thrown it away. All the other letters I wrote to you have been returned to sender, but I thought that this one might be different because you should know of my death by now. I assure you that my words serve no other purpose other than an apology.

I am sorry for not being a strong mother for you as a baby. You didn't deserve what I did, but by the grace of God you survived and are living a good life. You were not meant to be mine, but you were always meant to be a daughter, wife, and mother to others. Maybe you're even a grandmother now? I live each day in shame and sadness when I think about what I did to you as a child. But I have the same feelings when I think about what your life with me would have been like had I stayed your mom. I assure you, it was not likely to have been good.

I didn't realize it when I was young, but my mother was not a great mother. It could be argued that she wasn't even a good one. As a child, it was easier to overlook instabilities and be forgiving, but look where that got me? That could have been you too... But please know that I did then, and will always love my mother. While you may not believe this, she loved you too, even without having met you, and I know she loved me.

When we were still speaking, you never asked me about your biological father, but I'm sure you've wondered. I have learned that long-term wondering chips away at the soul, so, to put the issue to rest, I'm going to tell you three things that you will be the only living person to know. First, your biological father's name was Caleb Nixon and was a science teacher at my high school. Second, Caleb Nixon assaulted me just after I turned seventeen, an act which resulted in my pregnancy with you. I wholeheartedly believe that the trauma of being sexually assaulted, being a teen mother, then losing my own mother, all within just over a year, would be enough to cause anyone to break. Add in my inherited mental health issues lurking below the surface... I barely had a chance, and I thought you didn't either.

For a few years after my mother's death, I knew very little about what happened. Eventually, I found out that my mother had died while serving a mandated sentence for murder in a mental institution. This brings me to the third piece of information that no one else knows: Your grandmother killed your biological father because she knew what he had done to me. After the murder, according to reliable sources, my mother never spoke again, not even to defend what she did. I know that she couldn't bear the thought of someone, who did something so awful, having the possibility to be not only in my world, but also yours. Grandma Lottie—Charlotte Gertrude Miller, your namesake—loved you and wanted to protect you. Part of me wishes you had the opportunity to meet her, but another part of me thinks it's for the best that you didn't.

I often use the name 'God,' but if I'm being honest, for most of my life, I didn't believe there was one—until I met my you, my child who lived. Now I have hope that God will break the cycle that began with my mother—if not earlier—and continued with me. I hope it will not cause further pain for you or your children. Before I knew you, and even though I wasn't a spiritual person, I still prayed that you were in a better place, hoping that you had made it to Heaven, if there was one. When I met you—as an adult—it turned out you were in a better place, but not where I'd thought you'd gone. I am so thankful to the Whitmans for adopting, raising, and protecting you as parents should—something I could have never done.

I feel blessed to have learned that you did more than survive—you thrived. I apologize from the bottom of my heart that you had to learn who I was, meet me, and graciously accept me as a part of your adult life just to lose me again. If I had known any of *that was a possible, and that you had survived, I think I would have made different—and better—decisions. You being in my life made it so wonderful, even complete, but I know that my presence in yours had the opposite effect. I am aware that you likely have heard many terrible things about me over the years, and I regret to inform you that much of it was true, but that is not the whole of who I was.*

I wish I could find more ways to show my sincere apologies, but there are no amount of excuses or reasons, although true, that I could put on this paper, that would justify all the pain I have left in my wake. I know it seems backwards, but so much of what I did I believed I was doing for your benefit, not to harm you. For many years, I devoted my life to helping others feel well and being a contributing member of society. When you remember me, please try remember the good things.

CHAPTER 62

*C*hris,

    Lorie is gone. She held on as long as she could—and I did my best to hold on to her—but seeing you last week was the final straw. Now there's only me. I know you don't know me well, but I sure know you. And while I feel I owe you nothing, writing this letter is what Lorie would want me to do, and I owe her <u>everything</u>. Lorie made me a thousand times the person I could have become on my own, giving me a fulfilling and meaningful life. Dr. Delores Shaw was the me I was supposed to be, and she loved you very much.

    I know you hate me, but know that every second you cared for Lorie, I was there. It took practice and time, but eventually the person I was and the person I created fused into one. While Lorie might not have felt it, when you first met us, I was there. When you first kissed us, I was there. When you proposed, I was there. Lorie's mind may have felt there was a separation—that I could be suppressed, essentially buried alive never to return again—but I knew that couldn't last forever. Deep down, I am pretty sure she did too.

    I must say, even with all that I have done, you aren't without fault. You hurt Lorie, leaving deep emotional scars from your lies and deceit. You said she was your one true love. Having the life you created with her ripped away contributed to the state of deep denial she was in for the majority of our second stay here at WyldeWood. If you had just trusted us and not followed, I can only imagine we would be somewhere tropical enjoying our retirement together. Instead, you're alone out there and I'm alone in here.

Then there were the lies about your family—the ones you spun so convincingly. You told Lorie your family was dead: your mother, killed during a home invasion; your father, from a heart attack; and your brothers, Everett and Connor, perished in a car accident. Had you been lying to yourself for so long that you believed it was all true? And if that is the case, how can you not empathize with my situation? Imagine my surprise when I met a member of your own gene pool, right here at WyldeWood, who had their own version of events to tell. Not sure who I should believe, a known liar or a known criminal. Either way, I guess I will never find out the truth, but I am sure it will give you something to ponder...

Just so we're clear, I blame you for losing the two most important things in our lives: your love and the second chance I had with my daughter. Even with all the hatred I have for you, Chris, the love I still have for Lorie forces me to continue writing. I find myself almost as torn as I have ever been. Lorie always loved you—for long after you stopped loving her—and she wanted to protect you from the truth. I, however, don't particularly care for you, and would prefer to keep you from the satisfaction of knowing the truth. So where does that leave me? I am not exactly sure how I arrived at this conclusion; when the sum of both what Lorie would want and what I want does not add up to me sharing anything with you. But in spite of my desires, I feel it is the least I can do at this point in my life, which is to say, the end. So as my final act, I will tell you something you have been asking me about for years. I will tell you my truth.

I entered WyldeWood as a girl and left as an emotionally stunted woman thrust back into a society that never wanted me in the first place. Even though I was obsessed with getting out of WyldeWood, I felt it was a near impossibility. That thought process created a disconnect in my brain, preventing me from thinking about what life would be like should I ever end up on the other side of the institution's walls. Even so, I was thankful for the opportunity to leave, even more so because it was legal, and to start over. Upon my exit, knowing I had no means of support—in every sense of the word. In the kindest and most unexpected gesture, Dr. Castaneda, my psychiatrist, gave me a little over $300 of his own money to help me reenter the world. For a brief moment, I was reminded that books shouldn't be judged by their covers, and that there might be a chance for a bit of humanity in everyone… even me.

My attempt to start over was not a smooth transition; my emotions returned with a vengeance, and I had trouble reining them in, especially without the help of any doctors. Guilt, anger, betrayal, and yearning all swirled inside me creating a hurricane-like storm that was beyond my control. I returned to Roseville, where I quite literally had no home. The house was long gone. My mother was long gone. There was nothing there for me—not that there really ever was. All that was left in the town where I grew up were memories too painful to relive, and I had to leave. With nowhere specific to go, I decided to get back on a bus and let fate decide for me.

I felt numb as I looked out the window of the bus at the fleeting passing scenery, but I soon realized I was on a familiar path, and the bus was headed back to Kellerton. I felt relief wash over me as I knew I would be safe back at WyldeWood, but what was I going to do, ask to be let back in? Of course that wasn't the answer, but how would I get money? Who would hire me? I felt like I had five years before, trapped, alone, and abandoned, except now I had a criminal record to add to the list.

Some shameful money-making ideas entered my head, and I shudder when thinking of what might have happened, had I followed through with any of them. As I entered the limits of the town that housed WyldeWood, and knew my bus ride would soon be coming to an end, my body took over and gave my mind a rest. The areas around the edge of my retinas began to darken, causing me to literally have tunnel vision. It was the oddest sensation, made even more strange when at the end of the tunnel, all I could see was the face of Dr. Delores Shaw. I blinked and she was gone, but I then knew where I had to go. I continued on the ride until I made my way to Bateson, South Carolina.

It wasn't difficult to find Dr. Shaw. I heard employees at the institution talking about how she opened her own private practice just over an hour North of WyldeWood in Bateson, a town on the coast of South Carolina near Charleston. Since from WyldeWood, located in Southern Georgia, it was only another two-hour bus ride, I had the money for that. There was no internet then like there is now, so

I couldn't just look up her address. The bus dropped me off at the stop downtown, and I wandered the streets trying to devise a plan. After about two hours of aimless walking, I saw a small wooden sign hanging outside of an arts-and-crafts bungalow on one of the side streets. It said "Dr. Delores Shaw, Psychiatrist."

Before I found her, my mind was chock full of all the things I would say to her if I ever saw her again, but then, when I had the opportunity... My mind went blank. I wish I had a clearer head to formulate a better plan, but I guess, deep down I thought, as usual, things wouldn't work out for me. But there I was, standing so close to where she was, and all I had to do was build up the courage to ring the bell. I stood on the sidewalk in front of the bungalow until a neighbor came out of their house to ask me if I was okay. Not wanting to draw any further attention to myself, I nodded, then took a step forward, then another, and continued walking until I was at the door. I pushed the bell, and as it rang, I heard the bark of a large dog followed by footsteps.

A look of complete shock was on the face of my former doctor. Being the two-faced professional that she was, in an instant Dr. Shaw composed herself and said how nice it was to see me, then asked if I would like to come in. I accepted her invitation without saying a word. Once inside the house, which also served as her office, I was reminded of my childhood home, or at least what it might have looked like if my circumstances had be different. Dr. Shaw showed me to the room where she saw patients, a gesture that gave me a bit of déjà vu. I sat on the leather couch and she in a well-worn leather wingback chair. I just looked at her for the longest time, and she let me sit in my silence, something we used to do often, when I first started seeing her. Trying to figure out what to say—I thought about why she pretended to care about me, why she didn't tell me about my mother, why she left me—but the words just wouldn't come.

Dr. Shaw, sensing my emotional overload, but not fully under-standing the extent of it, called in her dog, Piaget, and instructed him to sit next to me. I'd guessed she was hoping to break the ice with the faithful companion. Not being much of a dog person at the time, I got up and walked around the room, looking at her books, plaques, and awards, wasting time until the right words came.

Without provocation, and like I wasn't in control of my actions, I picked up a brass paperweight on her desk—a small model of the human brain—and hurled it at the back of her head. A momentary look of pain and confusion crossed her face as she turned to look in my direction before she fell to the floor unconscious.

Stunned by what I had just done, I didn't move. I stood and stared at the doctor as she lay on the ground, bleeding from her head. After a minute, Piaget jumped down from the couch and lay next to his owner. The sweet gesture was the beginning of my affection for canines. After several minutes, I forced myself to take a step, then another, and another, finally standing next to Dr. Shaw. I crouched down and felt for a pulse, but there was none. I patted the dog on the head, and decided I needed to leave. I couldn't stay there forever, or even much longer, unless I wanted a one-way ticket back to WyldeWood, or worse. As I was leaving where the now dead woman was, I turned back to look at her for the very last time when it hit me. I'd felt for years she looked familiar, but I could never place who she resembled until right then. Dr. Delores Shaw bore a strong resemblance to… me.

It was as if I channeled all the feelings I had ever felt in my entire life into the force it took to throw the paperweight across the room. When it struck my former psychiatrist's head subsequently taking her life, I felt the crushing weight of the emotional distress I carried for as long as I can remember, leaving my body. I didn't mean to kill the doctor, although I am not sure what I meant to do, but I did not feel sad either. I mourned the loss of Dr. Shaw when I learned that she was leaving WyldeWood. I grieved for her again when I learned she didn't care for me like she pretended to. There was no more sadness for the doctor left in my body. I did not panic, because the plan I thought I didn't have made its presence known once I had the clarity to see it. After my initial shock, I was then able to focus. Other than the neighbor, no one knew I was there. I looked so much like Delores Shaw that if I were a brunette, wore glasses, and didn't live in this town, I could surely pass for her, securing my fresh start. The only hurdle left in my way was disposing of the evidence.

My actions were as fluid as if I had rehearsed them over and over before. I put a sign on her front door that said she was closed due to the flu, in case she had any appointments that evening. I then spent a while looking around the house for ideas as to what to do with her body. In order for me to become her, I could leave no trace that I was ever there, or that Delores Shaw had died. I knew there was not a single person who would be looking for me; my mother was dead, my father was dead, and my daughter was dead—as far as I knew. From that point on, Theresa was dead, too, and Delores was alive and well.

Drained after the adrenaline left my body, I made myself a cup of coffee and drank it while looking at the beautifully manicured backyard. The clouds began to part and bright rays of sun moved across the yard. First to illuminate was the bed of zinnias, then the Japanese maple tree. Finally, the warm glow settled on a set of storm cellar doors on the side of the garage. The lighting of the doors by the sun mimicked the lightbulb going off in my head. I abandoned my coffee and, looking to make sure no neighbors were watching, made my way across the yard to the sloping doors. As luck would have it, they were not locked except for a piece of wood at the bottom of each that could be turned to allow for the doors to open.

A wave of musty air hit me as I descended earthen steps. A little unsure if I should continue into the dark abyss of the cellar, fearful of what might be lurking down there, I charged on due to a lack of other options. Feeling with my hands in front of me, I bumped into a string which I pulled. A lone bulb lit the cellar revealing that it was empty, no surprise seeing as how there was no lock to protect any contents. Thinking this might be an obvious first choice for someone to look, if foul play was questioned, I turned to leave the small, damp room. On my way out, my eye caught sight of something on the dirt floor that looked different. A rusty, brown metal handle, partially in shadow, stuck up from the ground. Hoping it was more than a discarded piece of some long-removed apparatus, I ran my hands around the handle to find it was attached to a wooden door. I wasn't going to get anywhere without more visibility, so I returned to the house in search of a flashlight, which I found on a shelf by the back door.

Returning to the cellar with a light, I was then able to see the door and what lay beneath it. There was a hole, about three feet square, that was likely used long ago to store root vegetables or canned goods. The dust and dirt that covered the door led me to believe that it had likely also been long forgotten. The spot was perfect, especially if I topped it with dirt after I was done. I waited until I could use the darkness of night as a cover to move the lifeless body of Dr. Shaw to her final resting place. I would assume she is still there, so feel free to use this information to solve a fifty-year-old murder/missing person case that no one knew existed.

I waited until morning to clean up the house so no evening passersby would be able to see anything suspicious in the warm glow of lit windows. There was no need to remove evidence that I was there, as it would look like Dr. Shaw moved and was thriving in another part of the country. If all went according to plan, no one would suspect she was dead. I showered, dressed as the doctor, and found all the important documents—passport, bank statements, birth certificate. They were located in a file cabinet that was impeccably organized, making everything I needed all the more easy to find. I packed a bag with belongings that would be important to anyone leaving in a rush, and permanently. I found three thousand dollars in cash in the back of her sock drawer as well as an additional fifty dollars in her purse, which also housed her driver's license, checkbook, and check register.

After I had appropriately packed up, I replaced the "flu" sign on the door with one explaining how Dr. Shaw, AKA me, was moving for an opportunity I couldn't pass up. I apologized to the patients this affected and stated that this office was now officially closed for business, effective immediately. I tied a scarf around my head and under my chin to hide my blonde locks, put on a pair of sunglasses I found in her purse, put the leash on the dog, and headed out. I grabbed her car keys off the wall hook by the back door and got into the Volvo parked in the driveway. Just before pulling out of the drive, I had a thought and ran back into the house. Once in the office room, I grabbed her framed diplomas, certificates, plaques, and anything else an established doctor would have. I could not believe I almost forgot these important little details. If my plan was going to work, I needed to think of everything from that point on. Back in the car, I left town, headed West and never looked back. So you can check one thing off your list—you now know how the lives of Delores Shaw and Theresa Miller merged into one.

As for the other questions you want answered, I'm sorry, but I just can't. I have been told, over and over, what I did to my patients. I have been asked, over and over, what I did with their children. Hell, I now even can believe that I hurt my patients and stole their babies, because, let's face it, I have a track record that I actually can remember to corroborate. You might think I'm being spiteful by withholding from you now, but I swear on Lorie's grave that I cannot remember. I could tell you my motive, and that I have flashes of what feel like memories that must coincide with the murders and kidnappings. But as for the intricate details of the crimes, and where the children went, I just cannot say. Doesn't it make sense though? If Lorie could exist in a world so unaware that she was really me—and the Lorie I became was a figment of my imagination, blended with the most thorough kind of identity theft—isn't it possible that I could repress the heinous crimes I have been accused of?

In truth, I wish I could recall everything, because maybe Lorie would have been more stable had she been able to help you, once she—we were back here at the institution. All she ever wanted was what was best for you. If there is something I could have done to make her stay at WyldeWood more pleasant, trust me, I would have done it. The best I could do for her was to stay out of her way for the past few decades, I figured I owed her that much. Over the past twenty-three years, I have wrestled with the meaning of true love. I always return to this: true love is accepting someone in their entirety—the light and the dark, their angel and their devil. Everyone has an angel and a devil on their shoulders, but when you met me, the devil to Lorie's angel, you abandoned us both. Don't you think it's unfair for you to have judged us so harshly, when you never gave us the opportunity to meet your "devil?" Your "Theresa?" I'm sure he's in there somewhere… Find him, and you may better understand me. For Lorie's sake, I hope you find peace after you read this letter. Think of it as a parting gift from her, for the happiness you brought her long ago. With this letter, my final act as my true self, I unburden my conscience.

Theresa

P.S. When you see him again, tell your brother goodbye—for both of us.

CHAPTER 63

Charlotte Whitman-Sanchez exhaled a heavy sigh as she finished reading the copy of her mother's biography. She purchased it at a local bookstore, miffed she had to pay for a copy, when she felt she was owed one. But Charlotte had endured enough in her life not to lose sleep over such trivialities. Her expectations were low when she first started reading the book—something she had planned not to do at all—but then, since she already knew the ending, thought, *What further harm could it cause?* Plus, she knew that *everyone* around her would be reading it, and she wanted to adequately prepare.

Reading the book was more like preparational research for social conversations than anything else, and Lord knows that people would ask questions. She began imagining the kinds of things her peers might say and felt sick. Much like how soldiers are casually asked heavy questions such as, "How many people have you killed?"—the askers unaware of the weight those questions carry—people asked similar things of Charlotte. "Do you remember when your mother tried to smother you?" or "What does it feel like to be related to a murderer?" Charlotte knew that those friends, colleagues, and ignoramuses meant no harm because they just didn't know any better. Still, she could find little solace in that, because regardless, it was so wrong. She put on a smile and went about her life just like every other "normal" person, except she wasn't normal and she couldn't think of one person who would understand what she had gone through... except for Theresa—and now she was gone.

Charlotte had been wrong about the book—it did hurt. The author, her mother's nurse at WyldeWood, had stolen something precious from Charlotte—something she didn't even know belonged to her until now. A letter meant for her eyes only had been reduced to public spectacle, fodder for true crime junkies, entertainment. Reading Theresa's final thoughts about her added even more complexity to the already tangled labyrinth of emotions Charlotte felt about her biological mother. Charlotte knew her skin had always been thick, but now she would need to find a way to make it like armor.

Until Lorie came into her life, she appeared to wonder very little about her biological mother, which many found odd. The Whitmans were her family and she had a near-perfect life. Why waste time wondering about someone who didn't want her? Larry and Catherine had praised her for being so mature and adult about the situation, even as a kid, and she liked the positive reinforcement which furthered her stance. However, in secret, she wondered almost daily about her real mother. The love and respect she had for the Whitmans had her trying to "fake it until she made it" and Charlotte thought she had done a good job. But once she had a name and a face to go with the mythical person she'd thought about for years, Charlotte's thoughts went into overdrive and she could not let it go.

Finding out who her birth mother was—or who she *thought* she was—would forever change her world. As an adult, and knowing she might be able to get answers, she wasn't as easily able to brush off the fact that her own mother hadn't wanted her as a baby, and then hadn't wanted to find her later in life. It made her feel a twinge of resentment, but the feeling that grew and ultimately compelled her to meet Lorie was the *wonder*.

Charlotte had never been able to keep her wondering at bay. As a child, she would always search for her Christmas presents so she knew what she was getting before she opened the gifts. Menus were posted by Catherine at the beginning of each week, so Charlotte would know what to expect for dinner each night. She even asked her teachers for lesson plans as far in advance as they could provide. Larry and Catherine suspected that her need to know as much as possible may have stemmed from not knowing about such an important part of her past: her family. The Whitmans however, knew enough about her biological mother and the incident that brought Charlotte to them, that they hoped to keep that information from Charlotte indefinitely. The Whitmans loved Charlotte dearly and wanted to protect her from all the bad in the world, but what they wanted to protect her from most was Theresa, and knowing what she did to *their* child. As well-meaning as the Whitmans were, Charlotte thought they were also naïve; they should have known that curiosity is what killed the cat.

When Charlotte's brother had the family do DNA tests, Larry and Catherine hadn't thought much of it. Many years prior, the last they had heard was that Theresa Miller would never again see the light of day beyond the high walls of WyldeWood Mental Institution. Still, after the genetic geneal-ogy findings were in, they both held their breath a moment when Charlotte showed them her results. Thankfully, they were able to breathe a sigh of relief when they did not see any biological parents connected to their daughter. The couple never imagined that would change in the future, and they had no idea their child would receive an email with informa-tion about her biological mother. The email ignited a fire in Charlotte that she never knew existed and she wondered more about Delores Shaw than she had wondered about anything before in her entire life. Not wanting to upset her parents, Charlotte discussed meeting her birth mother only with her husband. Together, they agreed it could be done—with specific parameters.

Charlotte was able to determine that her mother was a psychiatrist in Wyndisburg, Colorado where she had resided for many years. The best plan she and Matteo came up with was that Charlotte could pose as a new patient, thus allowing her to meet her mother without revealing her true identity. Charlotte contacted the office of Dr. Delores Shaw to make an appointment three weeks from then. Matteo suggested that would be enough time to plan for her journey from San Diego to Colorado, yet not so much time as to allow her to overthink it and change her mind. She hoped three weeks was enough time to mentally prepare for meeting her own flesh and blood.

Dr. Delores Shaw looked strikingly like Charlotte, only with dark hair and glasses. Beyond that, she was fairly unremarkable. Because they shared a biological link, Charlotte couldn't suppress the hope for an instant connection. So the absence of recognition in her mother's eyes stung more than she'd anticipated. There was a fleeting moment when the psychiatrist's gaze seemed to linger just a bit on her new patient, but Charlotte dismissed it as a gesture she likely used with all her patients, to show them they had her full attention.

By all accounts, Delores Shaw seemed to be a good doctor, productive member of society, and a decent human being—which both comforted and frustrated Charlotte—and ultimately caused more *wondering*. Charlotte would ask herself, *Is she doing so well as an adult because she didn't have a baby to deal with? Did she try so hard because she wanted to prove she deserved to get me back?* Deep down she secretly hoped that Lorie wasn't doing all that well, and giving up her child was a gut-wrenching decision that had lasting effects throughout the years. Seeing her thriving was more painful than Charlotte anticipated. Deciding that her life was better before she cared about this woman, Charlotte did her best to get back to the normal she knew before she knew of Delores Shaw.

But of course, she just couldn't let it go. Charlotte scoured the internet, reached out to adoption agencies, and even, on occasion, searched her parents' house when they were out. Not sure exactly what she was looking for—just anything that connected her to the short life she had before becoming theirs. Not knowing where she came from, or which agency handled her adoption, made her quest feel like trying to find a particular grain of sand on a beach. The task of learning more about her birth mother was beginning to consume her life, and she was struggling to keep her frustrations in check. A mother herself, Charlotte knew the importance of being fully present for her children, and it was time to put the past behind her—or at least try to.

CHAPTER 64

Nearly six months after she stopped her fruitless searches, something completely unexpected happened. A nearly forgotten memory from twenty-seven years ago resurfaced, one that seemed trivial at the time but would ultimately alter the course of Charlotte's life. Charlotte was at her parents' house wrapping Christmas presents for her children when the childhood recollection returned. When she and Kevin were young, he was close to ten years old which made her eight, they played a game of hide-and-seek. When it was Kevin's turn as seeker, Charlotte found an excellent hiding spot in the back of her mom's closet behind her long dresses. It was a place she thought that, even if Kevin peeked into, he'd never see her because not even her toes were visible beneath the floor-length clothing. As she crouched against the rear wall, she felt something hard and round push into her back. Not wanting to turn on the light for fear Kevin would see it beaming under the door, Charlotte investigated in the dark. After another moment of blind exploration, she quickly determined the object was a doorknob. Not scared at all, because the idea of a "secret room" was beyond exciting to the young girl, she turned the knob, opened the door, and stepped into the dark unknown.

Thin stripes of light filtered through a vent at the far end of the narrow space. Not being able to see any other specifics, she felt for a light switch along the wall. Soon she bumped her head on something that felt like a low ceiling. When her attempts were unsuccessful to locate a light, and her hands were covered with what could only be the sticky fluff of spiderwebs, Charlotte ventured farther out into the room towards the source of the sunlight. About halfway through, she felt something brush against the top of her head… the bottom part of a light pull. She pulled the chain and the room became aglow in the warm, yellow light of a lone incandescent bulb. Once her eyes adjusted to the brighter room, she found she had hit the jackpot.

To her right were a plethora of wrapped packages in reds, greens and golds, labeled with either "Kevin" or "Charlotte" and "Love, mom & dad" or "From, Santa." She had found her parents' hiding place for her presents. And what could have been a core memory for her, learning Santa wasn't real, was quite the opposite. She remembered how she thought it was so clever of Santa to drop off his presents early to save time on Christmas Eve. Methodically, she opened each package with the precision and care of a surgeon, making sure not to tear any of the paper as to not leave any trace of her snooping. Knowing that Kevin was persistent and wouldn't give up until he found her, her dad was at work, and her mom was occupied with friends on the verandah, Charlotte figured she probably had more than enough time to take a peek at what all Kevin was getting too.

After carefully viewing and rewrapping all the packages, she began looking around the room to see what other treasures she might find. There was an old trunk with fancy, sparkly clothes in it. A cracked mirror and several empty picture frames leaned against the angled walls. Four cardboard boxes containing old pictures, medals, an ARMY uniform, and other memorabilia sat on the floor by the vent. Everything after the presents was so boring that she almost turned the light off and left. As she reached for the light pull, she noticed a shoe box that caught her attention because it had her name written on the top. Hoping it was a gift that had yet to be wrapped, she opened the box eagerly—only to find more boring stuff. The contents were few old papers, a photo of strangers, and a tiny bracelet meant for a baby. Giggling a bit at the thought of a baby wearing jewelry, she closed the box, placed it back in the dust-free rectangle from where she plucked it, turned out the light, and headed back to the closet.

The memory made Charlotte restless. She needed to get back into the secret room, but she had to find a way to do it without raising her mother's suspicions. Since Charlotte was far too old to request playing hide-and-seek, she had to come up with another way to get into that room. Knowing her mom well, Charlotte knew exactly how to buy herself some time in the secret room.

"Mom, you know what sounds amazing? Your molasses cookies. Do you have everything to make them?" Charlotte asked, fully aware of two things: her mother's love of baking for the family and she was out of molasses.

"I don't have *all* the supplies, but I am happy to run to the grocery and pick up what I need!" said her mom with excitement in her voice.

Charlotte also knew that as her mother got older, her children moved out, and she retired from her job, Catherine wasn't feeling as useful and necessary as she used to. In a way, Charlotte was doing her mom a favor.

"Oh mom, that's all right. You don't have to go through all that trouble!"

"Darling, it's no trouble! I'm happy to do it."

With that, Catherine Whitman headed to the store, leaving Charlotte with at least thirty minutes to reexplore the hidden room.

CHAPTER 65

T he secret room felt much smaller than Charlotte remembered—though, of course, she was much bigger now. It
had been years since the first, and only, time she was in the
small space, because the thought of the shoebox hadn't crossed
her mind since the day she found it. In addition, snooping
for Christmas presents as an adult lost its luster since her gifts
from her parents usually consisted of cash and gift cards. There
was no reason she had cared to revisit the room until that day.
With the gifts gone, and little else added over the years, it
didn't take Charlotte long to spot the shoebox, still in the same
place she remembered from many years ago. Although it was
coated with a thicker layer of dust than before, and the black
"Charlotte" was harder to discern, she knew it was the box she
was looking for. Holding her breath—partly so she didn't inhale
a cloud of dust, and partly because she couldn't recall just what
her eight-year-old self had seen and filed away in the back of
her brain—she was both hopeful and nervous about what she
might find.

Much like finding the hidden Christmas presents when she
was little, she felt like she had hit the jackpot in this room once
again. Inside the box was *exactly* what she had been hoping
for. The first thing she saw when she opened it was a swatch
of threadbare fabric. Upon closer inspection, it appeared to be
a small quilt. Also amongst the contents was a faded photo of a
group of girls, dressed in matching swimsuits. While Charlotte
did not recognize any of them, there was one who kind of
resembled her, but the coloring and setting of the image didn't

fit with any of her old pictures. On the back, there were names, which she also didn't know: N. Schneider, T. Miller, S. Daly.

Setting the photograph aside, Charlotte continued to look at the remaining items in the box, of which there weren't many. Her child brain must have added stacks of papers to the pile in the box because she lumped it in with all the other boring items in the attic, and what is more boring than paper? There was an address written on a half sheet of lined notebook paper for a place in Florida and a receipt for a car seat from Sears. The baby bracelet was still there, with three tiny block initials in the center: C. T. M. *Does the "C" stand for Charlotte?* she wondered. Next, she found a yellowed newspaper article with no photo. The headline read, "Local Teen Sentenced for Attempted Murder." Charlotte froze, and wasn't sure if she wanted to find out more, but she just had to know.

A seventeen-year-old Rose High School senior has been taken into police custody for the attempted murder of her infant daughter. The child's wails were heard by a postman, and after looking around the property for the child, he saw a woman lying on a bed, unresponsive, with what appeared to be vomit on the side of her face. With no infant in sight, and concerned for the woman's well-being, the good Samaritan gained entry to the house through an unlocked door. Upon further inspection,

he located the child, under
a pillow, on the bed near
the unconscious woman.
The pair were taken to St.
Joseph Hospital for eval-
uation. The infant exhib-
ited signs that she had
been harmed, and it is be-
lieved an attempt on her
life was made by the teen
mother, who remains alive
but unconscious. It is as-
sumed she tried to smoth-
er the child and then take
her own life. Due to the
nature of the scene, and
the injuries to both parties,
the teen has been deemed
an adult in the eyes of
the law and has been re-
manded to the Wylde-
Wood Mental Institution
for further evaluation and
possible incarceration.

The puzzle was starting to come together, but Charlotte needed a few more pieces before she could figure out what exactly was going on. She reexamined the information she had, and tried to connect at least a few dots. Looking over the photograph again, she held it closer to the light and squinted at the girl she thought looked a bit like her. Connecting the girl to her name in the lineup, Charlotte concluded that the person she resembled was T. Miller. Again she inspected the tiny baby bangle, this time saying the initials out loud.

"C. T. M."

She wondered, *Could the T.M. be T. Miller?* Thinking she had to be correct, because this box wouldn't just have random things in it… They *had* to be connected. Charlotte was optimistic because it seemed obvious that T. Miller had some connection to her, but she wasn't sure what. Delores Shaw was her biological mother, but no signs of her were in the box. *Could Theresa Miller be my biological aunt or grandmother?* Charlotte wished she could simply ask her parents, but she knew that was not an option. It would hurt them too much if she inquired directly about a life before them. There were no dates on the newspaper clipping or the photograph, so she had no way of knowing the timeframe when it all took place. *Was T. Miller the mother in the article?* All she could tell from her findings thus far was that whoever T. Miller was, she seemed pretty messed up, and none of it was making any sense.

The last item in the box was a tattered and folded piece of yellowing paper. Thinking it was another receipt for something, Charlotte almost tossed it aside, but she figured she'd come that far, so it would be best to leave no stone unturned. Even though she opened the folds with the utmost care, the paper tore a little with each movement. The pale gray writing on the document was so faded Charlotte almost couldn't discern what was written, but then a few key words made it clear what the paper was. At the top of the half sheet, there was a corner missing. The ending of a word that remained in spite of the tear, read, "ficate." Squinting and scrutinizing the document for any other clues, Charlotte was able to just make out the words "live" and "birth."

"Holy shit," Charlotte said, in a whisper as she realized what she had found.

It was a copy of her original birth certificate. Hoping to recover more of the information on the document that her naked eyes could not see, Charlotte took out her phone and snapped a picture. The photo app on her phone allowed her to adjust the image's brightness, shadows, coloring, and more. After a few tries, she was able to find a combination that allowed her to make out most of the very faded words.

Theresa Miller, age 17, had given birth to a baby girl—Charlotte Theresa Miller—on Charlotte's exact birthday. No name was listed under "father." Not sure how it was possible, but the evidence was right there in front of her: Theresa Miller was Charlotte's mother. She began to feel as though she couldn't catch her breath—likely the onset of a panic attack. This was probably her body's way of trying to reconcile what she just learned with what she had believed to be true, and possibly some distant memory of when she was a baby and couldn't breathe... Her biological mother tried to kill her as an infant and Delores Shaw was not who she claimed to be. *So then who the hell was Delores Shaw?*

If she thought she couldn't let "it" go before, there was no way Charlotte could stop searching for information about her biological mother now. After some online sleuthing, Charlotte was able to deduce that her biological mother, Theresa Miller, had likely changed her name after being released from Wylde-Wood. There wasn't any official documentation that supported that, but it was the natural connection of the points between Theresa Miller and Dr. Delores Shaw. With what Theresa was accused of, Charlotte understood the desire she must have had for a name change, and a fresh start far away. But the more digging she did, the more upset she became at the thought of what might have become of her life, or lack thereof, if Theresa's plan had worked. Larry and Catherine wouldn't have had her as a daughter. Who would Matteo have married? And her own children—Haden and Hadley—wouldn't even exist.

***

Reflecting on the time she first learned why she'd been available for adoption, Charlotte felt the same pang of regret: she should have let sleeping dogs lie. And even now, she had a second chance to let everything about her biological mother go when she died. But there Charlotte was, consumed once again by Theresa via the content of the biography. Even in death, Theresa managed to worm her way back into Charlotte's brain. Their relationship—especially after Theresa's second stint at WyldeWood—had felt more parasitic than symbiotic, excluding the brief time when Theresa—or Lorie—was an active part of Charlotte's life.

Charlotte often wondered, over the past two decades, whether or not she should visit her mother, and always came back to the conclusion of *no*. Her life and wellbeing had been threatened once by Theresa when Charlotte was an infant, and since coming back into her adult life, there were far too many others Theresa's reckless behavior affected—including but not limited to: her parents, Larry and Catherine, her husband and their children. Even still, Theresa was her flesh and blood, and that was a fairly constant nag at the back of Charlotte's mind. She had tried to mask the nagging voice with a myriad of possible solutions—alcohol, exercise, and meditation, just to name a few—but nothing worked. Once Theresa entered Charlotte's life, she should have understood long ago that she could never be rid of her mother.

In the end, the one thing that proved to be most cathartic was to write. Charlotte was never much for journaling, but writing a letter to her mother allowed her to get her feelings out. Her intention was never to give it to Theresa, but since the possibility was always there, part of the release was knowing that her feelings *could* actually be heard. But then again, they could also fall on deaf ears, and that might cause the whole healing process to backfire. While she hadn't written a new letter to her mother for many years, Charlotte would often take out the last letter she wrote to her and reread it, revise it, and rewrite it, changing some of the wording to make sure it was just right. There were at least two times Charlotte could remember putting the handwritten letter in an envelope, then sealing, addressing, and putting a stamp on it. One of those times, she even took it out to her mailbox and put the red flag up. Just a few minutes later, with the speed of a high school track star, she ran to the mailbox, retrieved the letter, and tore it to pieces.

A permanent copy of the letter was filed away in her brain, so the next time she wanted to edit it, she simply just had to put pen to paper and her words flowed. Several copies had been written, but none of the subsequent drafts had ever made it past her desk. In fact, she destroyed them as soon as each was finished to avoid any temptation to send one that she might later regret. Her words were too precious—and too risky—for anyone's mind but her own, yet keeping them trapped there felt almost as damaging as if they had gotten out, if not more.

One last time, she decided to get her thoughts out, then let it all go. With her mother gone. there was no point in continuing the ritual, as there was zero chance Theresa would ever read it. Charlotte went out to her patio and sat on the swing, rocking back and forth nervously, trying to prepare herself for what she already knew was coming, and hoping it would provide all the closure and release she needed. Though she knew the words by heart, seeing them etched in her own handwriting would make them undeniably real—once again. Charlotte drew in a deep breath through clenched teeth, and as the air reached her lungs, she began to write.

CHAPTER 66

M^{*other*,}
  While I find it difficult to address you as such, there is no denying that we are connected. We look so much alike that, if you were just a bit younger, or I a bit older, people might have mistaken us for twins. Our age difference, or the absence of much of one, could have people guessing we were more likely sisters than mother and daughter. I've told you before how finding out you existed was such a volatile experience in my life. Obviously, I knew I had a biological mother since I had known from the time I could understand that I was not born to the Whitmans. But putting a face and a name to what felt like a figment of my imagination made it all too real. From the moment I knew there was a possibility of getting to know you, a seed was planted that refused to stop growing. What I'd hoped would bloom into a beautiful flower became an invasive weed, creeping and curling into every part of my life. The weed was out of control and causing destruction in its wake, and I thought there was no way to make it stop.

  I knew long before you were a convicted murderer, that you were Theresa Miller, not Delores Shaw. Not long after I came to see you as a patient, I was able to find out your true identity and what you had done to me. What kind of person would want to kill a defenseless child? I tried to find out more about your family and what might have driven you to do the unthinkable. I was able to find the death records for your parents, which led me to finding out that not only is my mother a despicable human being, but I must come from a long line of them. The seed began to sprout.

The matter of how you became Delores Shaw was the next thing to consume me. I researched every Delores Shaw I could find on the internet. (Did you know there are 437?) During this time, my family began to notice that I was becoming distant and distracted. I didn't feel I could share any of this with anyone; it would crush my mom and dad, since I knew they had done their very best to keep me sheltered from, well, you. My children felt like they had done something to upset me and my husband was feeling like a single parent, even with me in the house. The seedling produced its first leaf.

Hours of scoring social media, public records, and business directories eventually led me to find evidence of a Dr. Delores Shaw. She worked as a psychiatrist at WyldeWood Mental Institution for a short three-year period. I followed the trail of Dr. Shaw from WyldeWood, to Bateson, South Carolina where she set up a private practice for two years. While business seemed good for her there, one day she up and moved without providing notice to anyone, even her patients. Through social media, I was able to track down one of her former patients, whom she worked with in South Carolina, who had reported the doctor missing. This person said they were frustrated because the police didn't take it seriously because there were no signs of "foul play."

Lo and behold, the not-so-missing Dr. Shaw turned up just a few weeks later in Wyndisburg, Colorado. I asked the patient if there would be anywhere she could think of that I could see a photo of Dr. Shaw. While she personally did not have one, she thought there might have been one taken by the mayor's office at the ribbon cutting ceremony for the opening of her small practice. I followed up with the mayor's office while in town, and the helpful secretary was gracious enough to dig through stacks of records in the city building's basement to look for the picture Luck was on my side as the photo was found, however it had not been properly stored and the image had degraded. Much of the image was faded and water-blotched, however the small area where you could see Dr. Delores Shaw, it was clear she looked like she almost could have been your double, or rather you hers.

I showed an image I had of you to the patient of Dr. Shaw's from long ago, and she said that she couldn't be one hundred percent sure it was the same person, but she was maybe ninety percent. All

I needed was that ten percent of doubt to let me know my gut was right, especially because Theresa Miller seemed to have disappeared off the face of the Earth after she was released from the WyldeWood. There was no record of her doing anything, as well as no sightings of her, after she was seen walking out the front doors of the institution. I'm not sure how you did it, but you got rid of the real Delores Shaw so you could become her. And out popped leaf number two.

Learning who you really were, then comparing it to the well-renowned, excellent doctor you had become, created a stark contrast in my mind that I couldn't reconcile. I became obsessed with the enigma that was you and it further consumed my life. I needed to find a way to release the anger I had likely been harboring, silent and undetected, for most of my life, that had grown into a beast of its own. I needed to do something that would make a difference in my life, or your life, or someone's life.

Then one night, as I tucked my youngest child into bed, I watched him drift off to sleep. His mouth was open, his chest was moving up and down with each breath, and he was clutching his cherished stuffed whale, Willard, without question feeling as safe and secure as a child could be. I wondered, "How could anyone want to hurt any child, let alone their own?" To my utter surprise, an idea blossomed amid the bramble of weeds I had been cultivating in both my mind and my soul. I decided that I was going to do what you couldn't do for me, and what your patients weren't likely to do for their children: I was going to save their babies.

How did I know about your patients, you might ask? On my first visit to your office, on my way out, your assistant left his desk unattended, I assume for what was only a short time, but I didn't wait around to find out. I seized the opportunity to take as much electronic information off of his computer as I could in just under two minutes. I logged into my cloud storage account and I uploaded copies of individual documents and entire folders without regard for what they contained. My hope was I could learn more about you and the person you'd become. Did you get married? Did you have more children? Were you a good person? Not wanting to risk being caught, I was logged in and out with no one the wiser.

Upon my return home, I combed through the information I retrieved. I was disappointed that there was nothing that pertained to you personally, but there was a trove of information about your patients. I didn't think much about it at the time, other than you seemed to really be helping people, but as I watched my child sleep, my mind recategorized many of the patient files into a "babies you were going to let die" pile. It didn't seem like you were doing much to stop what was to come for those children, and I questioned whether you even wanted to.

I reread all of your records with a new, scrutinizing eye. Any that seemed to have trouble parenting their children went right to the top. From that group, I sifted through again until I had found the most dire situations and the most vulnerable of humans, that is to say the babies I was going to save. At first, my crusade was just about trying to right the wrongs of your past, to help me find a productive way to cope and I suppose mixed in, was a touch of survivor's guilt. While I should have had the foresight to see the avenues down which my actions would lead, I either couldn't see or chose not to think about them. I just needed to do something to get all this out of my head so I could return to my once normal, obviously idealistic and dull life.

So many of your patients seemed to genuinely be getting the help they needed from you, ironic considering what you did to "help" yourself. However, there were a handful that based on your past and their states of mind, I just couldn't risk them doing more damage. The who, I had: Juliana Stevens, Brandie Amstell, Abby Darrow, the Taylor couple and Daniela Ortega. The why, I had: they needed to be stopped before they made a colossal mistake and harmed their children. But the how and the where were more difficult. I despised the thought of harming someone. I had never been violent a day in my life, but I felt I had no other option.

In order to make sure I stayed the course I had begun, I always kept with me, whenever I carried out the more difficult parts of my plan, the baby blanket I'd found hidden away in my parents' attic. I was concerned that fibers from the disintegrating piece of fabric would somehow end up in evidence, and could eventually be connected to me. Ultimately, I deemed it a necessity to keep what could have been my burial shroud with me as a reminder of what could have become of me. It was worth the risk. I know that I have killed, but at my core, I am not a killer. I look at what I did similarly to someone who kills in self defense, only I wasn't defending myself, I was defending those who could not protect themselves.

As I began the preparations for executing my ideas, I did research on family annihilators, mothers who killed their babies because of postpartum depression, and deaths of children at the hands of their parents due to other forms of abuse. If I had any doubt as to whether I was doing the right thing, what I found solidified that the course I was charting was correct. People are deplorable, and you were not to be excluded from that population. The gruesome and upsetting results did prove to be beneficial because, as I already had my "why," it helped me develop my "how."

Each parent whom I would spare from a fate far worse than death—living with the knowledge they murdered their own child—would die in a manner similar to innocent children who had been killed by their parents in the past. Drowning in a bathtub, stabbing, strangulation, drowning in a vehicle, and abusive head trauma to coincide with what a shaken baby would experience. Figuring out how I was going to bring an end to these adults, these future murderers, oddly enough, made me feel more at ease with my decision to move forward.

You mostly know the rest of each story; obviously each story had its few minutes of fame, but I also learned you were helping with each case. It turns out you were more intimately aware of the details than I had expected. I am sure you are wondering about the one person from my list who is still alive… Daniela Ortega. While I had plans for Ms. Ortega, just like the rest of them, my life took a very unexpected turn when you—well, the you that was Dr. Lorie Shaw—wanted to have a relationship and be a part of my world.

I had planned to completely close the book on anything related to Theresa Miller/Delores Shaw after I had sufficiently satisfied my need to, in a sense, rewrite the past by changing the future. But your courage in seeking me out—despite the risk of the worst kind of rejection—and the fact that our connection felt less like a mother-daughter relationship and more like a friendship, stopped me in my tracks. Getting to know the person you were in that moment, *leaving all the past behind, was more therapeutic than anything I had tried up to that point. Your appearance on my doorstep that day in early October spared the life of Daniela Ortega, and thankfully her child survived too.*

Accepting you into my life, and forgiving you your past, as I hope you would forgive me mine, was the catharsis that I had been desperately needing my entire life, but didn't know it. Now that I'm older and wiser, I can see why a teen girl without means, support, or guidance wouldn't make for an ideal mother. I'm sorry that I didn't give you a fair chance. Seeing how you showed so much care and love for not only me, but also my children and husband, made me realize that maybe reformation was possible… for everyone. But the past is done and cannot be changed. While I sometimes questioned my actions, I didn't dwell on the possibility that those I euthanized might have recovered, like you did, and become better parents. In order to return to the mother, wife, and daughter I was before learning about you, I chose to take comfort in the facts, not the "what ifs." The fact was the children I had relocated were thriving.

To answer another of your unasked questions, I assure you, the babies—now adults—are all safe and living good lives. There are many people, good people, so desperate for a child, they will seek any means necessary, even the less-than-legal kind. A search on the dark web provided me with site after site of childless couples looking to make a family. I vetted these people virtually, ensuring they had financial means, no criminal record, a good home, and the ability to provide the children with a safe, happy life. Part of the agreement I made with the new parents was that I needed yearly proof of the children thriving thus further solidifying that I made good choices all around, and each family kept their promise.

I have an untraceable email account in which each child has a file with all of their documentation over the years. None of these now-adults know what happened to them, as far as I am aware. They may or may not know they were adopted, but I don't believe they realize they were taken. I will provide you with the login details for the account, and the new names of each child. I feel it is well within your rights to know what good came from the crimes you were blamed for. I caution you, however, to think very carefully before releasing this information to anyone, especially Chris. In doing so, you would likely destroy the lives of all those who were taken and the families they were placed with. It may ease the minds of their biological family members, but other than that, is it worth it? I am surprised the truth hasn't already come out considering the prevalence of genetic genealogy, but as far as I know, the children I took are blissfully ignorant to their beginnings. And look what knowing the truth did to the previously idyllic life of yours truly. Sometimes the truth, much like Pandora, is better left in the box.

If you have any way to obtain email access, the email address you need is thestork@xmail.com with password HSHS#1112. In case you aren't able to view the account, I can tell you that Huxley Stevens is now Jason Minnick, Corie Wicklow is now Ashley Anders and I kept the Taylor girls together; Miley and Maura Taylor are now Kara and Karly Speakman. Within the folder for each child-turned-adult, there is a yearly photograph and letter, sometimes even more. Of all the families, the Speakmans have been the most grateful. Graciously, they have provided me with an update every time one of the girls reached a milestone or had an accomplishment, almost the way they would have shared with their daughters' birth mother, had circumstances been different.

The information about the children served two purposes: first, it eliminated any doubt as to whether or not I had done the right thing for those children. Seeing them happy, healthy, loved, and provided for was all the reassurance I needed to rest easy each night. And second, it helped ease the pain of knowing what I did, and how it affected the lives of those around me, especially you. While I never intended for you to take the blame for what I had done, when it all began, I hadn't thought through the plan well enough to think about anyone taking the blame. When I had heard that Alise Jenks had been arrested, a wave of relief washed over me because it wasn't me—and it wasn't you. At that time, you and I had such a good thing going, and I didn't want it to end. Alise was the perfect sacrificial lamb because she'd escaped justice before.

When you got caught in your own web of lies, I was heartbroken—both for myself, and for Matteo and our children—since they were growing to love you just when you were ripped from our lives.

There were many times over the years when I wanted to tell you not what you'd done, but what you hadn't done. The uncertainty surrounding that outcome, and how you would have reacted, just made it too risky of a move. I would like to assume that you would have still served the time, considering it payback for nearly taking my life so many years ago. As much as I felt like I came to know you, I didn't definitively know what you would choose, and I couldn't take that chance. However, I was certain that if one of us deserved a life sentence in Hell, it surely wasn't me.

There are days when I do feel badly that I abandoned you after your conviction. There was simply no way I could justify continuing our relationship to the people who mattered to me most, and if I am being completely honest, you were not in that small, select group. My life began with you, and when you were not part of my world, I thrived. Would my life have been easier had I never known you existed? Probably, but I cannot definitively say that I wish I had never met you. I believe inside every adopted child is the desire to know where they came from, and if their proverbial apple fell far from the tree. If our paths had not crossed, I still would have had questions that may have never been answered. Over time, I'm sure that would have chipped away at the very fundamentality of who I am, and would have seeped out affecting the lives of those around me. Would it have made me kill? Probably not.

As difficult as it is for me to admit, now it appears in our situation that the apple fell closer to the tree than I would have hoped, considering the tree. Let me be clear: while I don't think you and I are one and the same, I also don't feel you are the metaphorical tree from which spoiled fruit fell. Instead, I believe we're both apples, dropped from a tree that was rotting inside, yet kept producing fruit. Meeting you awakened things buried deep inside me—things that, until then, had been dormant. Now I have a better understanding of who I am. From the point our lives first diverged when I was an infant, until we were reunited, my life was near perfect. And after our paths separated a second time, when you were convicted of murdering your patients, my life returned to its aforesaid state. Albeit, I now carry some baggage that I previously did not, but all of it made me into the person I am today.

There was an adjustment to a "new normal" when I allowed you into my life, and again after we cut ties when you went away. My children were confused and upset to lose a grandmother that they barely knew they had. Now, my children are well-adjusted grown adults beginning families of their own. I have watched them closely over the years for any signs that they share the same defective genes as you and I. It appears they do not, and hopefully, the cycle has been broken. Although, we both know how one can keep their true self hidden, so I can never fully relax when it comes to the worry I have for my own offspring.

There will come a day when our paths will likely cross again—in another time, another life, or some otherworldly place. If that happens, I hope we can pick up where we left off the last time we were in each other's presence—in a loving, forgiving relationship. It has been interesting being your child, Theresa Miller, to say the very least. I hope the knowledge this letter brings you allows you to find peace of mind, knowing that you did not commit all of the horrible things of which you were accused. By being there, you allowed my family and me the luxury of remaining whole, and for that, Mother, I thank you.

Charlotte

When she finished writing, Charlotte carefully folded the letter and placed it in an envelope, sealing it shut, as if she intended to send it after all. Standing, she retrieved a lighter from her pocket and flicked on the flame. The corner of the letter touched the tip of the fire and ignited the paper. Charlotte held the letter until she felt the tips of her fingers begin to singe, as if she wanted to feel a physical manifestation of the emotional torment she'd experienced as the words poured out. When the heat from the fire was more than she could bear, she tossed what was left of the letter onto the stone pavers and watched it until there was nothing but smoldering ash. Using her shoe, she spread around the ashes.

As she turned to go back toward her house, where her son, daughter-in-law, and new grandbaby would soon be arriving for dinner, she glanced at the ground. To her surprise, the

ashes formed a deliberate image—or perhaps a subconscious
expression: a heart. Innocent to any onlooker, but it caused
Charlotte pause. Maybe she had more love and forgiveness
in her heart for her mother than she thought. Or possibly, it
was just a coincidence. With one last swipe of her shoe, she
destroyed the heart, much like she felt hers had been from the
moment Theresa came back into her life.

EPILOGUE

A few years passed since I held the "let it go" ceremony, and I believe it worked. After burning the letter, I actually felt lighter—finally understanding what people meant when they said that a metaphorical weight could feel physically lifted. The past was left in the past, and on the rare occasion a memory would creep its way back into my mind, it was almost as if it were faded recollections of a past life... which was manageable.

A few times, I considered making the journey to Georgia to visit the grave of Theresa, but decided against it. The simple grave would likely be difficult to locate amongst the many others who perished at the facility, whom no one would claim. No doubt, each grave looked exactly like the next—without adornments, and unlikely to have ever had even a single flower laid to beautify the spot or indicate that a meaningful and sorely missed life had been lived. Afraid that a visit would upset the delicate balance of the truth about my life and the reality I created, I opted to stay away.

One day, I searched my kitchen island for the day's mail, only to realize that I would have to retrieve it myself. Fetching the mail, an ordinary task, felt monumental. Matteo had always handled it, and since his recent passing from brain cancer, I was still adjusting to the void he left behind. When a thirty-five year marriage ends, it's surprising how the mundane tasks one takes for granted can become so significant. I let out a long sigh, feeling like I was about to begin a trek of many miles, instead of the fifty-foot distance it would actually take to get to my mailbox.

Rifling through the bills, junk mail, and catalogs took a bit, but when I finally came to the last piece of mail, I paused. It was addressed to me, in messy handwritten cursive, and the return address was one I couldn't initially place. *C. Carpenter, Miami, Florida.* The name sparked a flicker of recognition, though I couldn't recall knowing anyone by that name—or even anyone who lived in Florida. I opened the envelope, and inside was a single sheet of folded notebook paper, with a blue sticky note attached. The note read:

Over the past few years, I have thought a lot about the decisions I have made in my life. There are two that I still wrestle with as to how I feel about what I did. The first, taking your mother's letters. Well, I suppose they weren't so much hers as they were yours and Detective Greyson's. I am a bestselling author primarily because of those two documents, but never before and never since have I been a thief. I am not proud of what I took from you; however, I believe you might come to appreciate my actions. I figured that I owed it to your mother to send you the other part... The part I chose not to publish. The second decision that I struggle with is my years of silence, and I hope every day that no further carnage was left in its wake. Charlotte, while I don't know you, I knew your mother well, and I chose to believe that the same goodness I saw in her is present in you. I hope this helps you forgive her, and that you can find a way to forgive yourself.

Ruth Carpenter

I let the letter fall to the ground as I said in a whisper, "Ruth Carpenter."

I *did* know that name. Equally curious and terrified by this *other part*, I bent down to retrieve what I had dropped, but was hesitant to touch it, as if it were as sharp and dangerous as an unsheathed razor blade. My first instinct was to shred the unopened letter and throw it away, sparing myself the torment of reopening an old wound. But I knew better—throwing it away would haunt me. I'd fixate on its contents until I pieced them back together. In order to save myself time and effort, I decided to read what nurse-turned-biographer Ruth had taken the time to send me.

First, I wanted to reread Theresa's letter to me that was in Ruth's book, that I now knew was just an excerpt. I had to dig deep in my closet to find the publication, because it was something that I told Matteo I never had and never wanted. Feeling a twinge of guilt for lying to my sweet husband, I then remembered it was one of the smaller lies I'd told him—a sickening thought. Why not add to the nausea by rereading Theresa's biography?

It didn't take long for me to locate the letter and refresh my mind with the apology from Theresa which brought back all the same complicated feelings as it did the first time I'd read it. Something stood out to me this time that before I hadn't thought anything about. While the letter to Chris had been signed, the letter to me wasn't. Now that I knew there was more to it, it all made sense. I felt foolish, or maybe careless, that I hadn't noticed the note seemed a bit truncated before. Bracing myself for the inevitable emotional impact, I carefully reopened the letter just sent by Ruth.

I am sure you are more than aware, being that you are a mother yourself, that a mother always knows. I didn't want to believe it, but for quite some time, I have known it was you. When I came to the realization, it didn't feel as good as one might expect to know that I was innocent of the most recent crimes of which I had been accused. But let me be perfectly clear about this: I take full responsibility for your behavior, and you owe me nothing. Your mental break was the direct result of mine. If I had known how to get help when you were born, or if I had known you had lived, I might have been able to break the cycle of destruction within our family. I would serve another lifetime in this institution if I knew it would keep you out of it.

For years, I convinced myself that if I could bury Theresa beneath the façade of Lorie, perhaps I was capable of the unthinkable—of taking innocent lives. It took years of scrutiny, thinking over and over about my motives and methods, and it just didn't add up. And it never sat well with me that Alise was responsible. I couldn't tell you exactly why, but I think it's that, as I said before, a mother just knows. I thought if it wasn't me, and it wasn't Alise, and considering the timing of it all... And who else would have a reason to want to hurt me, along with people who were in danger of harming their children? And the children... who were never found, dead or alive... Then it just clicked.

While I was horrified at the thought of what you had done, I took solace in the fact that I knew you would make sure the children you took weren't harmed. I knew your heart was in the right place regarding your actions, but your head just wasn't. Trust me, I know what that feels like. Wanting to end the life of my infant daughter so she could avoid the inevitable suffering the world would put upon her because I loved her so much... I've known for a long time that is not how life works, and that I should have protected you in other ways, but then, so young and so depressed, it seemed like our best way out.

There is something else I would like you to be aware of, because I know my eternal rest will be easier if you do. When I arrived at the home office of the ~~real~~ first Dr. Delores Shaw, I found she was already dead. I have no idea what happened, maybe she was attacked, or it's possible she might have fallen. Nevertheless, she was lying in a pool of blood that had come from a wound on her head. At first, I thought about contacting the authorities, but figured they wouldn't believe me considering my past. My second thought was to just get out without being seen. Then, the idea of a fresh start washed over me as I realized that I not only resembled Dr. Shaw in appearance, but I also knew how to mimic her mannerisms, the intonation of her voice, and even her treatment ideas from our years of intensive sessions together.

I looked at the woman lying dead before me, with a mix of so many difficult emotions that I felt numb. I was angry with her for lying to me. I was furious with her for leaving me. I respected her for treating me with respect. I admired her for helping me heal. And now, another emotion welled in my chest... gratitude. With her death, Dr.

Shaw was giving me life and a fresh start that may not have come otherwise.

I am guilty of hiding her body, and covering up whatever crime or accident happened to her, and I did borrow her identity—she did not need it anymore. I'm sure you are wondering why I didn't tell that version of my story to Chris. The truth is, I know that my lies and mistakes hurt him deeply. I told him the version of the story that I knew he had already assumed was true, and that would allow him to further let me go. I did that for the Lorie he loved, because she was also a person that I loved, and it's what she would have wanted. I am absolutely not without major faults in my life, but hopefully you see that I am not as bad as everybody thinks. I'm grateful and lucky to have had a life for so long as Delores Shaw. But ultimately, that was just many years of borrowed time before karma caught up with me.

Over the years, I have found ways to make peace with my life and cope with my perpetual stay at WyldeWood. I assume it will also be my final resting place, unless you decide to claim my ashes and move them closer to you. I wish we could have continued the long-delayed mother–daughter relationship that we began over two decades ago, and then I would know how it all turned out. But since we couldn't, I want you to know that you are not broken, you are my daughter whom I have always loved, and always will. I hope that you have been able to find joy in the only gifts I have been able to give you: the gift of life and the gift of freedom.

Mom

Nurse Ruth was right. This was just what I needed to forgive Theresa. Her sacrifice and silence along with the discretion of Ruth Carpenter, had given me freedom. I realized how close I'd come to losing the the chance to raise my own children, and I began to understand the choice Theresa made at the young age of seventeen, when attempting to *give up* her own parenting rights. Cringing at the thought of what could have been, I understood what a waste it had been spending so much of my adult life blaming Theresa. Although I was thankful for the short, happy time we got to spend together getting to know one another, it was tainted by the before and after.

The nurse had known Theresa in ways I never dared to. What's more, the secrets Ruth had been harboring about not only my guilt, but also Theresa's innocence, lent an even more intimate feel to their nurse-patient relationship, an intimacy that I had denied myself, and Theresa. In that moment, an unexpected jealousy of Ruth Carpenter surfaced. Though surprising, for the second time in my life, I was feeling less ambivalent toward Theresa and said a silent prayer for her soul—and my own. Rarely had I found myself thankful that I was the daughter of such a woman, but the overwhelming sense of gratitude I now felt was amplified by the fact that it was too late to show it.

***

Three days later, I found myself wandering the monotonous aisles of the WyldeWood cemetery. Sadly, it was almost exactly as I had pictured, and while it was well groomed, all the graves looked lonely. The flat slabs of granite could not be discerned until you were close enough to read the individual names, so it took a while to locate Theresa's. The director offered to show me right to the site, but I figured the walk and fresh air would be necessary before I did what I came to do. After about fifteen minutes, I found what I was looking for. In stone, the culmination of a complicated legacy was etched, although there was only a name along with her birth and death dates.

I stood before the grave for several minutes, not knowing what to say. For a moment, I thought maybe it didn't matter, after all, Theresa was dead, and there was no one around to hear me. Still, I remained silent. I stayed at the site for a long time, never saying a word. Finally, as dusk approached, I was broken from my trance by a voice calling out.

"Mrs. Sanchez? Ma'am? Are you alright?"

I turned to see the director walking toward me.

"I'm fine. Thank you for checking on me," I replied.

"I would have been out sooner, but to be honest, I forgot you were out here. We so rarely get visitors for the living residents here, and we get even fewer for the dead," said the director.

"I can see why. I thought a traditional cemetery was depressing…"

The director shrugged in agreement and said, "My apologies, but we are closing the grounds for the evening in five minutes. Can I walk you back to your vehicle?

"That would be fine. Can I have just one more minute? I will meet you at the cemetery entrance," I said.

The director nodded and turned to leave me. I brought with me a windchime as a gift, even a peace offering, to place on her grave. Part of me felt like it was way too little and certainly too late, but as I bent to place the chime next to her headstone, I felt an unexpected calm. Looking back, I believe it was probably closure. Not that I forgave myself for the things that I had done, but rather I was able, for the first time, to completely absolve Theresa. Now her grave would stand out from the rest and show that someone, a good person—*no, an incredible person*—was buried there.

After I placed the offering, I had a thought—one that truly had never crossed my mind before. I took out my phone, searched for a number I had not used in years, and made a call. The director waved at me, indicating that my time was officially up, and I held up my finger indicating I needed another minute. I hung up the phone and began to walk away—slowly. I needed to buy just a little more time. On my way back toward the main building on the WyldeWood campus, I turned to look at the grave I would likely never see again. The windchime's clapper, a metal disc engraved with the word "mom," moved in the gentle breeze. The somber melody was a fitting soundtrack to the scene. The tribute to her was one I thought she would have loved, since I had never once before called her "mom."

In the nearly dark of the evening, even when faced away from the institution, I could tell my ride had come and it was finally time to leave. The telltale red and blue flashes from the police cruiser illuminated the entire area. I had asked Chris to work fast so I wouldn't have time to change my mind, and he did. The Georgia State Trooper he had called showed up in a matter of minutes, and was ready to take me to meet my fate. Chris had told the officer I would not put up a fight, so there was no need to cuff me. I inhaled deeply as I willingly surrendered my freedom and climbed into the back seat of the cruiser—Miranda Rights echoing in my head. Part of my bargain was that I would be able to call my children and explain, or at least warn them, about what was to come. Chris Greyson was shocked to hear from me, and there were likely no words to describe how he felt about learning the truth. When he asked me why now—or why at all—when the story could have died with my mother, I told him it was simple. It was time, and I owed her. My mother had done her penance, and in order to clear her name, I had to do mine. I got what I wanted out of my full life being a wife, mother, daughter, sister, and friend, but in order to fully experience the closure I had been searching for my entire life, I had to atone for my sins. Secretly I hoped that in some way, some backwards and messed up way, I had made her proud—all of her... Dr. Delores Shaw... Theresa Miller... and my mom.